I0831353

THE FETCH

THE FETCH

JOSEPH SHEARING

'A ghost, shrouded and filled up
In its own formless terror.'
P. B. SHELLEY

Edited and with an introduction by
Gina R. Collia

Published by Nezu Press
Queensgate House,
48 Queen Street,
Exeter, Devon,
EX4 3SR,
United Kingdom.

This edition published 2025

The Fetch first published by Hutchinson & Co. (Publishers) LTD., 1942.
'The Ambiguities of Miss Smith' is taken from *The Fatal Countess: And Other Studies* by William Roughead. Edinburgh: W. Green & Son, Limited, 1924.

ISBN-13: 978-1-917113-13-7

Cover: 19th century illustration after the painting *Der neueste Roman (The Latest Novel)* by Conrad Kiesel (1846-1921).

In the interest of preservation, the punctuation and spelling of the original UK first edition texts have been maintained, and the original formatting has been used wherever possible. Only minor publisher errors and spelling inconsistencies have been silently corrected.

The first edition of *The Fetch* contains a few significant errors. To correct these, the US first edition (retitled *The Spectral Bride*) has been consulted, and details of the corrections made have been highlighted within footnotes.

'The Ambiguities of Miss Smith', is taken from *The Fatal Countess: And Other Studies* by William Roughead, published by W. Green & Son, Limited, in 1924. The endnotes that accompany this essay were written by William Roughead and appeared as footnotes within the *The Fatal Countess.* The placement of endnote reference numbers follows that used for the original footnotes. However, the system of numbering used for footnotes in the 1924 text, which reset to no. 1 on each new page, has not been used for the current edition.

CONTENTS

'Miss Marjorie Bowen'
The Bystander, 5 September 1906.

'I have used many names for business purposes, but they were none of them of my choosing and seemed rather to be fastened on me like a series of masks.' - Margaret Campbell, *Myself When Young: By Famous Women of Today*, 1938.

Margaret Campbell
The 'Lady with the Hundred Names'

by Gina R. Collia

Margaret Gabrielle Vere Campbell was born into poverty, in a house belonging to an elderly lady named Mrs Cole, on Hayling Island, off the south coast of England, on 1 November 1885.[1] She was the second child of Vere Douglas Campbell (1853–1906) and his wife, Josephine Elizabeth (née Ellis, 1860–1921); Josephine had been pregnant when she married Vere in the summer of 1884, but their first child, Dorothea, had died in infancy in a London lodging house a year before Margaret was born.[2] A third daughter, Phyllis Gertrude Bowen Vere Campbell, was born in the summer of 1890, when Margaret was four years old.[3] Of Irish descent and 'handsome, intelligent, attractive, a giant in stature', Vere was the third son of Dr Hugh Campbell (1823-1902) and his wife, Henrietta (née Johnson, 1826-1912).[4] Josephine was the third daughter of Reverend Charles Bowen Ellis (1821-1887), a West Indies-born Moravian minister, and his first wife, Priscilla (née Bayly, 1829-1879).[5]

Vere and Josephine Campbell's marriage was not a happy one. Vere was an alcoholic who, though he had always been kind to his daughter, disappeared from Margaret's life almost entirely by the time she was five years old.[6] Josephine, to whom Margaret was never close, was prone to 'hysterical ill-humour';[7] she scolded Margaret frequently, regularly made her stand in a corner with her hands on her head, and repeatedly told her that she 'ought never to have been born.'[8] Though Margaret's very early memories were happy ones, as she got older and became more aware of the people around her—of those who had complete power over her—she found that they 'began to be terrifying', and her mother's 'gusts of rage' bewildered and alarmed her.[9]

> 'I heard shouts, quarrels, echoes of scenes—battles or fights, they seemed to me. I was hustled from one room to another, shut in sometimes for hours together, very much afraid and wondering what was happening. Someone would open the door and push in a glass of milk and a slice of bread and butter, and once, I remember, a rag doll, and tell me to be quiet or to "efface myself," or to "run away and play, there's a good girl." '[10]

Margaret received no formal education as a child. Her mother, an aspiring writer and playwright, attempted to teach her to read and write, but each lesson 'exploded in a scene', which only served to increase her frustration and annoyance towards her daughter; five-year-old Margaret was often slapped on the backs of her hands with a hair-brush or shut in a room without any food as a punishment for 'refusing to spell out of obstinacy.'[11] Eventually, Marion Piggott, the family's nurse-cum-housekeeper, who was always referred to as Nana, succeeded where Margaret's own mother had failed. Nana also 'loved to

Josephine Campbell, *Morning Leader*, 1907.

dilate upon murder cases, even taking her charges to see the house where the dark deed was done', inspiring in Margaret an interest in actual murders and celebrated poison cases that 'began to ferment in that young mind of hers' and, many years later, found an outlet in her novels.[12]

During her early years, Margaret had little access to books.[13] Her family moved from one London lodging house to another, to avoid settling debts, and she made use of whatever she could find to read on the current landlady's bookshelf. When the family moved to Kensington, Margaret began to educate herself with books borrowed from the local library, and when, having been evicted for non-payment of rent, they moved again to lodgings on Vauxhall Bridge Road, she began visiting the National Gallery, the British Museum and the South Kensington Museums.[14]

In her teens, Margaret dreamed of becoming a great artist, and one of her mother's friends suggested that her passion for art should be encouraged as there might be money in it. She applied to attend the Royal College of Arts in South Kensington, but she failed the entrance examination.[15] Then, after several more moves to new lodgings to avoid paying yet more creditors, her mother decided that she should attend the Slade School of Fine Art, which she did from 1901.[16] But her work was regarded as poor by her professors, she failed both of the examinations she took whilst there, she was perpetually embarrassed by her mother's failure to pay her tuition fees on time, and she 'began to be aware of the disability of sex.'[17] As a result, she lived in a 'constant state of depression and terror.'[18] She went without food on a daily basis, was embarrassed by the state of her poor clothing, and she felt that every other student was a better artist than she was. Deflated and despairing, she turned to writing and, as there was no money to buy paper, took to scribbling out stories and notes on the backs of her own drawings.[19]

Following several more house moves, Margaret's family took lodgings in a street off Russell Square, and she managed to get some work carrying out research and fact-checking in the British Museum.[20] By that time, she had nearly finished writing a novel and had completed a number of poems and short stories, but her mother, who had failed to secure any interest in her own writing, attempted to persuade her against pursuing a literary career. In an attempt to force her to focus on her painting and drawing, she sent Margaret to Paris, but she failed to provide enough money to pay for lodgings, let alone tuition costs for art school classes.[21] Despite her circumstances—'I was hungrier then than I had ever been'—Margaret enjoyed her time in Paris, visiting museums and galleries and adding to her knowledge of art and history, but she made no progress in her career as an artist and returned to writing.[22]

When she had been in Paris almost a year, Margaret's mother sent for her to return home.[23] Once back in London, she showed some of her writing to her mother; Mrs Campbell's response was to declare it 'hopeless'.[24] This did not, however, prevent her from sending her young daughter's novel, the swashbuckling historical romance *The Viper of Milan,* to an agent. His response was not encouraging: the story was not believable, he disliked the unhappy ending, and it was 'not the kind of thing… that a girl was expected to write.'[25] Her mother suggested that, as she was a girl, she should write a 'pleasant tale', possibly 'something simple', if she wished to be published, but this proved an obstacle for Margaret; the tales she wanted to write were 'often full of dark and sinister shades.'[26] She wrote to escape the world she was forced to exist in, and by writing of dark subjects she managed, to a certain extent, to rid her mind of her own troubles.[27] Margaret's novel went on to be rejected by eleven publishers, and Mrs Campbell suggested that her daughter find an alternative way of making a living.[28] But it was eventually picked up by Alston Rivers Ltd. and published in 1906, when Margaret was twenty years old, and very much to everyone's surprise, not least of all Margaret's, it became a bestseller.[29]

'Miss Marjorie Bowen',
The Tatler, 12 September 1906.

To avoid possible confusion, as her mother wrote under the name Campbell, *The Viper of Milan* was published under the name Marjorie Bowen, the surname being taken from her grandfather, Charles Bowen Ellis. Margaret later wrote that the decision had not been hers; she had wanted to write under her own name, the pseudonym chosen had been odious to her from the outset, and 'this use of two names unfamiliar and even slightly distasteful to me helped to divorce me from my own work.'[30]

By the end of October 1906, only two months after *The Viper of Milan's* publication, demand for the book was so great that a sixth impression had already been published, and lending libraries were forced to increase their orders for it by the day.[31] And as a result of the success of her first book, 'the literary sensation of the autumn season',[32] Margaret received a cheque for sixty pounds—the money going straight to her mother—and entered into a new contract with the publisher for two more books.[33] Mrs Campbell ceased the little work she had been doing to support herself and her children, Phyllis 'did not believe in work', and Margaret became the family's only breadwinner.[34] However, her income was not quite enough to keep four people, and she found herself 'harnessed to a career of hard work' and forced to 'chase every odd five-pound note in order to keep up with expenses.'[35] Loans had to be repaid, her mother's friends had to be 'helped', and Phyllis wanted singing, dancing and riding lessons; before a year had passed, her earnings had been spent.[36] And nobody was happier for it; in fact, Margaret felt that they were unhappier than they had been before.

Josephine Campbell was bitterly jealous of her daughter's sudden literary success, having failed to achieve any for herself.[37] Critics had questioned why she had bothered to write her novel *The Crime of Keziah Keene*, published in 1889, one calling it 'downright nonsense', another describing it as having 'very little narrative and no plot.'[38] The reviewer for *The Academy* expected it to sink 'into well-deserved oblivion.'[39] And her novel *Ferriby*, published a year after Margaret's first great success, was described as leaving 'an unpleasant taste on the intellectual palate.'[40] Her play *Mizpah Misery*, staged in 1894, was described as 'sorry entertainment', and *The King's Password*, put on in 1900, failed to be 'convincing, satisfying, or even coherent'; it was described by the reviewer for the *Liverpool Mercury* as 'crude', 'artificial', and 'rhapsodically melodramatic', with the occasional carefully-written line 'drowned in verbiage.'[41] After years of trying and failing to make a name for herself, she had 'the galling experience of having to stand aside and be congratulated by foolish tactless people on her "clever daughter".'[42]

Shortly after the publication of *The Viper of Milan*, Margaret's father died; he had been found dead in the street with his wife's address in his pocket.[43] Margaret, with the assistance of her father's brothers, arranged for him to be buried in Kensal Green Cemetery.[44] His wife, though they had been separated for some years, went to pieces and never recovered from her loss, and Margaret, desperate to gain some freedom from her increasingly difficult and volatile mother, returned to Paris.[45] She found that she could write there easily, and she began to make a life for herself, away from the stifling influence of her mother. But Mrs Campbell was not about to let her daughter break away; she followed her to France and insisted she return home.[46]

The Viper of Milan was followed quickly by two more novels, both successful and both issued by Alston Rivers, *The Glen o' Weeping* (retitled *The Master of Stair* for the US market), published in 1907, and *The Sword Decides*, which came out in 1908. These were followed by *A Moment's Madness*, which appeared in the Christmas number of *Cassell's Magazine* in 1908, *The Leopard and the Lily*, issued by Doubleday, Page & Co. in 1909, and *Black Magic: The Tale of the Rise and Fall of the Antichrist* published by Alston Rivers in 1909.

Yet no matter how hard Margaret worked, and no matter how much she tried to please them, her family remained unhappy and ungrateful. With more money coming in, though never enough to meet their expenses, they moved to a flat at 55a Maida Vale, near St. John's Wood, the ground floor of which was occupied by the London and Provincial Bank.[47] Margaret found her new home 'extremely gloomy and depressing'; life there was 'untidy, humdrum, and unsatisfactory', and the 'atmosphere was one of constant nervous hysterical storms and tension.'[48] Additionally, the house was haunted, so much so that Mrs Campbell arranged for an expert from the Society for Psychical Research to stay there and investigate while the family escaped to a cottage in Cornwall.[49]

Phyllis Campbell, *The Tatler*, 4 August 1915.

Phyllis and Nana slept in rooms at the top of the Maida Vale house, and it was this top floor that was the focus of the ghostly activity at first; there were groans, footsteps on the stairs, knockings on the doors, and the sound of someone pacing to and fro.[50] Phyllis refused to sleep in her room and moved to the floor below, and the man-of-all-work, a fellow by the name of Frederic Payne, began complaining that the basement was 'overrun by supernatural creatures.'[51] Lights and water taps were switched on and off, windows were flung open, and Margaret's mother, who had begun hearing scufflings and moanings, saw 'a wheel of light whirl down the stairs.'[52] At first, Margaret saw and heard nothing and did not believe in the haunting, but by the time the Society for Psychical Research was contacted she too had begun experiencing ghostly goings on. One evening, when she was alone in the house and the light was beginning to fade, she opened the door of the drawing room and saw 'a gigantic figure, hooded and cloaked, with very square shoulders, passing into the little room on the stairs that had been turned into a bathroom.'[53] Then, not long afterwards, she awoke in the night and felt 'oppressed by a feeling of unreality.'[54]

> 'There seemed an oppression of something intensely evil, an abstraction and yet something in concrete form. As she

lay quite still she saw in the air two objects rather like a pestle and mortar or a bulbous-shaped medicine glass, something with a black body and a long neck, lying in a bowl. They were of a blue colour and seemed to be of thickened glass.'[55]

Margaret was later told that the Maida Vale house had once been a private lunatic asylum, that an 'unchronicled tragedy' had taken place within it, and that after the event the doctor who lived there had moved in a hurry.[56] In truth, the house had been a private nursing home, and the tragedy had been the death of a female patient under the influence of chloroform in December 1902, for which the inquest returned a verdict of 'death from misadventure'.[57]

It was at this time, while her mother, sister and Nana were preoccupied with ghostly goings on, that Margaret met Zefferino Emilio Costanzo (c. 1882-1916), a Sicilian who had lived in London for several years.[58] Her family did not like him, and she liked rather than loved him, but he offered a means of escape; he was going back to Italy and might be there for some years, and he wanted her to go with him. And despite her mother's opposition to the match—she opposed the removal of the family breadwinner—Margaret and Zefferino were married in the October of 1912.[59] Zefferino was given a position with a company that was building a railway in the Carrara district of Lucca, and the following year the couple set out for Italy, taking a furnished house in Lucca Reggio, a two-hour train ride from Florence.[60]

For a time, Margaret was quite content in her new life. She learned to sew and, like her new Italian neighbours, kept hens and pigeons, though hers were not for food; she loathed meat and none was allowed in the house.[61] At the beginning of their married life in Tuscany, the couple lived on Zefferino's income; his wife's earnings continued to support the Campbell family in London. But when the railway in Lucca was completed in 1919, Zefferino lost his position and fell ill as a result, and the couple were forced to live on Margaret's income from writing. In an effort to reduce their outgoings, they moved to Florence and took an apartment in a large farmhouse near Santa Margherita.[62] Their rooms were uncomfortable, and Zefferino, who by then had acquired a constant cough, became increasingly violent-tempered; Margaret felt that all her hopes for a new, different life, away from the petty arguments and miseries of life with her mother, had been crushed. Then, on 4 August 1914, they received the news that England had declared war on Germany.

Margaret and her husband made attempts to get back to England, but their efforts came to nought.[63] The banks restricted withdrawals almost immediately; it was possible to get enough money for basic living expenses but nothing more.[64] Food prices increased, there were riots in Florence, and receiving accurate news from, or sending news to, England was next to impossible. In October, now heavily pregnant, Margaret journeyed with her husband to Sicily to his family home; she grew fond of his father and sister, but she detested the island itself, the way of life there and the disputes that everyone around her seemed to be embroiled in.[65] As she had remained the sole breadwinner of her family in London, she had continued to be productive throughout her marriage—she had produced two or three novels per year since the publication of *The Viper of Milan*—but now she had difficulty acquiring paper to write on or the time in which to use it.[66]

Following the birth of her baby daughter, Giuseppina, on 6 November 1914, Margaret became determined to return to England, and she and Zefferino finally began the long and arduous journey three months later.[67] They arrived in London one wintry day in February 1915, and Margaret found her mother and sister much as she had left them.[68] It soon became apparent that there was no place for Margaret's new family with her old one, so she and her husband moved into a farmhouse above the Kentish marshes, taking old Nana with them, and Zefferino took up poultry farming.[69] But during the cold winter months his health deteriorated.

On 19 May 1915, after a very brief illness, Giuseppina, then only six months old, died, and Zefferino was so affected by the loss of his daughter that his health deteriorated further still.[70] In the hope that milder weather conditions would be beneficial, Margaret arranged for them to move to South Devon.[71] She had continued to write—she was, after all, the only breadwinner for two families now—and was receiving an income which, though not quite as good as it had been before the war, was enough to sustain them. But it was shortly after their arrival in Torquay that she received two life-changing pieces of news: she was pregnant for the second time, and her husband would live no more than six months if he did not return to the warmer climate of his homeland. So, in October Zefferino sailed for home while Margaret remained in Torquay, awaiting the birth of her second child, Michael Birillo Vere, who was born the following January.[72]

One month after Michael's birth, Margaret received bad news from her husband; he was more seriously ill than she had thought, had fallen out with his family in Sicily and moved to Tuscany, and he wanted her to go to him with their baby son.[73] It was, of course, impossible to take a newborn baby on such a journey, so she left Michael in England and travelled to Italy alone. She nursed her husband, with very little help from another soul, until his death. Zefferino died from tuberculosis on 5 November 1916 at the Villa

Margaret in a 'Belle Alliance' dress. *The Sketch*, 10 March 1915.

Ceciale, in the sea town of Forte dei Marmi, in Lucca.[74] Margaret returned to England at the beginning of 1917, to her mother and sister, who still very much disapproved of everything she did, and to the infant son who, after so long a separation, did not recognise her as his mother.[75]

The little family left Torquay and moved to Hampstead Heath, and, in the October of the same year, Margaret entered into her second loveless marriage.[76] Arthur Leonard Long (1886-1983) was aware from the very beginning that his wife did not love him—'her story and her feelings had been fully explained'—but the marriage appears to have been fairly successful; it was a 'singular and pleasing union, to end only with their deaths.'[77] Her second marriage produced two sons—Athelstan Charles Ethelwulf was born on 2 Jan 1919, and Hilary Blaix Winch Vere was born on 24 June of the following year—both of whom, along with their half-brother, Michael, Margaret schooled at home until they were eight years old.[78] As with her first marriage, her second was supported by her writing income, and, as she had done since the publication of her first novel, she remained incredibly productive. In December 1921, Margaret's mother died—'a bitter death that was the direct outcome of her frustrated, unfortunate life'—and 'her sister went away and they saw no more of each other.'[79] From then on, she was no longer weighed down by the troubles and temperaments of her mother and sister, and she was responsible for the support of only her own household.

Articles published in the *Weekly Dispatch* in 1930 and *Sydney Morning Herald* in 1932 give us an insight into Margaret's working methods.[80] She used an ediphone, which she found 'an inspiring helper';[81] considering her prolific output, without it, she explained, 'neither my eyes nor my hands would stand the amount of work'.[82]

Margaret at her Kent home with her three sons: Michael (left), Athelstan (right) and Hilary (centre). *The Graphic*, 3 November 1923.

She narrated her story aloud, 'as though she were reading it from a written page'; once the story was completed, she transcribed it to paper, 'developing and colouring characters and scenes' as she went along.[83] She also took inspiration from listening to music; it was while listening to Beethoven's *Leonore* that the story of *Captain Banner*, a three-act drama written under the pseudonym George R. Preedy, first began to take shape in her mind.[84]

Margaret employed several pseudonyms during her career; in addition to her most well-known pen name, Marjorie Bowen, she wrote as Joseph Shearing, Robert Paye, John Winch and George R. Preedy. These appear to have been adopted to set certain works apart from those issued under the Bowen name, and with Preedy and Shearing there was some effort made to conceal the author's true identity for several years. *The Tatler* reported in 1952 that, a few years earlier, 'these pseudonyms were among the most jealously guarded secrets of the publishing world.'[85]

Margaret explained, many years after Preedy, Shearing, Paye and Winch first appeared in print, 'I became bored with the success of very early years. I felt I was living on another's reputation, so changed was I from the girl who had written "I Will Maintain!".'[86] And it's not terribly surprising that she should attempt to cast off the Bowen pen name for a time; it had been foisted upon her at the beginning of her career, and she had always detested it. 'The name Marjorie Bowen has always annoyed me,' she explained to a reporter in 1931, and she had found it impossible to express her 'second individuality' when using it.[87] In addition to the fact that she very much disliked her first pseudonym, she also felt that, when using it, 'her work was not receiving the close attention of the critics and the public', and that there was still 'a prejudice against women writers.'[88]

> 'When I am writing as George Preedy my whole personality definitely changes. The books I write as George Preedy are no effort whatsoever to me, but those of Marjorie Bowen are difficult and cause trouble.'[89]

Margaret wrote two novels as Robert Paye: *The Devil's Jig*, which appeared in 1930, and *Julia Roseingrave*, published in 1933; the former was still being advertised as an exceptionally successful 'first novel' by a new author when Paye's true identity was revealed in the autumn of 1930.[90] *Idlers' Gate* was published under the name John Winch in 1932, and that author's identity was made public the following year.[91]

The first title written under the name George R. Preedy was *General Crack,* published in 1928. The novel was a bestseller and immediately set the literary world speculating about the true identity of this talented new writer; Arnold Bennett, H. G. Wells, and Rafael Sabatini were all suspects.[92] Preedy was, according to the *Sunday Express*, 'the most retiring author in existence'; all efforts to get in touch with him failed, and appeals for him to reveal himself received no response.[93] He was obviously an expert in eighteenth-century history, and his only rival, according to the same newspaper, was Marjorie Bowen, whom they suggested Mr Preedy should meet.[94] The *Daily News* printed stories by both authors—Preedy's 'A Tune for a Trumpet' and Bowen's 'The Globe of Glass'—just days apart, to 'enable readers to make a comparison for themselves'.[95] It then sent samples of the two authors' handwriting to Dr C. Ainsworth Mitchell for 'microscopical examination', to discover if they were produced by one hand, but the good doctor concluded that there was 'not enough material upon which to base an opinion.'[96]

Speculation continued until the next Preedy novel, *The Rocklitz,* was dramatised in 1931. A reporter spotted Margaret, 'huddled, shyly, in a corner', altering Mr Preedy's script at the Duke of York

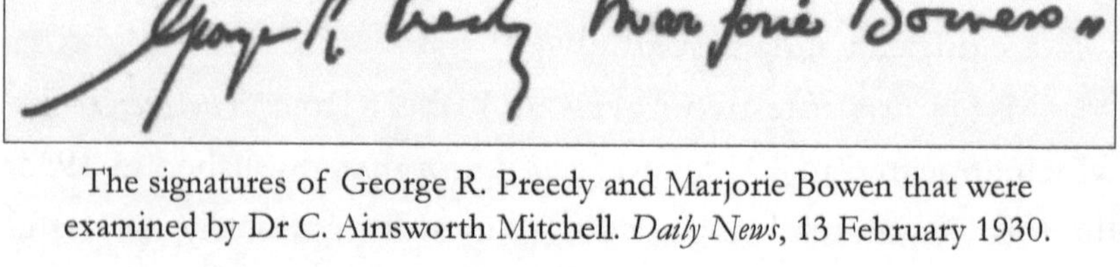

The signatures of George R. Preedy and Marjorie Bowen that were examined by Dr C. Ainsworth Mitchell. *Daily News*, 13 February 1930.

Theatre in London, and the jig was up.[97] 'I was trying to work a hoax,' Margaret explained; 'I wanted to get away from the type of writing done by Marjorie Bowen and to write something different as George Preedy.'[98] Not that this revelation prevented people from continuing to question the Bowen-Preedy connection. The following year, under the heading 'Tales under Two Titles: Bowen-Preedy Riddle Deepens', the *Sunderland Daily Echo* pointed out that, though 'it used to be admitted they they were one and the same person—a Miss Jekyll and a Mr Hyde', *Who's Who* had nonetheless continued to list them as two separate authors, with different biographical details, addresses, and interests.[99]

As Joseph Shearing, Margaret wrote historical novels with a true crime element; these were described as 'evil, sinister, ghostly, strange, baleful, terrible, relentless… and malevolent.'[100] The first Shearing novel, *Forget-me-Not*, was published in 1932, and from the moment of its appearance there was 'a definite and devoted cult of readers of this writer.'[101] Whilst there was much conjecture regarding the author's identity—at first, Mrs. Belloc Lowndes was the prime suspect—it remained a secret for a decade.[102] Joseph Shearing was 'one of the impenetrable mysteries of the day.'[103] It wasn't until 1942, when *Twentieth Century Authors: A Biographical Dictionary of Modern Literature* was going to press, that Margaret finally confessed to the fact that she and Shearing were one and the same person.

In 1939, the autobiography of 'Marjorie Bowen', *The Debate Continues,* was published by William Heinemann under her real name: Margaret Campbell. However, at the time, to make matters more confusing, she was often referred to as Gabrielle Long and Gabrielle Campbell. In 1949, a reviewer suggested that if Lon Chaney was billed as the 'Man With the Hundred Faces', Margaret should likewise be described as the 'Lady With the Hundred Names'.[104] The *Bookseller* considered it necessary to print a glossary of her noms de plume, and the *Evening Despatch* suggested jokingly that it was only a matter of time before Margaret announced she was also 'H. G. Wells, Arnold Bennett, Noel Coward, and Edgar Wallace'.[105] The author herself 'often thought of herself by the name Margaret under which she was baptized, a name borne by many Scotswomen since a royal saint made it popular.'[106]

Margaret achieved a great amount of success during her lifetime; her books sold extremely well for years and several of them were adapted into films and plays: her 1928 George Preedy novel *General Crack* was adapted as the film *General Crack* (1930), starring John Barrymore, her 1939 Shearing novel *Blanche Fury* was adapted as the film *Blanche Fury* (1948), starring Stewart Granger, and another of Shearing's, *For Her to See* (1947), became the film *So Evil My Love* (1948), starring Ray Milland, Ann Todd, and Geraldine Fitzgerald. Margaret was also one of the writers who worked on *Under Capricorn* (1949), the adaptation of Helen Simpson's 1937 novel, directed by Alfred Hitchcock and starring Ingrid Bergman, Joseph Cotton, and Michael Wilding.[107]

Margaret was described as a 'quiet, cultured woman';[108] she was 'a tall, shy, pleasant woman', 'always considerate and punctual for appointments', who, though she made a lot of money from her writing, 'lived modestly' and did 'much of her own housework'.[109] 'There is no vanity in the personality of Marjorie Bowen', wrote the reporter for the *Sydney Morning Herald* in 1932; she was a 'gentle-voiced woman' who was so lacking in self-importance that she answered her own doorbell.[110] Towards the end of her life, she lived quietly in a flat off the King's Road in London, where 'few of her neighbours' knew her 'well enough to point her out and say "That is Marjorie Bowen".'[111] When she was not writing, she had her hobbies; she still enjoyed painting, she was a skilled embroiderer, she particularly liked making dolls, for which she knitted petticoats, and she made many of her own clothes.[112] 'Life without a hobby,' she said, at the Diamond Jubilee Convention of the British Amateur Press Association in 1950, 'would indeed be barren. It is part of the English character to be an amateur and a little eccentric. If we weren't we should cease to be British people.'[113]

In the summer of 1952, Margaret suffered a broken arm.[114] In September, she spent two weeks in Ulster, trying to catch up with work on her novel *The Man with the Scales*, which her publisher had been urging her to finish.[115] She stayed with her friend May Morton, the Irish poetess who in her poem 'Gabrielle', written the previous year, had described Margaret as 'A sword of flame—a mind that probes and flares… A slender willow tree—a form of grace'.[116] With the author herself incapacitated, May took on the task of writing down Margaret's dictation, and the novel was finished while she was in Ireland.[117] It turned out to be the last that Margaret wrote.

On 3 December 1952, Margaret suffered a fall on the parquet floor of her bedroom. She took to her bed and, according to her youngest son, her condition appeared to improve for a while, but on 22 December she collapsed, and she died the following day in St. Charles Hospital, Kensington. She had suffered a haemorrhage due to having fractured her skull during the fall.[118] She was sixty-seven years old. At her death, she left behind more than a hundred and fifty novels and two hundred short stories. She once admitted that she herself was not certain how many books she had written.[119] Sadly, most have never been republished.

Notes

1 *1939 England and Wales Register* for the date.
With regard to her name: the *England & Wales, Civil Registration Birth Index, 1837-1915* and the *National Probate Calendar* record her name as 'Margaret Gabrielle', while the *England & Wales, Civil Registration Death Index, 1916-2007* and the *1901 England Census* have her down as 'Gabrielle Margaret'. Numerous death notices referred to her as 'Margaret Gabrielle Long'. I have chosen to refer to her by the name she chose in her own autobiography: Margaret.
Name of the cottage's owner, see Margaret Campbell, *The Debate Continues: Being the Autobiography of Marjorie Bowen*. London: William Heinemann Ltd., 1939, p. 1. Mrs Cole was most likely Frances Cole, who lived at 6 Clarendon Road and died in the autumn of 1885, just before Margaret's birth, at the age of 79. *See 1881 England Census.*

2 Marriage: *England & Wales, Civil Registration Marriage Index, 1837-1915.* Dorothea's birth and death: *England & Wales, Civil Registration Death Index, 1837-1915.* Location of Dorothea's birth: Campbell, op. cit., p. 1.

3 Born 1890, died 1982. *England & Wales, Civil Registration Birth Index, 1837-1915*, and *England & Wales, Civil Registration Death Index, 1916-2007.*

4 Description of Margaret's father: Campbell, op. cit., p. 50.
According to the information provided to medical directories at the time, Hugh Campbell studied at Edinburgh and Trinity College, Dublin. So far, I have found no record of him having studied at Trinity College. He passed the necessary examinations at St. Andrews in 1863 (see the *Sun*, 11 May 1863, p. 20).

5 *1871 England Census.*

6 Campbell, op. cit., pp. 7-8.

7 Ibid., p. 9.

8 Ibid., p. 7.

9 Ibid., pp. 2-3.

10 Ibid., p. 8.

11 Ibid., p. 11.

12 *Kensington Post*, 7 June 1947, p. 5. In her comments, Margaret refers to her childhood nurse without naming her, but Nana was her only nurse.

13 Campbell, op. cit., p. 11. Marion Piggot is recorded as the family's housekeeper in the *England Census* for 1901 and 1911.

14 Campbell, op. cit., p. 32.

15 Ibid., p. 42.

16 Ibid., p. 64.

17 Ibid., p. 65.

18 Ibid.

19 Ibid.

20 Ibid., p. 70.

21 Ibid., p. 77.

22 Ibid., p. 79.

23 Ibid., p. 83.

24 Ibid., p. 84.

25 Ibid.

26 Ibid.

27 Ibid., pp. 84-85.

28 Ibid., p. 85.

29 Newspaper reports often claimed that *The Viper of Milan* was published when Margaret was just sixteen or seventeen years old, but when it appeared, in August 1906, she was three months shy of her twenty-first birthday.

30 Campbell, op. cit., p. 91.

31 *Daily News* (London), 19 October 1906, p. 4.

32 *Daily Mirror*, 8 September 1906, p. 5.

33 Campbell, op. cit., p. 93.

34 Ibid., pp. 83 and 94.

35 Ibid., p. 95.

36 Ibd.

37 Ibid., pp. 95-96.

38 *Scottish Leader*, 26 September 1889, p. 2, *Ross Gazette*, 5 February 1890, p. 3, and *The Saturday Review*, 28 September 1889, p. 356.

39 *The Academy*, 19 October 1889, p. 250.

40 *Bath Chronicle*, 5 September 1907, p. 6.

41 *Birmingham Evening Mail*, 13 March 1894, p. 4, and *Morning Post*, 29 May 1900, p. 5, and *Liverpool Mercury*, 22 May 1900, p. 8.

42 Campbell, op. cit., p. 95.

43 Ibid., p. 99.

44 Ibid., and the burial register for Kensal Green Cemetery, London.

45 Campbell, op. cit., p. 99.

46 Ibid., p. 100.

47 *1911 England Census.*

48 Campbell, op. cit., p. 102.

49 Ibid., p. 116.

50 Ibid., p. 106.

51 Ibid., p. 107. Margaret remembers that the man-of-all-work was called Palmer. However, according to the *1911 England Census* his name was Frederic Payne.

52 Ibid.

53 Ibid. p. 116.

54 Ibid. p. 117.

55 Ibid.

56 Ibid. p. 127.

57 *Hastings and St Leonards Observer*, 20 December 1902, p. 2.

58 Campbell, op. cit., p. 118. His name is not given in Margaret's account of her life, *The Debate Continues*; in various other sources it is given as Zeffrino Costanzo, Zefferino Costanzo, Zeffirino Costanzo, and Zeffirine Costanza. In November 1918, Margaret's second husband, Arthur L. Long, wrote to the *New York Herald* to correct a piece about his wife's book, *The Third Estate*, and in that he refers to 'Zefferino Costanzo' (see the *New York Herald*, 17 November 1918, p. 43).

59 *England & Wales, Civil Registration Marriage Index, 1837-1915.*

60 Campbell, op. cit., p. 132.

61 Campbell, op. cit., p. 136.

62 Ibid., p. 151.

63 Ibid., p. 156.

64 Ibid.

65 Ibid., p. 158.

66 Ibid., p. 163.

67 *UK and Ireland, Find a Grave Index, 1300s-Current.*

68 Campbell, op. cit., p. 174.

69 Ibid., p. 175.

70 Ibid. Giuseppina Costanzo was buried in the churchyard of St Mary the Virgin, Stone-cum-Ebony, Ashford, Kent, England.

71 Ibid., p. 182.

72 *England & Wales, Civil Registration Birth Index, 1916-2007.* Full name: birth certificate (registered in Newton Abbot).

73 Campbell, op. cit., p. 188.

74 *England & Wales, National Probate Calendar (Index of Wills and Administrations), 1858-1995.*

75 Campbell, op. cit., p. 288.

76 *England & Wales, Civil Registration Marriage Index, 1916-2005.*

77 Campbell, op. cit., p. 290.

78 Birthdates of her sons: birth certificates, *UK, World War II Allied Prisoners of War, 1939-1945. WO 345*, and *England and Wales, Death Index, 1989-2021*. Schooling: *Sydney Morning Herald*, 27 August 1932, p. 9.

79 Campbell, op. cit., p. 291, and *England & Wales, Civil Registration Death Index, 1916-2007.*

80 *Sydney Morning Herald*, 27 August 1932, p. 9.

81 Ibid. A recording device for oral dictation where sound was recorded on a wax cylinder. The machine marketed by the Edison Records Company was trademarked as the 'Ediphone'.

82 *Weekly Dispatch*, 14 September 1930, p. 1.

83 *Sydney Morning Herald*, 27 August 1932, p. 9.
84 Ibid.
85 *The Tatler*, 13 August 1952, p. 13.
86 E.g.: *Torbay Express and South Devon Echo*, 27 December 1952, p. 5.
87 *Weekly Dispatch*, 1 February 1931, p. 11.
88 *News* (Adelaide, Australia), 3 February 1931, p. 9.
89 *Weekly Dispatch*, 1 February 1931, p. 11.
90 *Weekly Dispatch*, 14 September 1930, p. 1.
91 *Liverpool Daily Post*, 30 September 1933, p. 6.
92 *Weekly Dispatch*, 1 February 1931, p. 1.
93 *Sunday Express*, 9 February 1930, p. 4.
94 Ibid.
95 *Daily News*, 15 February 1930, p. 5.
96 *Daily News*, 13 February 1930, p. 7.
97 *Weekly Dispatch*, 1 February 1931, p. 1, and *Daily News*, 2 February 1931, p. 1.
98 *Daily News*, 2 February 1931, p. 1.
99 *Sunderland Daily Echo and Shipping Gazette*, 10 January 1933, p. 6.
100 Stanley Kunitz and Howard Haycraft, *Twentieth Century Authors: A Biographical Dictionary of Modern Literature*. H. W. Wilson Company, 1942, p. 1272.
101 Ibid.
102 *Daily News*, 3 June 1932, p.4.
103 *Daily News* (London), 19 October 1906, p. 4.
104 *Ireland's Saturday Night*, 26 March 1949, p. 2.
105 *Evening Despatch*, 2 February 1931, p. 6.
106 Campbell, op. cit., p. i.
107 Donald Spoto, *The Dark Side of Genius: The Life of Alfred Hitchcock*. Boston: Little Brown, 1983, p. 309.
108 *Derby Daily Telegraph*, 26 February 1931, p. 4.
109 *Evening Standard*, 27 December 1952, p. 2, and *Belfast News-Letter*, 16 March 1953, p. 3.

110 *Sydney Morning Herald*, 27 August 1932, p. 9.

111 *Evening News*, 10 March 1947, p. 2.

112 *Belfast News-Letter*, 16 March 1953, p. 3.

113 *Bromley & West Kent Mercury*, 22 September 1950, p. 4.

114 *Newcastle Journal*, 4 August 1952, p. 3.

115 *Belfast News-Letter*, 16 March 1953, p. 3.

116 May Morton, 'Gabrielle', in *Sung to the Spinning Wheel*. Quota Press, 1952, p. 18. Though the poetry collection was published in 1952, the poems were written the previous year, see *Belfast News-Letter*, 19 November 1951, p. 3.

117 *Belfast News-Letter*, 16 March 1953, p. 3.

118 *Belfast Telegraph*, 29 December 1952, p. 1.

119 *Evening Standard*, 27 December 1952, p. 2.

A SMALL OFFERING, WITH MUCH GRATITUDE

FOR

WILLIAM ROUGHEAD

WITH DEEP ADMIRATION FOR HIS PECULIAR GENIUS

AND INADEQUATE THANKS FOR HIS KINDNESS

JOSEPH SHEARING

London, 1942.

INTRODUCTION

THE FOLLOWING NOVEL is based on *The Ambiguities of Miss Smith*, a masterly essay by William Roughead. The author knows of no other account of this strange affair and wishes to give all due tribute and gratitude to the writer of *The Ambiguities of Miss Smith*.

It may be pointed out that the period of the story is in the 1870s and that the matters dealt with are considered in the light of knowledge common in that period. Spiritualism and other subjects touched on are therefore to be understood as being dealt with as from the point of view of seventy years ago.

PART ONE
PINK BONNET

Cold blows the wind, sweetheart,
  Cold are the drops of rain;
The first true love that ever I had
  In the green grove she was slain.

'Twas down in the garden-green, sweetheart,
  Where you and I did walk,
The fairest flower that in the garden grew
  Is withered to a stalk.

The stalk shall bear no leaves, sweetheart,
  The flowers will ne'er return,
And since my true love is dead and gone,
  What can I do but mourn?

A twelvemonth and a day being gone
  The spirit arose and spoke,
My body is cold cold, sweetheart,
  My breath smells heavy and strong.
And if you kiss my lily white lips,
  Your time will not be long.

Old Ballad. Collected by Robert Hunt

"A PINK bonnet," said Mrs Fenton, "a pink bonnet with long satin strings."

She smiled foolishly and looked vaguely out of the window while Adelaide held before her the fashionable headgear that provoked this comment. It certainly was a charming creation—

"What the French term a 'chiffon,' " simpered Adelaide. "You have seen the plates in the *Fashion de Paris*, have you not, Mamma?"

"I don't think you've showed me the last number," replied Mrs. Fenton, without any change in her dull blank glance, "but it's a very pretty bonnet, dear, and must have been expensive, too. Yes, long, pink, satin ribbons and two rosy-coloured ostrich feathers, and a little wreath of velvet flowers inside the brim—most becoming for one of your complexion, too, Adelaide, my love."

"Do you think, Mamma, it is really becoming?" asked the girl eagerly. "I haven't tried it on yet, you know. It only arrived from the mantua makers this morning.[1] Expensive, do you think it would be expensive, Mamma?"

"Well, I don't suppose it would cost less than five or six guineas, do you, my love?" Mrs. Fenton withdrew into placid complacency, folding her large hands upon her thick waist and gazing into the clear bright flames behind the polished steel bars of the grate. The kettle was steaming, the drowsy tabby cat was purring, and the atmosphere was one of good will and content.

The little parlour was clean and burnished, the prints of imaginary palaces showed in insipid inoffensiveness behind well-polished glass, the Staffordshire ornaments, black and white grinning dogs, black and white grinning ecclesiastics, were washed and lustrous on the narrow mantelshelf. The round table was set with a substantial meal, blue plates, narrow silver knives and forks, dough cakes, a brown loaf, a pat of pale butter, a jug of cream, and primly folded napkins.

Mrs. Fenton glanced around with a sudden flash of animation

---

[1] The mantua was a type of loose gown worn from the mid-17th to mid-18th century. It became so popular that dressmakers in general were referred to as mantua-makers.

that was caused by satisfaction at her surroundings; everything she could do she had done, and well. Her domain was small, but it was specially kept; within the range of her own limitations nothing was lacking. She peered at the polished iron kettle, now beginning to hum, a fine kettle with a large convenient handle and a shining base squarely set on the clear coals; she peered at the neat tea-table on which no detail of comfortable service was lacking, and then again at her daughter, who was standing in the window-place holding up the rose-coloured bonnet, so fashionable, so neat, with the long streaming ribbons of flesh-coloured satin, with the rosy-coloured ostrich tips, with the lining of fine French gauze.

Mrs. Fenton gave a faint sigh and her eyes, so stupid in expression that it seemed there must be some slyness behind them, hovered towards the cardboard box on which was written the name of Miss Herle, the most fashionable mantua maker in Mullenbridge, to the countenance of her daughter, who was turning the bonnet about with a satisfied air.

"Who sent it to you, Adelaide?" she asked, as if the question was not one of great import.

"No, Mamma, I mustn't tell you that, it would be giving away a secret."

"Perhaps, if you've got any secrets, Adelaide, you'd better tell them to me." Mrs. Fenton's voice had a touch of shrewdness; she turned away from her daughter as she spoke. "Or to your father," she added flatly.

The girl laughed, a laugh that sank into a giggle and a simper.

"Father! He's been dead this twenty years!" Her look of cunning was transferred like lightning to Mrs. Fenton. The women exchanged a half-glance, as if they understood and condoned one another.

The girl returned the bonnet to the box with the silver paper and tied the strings neatly.

"I need a pelisse," she remarked, "of white or rose-coloured cloth to wear with that, and sandals, too.[2] Don't you think it would be very becoming for me, Mamma, to be in white and rose-coloured throughout?"

"Very becoming, indeed," assented Mrs. Fenton, in a drowsy tone. "And now, dear, it's time that you set the tray and took your father up his tea."

"Oh, it's Caroline's turn to take Father up his tea," replied the girl with a pout.

"Is it? I'd forgotten." Mrs. Fenton had a lazy, slumbrous air. "Anyway, you might do it, out of good nature, might you not? I suppose," again the slyness flashed into her look and tone, "you've nothing else to do?"

"I might go for a walk," remarked Adelaide, "in the woods." She lifted her chin and smiled into the window-pane as if she looked into a mirror.

Her mother contemplated her, but made no comment and turned again to the fire where the kettle was now humming briskly and lifted it, using a patchwork holder, to the hob.

"Well, you could make the tea, dear, at least, and take the scones out of the oven. The buns are all spread with jam and cream. I'm sure Susan has put everything ready—it's her day off, you know," Mrs. Fenton continued in a slightly apologetic tone, "or I should not have had to trouble you at all. Yet," she added with a sudden briskness, "you're a lazy girl and why shouldn't you do something?"

---

[2] Pelisse: a long coat or cloak.

"Oh, Mother, I do a great deal, indeed I do! I write poems and paint pictures and read and——"

"Oh, and! and!" parried the mother, lazily. "Well, never mind! You're no use about the house, but you're a well-set-up girl and I suppose you will find a husband in time and that's all that any mother can expect."

"Is it?" asked Adelaide. "That seems to me a question! Do you know, Mother," she came to the table and almost automatically set out the tray for her bedridden father—plates, knife and fork, jug of cream, pot of jam, napkin, "a great many questions have come into my mind lately. I've been thinking about a number of matters."

"That's a mistake," announced Mrs. Fenton. "I've got on very well, and I'm fifty-five in a week or two, without ever thinking of anything. Don't think, Adelaide, just take things as they come."

"That's so dull, Mother," muttered the girl in a slow protest. "Take things as they come! Why should I? Why shouldn't I make things come the way I want them to be?"

"Nobody ever did that I heard of," answered Mrs. Fenton flatly. She leaned forward and raised the kettle by the small brilliant patchwork holder. "At least," she amended, "not since the days of the witches, who used to make spells and incantations, and who knows if one can believe in them or not? No, it's no use, Adelaide, one can't make *things* come the way one wants—just by wishing."

"Can't one?" asked the girl, quietly. "I wondered."

"Well, you stop wondering about nonsense like that and tell me where you got that bonnet," declared Mrs. Fenton. She rose, suddenly formidable, for she was a tall, heavy woman, well-dressed in her afternoon gown of black corded silk, with her cameo-brooch and gold chain and her banded iron-grey hair. "You tell me where you got that, my girl. Your father will want to know."

"Oh, Father!" Adelaide tossed her head and then checked the gesture as if she realized it was not lady-like.

"Yes, you may mock like that, knowing that your father's been bedridden and no good to anyone for a long while. But he is your father and I can make him act like it if I choose."

The two women faced one another and Adelaide's strong hands tightened on the rim of the black tray with the painted bunch of flowers. The elder woman looked down at them as if she studied the well-formed white fingers, strong wrists, and firm knuckles.

"What are you trying to do, Adelaide?" she asked, in a lazy voice. "Get above your class, that's clear, but how?"

The girl hunched her plump shoulders.

"Oh, I don't know, Mother. It can be done, I suppose. I've got my methods."

"Have you?" the elder woman gave her a shrewd glance. "You read a lot of romances, don't you, some two or three at a time from the circulating library? I wonder sometimes if they don't—well, go to your head, like gin or spirits."

"I've never tasted gin or spirits," sneered Adelaide. "They ain't genteel."

"But those romances—it seems to me they are much the same. They give you dreams, I suppose, make you think things are like you want them to be, don't they?"

"Maybe they do and maybe they don't. But what's that matter, Mother? I'm a good girl, behaving myself, aren't I? Look—here's Father's tray all ready, and the kettle's boiling and you still waiting. Make the tea and I'll take it up to him."

"First you'll tell me where you got that pink bonnet," insisted Mrs. Fenton. "We've always been honest and respectable."

"And we're always going to be, I'm sure," simpered Adelaide.

"Why shouldn't we be, indeed! Just because a gentleman chooses to make me a little present there's no reason why you should begin to talk like that. It shows ill-breeding. I declare it does, Mother."

Mrs. Fenton was baffled. She had touched on codes and standards that were unknown to her; she bit her lip, feeling her way. She was an ambitious woman who had always been sharp on her own advantage, but who had been early thwarted by a husband who had been always stupid, and finally a 'hopeless,' as she termed it, invalid. The small interest from Consols on which she lived had been no more than sufficient to keep the family of four people in that 'respectability' of which she had spoken; they were humble folk in a little way, who were able, in her own term, 'to hold their heads up among their neighbours,' but no more.[3] She said they could claim, on her mother's side, some genteel descent, there was talk, if it was no more than talk, of 'coat armour gentry on the distaff side,' there were little affectations of gentility and the traditions that come from good descent.

But Thomas Fenton—there was no means of glossing this plain man's antecedents. He was no more than the chief clerk in a tea-merchant's business in the City, who had been pensioned-off in his fortieth year, owing to failing health, by the generous firm who had employed him and who since that date had lain in an upper room in his bed, or in his chair; a 'drooling half-wit' was his wife's secret definition of his condition.

Mrs. Fenton's ambitions, always suppressed, had died, it seemed, for lack of nourishment. She had acquiesced in her dull destiny, she had kept her tiny domain beyond reproach, correctly, she had educated her daughters on orthodox lines. Adelaide and

---

[3] Consols: consolidated annuities, British government stock.

Caroline had been sent to a boarding-school for gentlewomen, an establishment that the younger girl, aged sixteen years, had only lately left.

Mrs. Fenton had vaguely considered a finishing-school for both of the girls in Brussels, or possibly Paris, but the fees were not only expensive, but the scheme beyond her scope; she could not face the difficulties attendant on such a course of action. There was the foreign language for one obstacle, the foreign travel for another, the question of a chaperone or a companion, what one did and how one did it, in fact. She was a woman who had never made many friends among her own class, who were slightly afraid of her and altogether hostile to her, and who had never been accepted by those above her. She remained in a prim, and even sinister, isolation, for she had not discovered her mind to anyone. Well-behaved, neatly dressed, well-built, with a locked face and closed lips, she went her way in the small town of Mullenbridge, neither listening to nor offering gossip. A woman not respected, for she was supposed to be mean and proud; not liked, for she was supposed to be hard and dull. But feared a little, for she had a curious, indefinable quality considered by her neighbours formidable. There was something, they said, when the subject of Mrs. Fenton arose (which was not very often), about her look, the way she turned her head, about even her silence, that was not at all agreeable but had indeed a certain menace.

The girls, Adelaide and Caroline, were sometimes discussed among the same neighbours. What was the queer mother intending to do with them? Surely they should be maids to some fine lady, since it might be considered they were above waiting in an inn, bringing the coals into the warming-pan and showing the guests up to their chambers; yes, nice, genteel maids, perhaps in a great establishment.

But there was no indication that Mrs. Fenton wanted to find such desirable posts for her daughters; no, indeed, she seemed to be endeavouring to give them an education far above their station, sending them to a boarding-school for the daughters of gentlemen, indeed! How did she find the money? Then the rumour went round that the conceited girls were, silly as this seemed, to enter some finishing-school. But they did not go.

Now Adelaide must be nineteen, and she was at home, doing, as it seemed, nothing, except what could be covered by the loose phrase, 'helping her mother to look after her father.' And there was Caroline. She had left her school, when three years younger than her sister, and she also was idle at home. Could Mrs. Fenton indeed afford to keep these healthy girls loitering in a parlour? Had Mr. Fenton so handsome a pension, had Mrs. Fenton so reliable an income from Consols or some form of gilt-edged securities that these two young women could live like their betters? This would have been the course of the neighbours' comment had they been able to put it in such a coherent form.

But the Fentons gave no cause for offence, therefore no case for definite gossip. People watched and grumbled, and a little wondered. And the point of all this spying, tattling, and criticizing was that Adelaide was extremely pretty and therefore the suspicion grew, especially in female minds, that Mrs. Fenton intended, in some devious ways, to exploit this feminine charm.

But how? Those who most keenly entered into this local problem could not answer this question. How could Adelaide Fenton, daughter of a bed-ridden clerk of a large tea merchant, hope to make anything of her graces which, if she had been able to obtain entry to the balls in the Assembly Rooms, if she had been of a quality to be received in the parties and dances of the neighbouring gentry, might have brought her some substantial return in the form of a good offer? Not, of course, from a gentleman, but from a yeoman farmer or possibly some upper servant like the butler to Lord Seagrove, for the privileged were permitted to attend these Assembly dances and balls, although not allowed any contact with the upper classes. A rope of red silk marked off the upper part of the rooms, where the nobility and gentry of the county met, from the lower portion, where the well-supported, the well-accounted-for, were allowed to render decorous homage.

The privilege of attending, even beyond the scarlet silken rope, these gatherings was one keenly striven for and one to which Mrs. Fenton and her daughters had never attained. How, then, asked the gossips, could that women, however cool and managing she might be in her own secretive and humble way, hope to secure for her girls any marriage beyond that of a tailor's assistant, a young man from behind a haberdasher's counter, or, at worst, a farm labourer who might in time, with thrift and diligence, save enough to obtain a cottage of his own?

Thus the cogitations of the neighbours. Mrs. Fenton never discussed these possible speculations with her daughters. What people thought of her or what she thought of them was never the subject of her slow conversation; she remained closed, even secretive, and so did the girls when in her presence.

Even now, with this considerable excitement of the pink bonnet, with the glossy box of shining white cardboard between them, no keen or lively comment was offered by either woman.

The tray was ready; Mrs. Fenton flicked a speck of dust from the prim bunch of scarlet and green roses painted in the centre of the black lacquer.

"I'll take it up, Mother," smiled Adelaide.

She picked up the load of food with an air of grace and left the room, holding it as if it were an oblation to the gods, high and gallantly, with swift movements of the hips that the mother noted with a stealthy and perhaps an approving eye.

As the elder girl left the parlour the younger entered it from an inner door. She smiled at her mother, seated herself at the table, and proceeded to eat steadily, collecting with cool precision, scones, jam, cakes, bread, butter, tea, and cream, She was so absorbed in her gluttony that she paid no attention to her mother's glance that was over her obliquely but keenly.

Caroline was a well-favoured girl, plump and blonde, with a pure complexion and close ringlets of a bright brown hair that those who admired her might have termed gold. Her features were good but too small for the contours of her face; her figure, for her age, was over-well-formed.

Her mother noted these advantages and defects with a cool and appraising eye, then returned again to her rocking-chair by the fireside and stared with a steadfast eye at the kettle and the flame. No word was spoken between the girl and her mother and no sound was heard save the gentle footfalls of Adelaide on the stairs as she approached to the upper room; there was silence until she returned.

"How did you find your father, dear?" asked Mrs. Fenton, using her conventional tone for the conventional phase.

"Father was the same as usual," replied Adelaide. "He said he liked the tea, enjoyed the cake, and next time could he have some more sugar, please."

Caroline glanced up at her sister, smiling with firmly curved lips, and asked: "Where did you get the bonnet, Adelaide?"

This seemed to be the question that the elder girl was expecting, for she gave a little sigh that might have been of satisfaction, touched the cardboard box and replied: "Oh, I don't suppose I should tell you, Carrie, should I? I think it's a secret. It's from a gentleman, you see, from an admirer."

The last words were echoed by the mother and the younger daughter: "From a gentleman! From an admirer!" Adelaide having a present from a gentleman, from an admirer . . . .

"Well, why not?" simpered Adelaide. She sat down at the table and selected, daintily, a cake. "He is going to marry me, of course, Mother. I'll tell you all about it some day, but now it is a secret."

"A secret!" said Mrs. Fenton

Caroline laughed rudely.

"It's a pretty bonnet," she commented. "Who is the gentleman that is going to marry you, Adelaide?"

"I can't tell you, it's a secret," repeated the elder girl, with a touch of sullenness. "You trust me, don't you, Mother?"

"Trust you? I don't know what you're talking about! You'll have to take these matters to your father. You've met a gentleman who's going to marry you and he's given you the present of a pink bonnet, and I'm to trust you. Well, well!" Mrs. Fenton rocked herself to and fro in her worn easy-chair. "Of course, you're a good girl, well brought up, Adelaide, and of nice behaviour and always at home early in the afternoon, and you say your prayers and go to church. Well, well, a gentleman, and he's given you a pink bonnet and you're going to marry him."

"Don't tease, Mother," pouted Adelaide. "What I say is quite true."

"Is he rich?" sneered Carrie, putting more heavy cake to her mouth. "Will he take you away, perhaps to London or to Paris? Will he buy you any amount of fine clothes?"

"Will he give you a chance to make as good a match as he is himself, you mean, Carrie?" retorted Adelaide sharply. "No, I'm not going to answer any of your questions. It's a secret, a mystery, I mustn't say anything. But you can see for yourself—here's the bonnet!" She took it out of the box as she spoke and placed it on her well-shaped head, drawing, with tight, crisp strokes, the wide strings under her rounded chin.

She stood for a while with an air of ease, enjoying the admiration of her mother and sister. She was charming, tall and graceful in her gown of white dimity with tiny sprigs of roses that was well made and freshly laundered, with her fichu of clear muslin folded over her rounded bosom, and the fashionable bonnet, incongruous because it was of satin and designed to be worn with an elaborate afternoon pelisse, but very pretty, set gallantly and daintily upon her well-set head.[4]

Adelaide was, in the opinion of her neighbours, a handsome girl, a delightful girl, or a charming girl; the adjectives varied according to the speakers.

She was slightly above the common size and very finely curved in shoulders, neck, arms, and bosom, with that rippling line of flesh and muscle that conveys a lively voluptuousness. The contours of her face were, like those of her sister, firm and freshly coloured; her lips and nostrils were deeply cut, her eyes, slightly deep-set, slightly near together, but bright and sparkling with red-gold lashes. Her rather coarse brown hair was abundant and lustrous. Indeed, she appeared to lack none of those charms and graces enjoyed by the favourites of Venus.

---

[4] Dimity: lightweight, sheer white or printed cotton fabric with two or more warp threads thrown into relief. Fichu: a small, triangular shawl worn round the shoulders.

And the costly bonnet became her very well, her mother's nod said as much, Caroline's cool stare admitted as much. The girl glanced at herself in the mirror in the imitation tortoiseshell border that hung between the Staffordshire dogs on the mantelshelf, and thought as much to herself, a bonnet of rose-coloured satin with the white lining, with plumes and flowers, the bows tied under the chin . . . .

"Fit for a gentlewoman," commented Caroline, with a sneer too subtle for her age.

"When I wear it I shall be a gentlewoman," retorted Adelaide with a teasing indifference.

She daintily removed the headgear, as if she had practised the gesture, with no hurry, no embarrassment; it was an elegant action gracefully performed.

"I wish you'd say who is the gentleman." Mrs. Fenton spoke in an easy abstracted murmur as if she addressed the fire.

"He will come to see you soon, Mother." Adelaide smiled in a self-satisfied manner as she swung the bonnet on her hand.

Caroline, wiping her lips on a thick napkin, asked: "Was it he you was walking with in the Folly Woods yesterday?"

"Well, if you saw me walking with a gentleman in the Folly Woods it was he. But what were you doing there, Miss—spying?"

"Now, now! Come, come!" scolded Mrs. Fenton, lazily. "Carrie's as much right in the Folly Woods as you, Adelaide. And you shouldn't either of you have been there alone."

"I wasn't alone, I was with a gentleman, the gentleman I'm going to marry. Don't question me any more, Mother. It's a splendid match and you may spoil everything yet. Look at this present! You can see how genteel the bonnet is! And I can show you other gifts, too. And see what I'm making for him."

She drew from the reticule that hung at her waist some handkerchiefs in which were initials embroidered in her own hair.

"See, I've been working these for him, and I am going to send them with a letter. Now, you must not ask me anything else." Her voice dropped. "You trust me, do you not, Mother? I am not a silly girl, I listen to your good advice. Carrie, go and sit with Father. It is time he had his reading."

"He does not care about the reading," remarked Caroline, rising slowly and brushing the sugar from her fingers.

"Well, then," put in Mrs. Fenton sharply, "if you do not want to read to your father, you can remove the tea service, miss."

"I would sooner go upstairs," replied Carrie, with a hunch of her plump shoulders.

She left the room, closing the door noisily.

"Lazy and greedy," grumbled Adelaide. "Why won't she clear the tea things? That means I've got to do it, I suppose."

"Susan has one half-day out a month only," remarked Mrs. Fenton smoothly. "One of you must make the parlour tidy; you do not do much work. Look at your hands, how white and smooth they are. You do not even sew much, or starch, or goffer, or iron, do you, Adelaide?"[5]

"No, neither does Carrie. You have brought us up to be ladies, haven't you, Mother?"

"To be ladies." Mrs. Fenton repeated the words. "What does that mean?—sitting on the settee in the best parlour and reading novels from the circulating library and thinking up lies, Adelaide?"

The girl returned her mother's steely look with a glance equally hard.

---

[5] Goffer: crimp or flute a lace edge or frill with a heated iron.

"I've never told you any lies, Mother."

"The bonnet, Adelaide, and the gentleman in the wood! I suppose now Carrie's upstairs we can speak freely."

"Perhaps she's listening at the door," suggested Adelaide.

"Oh, no, she won't be. She knows that I've got sharp ears, and I've heard her going upstairs and her steps overhead. She'll be sitting by her father reading *Pilgrim's Progress* or the Bible, what does it matter?"

"What, indeed!" sneered Adelaide. "As long as she is out of the way."

"Now, then, my girl—these lies, or—well, whatever you like to call 'em. Walking out with gentlemen, taking presents——That bonnet cost five guineas if it cost a halfpenny. I'll go to Miss Herle to-morrow, to find out the truth."

"The truth!" repeated Adelaide. "All Miss Herle knows is that the bonnet was ordered, that she made it for me and delivered it to me. And do you think she'll tell you who was responsible for that?"

"We're old friends."

"That don't mean she'll tell you what's against her interests." Adelaide moved to the table and slowly and reluctantly put the soiled china on the tray. "Mother, can't you let me alone? I know what I'm about. I've had a good education, I learnt something of the world at school from the other girls and their parents."

"Did you?" asked Mrs. Fenton, with an intense interest, looking over her shoulder. "Did you?"

"Yes. More than you ever learned when you were young, Mother. You were a farmer's daughter, weren't you, brought up in the country?"

"Yes," agreed the elder woman, stolidly. "Brought up to tell the truth and to be respectable."

"Brought up to marry Father and nurse him for twenty years, paralysed."

"Not brought up to that, miss. That was my fate, it overtook me. Look out that yours doesn't overtake you."

"I suppose it will. They teach you that in church, don't they?" replied the girl, sulkily. "Or what do they teach you? I'm sure I never listen either to the sermons or the prayers. I've got my own thoughts all the time. Fate, that's a queer word! Providence! What's it mean, Mother?"

"Don't ask me, Adelaide. My puzzle is just this, I suppose—that we're not gentlefolk and not servants, not even little tradespeople. I had the money when Father died to give you and Carrie a genteel education, but haven't had enough education myself to know if it's done you any good."

"You've got some sense, Mother."

"Sense! I don't know if that's going to help. I know what people think—that you two ought to be chambermaids at the 'Seagrove Arms,' or serving behind the haberdasher's counter. And so you ought, I suppose, if you'd been brought up the same as I was."

"Yes, Mother," said Adelaide slowly. "It is true you've not been able to give me any good advice; I've had to look about me for myself. Why not?"

"Why not, indeed."

"I've got no relations," continued Adelaide. "There's Aunt Martha, but she's far away and hasn't been to see us for three years, has she?"

"No, she hasn't, Adelaide. But I write to her—and she to me."

"And I suppose I've some cousins—Jenny and Anne, aren't they? Uncle Simon's daughters?"

"Yes, but never you mind about them." Mrs. Fenton's tone

was masterful. “No, never mind about them. I suppose they’ll be servant girls, chambermaids—well, let it go. Their parents are dead. Your aunt did what she could—she runs a little farm.”

“Why did you give us such a good education, Mother? What do you think we could do?”

“I suppose I was ambitious. I saw you was going to be pretty, both of you. I’ve nothing else to think of but you two, your father being like he is. And there was just enough money, we living quietly——”

“But you didn’t think beyond that, what would happen when we’d had the education, been taught how to behave ourselves and come back here and nobody know us—too good for the little people and not good enough even for the people who are just the hangers-on of the big people.”

“Don’t talk like that, Adelaide. A fine bouncing girl like you—well, you’ve got the looks and the education.”

“Do you think that’s enough, Mother? This education you keep talking of?” asked Adelaide as she took the piled tray out of the room; she returned quickly and lightly.

“Well, it seems to me if you’ve found a gentleman to walk in the woods with and talk of marriage and give you a pink bonnet——” continued Mrs. Fenton.

“And other gifts besides.” Adelaide suddenly slid her plump hand into the bosom on her thick white frock and pulled out a string of glittering pink paste that she cast on the table. “It’s pretty, isn’t it? You wouldn’t get it in Mullenbridge.”

And the girl snatched it up greedily, eagerly, to display it, and Mrs. Fenton’s eyes flashed grey fire. It was a long time since she had seen so delicate and charming an ornament. She had her own necklets of jet and pinchbeck, her lockets and cameo brooches, her thick silver bracelets engraved with swallows and ivy; but this trifle was different; it was like the bonnet, rose-coloured; it glittered and gleamed, drops of pink backed with silver—sparkling—"like diamonds," said Mrs. Fenton at last.

"But not diamonds," corrected Adelaide quickly. "Paste, French paste, made in Paris. It shows sweetly on my neck, doesn't it?" she aded eagerly, as she clasped the necklet round her white throat and looked at herself in the dim glass.

"How much did it cost?" asked Mrs. Fenton heavily.

"Oh, I don't know." Adelaide seemed again both sly and stupid. "One doesn't ask gentlemen how much their presents cost!"

"If he wants to marry you," said Mrs. Fenton, leaning forward and looking into the fire, "why don't he come forward and say so; why don't he see your father?"

"Would it be any use any gentleman coming to see Father? Besides, he's got his parents to think of—they won't let him betroth himself until he's of age, and there's six months to wait. He's got to be prudent. Discreet, he calls it."

"Ah! Prudent! Discreet!" muttered Mrs. Fenton. "Meanwhile there's presents, walking in the Folly Woods——That's not what we'd have called prudent and discreet in my young days."

"You were a dairymaid, Mother, a farmer's daughter, and I've been brought up like a lady. I know how to manage these affairs."

"Do you?" Mrs. Fenton was half shrewd, half baffled. "It's a pretty bonnet," she added vaguely, "it's a pretty glittering string of pink stones."

"I'll read you some of his letters one day, Mother," conceded Adelaide. "Not now. I've got them upstairs."

"Oh, he sends you letters, does he? And how do you get them, my girl, without my knowing of it?"

"Oh, you thought you had me watched, didn't you, Mother?" Adelaide checked herself up as if conscious that a common note had come into her tone. "Well, I don't suppose you would understand. Sometimes he puts them in a hole in a tree in Folly Woods, in Seagrove Park."

"Oh, you go there, do you?"

"Yes, round the old Folly. That's where he leaves the messages for me, where I leave mine for him. To-morrow there's to be a ring—that's to show that he intends to marry me."

"He'd better see your father," insisted Mrs. Fenton sullenly. "Why don't you tell me his name? All this about his coming of age——"

"He has only a grandfather, and he's an old man, and there's lawyers to look after him, and a tutor who's a clergyman. My sweetheart's a boy not much older that I am and he loves me very much."

Mrs. Fenton was silent, she moved her lips as if conning over some reply, but it remained unuttered. Adelaide sighed and put her bonnet into the cardboard box with the silver paper.

"You'd like me to be a lady, wouldn't you, Mother? You'd like to see me with a great deal of money, with fine clothes and a carriage? You shall have some luxury, too, Mother. I'd see that you were well treated."

"And what would happen to your father?" asked Mrs. Fenton. "Twenty years he's been in bed. Doctor Barton said it might be another twenty——There's something to look forward to, Adelaide—another twenty years of your father there in bed, paralysed, an imbecile——"

"But he's not always imbecile. He often knows what he's talking about. Sometimes he can speak more sense than you or I,

Mother. Well, if I'm a lady married to a great gentleman——"

"A great gentleman!" repeated Mrs. Fenton quickly.

"I said *if* I was a great lady married to a great gentleman," and Adelaide tossed her head, "I'd have someone to nurse Father so that you needn't have any trouble, Mother." She crossed over to the elder woman and put her arms round her neck. "Come, now, help me!"

"Help you! You don't seem to want any help! You seem to have done well enough for yourself!"

"But I do, Mother, I do—Carrie is watching me. She's spiteful, jealous; of course she would be, wouldn't she?"

"Carrie's just as good-looking as you are, and I dare say will have just as much luck; it's only that she's three years younger."

"I know. I dare say she'll be prettier when she's my age. But now—well, Mother, she's watching me and you can see she does! And tell her what I say is true, and tell Father that I've got an admirer, a gentleman who wants to marry me, that he's even sent me letters—oh, I can *show* you the letters—and that I'm making him handkerchiefs with his name embroidered on in my hair! Mother, you will, won't you? You see, it's difficult. It's a question of his guardian, his grandfather's consent, and the lawyers. He's got to be quiet for a while. But he loves me truly, indeed he does."

"I wonder, my girl, if you know what you're talking about?" asked Mrs. Fenton, putting her daughter aside.

"Oh, don't wonder, Mother; just trust me."

"He bought you the bonnet, a string of pink stones——"

"Only paste," sighed Adelaide, rising. "But one of these days he'll give me diamonds—a diamond ring and a diamond necklace, and diamonds in my hair, and even diamonds on my shoes, Mother."

"And what will there be for me?"

"Oh, anything you like, Mother; why not?"

"Why not, indeed! I've heard stories like these—they used to be called fairy tales in my time."

"Tell Father and Carrie it's true, please, *please.*"

Mrs. Fenton rose and in her ungainly person there was a power that made the homely room drab and shrunken.

"I'll tell Carrie it's true, I'll tell anything you like to your father—it doesn't matter what I say to him—if you will let me know all about it yourself, Adelaide. So far you haven't told me anything, you know. It's only just tales. And now, to-day, the bonnet——"

"Yes, I'll tell you, Mother. *He* will come and see you, I'll take you where you can see *him.* You can watch us walking together. He often says: 'Dearest Adelaide, I must be presented to your mother! I admire her so much!'"

Mrs. Fenton's eyes flashed, but she did not reply to this, for the door opened and Carrie entered the room.

"I heard your step on the stair, my girl; creeping down, you were, trying to listen, but you stumbled on the last rod and so had to open the door and come in. Oh, I know all your tricks."

"Why should I want to listen?" asked Carrie sullenly. "There's nothing interesting being said. Oh, Adelaide, you've cleared the tea service away!"

"She's not washed up the china or cutlery," said Mrs. Fenton. "It's all been left in there for Susan, and that'll mean trouble to-morrow. Never mind. Come here, Carrie. I've got a word to say to you. Has your father gone to sleep?"

"Yes, Father's asleep, same as usual. When's Doctor Barton coming?" The girl glanced at the clock that had a pale, moonlike face on which were painted wreaths and blue flowers.

"You go upstairs, Adelaide," commanded Mrs. Fenton, and

the girl obeyed at once, as if she responded, not to the mere words, but to some inner meaning conveyed by her mother.

Caroline picked up a copy of *The Family Friend* that lay in the window-place. "Don't look at that so scornfully," protested Mrs. Fenton. "I suppose it is worth twopence a month."

"Is it?" The girl, in flat accents, read out the cover of the magazine that she held: " 'All that is excellent and elevating in literature, happily mingled with all that is useful in life, while the price places it within the reach of all'—what does that mean, Mother?"

Mrs. Fenton's heavy face had a cloudy expression; she replied sullenly to what she knew to be a taunt.

"It is for ladies—you see what people who know say about it——"

Caroline read out in a high-pithed, expressionless voice from the letterpress inside the front cover of *The Family Friend*: " 'Thirty-two closely printed pages, price twopence monthly. It is emphatically a magazine for the family. Its pages present something for all, there is no member of the domestic circle forgotten, and no class of society overlooked. It is in itself a *Gentleman's Magazine*, a *Lady's Magazine*, a *Mother's Magazine*, a *Youth's Magazine* and a *Child's Companion*. It is, as its title correctly declares, a Magazine for Domestic Economy, Entertainment and Practical Science . . . .' "

"You are making a fool of me," put in Mrs. Fenton grimly. "Ladies ought to understand these things, and I've paid away good money, that my father earned *hard*, to have you educated as ladies."

Ignoring this, Caroline continued to read aloud.

" 'We have received it into our home circle with great pleasure, for it is not only a *family visitor*, but a *family friend*—it is a work especially adapted to cheer the happy fireside of home, and to aid the development of social affection.' "

"You know I can't understand that," protested Mrs. Fenton sullenly.

"Why do you pay twopence a month for it?" asked Caroline. "You've no common sense."

"That's a way to talk to your mother! Just because I've brought you up above my own station in life! That is a magazine for gentlewomen; well, I wanted you both to be that. I've done my best."

"Your worst, I think."

"What is your meaning, Caroline?"

"Too late to explain now, Mother."

"Too late—and you sixteen years only, Caroline!"

"Never mind. I dare say it was too late before I was born——"

"I don't know what you mean."

"You don't want to——"

"Talk respectful, Caroline."

The girl turned her back on her mother and tossed over the pile of books that lay among the worn cushions. "*Treasures in Needlework*, *Elegant Arts for Ladies*, the *Wives' Own Book of Cookery*, and *The Practical Housewife.*"

"Well, I bought them for you because I wanted you to be *ladies*," declared Mrs. Fenton defiantly.

"*Ladies*," emphasized Caroline. "Well, I suppose so—but what is the mystery about Adelaide; has that any connection with—genteel accomplishments?"

The mother replied obliquely.

"You've a sharp tongue, Carrie; it won't get you a rich husband—"

"Is there nothing else in the world worth having but rich husbands?"

"And you only sixteen! I don't know where you get it from! We were always respectable, God-fearing people——"

"The devil is more to be feared than God," smiled Carrie. "What can *He* do?"

"You wicked girl!" But Mrs. Fenton laughed slyly. "But to come to practical matters—Adelaide has a rich sweetheart—a gentleman. Your sister has been telling me about this admirer, this gentleman who gives her the presents," added Mrs. Fenton steadily. "It's true, Carrie, I know it's true. You are not to make jokes about it or to mention *him*. It's something important that's going to mean a great deal to all of us. It may be you'll get a good marriage out of it yourself. So hold your tongue, do you hear? Or I'll find means of making you."

Caroline did not reply to this threat. She was moving carelessly the pile of books in the window recess.

"Adelaide never looks at these," she remarked, "and they cost eight shillings and sixpence each."

"Well, *you* read them." Mrs. Fenton was defiant.

"The needlework and cooking, those are useful—but it is silly to try to make wax fruit, pictures in sand or bugle work."[6]

"Adelaide *did* try—*and* the porcupine quill frames—*and* the seaweed pictures."

"There was a horrid mess, and a deal of money wasted," smiled Caroline. "Adelaide only tried because she thought it genteel and elegant—the same reasons as those you bought the books for."

"She was right. Ladies have those books and those accomplishments. I wish I had a pianoforte. Adelaide was clever at her music. Miss Fullam said——"

"Miss Fullam flattered you because she was charging too much for our schooling. That was a miserable place at Clapham,

---

[6] Bugles are tube-shaped beads usually made from lengths of glass cane.

Mother. I wish you had not sent us there. I would rather have had the money. Besides the pupils weren't really ladies."

"They seemed so—and Mr. Bisset recommended the establishment."

"You don't know, Mother. I do, even going about Clapham a little, and once or twice to London. Mr. Bisset wanted to oblige Miss Fullam—he's her lawyer, too."

Mrs. Fenton looked startled for a second, then her face became again drab and dull.

"You don't speak correctly—after all I've spent on you—I do as well myself, just by listening to the Bissets, and to the gentry coming out of church—and—other ways."

"Adelaide reads too many silly books—she did at school; why do you allow her to join the circulating library?"

"Ladies read these tales. I've looked at them myself; there's no harm in them." Mrs. Fenton defended herself obstinately, then suddenly perceiving how she had been drawn from the important subject she had been discussing, she added sternly: "You're only sixteen, my girl, and pert; you keep your tongue between your teeth. I *know* that what your sister says is true."

Carrie was unimpressed; almost alarmed, her mother peered at her, and tried to follow up her advantage.

"Adelaide's love story is a secret, but it's true."

"I like mysteries and secrets," conceded Caroline. She glanced at the table now cleared of the cloths and dishes, took down her sewing basked from the side and began to wind up spools of tangled bright-coloured cottons.

"It's true," repeated Mrs. Fenton heavily.

The girl did not answer.

"You're to believe it's true, and you're not to tell anybody about it, do you understand?" continued her mother sternly. "It's a question of being careful for a little while, and then, as I say, all the good fortune that I hoped for when I gave you both the education of ladies will be yours."

Caroline picked over the cottons with her plump, smooth, white fingers.

"I don't think Adelaide's so very pretty," she remarked, reflectively, without spite or jealousy. "I've seen them walking in the woods," she added irrelevantly.

Her mother turned with a quickness surprising in one so heavily built.

"Seen who walking in the woods?" she demanded. "You said so—but I wondered."

"Why, Adelaide and the gentleman, the gentleman who gave her the pink bonnet. The woods by Seagrove Folly—*you* know. You said you knew everything, that it was *true*."

Mrs. Fenton was sullenly silent.

"I should tell her to be more careful, Mother, if it's a mystery or a secret. Other people might see them, might they not?"

"You're to mind what I tell you, and never bother about what others do."

Mrs. Fenton spoke clumsily, with the labouring attempts at elaboration of one who has been shocked and tries to delay action; she rose from her rocking-chair, moved the kettle farther back on the hob so that the jet of steam did not hiss so loudly, and went slowly out of the parlour leaving Caroline turning over her sewing materials.

* * * * *

On the first landing of the small house Lucy Fenton paused with a sigh that expressed more than exhaustion of her stout person that she had so painfully heaved upstairs. There were two doors facing her—one led to the room that she shared with her husband, that with the small adjoining closet was all that she had of privacy from her daughters and Susan Keen, the maidservant. The sick man hardly counted for human intrusion on this retreat; when she drew his bed-curtains together she could forget him and by the hour together. The other room was that shared by the girls. Above were the two small attics, in one of which Susan slept and the other which was used for storage.

Downstairs were the front parlour, the back kitchen and the scullery; there were no more rooms in the entire house. Not many means here for pretensions at gentility, not much with which to impress a doubtful superiority on a sneering neighbourhood.

Mrs. Fenton frowned, struggling with her own ignorance, her own lack of knowledge of the world. Naturally she was quick and shrewd, active-minded, ambitious, but thwarted and frustrated at every turn by her lack of money, her restricted ambience, besides the facts that she was uneducated and had to fight a sluggishness in her disposition that prevented her from making those strenuous and desperate efforts that others in her situation might have undertaken. Some women in the position of Mrs. Fenton, with the advantage of her steady income, her small capital and her two pretty daughters, even if handicapped by a sick husband and a provincial upbringing and a poor background, would have contrived something better than Mrs. Fenton had contrived. She knew this and it increased her antagonism against what she vaguely termed her destiny.

Without knocking she entered her daughter's room. Adelaide was seated at the window, the chill light—it had been a winter of bleak winds and was a late-flowering black spring—was beginning to thicken into darkness and a pearly glow, half-silver, half-dusk was over the figure of the girl in her flowered dimity frock; she had a curious, solid, almost heavy effect as if she was a well-formed statue. The bonnet, looking fantastic in this chamber and by this light, half-covered her lustrous ringlets.

'Dressed too thinly for the season, like all young girls now,' thought Mrs. Fenton mechanically, 'thin shoes and cotton frock, no mantle even when she goes out. She looks healthy, though. I wonder if she *does* go out, after I'm in bed, out to the Folly Woods?'

She smoothed her apron with her hands, that were like her daughter's, white and comely but now curdling into the soft ripples of late middle-age.

"Where are the letters you spoke of, Adelaide? You ought to show them to me."

"They're in my drawer—I wish I had a desk." The girl simpered; the full face turned on her mother was moonlike beneath the pink bonnet; she seemed now too heavy for beauty.

"Take that rubbish off your head," commanded her mother, sharply, "you look like a clown at the fair. I'm going round to Miss Herle's to-morrow to find out the truth about the matter."

"You said so before, didn't you, Mother?" replied the girl, lazily. She slipped the bonnet from her head and hung it on the polished arm of her rush chair. "And I tell you she can't tell you the truth but only that little bit of it she knows."

"You're trying to confuse me," protested Mrs. Fenton doggedly. "*You* could tell me the whole truth, and I'll have it, Adelaide, now."

"Oh, will you?" The girl lifted her plump shoulders. "You'd better let me alone, Mother, or you'll be losing the best bit of fortune that's likely to come your way."

The mother sighed, baffled, resentful, yet impressed; her daughter was better educated than she was herself. Lucy Fenton knew the value of that. She was, moreover, just as shrewd as she was herself and had, Mrs. Fenton believed, that curious quality that in her idiom she termed—'knowing how to manage the men.' She had observed Adelaide with a few male visitors who came to their house, with the shopmen, with the tradesmen, with the youths who had grown up from childhood in the same lane.

Yes, Adelaide knew how to lead them on and hold them off. Perhaps she was to be trusted, yet this secret affair seemed difficult, dangerous to this woman, more unfortunately placed, as she bitterly reminded herself, than if she had been a widow.

She tried a wheedling tone that she used with ill effect and that was against her nature. Seating herself on the other rush-bottom chair placed between the two long beds with the white crochet covers she coaxed.

"Who is it you walk in the woods with, dear? Caroline has seen you and maybe others have, too. Won't you tell me all about it and let me help you?"

"You couldn't help me, Mother." The girl spoke sullenly and with an edge of defiance. "You stand in the way, and you know it. I have to be careful what I say about you, and Father. I don't want to be undutiful or to say things that will wound. My Basil is a fine match"—her voice trembled and she put her hands over her eyes. "I've his letters here. You can see them, one day. There's his seal on them and his name underneath. Let me alone."

"You don't speak so genteel as you used to," said Mrs. Fenton sharply. "If you say I stand in the way, it seems to me you soon forget your manners yourself."

"He's not thinking of manners," retorted the girl, passionately, "he's thinking of me. He loves me, he's going to give me a white horse, an Arabian horse, he's going to build me a summerhouse, a pavilion that will be painted with convolvulus and wild roses on a blue lattice-work. He's going to have a new wing put on to the house, which is like a palace. There's going to be a conservatory, what you call a stove-house, built, and there'll be all manner of exotic plants in it."

"What do you mean by exotic?" asked Mrs. Fenton suspiciously.

"As if that matters!" Adelaide was contemptuous. "It means foreign."

"You got it out of one of those books you read. I don't see that opening a circulating library in Mullenbridge is any good for anyone."

"You don't understand."

"That's what the young ones always say to the older ones," replied Mrs. Fenton, without malice. "Sometimes it's true, sometimes it's not. I'd understand all right if you'd give me something to understand. You're trying to get married to a young man who's above you in station and you're managing the affair secretly. Well, I admit I've not home to receive a gentleman in, and your father—when he is in his senses—is no use to anyone."

"Basil," commented Adelaide, "is sorry about that. He doesn't like to think of me nursing a bedridden man for so many years."

"Oh, you managed to say that, did you, to this Basil—is that his name?" Mrs. Fenton searched her mind, briskly, keenly; she knew no Basil in the neighbourhood.

"I call him Basil," said Adelaide, evasively. "And he calls me Carina."

"I never heard of that. Is it a Christian name? Light a candle, Adelaide; it's getting dark."

The girl rose and lit the two candles of plain mutton-fat in the simple pewter sticks that stood on the little table that was used for both toilet and writing.

"It's a foreign name. You wouldn't know what it meant, any more than you did about exotic."

Adelaide did not give any further regard to her mother; she was staring at the reflection of her face that was shown like a flower blooming above a dark lane in the depths of the sombre mirror that was filled by all the shadows of the darkening room and the flames of the candles that illuminated her glowing, soft countenance.

Her mother also studied this reflection with the detached, keen, almost greedy air of one who views a treasure, possibly her only treasure.

The girl, well, perhaps the two girls, were her sole capital; through them lay her only chance of attaining some passionately held but most vaguely defined ambitions.

Her life had really been no life at all, a mere existence—childhood, girlhood on a small farm, the marriage to a man a little 'above her,' confused hopes and wishes (crossing and re-crossing one another) of seeing something, of doing something more than she had seen or done before, of contriving, by some means she knew not what, to emulate those she saw enjoying all that seemed to her desirable—women who were easy, luxurious, flattered, admired.

The birth of her two children, the increasing anxieties of supporting them on a small income, her husband's miserable health, then his long illness, all this had combined to stifle Mrs. Fenton's ambitions that had never, even to herself, been clearly formulated. Her ignorance and her sluggishness had hindered her from defining even her aspirations.

She had gradually transferred this medley of blurred desires, of vulgar ambitions, to the girls, and there again she was thwarted by her own lack of knowledge, her own slowness and apathy, by the pressure upon her of distressing circumstances. Mr. Bisset, her attorney, had been the only person to whom she could go for advice and perhaps he was not so clever.

Yet Adelaide might be lucky, she certainly was educated in a genteel manner, and Mrs. Fenton had a blind faith in education.

"Well, I have done all I could for you," she protested, as if she put forward her merits as a plea for favours. "I've spent every halfpenny on you that I could, all the little bit that Father left. I never had more than two gowns a year, one for winter and one for summer, and I've not changed them more than once in every ten years or so. I even cut down on your father's medicines and the dainties Dr. Barton said he ought to have, in order to keep you up in your music and your painting. They were extra, Miss Fullam said."

"And what's the good of either one or the other when there's no pianoforte in the house, and no money to buy water-colours with?"

"Never mind, dear," replied the mother, and her tone was half servile, half threatening. "If you're to marry this gentleman who's to give you a boudoir, or a pavilion, or a stove-house, or whatever it is, and a white Arabian horse——"

"All that and everything!" cried Adelaide, with a triumphant interruption. She was re-arranging the candles so that they cast a double glow upon her in the dusky depths of the mirror, totally absorbed in her own reflection, answering her mother with her lips only, with the first words that came as she watched the changing colours of pearl, rose, gold and bronze in her face, neck and throat.

"Well, then," persisted Mrs. Fenton, slowly, "it won't matter if you don't have a pianoforte here, but you'll be glad I taught you how to play one, won't you? But what's the use of a horse to you?" she added. "You never had one all your life and couldn't ride it. I had a mare, old Dolly, on the farm."

Adelaide did not trouble to answer. She sat down at the little table that she had made as attractive as possible with a few trinkets of glass and china and, pulling open a drawer that had long brass fuchsia-shaped handles, she held up before her mother's eyes a packet of letters tied with a lavender-coloured sarcenet ribbon.[7]

"There they are, Mother, you can look at them from here. They're from Basil, but to-day you're not to read them. Did you tell Caroline to believe all I told you?"

"Yes, I did. She said she would. But you can't trust the girl. She's quick-witted too. She'll be watching you to see if you, or I, or both of us, are lying. She said she'd seen you both in the Folly Woods, too."

"Well, what does it matter? A lady can walk with a gentleman in broad daylight."

"Not without people talking. And who is this gentleman? I don't know many in the neighbourhood."

"You're thinking them over. There's the doctor's young son and the lawyer's son—one helping his father in the dispensary and the other articled to his——"

"Oh, yes," interrupted Mrs. Fenton, rising impatiently, "and there's a good many likely young men in the town. But they're not gentlemen, they'll not be able to buy you white horses and stove-houses, with foreign flowers in them, or whatever the nonsense is. Give me those letters, miss, let me see who's written them."

"They won't tell you anything, they're signed Basil." Adelaide thrust the packet back in the drawer and looked at her mother over

[7] Sarcenet: a thin, soft silk used for linings, ribbons, etc.

her shoulder. "Can't you trust me? It won't help you if you don't. I'll run away!"

"You wicked girl," said Mrs. Fenton slowly.

This was exactly what she'd done herself—run away with the pale clerk who had come 'for change of air' to the village where her father had his little farm; 'a lot of good it has done me, I'd better have married Thornhill's son, who had a little property better than my father's. The two farms might have been joined and I might have been comfortable now, if not genteel or lady-like. Yes, the two little properties together would have been worth having. But I ran away with someone who was above me and young Thornhill married someone else. Why do I ramble on about my own past? It doesn't matter any more to anyone.'

"Run away if you like," she added with an indifference that caused the girl to turn and face her. "But you've no money, and if this fine gentleman's under age he won't have any either. Remember, too, that your father, imbecile though you may think him, has got to give his consent to anything that you do before you're of age yourself."

"I don't want you to be angry with me, Mother," said Adelaide. "I don't mean to run away, of course I don't, and I want you to share in all my good fortune. Just let me alone a little for a few days."

"A few days," said Mrs. Fenton, eagerly. "You'll tell me everything then?"

"Yes. Only keep Caroline off, and Father, too. Sometimes, you know, when he's sensible, he asks questions. Don't go to Miss Herle about the bonnet, it'll only begin a lot of talk and there's no need."

"You won't be able to wear it in Mullenbridge," remarked Mrs. Fenton, lifting the latch of the door and peering through the shadows.

"No, I know I shan't. And I haven't the pelisse or a reticule or slippers or anything that I could wear with it. But I'll keep it."

"What did he want to give you a bonnet for that you can't wear, and a string of stones that you have to keep inside your frock? It seems to me he is a fool."

"He is young, and very much in love," cried Adelaide. "Good night, Mother, I'm going to bed now."

"Don't you slip out at night, miss, to the Folly Woods, or wherever it is you do go! Yes, they may well call it Folly, anywhere you take your walks, I'll swear."

"How could I go out? You lock the door."

"So you know that, do you, miss? You've tried it!"

"Well, I hear you go down every night. And if it's not you, it's Susan. And how could I go out with Miss Caroline watching me, and you and Father just across the landing, and Susan overhead, and all the neighbours."

"It sounds as if you've counted over the chances, and the risks, miss."

"Maybe I have. Any girl would. There's the moonlight over there, you can see the woods from the window."

"Well, go to bed," said Mrs. Fenton, in non-committal tones. "I'll see what I'll do. I'll talk to your father when he's well enough. And you be careful how you manage young Carrie. She's a bit more clever than you think, perhaps more clever than you are yourself."

"Don't open the door yet, Mother, I want to ask you something—isn't there some good blood somewhere in your family? You used to talk of it when we were children, now you never do."

"What's the use?"

"Is it true? Miss Fullam always spoke as if you'd married above you."

"Did she? Well, I thought so, too. The Fentons have always been city workers, but never more than clerks—humble, too, but your father seemed to me . . . " She checked herself. "You ask your aunt, she'll know better, it's all stories. My mother was a Heslop, they held themselves better than the Mortons—they had come down, there was coat armour gentry somewhere."

Adelaide pressed for facts.

"Nothing in the Church—no Bible with names, no crested silver?"

"Nothing," replied Mrs. Fenton. "Don't you concern yourself about these old tales, plain lies, I dare say—I put them about to shut people's mouths. You're from humble folk—both sides. It's yourself you've got to look to . . . . "

"I know, and Basil don't care."

"I gave you both a genteel education, I keep you in idleness. I can't do more," sighed Mrs. Fenton.

With this Mrs. Fenton left the room and Adelaide stood for a while listening to her mother's heavy footfalls on the ladderlike stairway. This was the tiresome part of a tiresome day—what to do between now and bedtime . . . . Of course, there was work, she could sew or patch, she could call on a neighbour, sit with her father and read to him again another chapter of the Bible, those verses that he seemed to like even when he was in his most lethargic moods and his mind was clouded, and she would believe him senseless until by a twitch of his pale lips or a flutter of his bony fingers on the clean coverlet he would make a sign that he approved and desired that she continue.

"I've done enough of that to-day," decided Adelaide, with a toss of her head. She put the two candles on the little table by the bed, threw herself on it, and taking from under the pillow a novel,

Daughter of the Night, began to read, moving discontentedly and restlessly as her position became uncomfortable and awkward, holding the book with difficulty so that the fluttering flame cast a light over the closely printed pages.

When Caroline entered the room that the sisters shared, Adelaide was completely lost in the story. It was not with a feigned absorption that she remained inert on the pillows, never turning her head as the younger girl entered, impatiently complaining of the smell and the smoke from the flaring wicks of the unsnuffed candles.

"How wasteful you are, Adelaide, and how careless! The candles guttering like that. I declare one is making a winding-sheet, and that's an ill-omen *you* would say. The window's not properly closed and there's a draught. And how can you read in such a light?"

Turning with a sigh from her delicious reverie, Adelaide clapped the book together, dropped it and sank back on the pillows, clasping her hands behind her head.

"Are you ill? Does your head ache?" asked her sister, approaching her and gazing at her keenly. "You'e very flushed. Why don't you go to bed? I think it's untidy to lie down in one's clothes. Have you washed yourself?"

"I'm not going to wash to-night, the water's too cold."

"Susan will heat some if you wish."

"Don't go down and ask her to——"

"I don't intend to, I'll wash in cold water myself. It's quite good enough for me, but your complexion is rather greasy and you'd do better with the warm water than all those lotions on which you waste the money that Mother gives you for other purposes."

"You know perfectly well," retorted Adelaide angrily, "that those lotions are not for my complexion. I buy them to cure me of sickness. I often feel sick when I stoop or do much housework. I have attacks of giddiness."

Caroline laughed coolly.

"Everybody knows what's in those pots and bottles you buy from Mr. Gilbert. I wonder he humours you and sells you the stuff. I suppose it's because we spend so much money there through father's illness."

Adelaide now dropped all pretence and sighed: "I've seen some advertisements in the Annuals of lotions one can get in Bond Street, London. They come direct from Paris and are the most elegant preparations. Yet really, at my age, one needs nothing. I am in the bloom of youth, that, in itself, is Venus's finest adornment."

"You talk in a strange, nonsensical way," remarked Carrie contemptuously. "I suppose that's the rubbish you get out of those romances you're always reading."

"It's the way ladies talk," replied Adelaide. She rose discontentedly and glanced at the trim, neat, untouched couch of her younger sister as if she longed to exchange it for her own, that was tumbled and tossed. "Mother believed all that I told her about my lover," she stated proudly. "She approved of my conduct. I have assured him that in a short time I shall be able to present him to my parents."

"I said I'd seen you both walking in the woods," remarked Carrie, "and now you must give me the paste clasp Aunt Martha sent you last Christmas. You promised you would."

"But you *did* see us walking in the Folly Woods, Carrie. And why should I give you my paste clasp for merely telling the truth?"

Caroline took off her clothes, quickly yet carefully, arranging her garments precisely on the rush bottom chair in which Mrs. Fenton had sat. The girls were silent; each engaged in an inner debate, then Carrie said, as she snuffed the candles out, then slipped into her cool, unruffled bed with a little shudder as the linen sheets and her cotton gown chilled her warm flesh: "You'd better give me the paste brooch, Adelaide, or I shall tell Mother that I was telling lies. And once she thinks that I never tell the truth, why she won't believe anything I say, will she?"

The core of this confused statement was very clear to Adelaide. She believed that she was defeated, but still tried to defend her treasure. How mean it was in Caroline to bargain for the red paste before she would undertake to do what she ought to have done, out of good nature, without any payment at all!

"I'll read you the letters instead."

"I've heard them before." The younger girl's voice came insolently out of the darkness; there was no moon and the night was cloudy. Only the faintest blur showed in the space of the window from which the thin curtains had been drawn aside by Caroline before she put out the lights.

"You haven't heard all of them. Some came yesterday."

"Did they?" questioned the younger sister. "I didn't see anyone bring them."

"Oh, it was the manservant, Humfries. It was when you was out."

"Yes, and Mother was out, too, I suppose?"

"No, Mother was there, looking out of the window, and she saw him, you ask her if she didn't see him. And then there was another *billet-doux* in the old beech tree nearest the Folly."

But Caroline was not tempted.

"They're all the same." Adelaide could hear that she was yawning. "They're like those in the books you get from the library, word for word very often."

"Gentlemen in love," retorted Adelaide, in a whisper, "always use the same terms of endearment."

"I suppose so." Caroline was not interested. "I don't like those romances. They're about things that never really happen."

"You are a prosaic little puss. Nothing romantic'll happen to you while you have those ideas, Caroline."

"Romantic! You've got to give me the red paste."

"What will Mother say," Adelaide put up her last defence, "if she sees you wearing it?"

"I don't know. What does it matter? You can tell her you gave it me for my birthday. Put it in my drawer to-morrow, Adelaide, or I shall say that I didn't see you both walking in the woods."

The other girl replied sullenly. "Very well, I promise. I give my word."

"Oh, I don't care about your promises, or your word," replied Caroline, "just see that the paste in in my drawer there. If it isn't, why then, I shall just tell Mother I was lying."

The girls turned on their pillows, Caroline to sleep, Adelaide to dream.

* * * * *

Mrs. Fenton made, with due deliberation, her visit to Kitty Herle. The milliner was a prim and smart little woman who ran a brisk business with the wives and daughters of the upper tradespeople, the wives and daughters of those men who had retired from nondescript professions, who might by a stretch of courtesy be called on the fringe of the gentry.

She received Mrs. Fenton very pleasantly. That lady was not among her customers and not, as she would have said herself, 'her style,' since her bonnets were of the plainest and always too well worn to have retained any elegance even if they had originally possessed any. But there seemed promise both of future business and future subject for gossip in Miss Adelaide.

“Miss Herle, you made a bonnet for my daughter,” stated Mrs. Fenton, as she glanced with a slowly awakening curiosity round the show-room. On polished stands were displayed what the milliner termed ‘Parisian models’; pinned to the ribbons was the print or drawing from which they had been copied from some modish French magazine.

“Yes, I hope it suits her, I hope you like it. I would have wished to see the pelisse that it was designed to go with,” the little woman spoke slyly, with her head on one side.

“My daughter hasn’t got a pelisse or a mantle fit to be worn with that bonnet. It’s just luxury, an extravagance, I suppose you’d call it, a present. I daresay you think my daughter shouldn’t be taking presents from men.”

The milliner’s eyes glittered.

“That wouldn’t be my affair,” she replied primly. “I understood Miss Adelaide to say that the bonnet was a gift from the gentleman to whom she was engaged to be married, that it was all to be a secret until she came of age.”

“That’s so,” agreed Mrs. Fenton, “but I thought I’d let you know that I was aware how matters stood and that I approved. My husband’s an invalid, as everyone in Mullenbridge well knows, and I have to take these duties upon my own hands.”

The little milliner turned up her lip and flicked with expert fingers at one of the muslin roses on a large hat of white stiff straw that hung near.

“The price of the bonnet,” she remarked, “is five guineas. I can’t give the gentleman very long credit, you know. Of course, it’s a trifle for a man in his position, but when you next see him you might tell him—well, just that—that I can’t give very long credit.”

Something seemed wrong here to Mrs. Fenton, there was a touch of vulgarity, surely, about this commercial transaction . . . . it seemed to jar on this mysterious romance.

"Why don't you tell him yourself?" she asked bluntly.

"Oh, I shouldn't care to write like that," retorted the other woman. "I've never seen *him*, you know. *He* didn't come here, it was just Miss Adelaide, alone. She said *he'd* pay, and if I'd oblige her by letting her take the bonnet away at once I should have all her custom after she was married. I'm only in a small way, though I'm sure I've got talent above the ladies of Mullenbridge, if you will forgive me, Mrs. Fenton. If *you* know about the pink bonnet, I suppose it's all right."

"It's quite all right."

"You've seen *him*, then?"

"Why, yes, I've seen him, and Carrie's seen him."

"And everything's arranged, quite properly? Excuse my curiosity and don't think I'm prying, but of course I'm very excited and pleased at the young lady's good fortune."

"She didn't tell you his name, I hope. That was to be a secret."

"No, she didn't tell me his name," admitted the milliner. "But I suppose one's allowed to guess."

The baffled mother rose, her natural shrewdness that had been rusted by long inactivity was not equal to this combat. Was the little milliner lying, like she was lying herself? Had Adelaide's lover really once stood in this smart little parlour, admired the models and chosen the stiff pink bonnet for his beloved's head? It was not very likely, too many people would have known, gossip would have been started . . . . No, the girl had come alone and contrived to get the piece of finery by saying that this mysterious unseen, and unnamed lover would pay for it; Adelaide certainly had a way with her. Yet it was a stupid piece of recklessness, for it was impossible for her to wear the bonnet in Mullenbridge, even if she had suitable clothes it would attract far too much attention; but then Adelaide seemed determined to attract attention . . . .

"Well," said Mrs. Fenton, with a clumsy slyness, "I just thought I'd come and tell you it was all right. And as for your money—well, I'll tell him next time I see him. Everything will be open quite soon. One has to wait a little, prudence and discretion, you know."

"His parents, I suppose?" the little milliner had her head on one side again and was tapping her front teeth with her rounded shining nails. Mrs. Fenton remembered what her daughter had said . . . her instructions.

"No. His grandfather, his guardian, lawyers, you understand—"

"Oh, ho!" Kitty Herle's eyes sparkled and the blood, to Mrs. Fenton's astonishment, burnt in her cheeks. "Then my fortune *is* made, and I shall have a *wonderful* client, after all!"

Mrs. Fenton hardly knew what the milliner meant, but acquiesced with a smile and a half-curtsy and returned heavily with a musing air to her home.

This stood in one of the cheaper but pleasanter suburbs of the town, on the verge of the country, in a small garden, similar houses being on either side, beyond the lane ran into fields. At the back was a churchyard on a slope that was crowned by the church of St. Jude. It was a peaceful scene Mrs. Fenton saw as she came home, the weather was still bleak and dull, but there was some azure showing behind the wisps of yellowish-grey pearl-coloured vapour in the sky and late blossoms were showing at last on the laburnum, hawthorn, and apple trees in the gardens. Susan was pegging out the clothes in the small paddock at the back of the house. Two elderly, quiet, and amiable women who lived in one of the neighbouring houses, Miss Priscilla Groom and Miss Dorothy Groom, were peering among their gooseberry bushes for the first trace of the hard green fruit.

Mrs. Fenton nodded to them and went along her own neat brick path; she glanced instinctively up at the window of her bedroom; like everyone who has had care of an invalid, this burden was constantly before her mind. He might, one day when she came home, be dead. Well, it was not so to-day, or the blinds would have been down. How strange it would be if, after all these years, she should one day find him a corpse. The thought of inescapable death for herself and for all she knew came on her with a sharp stab of unexpectedness.

Caroline came down the garden to meet her; the girl looked fresh and pretty in her sprigged cotton gown. She smiled at the two elderly women who were so carefully and anxiously lifting the leaves of the thorny bushes.

"There won't be so much fruit this year, the frosts are late," remarked Carrie as she took her mother's arm and walked with her into the parlour with an air of cool importance.

"Why, what is it, Carrie? What's happened?"

"Oh, *he* came. I must tell you. *He* was with Adelaide in the parlour—for twenty minutes, I should think. *He* said he was going to buy her a pianoforte and come round and sing and play with her. Won't that be pleasant?"

"Carrie, you're lying!" Mrs. Fenton pushed the girl away from her, into the parlour, went in and sat down in her rocking-chair. "You're lying, Carrie! There's been no man here. It's—well, I don't believe it."

"Oh, don't you! And why shouldn't you, pray? Well, what did Miss Herle tell you, Mother?"

"It's all right, everything's all right, Carrie. Everything that Adelaide said is true."

"Well, then, why don't you believe that what *I* say is true, and that *he* came here now?"

"Who is he then?" asked Mrs. Fenton doggedly.

Carrie simpered and hunched her round shoulders.

"Adelaide called him Basil. He was a young, handsome, and very smart gentleman, and oh, so agreeable to me. He was very sorry that you were absent. He's calling again to be presented to you."

"I should have met him," said Mrs. Fenton, "I should have met him in the lane."

"No, you wouldn't," said Carrie, "he came over the path through the churchyard."

"Miss Priscilla and Miss Dorothy would have seen him."

"No, they wouldn't. They've been in the house and only came out just a moment ago, after he'd gone."

"Then there's Mr. and Mrs. Fry, next door—the other side."

"Oh, they may have seen him, or may not, I don't know. You can go up and down the lane if you like, Mother, and ask everybody, even to the urchins in the road, if they've seen a handsome young man coming here. But that would seem rather disgraceful, don't you think?"

"It seems more disgraceful that young men should come here and I know nothing of it—to be made a fool of like this!"

"But you said it was all right to the milliner, that Adelaide had told the truth there. Why shouldn't I be telling the truth now?"

Mrs. Fenton was silent, she had not thought out her plans.

"Where's Adelaide?" she asked stubbornly. "I won't have your father bothered with this."

"Oh, Adelaide's told him."

"Told your father?"

"Yes. She wants him to consent to their betrothal. I think she took him up a paper to sign, or a letter to show."

"I won't have your father disturbed."

"It doesn't disturb him. Father said he likes *him*, said he was glad his little girl was going to get married, and he hoped I'll be next."

Mrs. Fenton rose; as she was leaving the room she asked sharply: "Why are you wearing the paste that your Aunt Martha gave Adelaide?"

"Oh, it's a present for my birthday."

"But your birthday's two months off."

"I know. But she promised it me, and I begged that I might have it now and wear it."

"Well, you're *not* to wear it. It looks foolish on a sprigged cotton. Where did it come from? I didn't see it when you were running out to meet me just now."

"I hadn't got it on, I didn't want those silly old women to say anything about it. I had it inside my frock. I pulled it out just now to look at it. Why shouldn't I? Adelaide had the pink stones in her dress, this necklet is different. It came from my sister, and she had it from her aunt, and I suppose it's all quite genteel and proper, isn't it, Mamma?"

"I don't know what's right and proper," muttered Mrs. Fenton, "but I'll find out."

She went heavily upstairs, opened the door of her chamber and saw what she had expected—Adelaide sitting beside the sick man's bed. Mrs. Fenton's slow but practised glance went round the room—everything in order, neat and clean. She and Susan saw to that, not only out of love of good housewifery, which was inherent in her nature and her upbringing, but because routine, cleanliness, and discipline made some objects in her life that otherwise was, or had been until lately, objectless.

Adelaide wore her white gown with green ribbons lacing on the bodice, which became her, Mrs. Fenton knew, very well. She had recently bought another green ribbon that did not quite match the other and had tied it in her hair; she had a letter in her hands and the pale, uncertain sunlight fell through the window on to her figure, that was stolidly graceful, as if she was something massive and permanent.

The sick man was propped on his pillows, on his face, distorted by palsy, was an expression of pain now relieved by a gleam of interest in the bright young figure that sat at his side.

The curtains that Mrs. Fenton and Susan had made of coarse white cotton lined with a yellow of a tea-rose colour were drawn away from the end of the bed, and pulled back on the tester. The patchwork quilt, elegantly and skilfully worked by Susan and Mrs. Fenton, was tautly and neatly in place. A grey shawl of a honeycomb pattern was over the invalid's shoulders.

A faint sparkle of recognition came into his dull and sunken eyes as his wife came round the bed.

"What are you reading to your father, Adelaide?" she asked, softly. "What are you disturbing him with?"

"It's a letter from Basil. Basil's been here, Carrie saw him."

"Carrie *said* she saw him," corrected Mrs. Fenton, in such a low tone that even Adelaide hardly heard her. "You know I'm not going to have any trouble in your father's room, I'll talk to you downstairs."

"Father likes to hear it," protested the girl in smooth, suave tones. "It pleases Father to know that one of his daughters is going to be settled, and well settled, too. Doesn't it, Father?"

She folded the letter up and placed it in her bosom. 'Where she's got those pink stones, I suppose,' thought her mother. Mr. Fenton stretched out his hand with a convulsive and uncertain movement.

"Has he had his supper?" asked his wife.

"Oh, yes, Susan came up and did everything." The girl spoke with a vague disinterest that came over her like a cloud every time that anything but her own immediate concerns were referred to or brought before her absorption.

"Did you bring your Basil up to see him?" asked the mother.

"Yes." Adelaide looked on the ground. "Basil came and stood at the door and Father smiled at him. They understood one another very well. But I didn't want to fatigue Father by a conversation, so Basil bowed and went away again. Carrie was there, too, she will tell you so."

"Come downstairs, I want to speak to you."

Mrs. Fenton pulled the bell-rope of tightly-woven bands of coloured wool, then mechanically shook the sick man's down cushions into shape and drew his shawl closer on his withered breast, and touching her daughter on the arm drew her away to the door.

Susan was there already, she had come out of her room at the sound of the tinkle of the bell. She moved quietly to her accustomed place beside the bed of the man she had helped to nurse for twenty years. She knew what to do and how to do it, she and mistress understood each other very well, though they never exchanged compliments.

"What did the milliner tell you?" asked Adelaide, on the stairway.

Before Mrs. Fenton could answer Carrie had replied, standing at the door of the parlour.

"Oh, Mother said that Miss Herle said everything was all right. She won't believe me when I told her that Basil was here, and declared that you ought to have a pianoforte and that he would come and play and sing on it. Now why won't you believe that, Mother?"

"But of course she will," said Adelaide. "She'll believe anything you tell her, won't you, Mother? You know that Carrie's a truthful girl. You promised that you wouldn't doubt her, didn't you, Mother?"

"Yes," agreed Lucy Fenton sullenly. "I suppose so—as you say——"

She had already decided, without much hope of success, to try to find out something from her husband and from Susan.

But the first was in one of his most lifeless moods; he stared at the yellow lining of the home-made curtains, without any response to the cautious questions that she presently put to him, when she fed him his sweet gruel.

With the timid, elderly maidservant she dared to be more direct.

"Did you see the gentleman who came here this afternoon, Susan?"

"I was upstairs, ma'am, doing the mending, the girls make a deal of darning——"

"The young ladies," corrected Mrs. Fenton, though she knew that the ma'am was a concession from poor humble Susan. "So you saw no one?"

"No, ma'am—Miss Adelaide sent me upstairs and said she'd set the tea."

PART TWO
'EXCEPT THE VISION AND ITS DETAILS'

'Second sight:—a singular faculty of seeing an otherwise invisible object, without any previous means used, by the person who sees it, for that end. The vision in question makes such a lively impression upon those who possess the gift, that they neither see nor hear anything else, *except the vision and its details*, as long as that vision continues.'

Glimpses in the Twilight,
GEORGE FREDERICK LEE.

THE Earl of Seagrove stared sourly at the stout ecclesiastic who stood before him in the shadows.

"James comes of an eccentric family," he remarked, adding defiantly: "The Daintrys have their history."

"An explanation, my lord, but not a remedy," replied the Rev. Timothy Chalmers.

"It would never have occurred to me," replied the Earl, "even to suggest a remedy, even to *think* of suggesting a remedy. The boy must *obviously* go his own way."

"The last of his family, sir. Permit me to remark that though your lordship——"

The Earl interrupted.

"I know what you're going to say, Chalmers. I know we've been odd, and even tiresome, with one disaster and another, but we're worth preserving. Well, I've done my best, I had three sons, is it my fault that all I've left is one grandson? And now you tell me tales about him that aren't, well—*satisfactory*."

"I don't know, sir—as you say, not *satisfactory*. I wanted a little advice. I think that my charge should have more company of his own age."

"Well, his relatives have taken him about in London, haven't they? And in Paris——" protested the old man, impatiently. "You've led him on the Grand Tour in the old way, you're pretty experienced in that, I believe, Chalmers, taking these raw lads on their travels. You've shown him what's to be seen, as I suppose, introduced him to experienced women and men of the world, to cabinets of curiosities, to princes, well, well, all the rest of it?"

"Yes, sir, I did my best as you declared you did. I was diligent at my task." The clergyman spoke flatly and stared down at his square-toed shoes.

"And no expense was spared. You had good servants, a courier, an equipage——"

"Everything, sir, everything."

"The boy was not particularly extravagant or wilful, didn't hang round the gambling-hells or *bagnios* more than is usual?"[8]

"No, sir, not in the least. But these terms are no longer used. What I have to remark upon is his abstinence from pleasures common to his age. It's my opinion, sir, and, I believe, of all those who are given the charge of youth, that it is good and even necessary that they should indulge themselves in some manner of diversion and so come to know their own world and their own kind. But Lord Manton held himself very much apart."

"A scholarly lad," sneered the Earl. "We have that in the family too——"

"Scholarship, sir, yes. My pupil was always proficient at his

---

[8] *Bagnios:* brothels.

classics, he was much interested in the antiquities of Greece and Rome. Nor did I regard his behaviour, when we were abroad, as in any way abnormal. He took a fair interest in what was passing about him, the company to which your introductions were a passport, the sights and amusements provided for one of his rank and breeding. It is since his return to England, sir——"

"I know, I know what you are about to say," interrupted the other with a touch of indifference and impatience. "Charters is too large for him, and Verities too old-fashioned, and there's no woman to keep them up as they ought to be kept. Housekeepers are cheats, and servants rob and steal, I keep changing the steward in vain. Well, the estate is not encumbered, he'll be able to put the faults to rights—I shan't concern myself very much with it one way or another. I mean to go to Portland Place and shut up Charters and Verities."

"But, sir, what is Lord Manton to *do*?"

"Let him *do* what he likes. He's a large fortune. He's relations here and there, or people who'd be only too gratified to entertain him. One of the best matches in England. He's personable, though he hasn't learnt all that I could teach him, or you either, for that matter, Chalmers," added the old man, with a leer. "I can't think of much besides my gout. My life's over. I shall be eighty years of age in the autumn on the third day of October."

"Lord Manton will have come to his majority by then—in August, sir, and I was disturbed, as one who has had the responsibility of his education since he left Eton, whether he's fitted to undertake the management of so vast a property, so much money, so high connection——"

"You end haltingly," remarked the Earl, frowning under his heavy brows. "You'd like to say—so *eccentric?* Shall we use that word, an eccentric? I suppose he knows the story of the Daintrys?"

"Yes, that's the worst of it, sir, he knows——"

"I choose that he should know." The Earl rose and walked up and down the long, sombrely-furnished room. Through the tall windows fell the pale shafts of the late May sunshine: the weather was chill, bleak and cold, a fire smouldered on the marble hearth; everything in the room was in good taste, having been added to by generation after generation of wealthy travelled gentlemen, the chamber had also an air of having been of late much neglected: there was the careless touch of the housekeeper and the steward in the arrangement of the books, the busts and the pictures; nothing had been set forth by interest or affection.

The old Earl, after a lifetime of varied adventures, most of which, though forgotten by himself, had been only too well remembered by the fashionable world in which he had once moved, had retired to Charters to pass the end of his life in the bitter indifference of philosophic and yet disappointed old age, dividing his time between visits from such friends of his manhood who still remained to him, journeys to Buxton where he took the waters in the vain hope of curing the rheumatic gout that crippled him, seasons in London, and the inspection of the new stove-house, as he called the glass building that his head-gardener designated by the new term 'conservatory.' Of all the divers interests that had enlivened the old man's life few remained, one of these was horticulture. By accidents that might be termed tragedies he had lost three sons and two daughters; four grandchildren had died in early childhood. His sole heir was his grandson, James Daintry, Lord Manton, who bore his father's courtesy title.

The old Earl, though bearing a by no means false reputation for eccentricity, had not been unduly extravagant and he had enriched himself with two good marriages, so that the estates the young man, who would attain his majority in the summer of this year, would inherit were of considerable value and extent and under the care of efficient stewards and trustees, while the properties of the two late Lady Seagroves had been as well looked after as their monuments in the chapel.

The Earl had also, according to his belief, 'done his best' by the young man who had received the education that his grandfather considered proper for his station; and if, in selecting the Reverend Timothy Chalmers to be his tutor and 'to bear lead him' through Europe the Earl had considered the favour he was doing to one who had been a friend and companion of his middle-age, the impoverished cadet of a noble house fallen upon poverty and some discredit, more than he had considered the interests of the boy, still it could not be denied that in many ways the Reverend Timothy was well adapted to the part that he had undertaken, and that he had fulfilled his task with tact and devotion, by no means to be balanced against the handsome pay and considerable advantages he had received.

He was a man of about sixty years of age, florid, with an air of good breeding, features empurpled but well-shaped, shown off by the crisp whiteness of his handsome hair that was still thick and lustrous. His thick hands were shapely, he was fond of displaying them, and of holding out the little finger of his right hand adorned with a handsome fashioned ring of dark green chrysoprase.[9]

The large number of people who were directly concerned, amused, interested or diverted by the character, fortune and prospects of James Daintry, Lord Manton, looked askance at the

[9] Chrysoprase: a gemstone from the chalcedony quartz group.

selection of the Rev. Timothy Chalmers to be the tutor of this favourite of fortune, but on the surface the man was unexceptional, at least, according to those old-fashioned standards the Earl upheld.

Mr. Chalmers spoke now with an air of sincerity, as one who considers himself the guardian of youthful honour, truth and security, and who has no concern at heart but the welfare of his pupil. The Earl was impatient with problems, he had had a lifetime of them and had not been able to solve any, and these failures reflected now, in the tarnish of his blighted old age, no satisfaction either to himself or the others involved. Better to let all go, better to be indifferent, cut the Gordian knot instead of endeavouring to untie it. . . .he had done what he could for the boy, Edward's son . . . .

He stared past the tutor, and his eyes, dimmed by the grey clouding of approaching cataract, saw those sons of his, James, Edward, Henry, their children too, his own girls, and sons' wives—all dead now, shadows, spectres, phantoms; they seemed to be noisy and protesting: shadows should be silent and drift away quietly into the dark; they had always been noisy, protesting and complaining—"complaining," he said, voicing his thoughts.

Mr. Chalmers, who had been waiting respectfully for his employer to speak, showed no surprise at this comment, he knew enough of his patron's past life to realize to what this word referred.

"It is the future we have to think of, sir. The young man is not twenty-one until August. What is he going to *do* with himself?"

"Why, marry, I suppose, there's good matches enough for anyone of his position."

"Don't you think, sir, *you* should arrange one of these possible matches?"

"Before I'm taken off to the Mausoleum myself, you mean?"

"Well, that, sir, if you care to express it in that manner."

"No. We won't have any lawyers' business here, we've had enough of that. What did those other marriages come to?—quarrelling on all sides, the settlements, the deeds, this, that and the other all tied up and then—somebody in a madhouse or——"

There was a pause; a cloud had passed over the sun and the light in the chamber was luminous but grey.

"Or hanged for murder," concluded the old Earl, rising stiffly. He paused by the white hearth and dangled the massive seal of his fob. He was still upright, a gaunt figure in the fashionable attire of the present day: he always followed the *mode* and did not, as so many old men do, remain constant to the garments and appointments of their youth or early manhood.[10] He had never been handsome, but the Daintrys all had a proud air, that came from the possession of unquestioned authority. In his careful attire, the precise work of a Bond Street tailor, the Earl seemed, to the amiable man who watched him, like a caricature of youth, an old, worn, creaking puppet in the garments of a lusty gallant.[11]

But the Rev. Timothy Chalmers dismissed these fanciful reflections; he was often visited by them, his commonplace book was full of curiosities, for he had carefully and often disdainfully noted down, from one time to another, oddities of nature, of human character and behaviour, a number of these entries, that he kept scrupulously locked away, had dealt with the history of

---

10 *Mode:* fashion.

11 Publisher error. In the UK edition, a line from the final sentence of this paragraph is missing; it appears at the beginning of the following paragraph by mistake. The sentence therefore reads: 'In his careful attire, the precise work of a Bond Street tailor, the Earl seemed, to the amiable man who watched him, [missing line] ments of a lusty gallant.' The US edition (retitled *The Spectral Bride*) does not contain this error and has been consulted to check and correct it.

the Daintrys . . . the carriage of my lord on this occasion might, the Reverend Timothy reflected, be the theme of more of these cynic jottings.

But this was not the time to be indulging in half-mused, half-contemptuous reflections on the idiosyncrasies and weaknesses of those who for long had called themselves 'the great ones of the earth.' Mr. Chalmers had a task to put through; wearisome it might be, but he did not intend to leave it until he had done what he could, achieved, according to his own standards and judgments, some satisfactory decision.

"Yes, hanged for murder, my lord," he repeated slowly. "That perhaps is the trouble."

"The trouble? You're speaking pretty boldly, Chalmers. Is there a *trouble*?"

The old man could not long, or with much ease, remain on his feet. He returned to his chair and sat there, his large, bony hands clasping the polished oaken arms.

"There are always troubles," he repeated, like a refrain. "I think I began by talking of a plot, a difficulty—shall we use that word? Lord Manton knows the history of his family. It was my wish that it should be imparted to him in his early years so that it should become familiar to him. After all, there is hardly a noble in the country that has not had one forebear who has met a—shall we say—violent death."

"Perished on the scaffold, my lord, I believe is the correct term. It is one of which what you term so rightly, noble families, noble in any sense of the word, sir, are justly proud. But to be hanged for murder at Tyburn is not by any means the same."

The old Earl sneered, looking sideways.

"He had a silk rope and his own carriage and four—they took

him away in an open coffin with silver-gilt mountings, and he lies in the Mausoleum with others of his family. The episode should be considered, shall we say, over? The story completed. It was, in any case," added he, with a sudden violence, "an unpleasant, and, I hold, a foul miscarriage of justice."

"You think the fifth Earl innocent, my lord?"

"I think he should have been *declared* innocent. How often do such mischances happen, and how seldom are they paid for, at least—like that?" Then, as if rousing himself from contemplation of this old and festering grievance, Lord Seagrove demanded: "Now, Chalmers, come to the point. We've had enough of this rigmarole. What are you trying to tell me about Manton?"

"This, sir—that despite all my attempts to distract him, he is brooding on this matter. He has taken to reading poetry, to writing it, too, I'm afraid, sitting alone in his rooms, refusing visits to London, avoiding company, walking too often near the Mausoleum and the Folly."

"They are both, I believe, very elegant buildings—perhaps Manton has a taste for architecture?"

The Reverend Timothy glanced at his patron very sharply.

"I can assure your lordship that it is not a taste for architecture that keeps Lord Manton so often in those solitary groves. He is, I tell you, of a melancholy disposition. He thinks far too much of this old story, which should, as you pertinently remark, have long ago been forgotten. He feels in himself the same—how shall I express it?—qualities that produced this tragedy."

"We've all got 'em," grinned the Earl, "lust and passion, violence, self-esteem. Well, you've been his tutor, you should have taught him how to control these—emotions."

"I've done what I could, sir, but sometimes hereditary tendencies are too strong for the most experienced and persevering of tutors."

The old Earl rapped his wasted fingers on the handsome ormolu desk.

"What is the young fool afraid of? What are you afraid of?"

"I'm not afraid of anything, sir, and I don't consider Manton a fool. And as to what he says or thinks, why, I could talk the hour and you not be any the wiser, by my repeating my record of one or my speculations on the other. But I'll tell you this much—there was a young woman in the case—I'll not repeat the word, which I daresay is offensive in your lordship's ears——"

"Offensive in that of any man of breeding," sneered the old man. "Well, what about her?"

"She was, unfortunately, buried in the churchyard of St. Jude."

"Yes, they ought to have been able to prevent that——The Rector at the time was out of hand, didn't know his place——There was a clamour, a public outcry. Never mind, her grave is forgotten, overgrown, neglected——Who remembers?"

"Lord Manton remembers, sir. He goes frequently, rather too frequently to the churchyard. You won't find that gave in such disrepair now. My lord, with his own hands, has put it in a decent state."

At this the Earl did look up, and with a jerking start, his jaw working, his thick coarse white eyebrows drawn down into an ugly scowl.

"You ought to have told me this before."

"I hoped it would pass, sir, I hoped I could get him away. It proved impossible. He's inclined to be romantic, he's read too many novels and poems—as I said."

The Reverend Timothy spoke with elaborate nonchalance, holding up his fine hand and gazing at the fine ring. He added:

"He thinks she might come back—your lordship will know the legend, it's common in most countries—the Spectral Bride, shall we call it? There are one or two novels written on that."

"Fantastic! He'll grow out of that nonsense."

"So I thought. If I still thought so I should not, sir, have disturbed you. But there is a girl who walks by the Folly and the Mausoleum."

"With him?"

"I haven't seen that. But he goes up there."

"Who is she?"

"I don't know. It's usually in the twilight, and I can't be seen openly watching. It's a difficult matter and there's no one in whom one can confide. It is, obviously, one of the town sluts, her head half-turned with the trash of the circulating library——"

"Well, then, why make any account of her?"

"Because, sir," replied the Reverend Timothy, in very level, prim tones, "Harriet Bond was no more—a town slut. These worthless pieces can be of great importance in the history of a noble family."

"What am I going to do?" asked the Earl rapidly. "What do you advise?"

"First, don't go to Buxton, sir, or to Portland Place. Secondly, get some stranger, from London, I should say, to watch."

"On my grandson?"

"I would not say as much as that, I'd say a watch on the young ladies, shall we call them?—of Mullenbridge. She might be romantic, foolish, or ambitious. One can only do what one thinks right," added the Reverend Timothy quietly, "no more, no less."

"Not, perhaps, so much," grinned the Earl. "What have we, my dear Chalmers, to do with what is right or wrong? It seems to me there's a great matter of, shall we say—moonshine—nonsensical fiction in what you say."

"Nonsensical fiction, my lord, especially that as purveyed by the circulating library, might be a very powerful influence in the lives of young people. Lord Manton has lately ordered a complete set of the Lytton Novels. He talks of setting up as a writer himself."

"Well, that will pass, no doubt. But this other—shall we call it a folly——?"

"Do not let us quarrel over terms, sir. One must use words that are somewhat harsh when dealing with a case like this—I am not so sure that it will pass. I think that it may perhaps continue until it becomes an obsession, until it eats up mind and spirit and enfeebles the body and intellect."

"You always use portentous terms, Chalmers, yet you were a good companion in your day. Well, let's put this vexation into plain terms."

"It's almost impossible, sir, to put it into plain terms. It must seem to you, as indeed it at first seemed to me, so much fantastic lightheadedness that would pass——"

"Tell me, sir, what you mean in the plainest words you can command, if not plain yet clear. I've noticed that my young grandson, well, there's a good many years between us, the youngest son of my second son—twenty years and eighty years have not much in common. I haven't been able to get very close to the youth, but I've observed that he has been moody and difficult, but it didn't seem to me to matter very much. I suppose he could be married whenever we chose. What of Lady Caroline Westland? Won't she ask him to Manchester Square? What of Lady Sybil Duncan?"

"Sir, all these expedients have been tried. All these kind

relatives have done what they can for Lord Manton, but he will return here, he will live at Charters, he will devote himself more and more to introspective studies, metaphysics, the science as he calls it, of the occult——"

"Alchemy and star-gazing, I suppose," interrupted the Earl petulantly. "Come to the young woman, that is the important part. Who is she?"

"I could not tell you, sir, as I told you before. I've tried to watch, but it's been difficult. It's most important not to attract any attention. It is also certain that she is a creature of no consequence. There are no young ladies in the immediate neighbourhood—if there were they would scarcely be allowed to wander alone in the Folly Woods at dusk or by moonlight."

"A hussy of the town, then, perhaps a servant girl, or——" Lord Seagrove grinned and his twisted fingers tapped on the ormolu desk as if he beat out a tune.

"Harriet Bond was a servant girl employed at the 'Seagrove Arms,' " Mr. Chalmers reminded him. "It is unfortunate that a portrait of her is preserved there."

"It should have long ago been destroyed, I thought I had given my orders?"

"I believe you did, sir. I believe it was supposed they had been carried out. Well, you know what it is—curiosity. People will pay high for a sight of a picture of a girl—well, who——"

"Don't run over the story, and don't think that I'd mind if you did. The girl was supposed to be murdered by a gentleman who was hanged for the crime—let it go at that. Who cares, at this time of the world's history? But I did not know they had a likeness of her there. I ordered everything of that sort to be destroyed when I came into the title. I did not find much then.

My father had seen to that before me, at the time there were the usual broadsheets, prints, vulgar nonsense."

"It is not a print, sir, but an oil painting about the size of a signboard, it is hid in a cupboard. On Lord Manton becoming interested in the old story, he went to the 'Seagrove Arms' and spoke to Fiske. Of course he knew his stories—the Fiskes have been there a century or more."

"Stories, most of them lies, I suppose!" interrupted the old Earl, fiercely.

"Of that you can be sure, sir. Such events, monstrous in reality, become even more extravagant when clouded by fiction."

"I daresay the painting is a forgery to be shown a penny a peep once."

"Maybe, sir." Mr. Chalmers was trying to be patient on a matter that provoked him, and clear on a matter that was intricate. "It has impressed Lord Manton. He considers that this female whom he sees walking in the Folly and near the Mausoleum or, as he declared once, in the churchyard, has a likeness to this portrait."

"Ah, does the young fool believe that he is communicating with the spirit of Harriet Bond? Is that what you try to say?"

"Not quite that, sir, not altogether that. I can best explain it by using an old country term. He supposes it is just possible that it is a fetch that he sees."

"A fetch," repeated my lord, quietly. "And what may that be?"

"Sir, the dictionary will give it to you as something 'that comes again, or is brought back.' "

The Earl rose and walked impatiently with the disordered steps of the old up and down the handsome room.

"Well, Chalmers, you brought me a pretty problem. What do you wish me to do? The obvious action, the sensible action, is to send the boy away and get all this cobwebby moonshine out of his head, keep all these metaphysics, as he terms them, this occult supernatural mummery out of his way."

"You'll never do that, sir," interrupted Mr. Chalmers, who also had risen out of respect to his patron. "If anyone wants a something as much as Lord Manton wants this, whatever it is I can give it no name, he will get it, especially when they have leisure and position."

"Well, you're a clergyman," the Earl's sneer was hardly apparent, "you're a man of God. Why can't you exorcise this spectre whatever it is? Prove to the boy that this piece is a mortal girl hanging about to entangle him. A fetch, indeed!"

"It might be dangerous to be so drastic," protested the clergyman. "Lord Manton might refuse to believe that the girl—should we be able to trace her and expose her tricks—was a human-being. To do this might be the very means of throwing them together."

"Well, then, what do you advise me to do? Why did you let the matter come to this pass before you told me of it?"

"I tried to stop it my own way, but suddenly it has taken a worse turn. When Lord Manton was in London he made the acquaintance of Dr. Lucas Perry. This Swedenborgian has had an influence over him that I cannot combat."[12]

As if weary of the whole subject, that was indeed a tangled burden to his distracted and aged mind, the Earl declared, resting against the heavy mantelpiece:

"We must pack him off to Paris or London. I'll get some

---

[12] Swedenborgian: a follower of the teachings of Emanuel Swedenborg, the Swedish scientist, theologian and mystic. After his death, his followers formed the New Church, a form of Christianity based on the teachings of Swedenborg and the Bible.

private inquiry agents to find out who this girl is. Meanwhile you can't do anything but watch him. I should leave him alone if I were you," he added, with a sudden flash of animation. "Don't let him see that we suspect anything or disapprove. Sometimes these illusions," he spoke as if he had experienced them himself, "are like so many fits of fever. They come, they go——"

"Ay," thought Mr. Chalmers as he, taking this for a dismissal, turned towards the door, 'they come and go. But one mustn't forget, sir, that there's insanity in the Daintry family.'

* * * * *

The subject of this conversation, which had begun so suddenly, continued so long and ended without any satisfaction to either party, was prosaically engaged in the largest chamber of the apartment assigned to his use in the round tower at the corner of Charters. James Daintry, by courtesy Lord Manton, was writing a letter to his lawyers, in which he demanded from them an exact account of the monies he would come into when he became of age in two months' time, for he was heir to a considerable sum due to him from his mother quite apart from the paternal estates.

This youth was tormented, like most young people of no special ability, gifts, or strength of character, with a keen and pressing desire for what he termed freedom. He longed to be rid of the tutelage of the Rev. Timothy Chalmers, easy and tolerant as that gentleman had been in the exercise of his duties, he longed to be away even from the occasional supervision of his grandfather, who seemed to him like a figure out of another world with a stiff body, a rigid mind locked in the past. He wanted to be away, even, from Richard Hackett, who had been his personal servant all his life and who was in every way respectful, obliging and efficient. He would be glad to be rid of the other old servants, too, of the housekeeper, Mrs. Serjeant. Oh, yes, they were all obliging and agreeable and put no restraint on him in any way. How could they? He was their master.

Yet he wanted to use that word so often repeated, so seldom understood—'to be free.'

Charters, the estate itself, which he knew so well since he had come to live there soon after his father's violent death, was different. He believed that there in the ancient house and grounds he would find the clue to the many secrets that at once stimulated and puzzled him. Long as he had known the old place, there was still much to explore—to ponder over: the chapel, the ruins of the Abbey, the Folly, the Mausoleum, the Orangery, the new stove-house that his grandfather had built twenty years before and that was not yet completely finished in all details. This love of horticulture—the term love was not an exaggeration, for this passion was the one link between the Earl and his heir; Lord Manton planned to bring a rare collection of exotic plants to Charters.

'I must be free and I shall not be—no, not even when I have attained my majority. I shall have to wait until the old man dies. He might live to be ninety or a hundred years.'

He checked his thoughts and tried to reason out his position. He was a studious and intelligent young man, a fine athlete, one who possessed many graces of mind and body.

'What do I want most of all? I want to get Lucas Perry here, but my grandfather would never permit that. Chalmers has already put many difficulties in the way. I want to be able to go alone, without fearing that maybe they are watching. It does not matter if I am riding or walking, there is always one of them finds an excuse to saunter by my path. Oh, they do not think I notice, of course.

It is very adroitly done, but it is quite obvious, too. I am not going to make a fool of myself,' he added, violently, leaving the letter, unaddressed, unsealed, lying open on the desk of burr walnut wood. 'There is something to be investigated here, and why shouldn't I be the one to do it? Lucas Perry is a sane, educated and intelligent man. He has been well schooled by life, too. Why should not he know what he is talking about as well as either my grandfather or Chalmers, who is a materialist, really, and cares for nothing save ease and pleasure. I believe he has been in many doubtful episodes in his time—at least, both he and my grandfather are of the last century, sixty years or so out of date—they think in terms of their own youth.'

The young man knew that this was not true but it pleased him to put up this specious defence of his own disagreement with good advice.

He could not, however, discover hope of solution of his own problem, which was how to combine complete freedom from those who, however kindly and respectfully, or even indifferently, watched him, with continued residence at Charters. There was Verities, the Daintrys' other large estate in Wiltshire. He might go there, take a staff of servants with him and entertain his friends, people whom he had met abroad, relations, the people whom Lady Sybil and Lay Caroline would bring at a signal from him; Verities was not so far away that he would not be able to ride or drive over every week, if he wished, to the Folly Woods; yet this did not altogether please; he sighed with the bitterness of idleness and confusion of mind.

Then, thinking of a never-failing distraction, he glanced round to make sure that he was alone; sometimes Hackett would come in, quietly, with unobtrusive tread and slow movements, sometimes

Chalmers, also light-footed, would turn the handle of the door and surprise him; he did not care to lock himself in, that was too conspicuous; but when he was serving his secret obsession he must be free from interruption.

He went to the press, unlocked it and took out a small, crudely executed oil-painting of a heavy-looking young woman with bright brown hair wearing a gown of thick material and a hood such as was usual to the peasantry in the mid-eighteenth century. The exact date of the portrait and the tragedy it commemorated the young man did not know; the records of the affair had been very efficiently destroyed. Everywhere he tried to make a search he was baffled by rebuffs and secrecy, the first courteously given, the last adroitly disguised. He did not even know what relation the unhappy man who had been involved in the death of Harriet Bond was to himself—a great-uncle, a great-grandfather? There was no pedigree, no genealogical table, no family trees in Charters or in Verities; there were gaps in the records of the family. It may have occurred a hundred and twenty, perhaps a hundred and thirty years ago; at the 'Seagrove Arms' where he had acquired the picture at a high price he had inquired from Fiske about names and dates, but though he had probed skilfully, and he did not believe he was lacking in prudence or art, he could discover nothing . . . . of course, they were afraid of the old man; all his tenants would be—gagged.

"What's the use, my lord," the innkeeper had protested respectfully, "of searching for something that was forgotten when my father was a child?" And he added with an intonation that was touched with cunning: "I wonder how you came to hear of it, sir? It's an ugly old story, and maybe not true at that."

"I heard it in Rome," Lord Manton had replied absently.

The memory had come so strongly on the words that he had not noticed the amazement on the man's face, quickly concealed with professional servility. Richard Fiske had wondered how the young man had come to hear this local story in Rome. It was well enough known in Mullenbridge but never mentioned, slurred now in the details since the present Earl, sixty or more years ago, had heard some rumours that documents relating to the case were still in existence, had sought them out, bought them at a high price and had them destroyed and let it be known that anybody who mentioned the affair should no longer be a tenant of his, and now the heir had heard of it in some outlandish foreign city.

But the young man had taken no notice of the effect that his words had produced. Rome was in his fancy now—the pale basilicas where design is made from light and space, the colonnades with gigantic distorted figures—as he, with the furtive movements of one with something to hide, held the painting in the window and studied it eagerly, then, swiftly replaced it, as he heard a step without. Hackett was there—without the opening of the door—in the half blended light and shade, it seemed to the youth's angry agitation, saying with his bland, well-trained, deferential lowering of the glance:

"Dr. Lucas Perry is below and wishes to see your lordship." The manservant spoke with that suaveness that may be considered either complete respect or a cynical contempt according to the nerves and sensitiveness of the person addressed.

But Lord Manton was not concerned with these expressionless manners, though the man's words and tones often irritated, exasperated, and even alarmed him. He exclaimed sharply: "Dr. Perry here! But I was not expecting him. Neither is the Earl——"

"Dr. Perry is below, sir, in a barouche. He seems to think he is sure of his welcome. Am I, my lord, to show him an apartment—the green chamber or that next to your lordship's in the tower?"

"The Earl should be consulted; I was intending to receive Dr. Perry."

The young man glanced at the letter to his lawyer; complete, unsigned, unsealed, this seemed a testimony to his irregular, careless, and simple life—so much begun, so little completed. What would Lucas Perry do to help him in his present pass? Yet he was glad that the man had come, he felt a sudden access of strength as if he had been fortified in a half-hearted rebellion, and that was why in instinctive self-defence he pretended to be vexed.

"Has Dr. Perry brought servants?"

"Yes, my lord, his man, Duncome."

"Give them, then, accommodation in the apartments near here in the tower. Everything, I suppose, is ready?"

"There'll be no trouble whatever, my lord, in the arrangements. And as for the Earl, he is abroad. He has left some half-hour ago for Verities with the Rev. Timothy Chalmers."

'To plot something against me, I suppose,' thought Lord Manton; his mood swiftly changed. He did not know if he was, after all, pleased with this sudden and unexpected visit that meant a new and antagonistic element introduced into Charters; perhaps it would have been easier, as well as wiser, for him to have made his own decision, unaided. Did he need this man, so much older, more experienced and subtle than himself, peering into his problem—perhaps despising him for having anything so fantastic on his mind?

He turned aside with a gesture of impatience that was clumsily concealed; he was aware of his own inconsistence. Even a few minutes before Hackett's entry he would have been relieved, overjoyed to have heard of the possibility of a visit from Dr. Lucas Perry.

He had no time for further debatings on his own uncertainty, for the manservant withdrew and returned with Dr. Lucas Perry.

This person was a mild-looking man of middle age in the most conventional costume. There was nothing about him distinguished nor unusual except perhaps his full-lidded eyes and deeply curved lips and air of uncommon composure.

He saluted Lord Manton easily and expressed his regret at having, as he termed it, "descended upon him so suddenly." But he had had business (he did not specify what) in the neighbourhood, and thought that it might be permissible for him to call at Charters and wait upon the Earl of Seagrove and his young friend.

The youth received this amiable and sincere apology with the courtesy instinctive to one of his breeding, yet he could not altogether conceal an embarrassment that the other soon perceived.

"If I put you into any difficulty, I will at once retire. The 'Mullenbridge Arms,' I believe, can provide a clean bed, a good meal, and, on occasion, affable company."

"Indeed, no, you will be my guest at Charters. Who could find anything against that? You find me, I confess, a little overwrought." He glanced down at the lawyer's letter. "Your presence has come too opportune, too pat, you understand—you were much in my mind. My position is, in many ways, unfortunate, you must concede me that——"

"I am willing to concede you everything. Why, sir, trouble yourself over matters that are, at the best, mundane and trivial?"

"You have much to teach me," declared the young man, obstinately. "But I am not sure that I wish altogether to permit you. There is a great deal that can be argued and discussed. I am tired, lack, perhaps, my dinner——"

"It is past the usual hour," remarked Dr. Perry amiably.

"I have been sitting here in this old room thinking of old stories. I have," he glanced towards the cupboard, "locked away a picture that—troubles, no, that is not the word—concerns me a good deal—I told you the history of it."

"The mystery of Harriet Bond?" smiled Dr. Perry coolly. "Well, it is, perhaps, unfortunate that I should have arrived at the moment when you were so absorbed in such a matter. Perhaps it may be that I can help you, yet I do not know to what pass in your trouble or absorption you have come. You know my tenets, what my leader taught. You know that I do not seek disciples, yet would always willingly welcome those prepared to join our sect."

"You see yourself to have found the way to peace of mind and contentment.

"Maybe. That is always an individual quest, an individual achievement. Content! The word is one that we mortals hardly dare to use. A certain measure of tranquility I have found."

"Why do you come here? I wished to keep your company for London. I can hardly, sir, credit your tale of chance. You have sought me out for some purpose."

* * * * *

Dr. Lucas Perry soon dispelled Lord Manton's ill-humour. The disturbance caused the youth by the gentleman's presence was more than compensated for by the prospect of amiable and sympathetic company. How agreeable it would be to transfer his introspective woes to the interested ears of another, and one who was not only able, but usually eager to help, one who could put his problems and difficulties on some kind of a basis that the young man would be able to deal with.

He pulled the long embroidered bell-rope and when Hackett appeared demanded that refreshments should be served in his own chamber immediately and supper set somewhat before the usual hour. Dr. Perry made himself the most amiable and obliging of companions; he had arrived, he declared, not on chance; he would not go into details with his host (whom he supposed he might consider his pupil), but merely hint that it had not been by any tangible means that he had been brought to Charters—"I could have reached Winchester by a short way."

From this it was easy for Lucas Perry to come upon what was disturbing the young man, though he would not admit such a definite term as 'disturbance'——He touched his 'problems,' usual enough, as he admitted shamefacedly, but none the less acute for that—his desire for freedom, the irksomeness of the guardianship of Timothy Chalmers and the old lord, and yet his desire to remain in this ancient house so peculiarly his own, where as he supposed and hoped some remarkable adventure might befall him . . . an adventure of the mind, the spirit.

He then drew Dr. Perry on to the legend of Harriet Bond and found, somewhat to his surprise and chagrin, that that gentleman was well informed about his ancestor's squalid tragedy.

"We must not," remarked Dr. Perry placidly, "make too much of that happening. It was one that was but too common—springing from the barbarous manners and impulsive passions of those days."

"Seduction and murder," smiled the young man sternly. "I suppose that might happen at any time—even to-day?"

"Yes, but it would be unlikely now among people of the quality of your ancestor. The Lord Seagrove who was concerned in this affair was in every other way, or shall I say in every way, for this licence too might be included in the list of his modish tricks, a man of fashion, one welcomed by the *bon ton*, a fine athlete, an exquisite classic scholar."[13]

"I know his virtues," Lord Manton interrupted with an impatience that he did not often show towards the man whom he had begun to revere. "Those are brought forward commonly enough. It is his tragedy, it is this story of his hanging," he brought the words out quickly, "that is kept from us."

"Look upon the dismal story as a mere accident in the history of your house. What can it matter one way or another once it is regarded with philosophy?" smiled Dr. Perry. "Many a worse crime has been unpunished; this was expiated. Why are you concerning yourself with it now?"

Spoken to thus frankly, Lord Manton replied bluntly: "You know that I have been attending occult experiments in London, that I have watched spiritualistic mediums—well, I will not go into these things."

"No need to do so," replied the other blandly, turning his glass about in his hand and admiring the reflection of the slanting sun ray in the brilliant wine. "I know something of your experiences and people with whom you have mingled."

"It is unjust the way in which these seekers of truth are persecuted," protested the young man. "What sense was there in repealing the laws against witchcraft, when anyone who endeavours to solve our most urgent problem may be persecuted as a vagrant——?"

"You consider it urgent—to know if the soul exists, if it be immortal? Not many at your age—do so—young, with so many advantages—and yet you are interested in the attempts of the adepts

---

13 *Bon ton:* high society.

to project their souls from their bodies." Dr. Perry was speaking rapidly. "But are you even convinced that there *is* a soul?" He drew a small book from his pocket, opened it at a marker, and, after asking—"Do you like this?" read—'The pictures are of those long dead, they seemed to me the only certain realities, we ourselves are but as shadows, never continuing in one stay and only catching faint glimpses in the twilight of friends long lost, who, we trust, now walk in white in a kindlier and better land.'[14]

"No, friend of mine," broke in Lord Manton, 'it is true that she wears white—but a kindlier and better land!" He laughed nervously: "How childish that sounds!" He gave a movement of repugnance as if something distasteful had suddenly closed in on him; Lucas Perry regarded him with a calm compassion; the youth was well-made, above the middle height, with well-proportioned features and bronze-coloured hair, thick, coarse, curling, and with an undertone of red. This warm agate hue showed in his brows, eyes, and the faint freckles across the bridge of his blunt nose; though he was healthy and had no look of pallor, his skin was thick, white and impervious to sun or wind; he appeared older than his years, and had that dignity that graces one well-bred who lives much alone and thinks independently.

Dr. Perry pitied him because of his heritage. The family was ancient, but not distinguished, no member of it had been prominent in Church, State or arms, had patronized the arts or encouraged commerce. They had always married prudently, and an occasional spendthrift had been allowed in a race of reasonable men. It seemed grotesque that the fifth Earl should have been hanged for the

---

14 From *Glimpses in the Twilight: Being Various Notes, Records, and Examples of the Supernatural* by Frederick George Lee, 1885.

murder of a servant girl, but the influence that could not save his neck from the rope had concealed his story from posterity. Even those most anxious that he should die shamefully had acquiesced in a decent respect for his name when he was dead. Party feeling, and the habit he had of making enemies, had helped to bring him to the scaffold, class feeling and the wealth of his heirs helped this tragedy to slip into oblivion—or nearly into oblivion. Dr. Perry checked his musings.

"This is not helping you much, James," he remarked thoughtfully, "—for me to sit here silently—"

"Shall we dine?"

"No—let us sit together awhile. You know we are unusual companions. You know what we have discussed. I was moved to come here to-day—yes, I turned out of my way to come here. I have some understanding of your—concern—tell it to me plainly."

He sat quietly, a quiet man, with wrinkled lids, cool grey eyes and grizzled hair, his large hands outspread on the arms of his chair.

"It is the little foxes that eat the vines," he remarked; "if one broods, and lives solitary—a small seed will grow swiftly."

"I have a curiosity only—why not about that as about anything else? It is at least as interesting as cards, horse racing, boxing, attending dances and *soirées*."

"But not so safe."

"Safe? If one is afraid of nothing?"

"Is that possible? I ask only. To fear nothing, James? Is not our utmost privilege to have a *choice* of fears?"

"Dr. Perry . . . " the young man paused, "I begin to be enthralled by my——"

"You will not say—delusion? Is it not always so? You see, I keep all I say at a question. We soon begin to lose what dupes us.

The encircling arms of the fog that pulls us through the reeds, the dancing light of the marsh fire——Yet, perhaps I can draw you back. Continue. I believe, indeed, I did obey Divine inspiration when I came here to-day."

"Hideous tales, dreary traditions mingle with my philosophic doubts, my dubious questionings. I suppose these moods could easily be explained. I live apart, I did not go to college, I care nothing for common pleasures, I have too much money, I have no ambitions."

"Let all that go," smiled the elder man; "we will take all that as said. I understand your character, your class, and your position."

This clarity soothed the young man, who was eager to dwell on his personal obsession.

"It has been supposed," he began hurriedly, "that this girl comes back, that she is, in the vulgar tongue, a Fetch, that she returns and haunts various places, among others a grave that I, lately, have had cleared—some work I did there myself. She lays in wait (I must use a vulgar term again) for the descendant of her murderer to revenge herself on him."

"That is an old, a universal fable. I believe you will find it in all folk lore—the spectral bride, the mysterious betrothed. Ah, yes, I remember when I was last in Scotland near Ayr, I heard such a tale—of a girl who had been lured to a lonely heath and murdered by a treacherous lover, she wearing a white frock and a green bonnet; she haunted that bleak moor until she had snared a grandson of the man who had destroyed her body. The bewitched youth fell in love with the spirit or fetch, was deluded into supposing her to be flesh and blood, they were betrothed and went to Ireland together in a spectral coach; those solitary shepherds who saw this carriage pass declared it was travelling at about sixty miles an hour——"

"No such ancient, dead moonshine is in my head now," replied the young man, frowning angrily and glancing with an air of apprehension at the thick red rep curtains that hung either side the high narrow window.[15] "I have seen a female, it is true, walking by the Mausoleum and the Folly and again standing by the grave, but there is no reason to suppose that she is not a village girl. Yet there are mysteries, and you, aware that I have no material cares, know that I could wish to investigate them."

"How should I help you to do that?"

"First, sir," the young man leant across the table, unconsciously raising and bringing down lightly his clenched fist, "by telling me this story of Harriet Bond plainly, as you know you say it; then I will tell you what I know."

"Yes, I know all that is commonly known." The Swedenborgian took again from his breast pocket his small book and opened it. "When I first made your acquaintance I took these notes of facts that are available to those who seek them, though kept very quiet in your immediate neighbourhood—nay, in all Wiltshire. If you wish, I shall tell it to you—it is a chronicle of what the world calls facts, I must repeat."

"Let me have them in the dryest possible terms."

"You may be sure that so I have put them down. I shall take but a few minutes to read them and maybe something here will set your mind at ease, for nothing festers so fast as an unsatisfied curiosity.

"Miss Bond, then," began Dr. Perry, first adjusting his square, silver-rimmed glasses and looking at the notes in the red-covered book that he held before him in the waning daylight, "was a

[15] Rep is a cloth woven in fine cords or ribs.

maidservant at the 'Seagrove Arms'; she came from a farm near Charters. She had an unusual beauty and lustre, a spirit and grace uncommon in her class, and it was soon noted to the great scandal of the neighbours that she was often walking near the unfinished Folly that was being erected on the Italian model, and the Mausoleum that had been copied from the Temple of the Four Winds—with the fifth Earl, when he returned from London in the spring—more than a century ago.

"He was then in his twenty-eighth year, a man who had much experience of the world; his Italian mistress had for a short while adorned Charters and left with a splendid equipage and magnificent presents. The Earl had been for twenty years a minor, but he had important and affluent guardians who were always assiduously engaged in endeavouring to procure for him a match fitting for his pretensions.

"Charters was continually filled with elegant and ostentatious company from London and sometimes with Italian and French noblemen whose acquaintance he had made when on his travels. It may be well understood that in these circumstances his occasional sauntering in some unlikely place with a village girl was not much taken notice of save by the vulgar gossips. Harriet Bond was warned by the Fiskes, who kept the inn, of the stupidity of her conduct, but kept herself aloof and seemed to disdain them all. Indeed, so proud was her manner and so handsome were the presents that she was able to display, antique brooches, coral bracelets and pearl combs, that a startling whisper went round Mullenbridge that the Earl was truly enamoured of the fair rustic and one day intended to make her his wife—the old legend of the king and the beggar-maid in modern times."

Here Lord Manton interrupted impatiently: "It might have

been true. It is not beyond human nature, supposing a man of rank and position did see some creature who seemed to him like a being of another world." He paused, clasped his hands round his knee and gazed again at the curtain, that swelled partly outwards and then was sucked in again.

"The window's open and it is chilly," said Dr. Percy, but Lord Manton said no, it was closed, that whatever breeze had disturbed the draperies must come from the interior of the room. He rose to show this was true. The window was latched.

"Pray proceed with your narration," he said; "I find it extremely interesting, for so far I have nothing but the barest hints of this tragedy."

"You will find it commonplace in everything but the rank of the principal actor," said the Swedenborgian. "Curious that I should have been mistaken about the window—my sight is not good, and these glasses are poor. Shall we not have the curtains drawn and candles in?"

The youth caught the curtains together, leaving the room lit only by the light from the other window, then pulled the bell.

"All is so old-fashioned here," he said nervously. "When the candles are lit, it might be in the time of your narrative"

Hackett brought in the silver sticks, set the tapers, lit the lamp, and asked when dinner should be served.

"In another hour," the young man spoke impatiently. "I should have told you, sir," he added. "My grandfather and Chalmers have gone to Verities; we shall be alone. Now continue," he urged, as Hackett withdrew.

Lucas Perry peered round: the flames burnt small on the hard wax of the candles, the wick of the lamp had been turned low, the achievement of the Daintrys over the fireplace was outlined in clear shadow—snarling heraldic beasts, a curt, arrogant motto.[16]

"Yes, in this mellow light, the room looks old, it is true—is old, probably has changed little since that spring——"

"About this season of the year?"

"Yes—the account I read—in *The Gentleman's Magazine* said—the spring, the exact date I did not note—no, neither year, nor months, nor days."

"That is odd! Are you sure your facts are accurate?" the young man asked nervously and again peered round the room as if trying to disentangle the various shadows that interlaced in the corners.

"I took some pains to verify them. The trial was duly recorded."

Lord Manton put his hand for a second to his throat and in a dry voice bade his friend proceed.

This Dr. Lucas Perry did, in a tone in which compassion and irony were justly mingled.

"The incidents followed the usual course. It was soon observed by the Fiskes that Harriet Bond was depressed and sick, and to the usual reproaches she responded with the usual tears. There was still nothing remarkable about the case until one day a Mr. Goodhart appeared at the inn; he was an acquaintance of the Earl's, somewhat inaptly named, a man not of his own rank but who had been seen often in his company at Newmarket and the *bagnios* of London.

"This gentleman explained to the servile Fiske that though my lord was in no way responsible for Harriet Bond's melancholy that he had observed on seeing her loitering in the lanes, yet out of compassion for one who was the daughter of his tenant, he would

16 Achievement: heraldic achievement, also known as a coat of arms. In the US edition, the word 'achievement' is replaced with 'crest'.

have the charity to send her and had made arrangements to remove her to a genteel house in Winchester where she could be trained for service as a lady's chambermaid, for she was in manners and person above her present situation—and hence her discontent and lowness of spirit.

"The Fiskes were much impressed by the visit of the Earl's friend on such a matter, and amazed that the Squire—as he was to them—should consider the girl of enough importance to invent such a story. They supposed that he was deeply enamoured of her and intended to provide for her handsomely in some secret apartments in the Assize town, which to them was a very grand place.

"Mrs. Fiske, however, thought that the girl's parents should be told; on this objection Mr. Goodhart declared that this had been provided for, and consent given; still Mrs. Fiske protested that a woman should be employed in the matter, and the girl, though only a serving wench, not go alone to Winchester.

"But Harriet Bond herself ventured into the parlour and declared that she knew of the place, that was with a Mrs. Pentriss, who did millinery, near the Close, and that this town life pleased her, and she would go."

"Here is much precise detail about a trifle," interrupted Lord Manton.

"I give it because it is the only precise detail that came out at the trial," replied the other mildly. "The Fiskes and the girl's parents were eager to clear themselves of the obvious charge of servility or corruption. Why had they allowed the girl to go? There were fellow-servants who saw her leave the 'Seagrove Arms' on a pillion behind Mr. Goodhart's servant.

"Harriet Bond seemed even glad to go; she kissed Mrs. Fiske and the maids affectionately, cast off her melancholy as she told them that she hoped to see them when she was happier than could now be supposed.

"There was something about this behaviour that impressed and even startled the Fiskes, and the whisper that had hitherto been suppressed began to swell again, not only in the inn but in Mullenbridge, that perhaps Lord Seagrove, fantastic and eccentric as he was known to be, intended to marry secretly this ignorant rustic.

"She left nothing behind, having taken in a bundle all the little presents that she had been displaying, and it was assumed the Earl had given her, and such clothes as she had worn in her service.

"It was a fortnight after her departure that a man by the name of James Thorpe, who had a small fulling mill on the Earl's estates, was, as he afterwards declared, startled by seeing the spectre of a woman faintly outlined in a silvery bloom (as he said in his account) and stained with a faint red colour, rising from the floor like a twist of vapour. Her dishevelled hair was hanging down and she bent her head to show five large gashes on the skull.

"Upon the fuller demanding who and what she was (and this he contrived to do though his courage was sunk very low), the spectre replied: 'I am the ghost of Harriet Bond.' She then said that she had been murdered by the Earl's emissary, Harry Goodhart, in the woods behind the half-built Folly. 'I was slain,' said she, 'with a collier's pick that was standing by the new building, it having been used to open a seam in the ground of hard rock.' She then indicated the spot where her body had been buried in the wood, and added that Goodhart had soiled his shoes and stockings with blood and concealed them near the corpse."

"None of this," muttered Lord Manton, "inculpates my ancestor."

"No, and there are many, sir, including your grandfather, I believe, who still hold his innocence, but have patience as I relate this story that now begins to be clouded with superstition.

"This fellow, Thorp, durst not go, as the spectre bade him, to the nearest justice of the peace and lay information of the crime, for he knew that Goodhart was a hanger-on of the Earl's, that stories went about in Mullenbridge of that nobleman's revengeful temper, and he believed it was as much as his tenancy was worth to lay an information that might in any way concern my lord.

"The spirit, however, continue to haunt him; he took great trouble never to be alone, especially in the dark, yet he had continually before his eyes the vision of the woman, and continually in his ears her repeated pleading and threats.

"On one occasion the apparition met him in a yet more terrible shape and spoke to him in words of yet more threatening menace. By now, too, the unhappy man was aware of the rumours that were passing among his neighbours. No one else had seen the apparition, but there had been no message from Harriet Bond, and her mother, taking the stage waggon into Winchester, to the address the girl had given Mrs. Fiske, had discovered she was not there, had never been there, nor was there any news of her; the Fiskes thought it was strange that one who had gone off so gaily and light-heartedly had not given any indication of her whereabouts or condition.

"Indeed Harriet was lost, and over a complete disappearance there alway hangs an air of awe and mystery, agreeable to the vulgar and horrible to the fastidious.

"Lord Seagrove had left Charters with his friends, the house was shut up in the care of servants and this gave an added air of gloom to the town and estates. Building, too, had been ceased upon the Folly, on the score, the steward declared, of the expense.

"Between the mutterings of his acquaintances and the

appearances of the apparition the fuller lost his dread of the great man, and one day in August and he solitary, that of the hour being about sunset——"

"Why," interrupted the young man contemptuously, "should this weakling at so unlikely a time have been alone? The tale is for the nursery—a fable."

"As to what is the truth or what a fable this is neither the time nor the place to debate," smiled the Swedenborgian. "I am telling you what was afterwards heard in evidence before the Peers, what Thorpe, sane or benighted, swore to upon his oath.

"So this spectre came to him as the light fled and so alarmed him that the next morning, after a night as he afterwards described it, 'of sleepless agony,' he went to a justice of the peace and told the tale, putting the blame of the murder of Harriet Bond upon Harry Goodhart.

"Under his direction the constables came from Winchester with a warrant; the clearing in the woods where the Folly was building was searched, and in a crevice behind some blocks of marble, well-preserved, were the shoes and stockings that the ghost had described, rotten with human blood. And in a deep grave under the foundations of the Folly which had been left when the workmen were dismissed was discovered the corpse of Harriet Bond, in the attire, white dress, green sash, sworn to by Fiske and his wife, that she had worn when she had gone away with Mr. Goodhart.

"No documents nor jewellery were found upon her body. On her head were the five wounds which the fuller had sworn in his evidence as having seen upon the skull of the spectre, and nearby was the collier's pick.

"Upon this evidence Harry Goodhart was arrested when

attending a prize fight. Overwhelmed by the totally unexpected charge (through the shutting-up of the Park he had felt safe), he confessed to a share in the crime and implicated the Earl, at whose orders, he said, he had enticed the girl away. The cause of the tragedy he supposed to be a promise of marriage that my lord, in his infatuation for the girl, had given her in writing, together with a present of handsome and valuable jewels.

"Now the apparition had not mentioned my lord's name, or, if it had, Thorpe, the fuller, had not brought it across his lips. The magistrate before whom Goodhart was brought was confused by so ugly a story and would have hushed it up. It was, however, beyond his power to do so, for the fuller, by then almost transported, cried out the crime in highways and byways.

"A warrant was granted against the Earl and his companion. My lord, however, on the instance of his powerful friends, was admitted to bail.

"He made a complete denial of the charge and warmly protested his innocence, as is the way," interpolated Lucas Perry, "of most criminals. His friends thought the whole affair monstrous, a mingling of spite, ignorant gossip, and an hallucination, for it was believed that the fuller was not in his right mind and that he himself was very possibly the murderer of Harriet Bond. The Earl, too, had powerful political enemies, and had affronted people with great influence.

"My lord's demeanour, to his family's dismay, did not support a supposition of a false charge. He appeared uneasy, in great agony of mind, and made an attempt to fly the country that was, however, discovered, and he was brought back from Dover.

"When confronted with Goodhart, who declared violently that he had received the offer of a thousand pounds, which had since been paid to him, for enticing away Harriet Bond, the Earl appeared confused, distracted in his answers.

"He did not deny an infatuation for the girl, whom he repeatedly declared was a remarkable and enchanting beauty. He denied, however, that he had given her any promise of marriage, or that it was possible for a man in his position to consider such a notion, or that he had exchanged more than a few words with her or given her presents.

"But everything he said was so distraught and seemed to proceed from a mind so bewildered, that little attention was paid to his statements by the disinterested while they much distressed those too nearly concerned.

"In the upshot Lord Seagrove was brought to trial before the Peers, with Harry Goodhart as witness for the Crown.

"By now, the whole circumstances of the atrocious story were known all over England and the greatest partisanship, excitement and enthusiasm were aroused by the case. My lord, being of such wealth, pretensions, and having so many friends and acquaintances, was warmly supported by many, not only of his own relations but by his own class; but, as I said, he had powerful enemies. Pamphlets and broadsheets went up and down the country about the affair, this and that aspect of it was canvassed.

"I cannot now, my lord, go into all the details. It would take a large volume to give the case with all *pros* and *cons*. There was much that was fantastic and even incredible in the affair. Everyone had his or her opinion of it; you may suppose what was said as to the difference between the station of the murdered woman and the man who was supposed to be her murderer; the unlikelihood of his getting rid of one so insignificant by a crime so abominable, the talk of the promised marriage of which no trace was found, his own confused and even bewildered demeanour, all seemed to be blighted and obscured by a most dismal mystery.

"What was said by one class was not heard by another. The gossip of the fashionable salons of London was not repeated in Mullenbridge.

"Well, Lord Manton, I fear I cannot go into further particulars without giving you pain. Reports of the trial and the execution of the sentence that followed have been as fas as possible concealed.

"Against Goodhart the case was strong; there were the stockings, the pickaxe, the evidence of Thorpe the fuller. Those who disbelieved in ghosts (and there were many, even in those days) supposed that he had been a witness of the crime, had not dared to reveal anything save by his pretence of supernatural revelation. Thus far the sceptics: those who credited Divine intervention in such matters were eager enough to declare that here the hand of God was plainly manifested.

"Nor can I," added the Swedenborgian, "who believe in the invisible world and that Heaven and Hell are about us as we move, pronounce one way or another. There were the stockings, there were the shoes, there was the pickaxe, there was the corpse, all exactly as the fuller declared the spectre had described. If he had come to his knowledge by some rational means and had chosen this device to expose it, I know not . . . .

"The Earl was put on trial, not before his peers, but before the criminal court. There was no evidence against him whatsoever. The fuller did not even say that the spectre had mentioned Lord Seagrove. All that was in his disfavour was the evidence of Harry Goodhart, his pander, his flatterer, a man of an evil reputation who had travelled Europe, leaving trouble and disgrace behind him. However, the Earl's reputation was not good; the Crown could bring forward several witnesses who were able to swear to his, shall we say, unfortunate disposition. The family, again, James, I speak from respect," and the Swedenborgian bowed suavely, "was known to be eccentric; many anecdotes of the strange conduct of the Daintrys were brought forward; the prisoner must have been surprised at the evidence that had been collected against him. One might imagine, were one a romancer, how the young man's horror and amazement increased as he discovered the mass of material to him, perhaps, unknown or disregarded, that was brought forward to prove him capable of a dismal, foolish and contemptible crime.

"He had little to say in his own defence, indeed disappointed the expectations of his own lawyers, for he was confused, bewildered, contradictory. He admitted to an admiration of Harriet Bond, yet declared that he had not known who was the creature he had met in the clearing made for the foundations of the Folly that he was building; he appeared somewhat unsettle in his mind by his experiences abroad and spoke of aerial beings whom he had encountered in the broken seats of the Colosseum at Rome and on the steps of the ancient temples of Greece.

"Enlarging on this theme he showed himself a good scholar and antiquarian; this went against him with the public, who regarded him as a man of education who had used his advantages basely.

"Judge Barne was much disturbed during the trial, indeed showed such a trepidation of spirit that many of the vulgar supposed that the spectre of Harriet Bond had appeared to him, demanding justice.

"I shall make my relation brief; there are many excursions into which I might go, I must not relate any of them."

"Your story has been long enough," said Lord Manton with

a sigh, again glancing towards the red damask curtains. "And yet I can make little of it as clearing up what to me has always been most obscure. But continue, continue!"

Dr. Lucas Perry glanced again at his notes.

"I have put it all down here very carefully. I knew that sooner or later you would broach this subject with me and I wished to be ready with my answers. You can accuse me of exaggeration or phantasy, but what I say is founded upon—well, facts, as they were related at the time. It all has a metaphysical turn and is confused with this rambling talk of ghosts and spirits.

"The evidence of the fuller, Thorpe, which according to his own account was entirely based on the supernatural, was admitted in a court of law. My lord's lawyers and advocates, engaged by some of the greatest families of the time, for his connections were affluent and powerful, astonished the public by bringing in a plea of insanity.

"The trial was soon over. The plea of insanity was rejected; Judge Barne, though obviously overcome by the horror of his task, summed up strongly against the prisoner and pronounced sentence upon him that same night.

"The sentence was duly executed and the prisoner died protesting his innocence, as, I believe, these unhappy beings always do. Who is there who, at this supreme moment, has admitted his guilt?

"That Harriet Bond was murdered and buried near the foundations of the Folly is without question. Whether or no her spectre appeared to the fuller, whether or no either Harry Goodhart or his employer had anything to do with the crime—who shall say now? The affair has been judged, justly or unjustly. It is over."

"But its repercussions come on me," protested the young man.

He rose, went to the window place and put his hand out as if he would hold down the curtain, though it showed no stirring. "There must have been," he added, in a cooler tone, "some very powerful evidence, some very strong feeling to make it possible for a man of my ancestor's—my great-uncle was he not?—breeding, being declared guilty of so foul, so mean a crime. As for the ghostly tale, well, let that go. It is not the matter that I'm investigating . . . ."

"Nay, you're already deep in it, sir, since you believe you see what you term a fetch, in otherwise, the spirit of Harriet Bond. Now I, though I believe that Heaven and Hell are about us and in the tenets of the Swedenborgian faith, can maybe prove to you that this creature whom you alternately cherish and dread, who alternately fascinates and repels you, is no more than a human being who has set her cap at what to her would be a remarkably brilliant match . . . ."

At these words, spoken with irony and in so different a tone from what Dr. Perry had used before, the young man was startled, he turned and bit his underlip.

"You make me a fool," he exclaimed suddenly. "I thought you were with me in this fantasy."

"Fantasy or reality, use what name you will. But I believe that this girl whom you have seen wandering in the churchyard, by the Folly or the Mausoleum, is not more than, as I say, an ambitious, silly miss."

"Mullenbridge is not a village, the people are not so rustic—so stupid. The girl that I've seen, well, she is like the old portrait. I've showed you that. I found it at the 'Seagrove Arms,' where it was hidden away—a large, handsome young woman in a white frock, heavily-built, beautiful, too."

"It may be a portrait of Harriet Bond—allow me to accompany

you one evening to this tryst and we will endeavour to discover if this female who so disturbs you is a human creature."

The youth was offended by this speech, little expected. Was it not Dr. Perry's part to be in every way sympathetic towards these supernatural experiences as he chose to believe them? It was with a very ill grace that he listened to that gentleman's account of a young female living in Mullenbridge, a Miss Adelaide Fenton, who greatly resembled the portrait that Lord Manton had on a previous occasion shown him of Harriet Bond, and whom on previous visits he had taken the trouble to observe.

"She is idle, romantic, educated above her class, and is known to wander about the woods, the churchyard, often with a novel from the circulating library in her hand. It may be that her mind, none of the best, I dare say, is already muddled with some echoes of this old tale. Now, James, I am speaking to you as your grandfather or your tutor would have spoken, not as your spiritual advisor or as one who sympathizes with your metaphysical tendencies."

The young man interrupted with angry surprise and impatience.

"Who are these Fentons? I know nothing of them whatsoever. The name seems to me to have a vague familiarity, no more."

Dr. Perry then, with as much dryness and as rational an attitude as if he had been the Reverend Timothy Chalmers or the old Earl, related the details of the commonplace history of Mrs. Fenton, her bedridden husband and her two daughters.

"The young man listened with distaste; all that impressed him about the relation was the coincidence that the girl lived on the verge of the churchyard of St. Jude and might possibly be the young woman whom he had seen by the grave of Harriet Bond, whose body had been raised from her grave in the foundations of Seagrove Folly and buried in holy turf. But that it was silly

Adelaide Fenton whom he had seen walking by the Folly or the Mausoleum he was not prepared to credit.

"What would be her purpose? Had she to meet a lover or even an acquaintance, why choose so lonely a spot? This creature whom I have beheld has always been solitary."

"She would be, James, if she were looking out for you."

"You do indeed speak to me as if you had been sent by my grandfather or my tutor. Indeed, sir, it was for another purpose I made your acquaintance. I'll not listen to you," added the young man, walking to and fro. "No, this is no comfort to me . . . . "

"You are enthralled by your legend, obsessed by the dismal story of your ancestor——"

"I do not know. It seems to me that the whole estate is haunted, but by what. By my family sins? Do you believe in sins? I feel spectres in the whole locality, Dr. Perry, in Charters, and Verities, the Folly, the Mausoleum. The cousin who came into the title after that wretched man was hanged built up the Folly, finished it in defiance of local opinion, and left it as it is to-day—but no one ever used it——"

"What are you trying to say?" asked Dr. Perry. "The conversation has been long enough. We can get no further. Come with me to London, forget the atmosphere of this place that, I think, is having an unfortunate effect on you. Why, of course there are stories about this old mansion house, as there are about every other old dwelling, many stories. How shall we trace them, and why should we be afraid of them?"

Unheeding this the youth paused before him and said eagerly: "Have you noticed, by the large walled fruit garden where the finest apricots grow, that there is a postern gate leading into the stable yard? Underneath the brick in a tiled channel there is a spring of fresh water. This is so delicious that it was used by the family—brought into the house late in the evening, so that it might be cool, you understand. A servant would go with yoke and pail before the household offices were locked up for the night and fill up all the vessels needed for drinking before the morning.

"On one clear evening, a maid was sent with pail. The moon was shining, there was no cloud, the smallest object was visible. When she returned into the pantry she was without the yoke and pail and whimpering with terror.

"She sobbed out that she was stooping over the spring when she found herself in the midst of a crowd of people who were carrying a coffin, which they set down at the gates of the stable yard——"

"Well," interrupted Dr. Lucas Perry, "it is a trivial tale, why recount it now?"

"Only because it remains vividly in my mind. I remember my mother, shortly before her death, telling it to me. You know that my father and mother both died suddenly, as did my uncles, and I'm the last survivor of a family who have met violent ends.

"Well, the household was so disturbed that one of them, I think it was a steward, went out and asked the gardener, who had a cottage near, if he had seen a funeral, and he smiled and said: "Who would have thought of a funeral at ten o'clock at night?"

"And what's the outcome of this fable?"

"Only that soon afterwards someone died unexpectedly, and was carried across near the spring, carried in the coffin. On that spot the Folly was afterwards built. I tell you the whole locality is haunted."

"Then, sir, leave it!" Tranquillize your mind with a visit to London."

"Have I not been already to London, Paris, Florence and Rome and to more outlandish parts of the world? No, sir, I remain here at Charters, and do you, a Swedenborgian, with your doctrines that hitherto I have found satisfying, venture to tell me that my intellects are disordered?"

"Nothing of the kind, sir. I would not cast any implication on what you say, only I intend to-morrow"—and Dr. Lucas Perry spoke primly "—to pay a visit to Mrs. Fenton and her two amiable daughters and see if I can, with what insight I might possess into this world and the next, disentangle fancy from fact."

* * * * *

Lucas Perry was well known in Mullenbridge and some vague and sinister rumours had been blown abroad that he was a follower of a strange religion; it was considered rather surprising that the old Earl allowed him so much in the company of his grandson. But Mr. Chalmers, the young man's tutor, seemed not only to tolerate Dr. Perry, but to be his good friend, and the two gentlemen were often seen in close conversation together walking in Charters Park.

Mrs. Fenton, then, knew immediately with whom she had to deal, and when she went down to the parlour to receive him, gratified pride disturbed her usual equanimity, yet she preserved her stolid look as she made her curtsey and waited for the visitor to open the conversation.

This he did and with a worldly ease that she found surprising from one whom she had considered to be scarcely a gentleman and supposed to be a member of a dubious set. Mrs. Fenton had even heard it whispered of him that he attended meetings in London where attempts were made to raise the spirits of the dead; Dr. Perry did not seem, however, now in the least inclined to touch upon any such curious matters, for he asked her at once and with an air of authority, as if he had been entrusted with an important mission, if her daughter had the acquaintance of Lord Manton.

Mrs. Fenton guessed immediately that something extremely important to the family fortunes was being touched on. She knew that she was far too ignorant to be able to deal with it, but she was not so stupid as to give herself away. She folded her lips closely and made a conventional reference to her husband.

"It is the father to whom you must go sir, for any talk of my daughter's suitors."

He glanced at her, she was angry to note, with a hint of amusement.

"Mr. Fenton is a permanent invalid, one, I believe, hardly in possession of his faculties."

"He knows what's good for Adelaide, sir!" Mrs. Fenton spoke with angry clumsiness: yet she was agitated, too, with a wild hope. What did this mean—good or bad fortune? She remembered, oh, so clearly, every word that both Adelaide and Caroline had said to her on this subject, she had guessed for some while that the mysterious suitor might be the Earl's grandson. Why not? These things had happened before, were indeed a common ingredient of old songs, legends, fairy stories . . . . She caught herself up on those two words, 'Fairy stories . . . .'

The Swedenborgian seemed to read her clearly, she was chagrined to note, for he remarked: "I am not among those, madam, who disbelieve in the power of youth and beauty and charm to overcome worldly disadvantages. Lord Manton is young and romantic and comes of a family noted for its eccentricity. Your daughter—I have observed her in Charters—is a delightful creature, well-bred, well-behaved."

"She went to a good finishing-school," said Mrs. Fenton sullenly, fearing a trap.

"Will you tell me what you know about this affair, that I think has been kept rather secret."

"Will you tell me, sir, what right you have to ask?" demanded the large woman, with some dignity.

"I have no credentials. I am here as a friend of the Seagroves, and your friend also, madam, I hope."

She feared and dreaded him, she winced from his presence; he was in every way her superior and her master; she longed to know the core of his motive. She muttered again that this was a matter for her husband to handle—and that he was not so ill that he could not handle it.

"I think your feminine wisdom, I think your motherly love will be sufficient protection of your daughter's future happiness," said Dr. Perry formally. He smiled, lifting the corners of his thin mouth, his wrinkled lids.

"What do you think about my daughter? What are you saying about her, Dr. Perry, sir?"

Mrs. Fenton spoke with an air of menace; she came a step nearer her visitor. He replied coolly: "I believe she wanders in those parts of the grounds that the old Earl has lately allowed to be open even to those who are not his tenants. She strolls near the old Mausoleum and the Folly, of which a sordid and unpleasant tale is told by those who ought to forget it, and that lingers in the mind of my young friend who is, as I told you, of a romantic disposition. It is this, and not the hope of meeting your daughter, Mrs. Fenton, that takes Lord Manton to the Mausoleum, the Folly and the churchyard."

She stared at him with dull hostility and replied: "It seems to me that you are talking very great nonsense."

"Your daughter, madam, if you do not have great care, may be doing worse than that. She may be play-acting very great nonsense."

"I don't understand you, sir!"

"You will, I think. I believe you are shrewd enough. I should advise that you send your daughter, who is so charming, so accomplished, away for a while, from this house, from Mullenbridge. Lord Manton may be himself going abroad again for a year or so, in my company and that of Mr. Chalmers. There will be no opportunity for him to correspond with, or even to recollect one who, when he was here, was nothing to him but a shadow of one long since dead."

After these unpleasant sentences Mrs. Fenton cowered; she could not hold her own, she did not know on what grounds she stood. It was very likely that the girl had lied to her, but then this man might be lying too. Of course, *they'd* do all *they* could to break off a match like that. But why shouldn't my girl manage it as others had, with no better looks or luck. The young man is a solitary, without the usual tastes of his class, melancholy too, it seemed, wandering alone like that. Well, that might be useful, it might give Adelaide her chance.

Lucy Fenton spread her thick fingers out, looked at them reflectively, then closed them.

"I know perfectly well what you are considering," remarked Dr. Perry. "I tell you that Lord Manton is going abroad, and by the time he returns he will certainly be engaged to marry. And that had already been arranged with a certain young lady whose family is connected with that of the Seagroves."

At this sentence Mrs. Fenton felt another chill of defeat.

"I'll speak to my daughter," she conceded grudgingly. "I'll get what I can out of her. You don't know what girls are . . . . "

"If I can understand the young lady, madam, and I think I can, it will be no use for you to speak to her. You must take her away, or send her away. It will be wiser, and happier, for her—for you all."

He gave the conventional and old-fashioned phrase an icy turn, but Mrs. Fenton further tempted her fate.

"What will happen if I refuse?" she asked with a sulky glance.

"Then," answered Dr. Perry pleasantly, "it will be easy for the Earl to make it impossible for you to remain in Mullenbridge. I do not think you are the type of person who would like to leave a town, in which you have long lived, under a darkness of suspicion, possibly of disgrace."

Mrs. Fenton was dismayed and baffled, but she flung back: "My daughter's done nothing to disgrace herself!"

"That depends, madam, on how we define the word. Will you think over what I have said and try to take my advice?"

He bowed stiffly from the waist, his tall hat held to his bosom, and was gone.

Trying to gather her mental strength, she peered after him as he walked with his light step along the garden path; inquisitive eyes were watching him from the gardens at the right—those two old women, always out under pretence of searching for the gooseberries, they must know that with so black a Spring as this they would not be worth gathering even now.

Mrs. Fenton moved away from the window. No, it would not be agreeable to have to leave Mullenbridge with a great number of people looking at her like that . . . . She went slowly upstairs.

Adelaide was sitting with her father; Mrs. Fenton listened at the crack of the door. She could hear the pleasant, monotonous voice reading pompous splendid words from the Old Testament.

Then she went softly, and she knew how to move without making a sound, into the next room where Caroline was seated by the window making rosettes out of strips of green ribbon and sewing them on to a white chip hat. Her mother put her finger to her lips as a sign of discretion, crossed the room heavily and sat beside the girl, who watched her in cool expectation of some excitement.

"Dr. Lucas Perry has been here," whispered Mrs. Fenton, breathing heavily. "I'll speak very low, I don't want your sister to hear what we're talking about."

"She won't, she's reading to Father." Caroline's response was very hushed; she listened, her needle and thread suspended in her plump fingers. "What's he been here for?"

"That's what I want to find out," confided Mrs. Fenton. "I wish I knew more about him, too. He's a queer kind of man, frightening."

"Oh, do you think so?" smiled Caroline. "I've met him, and spoken with him," she added, unexpectedly, her voice was the most discreet of low tones.

"You've spoken to him!" repeated Mrs. Fenton amazed.

"There's nothing in that, is there?" Caroline spoke primly. "He came upon me gathering plants to press in my book in the Folly fields, by the great gates, he stopped and spoke to me and was interested about botany, about other things, too."

"What did you tell him, Carrie?"

"Well, he talked of the invisible world, the spiritual world and the invisible mental world—yes, that's what he said. But he's a good Christian, Mother, he believes in God, and Heaven and Hell, though differently from what we do."

"Differently, indeed, I should think," muttered Mrs. Fenton. "I don't like the looks of him nor what you've told me about him.

He's come interfering in our affairs, Carrie. You girls—well, I don't know if you've been telling me the truth—but now it's important." She leaned forward and laid her heavy hand on the knee of her daughter's cotton frock. "Who was the young man you've seen walking with Adelaide, who came here that day and whom I just missed? Was it the old Earl's grandson?"

"Why shouldn't it have been?" evaded Carrie.

"Did he send her all those presents, did he promise to buy her a pianoforte and a white horse, and did she post to him those handkerchiefs she was working in initials in hair?"

"Well, I promised to keep it all a secret, Mother."

Mrs. Fenton groaned in her vexation and defeat.

"Is he going to pay for the pink bonnet?" she asked irrelevantly.

"I suppose so. And all the other presents. But what's it matter, Mother, why can't you leave it to Adelaide? She's quite shrewd and understanding. I wish I had come down when Dr. Perry was there. I like to hear him talk of the three Hells and the three Heavens and how each Angelic Society has its Infernal Counterpart."

"It's blasphemous talk, or the man's out of his mind."

"You know he isn't that, is he, Mother? You've only got to look at him to see how businesslike he is. Besides, I believe he is a clever doctor and has a great influence over the young heir."

"You're talking of what you don't understand, what can you have heard in Mullenbridge gossiping among foolish girls like yourself? I wish I had someone on whom I could rely, someone to whom I could turn. I told Dr. Perry I'd speak to your father—of course, it's impossible.

"Why don't you speak to Adelaide yourself? I suppose she'd tell you——" Carrie checked herself with a sly grin.

"The truth?" frowned Mrs. Fenton, "or some of that stuff she gets out of those novels? Why did they want to open a circulating library in Mullenbridge?"

"She's got the letters," whispered Carrie. "She keeps them in that drawer," the girl nodded towards it, "locked. She reads them to me now and again. I don't like hearing them, they're very tedious, all the same. Just like the letters in the novels."

"What's the handwriting?" demanded Mrs. Fenton.

"Oh, not a bit like Adelaide's," declared Carrie quickly. "Long and fine, what they call Italian copperplate, I think."

"The young lord's what they call eccentric, not right in his senses, I think," brooded Mrs. Fenton. "That's what I learnt from what that man was trying to tell me to-day what I've heard before. They're sending him away—abroad."

"Sending him away!" breathed Carrie, quickly. "Abroad! And for how long?"

"Two years, he said. Isn't it an odd kind of life for a man of his position? He don't see no company, he doesn't go anywhere much. He's been abroad before, but always living solitary and I understand with that clergyman, Chalmers." Mrs. Fenton's words came with hesitation for she was speaking of a society of which she knew nothing, but inherent commonsense and the little knowledge that she had picked up from the conversation of her betters told her that Charters was a peculiar household, that neither Dr. Perry nor Mr. Chalmers were the companions usually chosen for a young man of Lord Manton's position and prospects.

"They say he goes to places where they try to raise the spirits," she added guardedly, pressing her hand more heavily on her daughter's knee.

"Oh, Dr. Perry told me about the spirits. He said that in the spiritual world there is no space between the spirits, and so Doctor

Swedenborg, who founded this religion, could talk, when in his own bedroom, with the souls of men who were a long way off or were even on the moon and the stars."

"That's rubbish," decided Mrs. Fenton brusquely. "That's where the poor young man gets all these ideas from——"

"What ideas?" demanded Carrie, allowing needle and thread to fall into her lap; she put her fresh young face close to her mother's anxious countenance.

"Oh, something about an old story, some crime or other, hundreds of years ago, who cares? As if there was a spot in the country where there hadn't been something of the kind. Some foolish old tale that the young man allowed to take hold of him—supposing he saw a spirit."

"Perhaps he did," said Carrie, calmly, "but I don't see what it's to do with us or with Adelaide. Though perhaps she wouldn't like a husband who saw visions."

"Husband!" pounced Mrs. Fenton, jealously, as if she was counting over a treasure. "Her husband!" Then she stood up suddenly and shook her shoulders. "I don't like it!" she declared. "I don't like it! I'd better send Adelaide away."

"Oh, had you?" asked Carrie, with a precise and curious air. "Have you been warned to do that?"

"You know far too much for a girl of your age," sighed her mother. "I know it's no use my talking to you, but you're not going to tell me anything more. If I did get you to speak I suppose it would be lies."

"I haven't told you lies," declared Carrie, primly.

"Then you *did* really see that young man, that young fool, it seems to me he is bewitched or benighted, with Adelaide?"

"I told you what I'd seen."

Mrs. Fenton checked her examination of the girl. After all, it was not fair to involve the child too deeply in a matter like this, besides, she was sly—to think that she had met that crazy doctor, who had been talking to her of his Hells and Heavens! It would be wise, perhaps, to take both her daughters away from Mullenbridge.

'I suppose the old lord sent him to spy on 'em,' she thought, with gloomy resentment, and yet with a touch of fear. 'And I'd better be careful. Of course, he could ruin us. But she might go away—well, for a few months. I could afford that. I'll send Carrie with her, too. I must think of some excuse that won't make the neighbours talk. Perhaps they've said too much already. There's the pink bonnet to be paid for. If she's bought it herself, where did she think she'd get the money from?'

Bewildered and yet undaunted, Mrs. Fenton turned away from her young daughter and left the room. There was silence in the nuptial chamber; she lifted the latch cautiously and peered within. Adelaide was seated with the open Bible on her knee, a dreamy and sullen expression on her smooth, comely features. Thomas Fenton was asleep. His wife looked round to see that he lacked nothing; everything was in order, all was neat and tidy. Whatever happened, this man should not be neglected. She pulled the bell-rope and busied herself with small, unnecessary tasks, moving a glass here, a napkin there, pulling the curtains an inch or two closer in front of the window until Susan came to take her place.

Then she beckoned to her silent daughter and preceded her downstairs; she knew what she wanted to say, but had very little idea of how to say it. She wanted to be direct, express herself with clarity, she wanted, though she feared this was impossible, to get at the truth. She feared that she might be foregoing the possibility of a brilliant advantage; she feared also that if she did not take heed of the warning that had been so definitely and so coolly given her to-day, she might involve herself in a disaster that she would be quite incapable of averting or even of escaping for she had few weapons and few resources.

While she stood silent, pulling at the buttons on her gown and puzzling as to how she should frame what she had to say, Adelaide broke the uncomfortable silence by remarking: "The bill for the pink bonnet's come in, Mother, and Basil asks if you will pay for it——He's short of funds at the moment, having lost a great deal at cards."

Mrs. Fenton instantly compared this picture of a spendthrift young gambler who gave a girl presents for which he could not pay (a simple present, too, Mrs. Fenton was sure for the means of a 'young gentleman of rank and fashion') with the impression she had received of Lord Manton from Dr. Perry's talk as a solitary, rather morose young man whose mind was full of marvellous and rather unpleasant subjects. Basil—a fancy name, a fancy tale.

"Will you pay for the bonnet, Mother?" pouted Adelaide, holding out with a pretty gesture that seemed artificial the mantua-maker's bill. "It's very tiresome, Basil promised to send the money, but he is away at the races and much engaged in the fashionable world."

"Yes, I'll pay it," said Mrs. Fenton, slowly taking the paper and looking at the sum marked on it—two pounds fifteen shillings and sixpence—for a bonnet, a bonnet that could not be worn because it was too smart, because there was no dress, or pelisse, or gloves, or slippers, or reticule to go with it. "Yes, I'll pay it," she repeated heavily. "It's a pity he didn't get you something sensible, Adelaide, for I'm going to send you on a visit to your Aunt Martha, you and Carrie both. She lives near the sea and the air will do you good. It will freshen up your complexion, and perhaps your wits." And she laughed harshly.

This was so unusual in her, and her suggestion was so startling that Adelaide stared at her in trepidation almost as if she thought her mother had gone out of her mind.

"There's no circulating library there, it's a pity," added Mrs. Fenton, lifting her lip.

Adelaide shrank away behind the bed curtains.

"Will you pay for the bonnet, this afternoon," she pleaded humbly. "Miss Herle is getting impatient, it ought to have been paid a week ago. I didn't think to tell you about it before. I supposed that he had paid."

"None of your excuses, miss. Get your valise ready, I'll arrange for you to go to Devon as soon as I can."

"I don't want to go," cried Adelaide, with a flash of obstinacy. "I suppose it won't be for long? I know Aunt Martha is always keen for us to go and visit her. But she's an old maid, leads a dull life, doesn't she?"

"She's a vigorous woman, she runs a small farm quite successfully, she'll find you something to do. You'll have to go, Adelaide, and go quietly or I shan't pay for the bonnet. I shall begin to ask questions. Things maybe you won't like to hear will come out."

Adelaide was silent, she looked aside; her mother hoped that she had quelled her, but the girl did not easily accept defeat.

"It really don't matter," she protested, "whether I go away or not. Basil and I can always write to one another. I shall go to the beech tree at the Mausoleum and put my new address in the hole where we keep our letters."

"You'll commit no such folly, miss. And you won't go abroad without me."

"Oh, not even with Carrie?" Adelaide began to whimper with a sudden affectation of distress. "Aren't I to see Basil to say good-bye? How is he to know that I'm going to be faithful?"

Mrs. Fenton looked at the bill in her hand, then up at the girl. Adelaide was silent.

"You'll do as you're told, miss. You won't plague your father. You won't disturb Susan, you won't put foolish ideas into Carrie's head. Your Aunt Martha will take care of that."

"Very good, Mother. I'll behave as you wish me to behave as long as you'll pay for the bonnet and not let it get out round the town that——"

"That you told lies about him," said Mrs. Fenton. "I'll do what I can."

* * * * *

Dr. Lucas Perry returned from Winchester to Charters to find that some company had unexpectedly arrived and that there was more life and movement, more sounds of voices and even of laughter, than he ever remembered to have heard in the old mansion, that had never been sufficiently modernized to make it really convenient and comfortable.

Lord Manton seemed rather pleased by this unlooked-for society, as if he was glad to be rid of his own introspective moods and that though these gentlemen were not such as he had lately chosen for his companions, they were intelligent and well-informed. And some of them took a vivid interest in the most debated questions of the day, and the talk after supper when the old Earl had retired early to his chamber was easily turned by the young host upon some spiritual phenomena and *séances* that had lately been held in a house in a famous London square.

"You, I think," here interpolated one of the company, turning to Dr. Perry, "are a Swedenborgian, are you not?"

That gentleman bowed and said that Emmanuel Swedenborg had never founded a sect, but that he, Lucas Perry, belonged to the New Church signified by the New Jerusalem described in the *Revelations* which had been for some years organized as a sect, the founder of this in England being Robert Hindmarsh, a Clerkenwell preacher who had been one of the first followers of the mystical Swede.

"We," explained Lord Manton, "are apt to make gross mistakes about these Swedenborgians, as I must, sir, still name you, the other title being too long and difficult."

"We have nothing whatever to do with spiritualism or the raising of the dead," smiled Dr. Perry. "You have confused our knowledge of the spiritual world with vulgar legends, absurd superstition and even malicious mischief-making and self-seeking on which most of the supernatural tales rest."

"Self-seeking, self-love," repeated the excited youth. "I believe, sir, your Church declares that all who are thus afflicted go to Hell?"

"They are," replied Dr. Perry, bowing, "in Hell already."

PART THREE
THE NECROMANCERS

> 'The spectres uttered no sound, but above the figure of the lady, as if written in phosphoric light in the dusk atmosphere that surrounded her, were some words, intimations that, having never aspired beyond the joys and sorrows of this world, she remained earthbound.'
>
> *Haunted Houses.*—
>
> J. INGRAM.

A GROUP of people who considered themselves extremely enlightened, or at least of a very scientific and enquiring mind, many of them members of learned societies, was gathered together in the back parlour of a handsome house in Bayswater in the hope of participating in some supernatural or spiritualistic phenomena. One ancient word, magic, might have described what they were engaged in—that obscure and impressive practice that has been given many modern high and impressive names.

James Daintry (he preferred not to use his courtesy title), after a month of gloomy and sombre as well as purposeless wandering on the continent, had returned to London and renewed, though not on the same warm terms as before, his friendship with Dr. Lucas Perry, avoiding all the other companions who endeavoured to amuse him with those diversions and interests common to their age, rank, and disposition.

Dr. Perry was not, being a Swedenborgian, a spiritualist. Indeed, he was one of those who resisted the attempts of those fanatics, as he termed them, who hoped to raise 'spiritualism' into a religion.

He had, moreover, warned his young friend, who seemed to be even less cheerful than before, and to indulge too often in moody abstractions and to hold himself too remote from the ordinary distraction of life, that to concern himself in what might be rightly termed spiritualism might be perilous and that some who had tried to evoke the spirits of the dead at formal *séances* had lost their reason without being, however, confined to lunatic asylums. His pupil was not in the least depressed by these rebukes and warnings.

"I do not know how you consented to be a Swedenborgian if you can talk in such a manner," he retorted with some heat. "Reason! What is it? Do you not yourself often argue against it?"

"My religion is a way of life and the spirits with whom I converse are not those you seek to evoke." And he reminded his impatient listener of the disastrous effects of a public exhibition of spiritualism in a Scottish town where it was generally admitted some evil influence had prevailed, and the most dire alarm and grisly horrors had spread among the assembly.

However, Dr. Perry agreed to accompany the young man to this meeting, which seemed to himself commonplace and of little importance.

The room was handsomely furnished in the ordinary taste of the upholsterer, for this was the residence of a well-known physician with a comfortable practice as a consultant. The gentleman himself was present; he was a middle-aged man of a practical and well-bred exterior, a Scot by the name of Beattie and a Highlander on his mother's side; he was supposed to possess the second sight which is well known to exist in the West of Scotland.

There was also present Robert Oldham, a lawyer, an alert, shrewd, good-humoured man of middle age; Guy Coates, a serious young man of good birth who was studying for Holy Orders; two elderly ladies, each of a modest aspect and demeanour—Mrs. Raines and Mrs. Outram, and a Miss Cox, who had the appearance of an upper servant in a respectable household and seemed rather embarrassed by the superior rank of the people by whom she was surrounded.

This company sat at a large table that was covered by a chenille cloth of a purple colour; upon this stood a large lamp with a glass chimney and an opaque shade, a heavy bottle of Irish glass filled with water and a cut tumbler beside it—the only refreshment that Amelia Trent, the medium, declared herself able to take when about to go into a trance.

Dr. Beattie discoursed seriously with Lord Manton, whom he had not met before but whom he had invited to his house through the agency of Dr. Perry.

"Do not suppose," said he, "that because I allow these experiments to be made here that I have any blind faith in them. Indeed, I consider them as experiments, no more than that. You are too well read, I am sure, sir, for me to touch upon the antiquity of the subject that we are now, for so brief a while, studying."

The young man replied that while he had by no means taken up research into the occult, he was aware of the broad outline of this matter, which lay like a dark, unexplored, tangled undergrowth behind the serene surface of man's intellectual attainments.

The physician glanced at him quizzically, good-humouredly, and with a touch of compassion. He replied: "I must confess that I regard with a certain uneasiness the growing taste for so-called investigations such as these. We are all gathered here, no doubt, with the best of intentions, yet who knows if we may not be corrupted by our curiosity, that we are not in fact indulging in the willing worship of demons?"

The company were standing in the corner of the room, near the dusty rep curtains that concealed the November night, and spoke in tones too low to be overheard by the medium, who was composing herself for her communication with the invisible world, had her hands folded upon her broad bosom where a gold chain glittered on a grey poplin bodice.[17]

"I do not for one moment suppose that that good woman there, for she is in every way decent and respectable, is evil, but might she not become a—well, what she calls herself—a medium, through which evil would flow? Let us not be too sure," added Dr. Beattie, "that this may not end in real formal idolatry."

"Yes," the lawyer agreed, "it seems to me also that this is an idolatry, not perhaps in any of its old forms, and yet—let us not be too sure. I do not mean the worship of Mammon, with which saying we are very familiar, I don't mean that covetousness which is the servant of idleness, I mean the rejecting of God, or the goodness our heart believes in, the refusal to yield ourselves to be filled and guided by God—the turning to Him."

"To Him?" asked Lord Manton. "Who is He? Whom do you mean?"

"I mean some other," replied the lawyer, quietly. "Who knows—shall we say a Demon, something offensive and unintelligent, as we like to suppose? What has been may be again, we are not the wisest, bravest, shrewdest men who ever existed. Paris and London are not equal in culture and refinement to Athens and Corinth."

"Perhaps we *know* more now," suggested Lord Manton,

---

[17] Poplin is a plain weave fabric of cotton, wool, or silk, with very fine horizontal ribs.

nervously; "we have progressed in knowledge, if not in wisdom or shrewdness."

Dr. Perry said that they had not come there to discuss problems of this kind, but only to be witnesses of an experiment. "Let that word cover all."

"My young friend," he added, "has never before attended one of these *séances*. I have asked him to cast all preconceived notions and prejudices out of his mind, and also," added he, with emphasis, "any fantastic tales that he may be harbouring, or any crude and absurd ideas that he thinks will be clarified to-day, or any puzzles that he supposes may be very soon solved."

Guy Coates, the youth who was reading for Holy Orders, then asked if it might not be possible that the spirits were good; "may not these be revelations that come to us in God's own way?"

This Dr. Beattie denied.

"There may be some explanation such as mesmerism, hallucinations, and yet what is this but changing the terms? I have heard, on good authority, of these things myself—heavy articles turn about and run and skip, sofas and pianos raised many feet above the ground, gliding in the atmosphere, making a circuit of the room and gently falling into their places again, human hands floating in the air, spirit writings, spirit drawings, spirit recitals at the piano . . . ."

"Is that indeed true?" demanded Lord Manton, eagerly. "Have you seen them yourself, sir?"

"I've seen none of them. I do not pretend to understand it at all. I know multitudes of keen, shrewd, and observant professional men of all classes, aye, and ladies too," said he, bowing to those present, "who tell me these things, and I know that I have made certain deductions thereon which I would not think of boring you with now. But I say that *if* these things come—well, I'm a Christian and I've no doubt or difficulty in saying from *whence* they come."

"I do not think," remarked Mrs. Outram simply, "that we need fear this evil that you speak of, if you are indeed referring to a personal Devil, for I believe that he has no existence except as a distorted, deformed, and monstrous interpretation of the evil in each individual. And when I say evil," she added, speaking smoothly as one who has learnt by heart sentences from a text-book, "I mean everything in opposition to wisdom, goodness, and love. I know there are those who think that spiritualism is a satanic agency, but I cannot agree."

"One may be easily misled, madam, by sentiments and fancies, and by wishes and desires. Let us, however, return to the table and see if Miss Trent has gone into her trance."

It seemed as if this was so, for the medium had fallen back in her chair, having drawn her coarsely-crocheted wool shawl tightly round her head and face. Dr. Beattie and then Dr. Perry felt her pulse and gently laid her fat hand upon her sloping lap, declaring that she was now unconscious. Dr. Beattie then carefully lowered the wick of the lamp, leaving the room in a dim, diffused light that yet, however, was quite bright enough to enable all the objects in the room to be distinctly perceived. He then, as one who undertook a routine task, told everyone present to empty their minds of any apprehensions, expectations, or prejudices, not to cross their knees nor to fold their hands, but remain sitting without touching one another in a row facing the medium.

This they did, Dr. Perry and Lord Manton sitting either side of Dr. Beattie. Beyond them was the lawyer and the young theological student and, lastly, the two ladies, Mrs. Outram and Mrs. Raines, who before she had taken her seat had raised the lamp and smoothly withdrawn the cloth which she neatly folded and put over a chair that stood the other side of the room.

Lord Manton noticed that the chamber was bare of cupboards and that there were no curtains beyond those that concealed the windows; these lay flat against the dark glass. He had already examined them and found that there was not sufficient space between the draperies and the window for anyone to be concealed. Nor was there, in any part of the room, a door save that which opened on to the passage from which they had all entered.

Dr. Perry noticed with a smile this anxious scrutiny. He had told his friend before they entered the parlour that he would find it had been specially selected to guard against any possibility of crude fraud.

They remained for some time sitting thus silent and James Daintry thought how commonplace and ordinary they all looked. The medium herself appeared a most insignificant woman and was a displeasing sight, with her coarse head lolling on her bowed shoulders, her plump hands slack in her lap, her stout bosom rising and falling with her stertorous breathing.

After a few moments—he supposed it was no more—of close attention and complete silence, the young man began to feel slightly giddy and his senses began to swim. The forms of the room, the lines of the floor and the ceiling became less distinct, and there was a faint buzzing, like running water, in his ears so that it was not easy for him to distinguish any sounds that there might be—the breathing of the medium, the flutter of the flame in the lamp, the slight movement of his companions' feet as they moved them in subdued, restless shiftings one from another. Then he heard, like so many claps of thunder, loud raps that came from the table as if violent blows had been struck there by an invisible hand.

He turned his head and saw the table untouched but tilted at an angle of forty-five degrees. It continued in that position for almost a minute, then turned back and repeated the movement on the other side. Nobody was within at least five feet of the table.

The young man tried to move, but felt as if bound in his chair; there was a lethargy over his entire body that was accompanied by a dull, though strong sensation of terror. He saw his companions in slightly distorted shapes; they appeared a long way off like figures viewed through the wrong end of a telescope. The medium seemed to rise in her chair to the height of several inches from the ground and then slide back again. This was repeated several times.

Meanwhile the room had become blurred as if a thick mist of an equal density was obscuring it. This dull vapour, that was of a uniform greenish hue, was dissipated with a suddenness equal to the suddenness with which the unexpected and violent blows on the table had occurred, by blazes of light of various magnitude and intensity; some seemed to be no more than a faint phosphoric that had the appearance of a small bud of fire. Others, and these were higher up in the room, were enormous bubbles that appeared as dazzling as the sun and gave off cascades of sparkling light. One of these brilliant balls spread into the shape of a luminous hand which hovered near the young man as if making an attempt to caress him, then faded away into the mist.

These lights continued to float about the room, further lulling and soothing the young man's senses and increasing his lethargy, but rather increasing than quelling the core of terror that burnt behind his immobility.

One of the lights, at least, appeared to be solid, for it came down on the table, and struck it with a heavy blow.

The medium seemed to be deeper in her trance and was falling back as if in a state of complete insensibility in her chair, while the different points of light were dancing about and settling on the heads of the company, resting on the snuff-coloured locks of Dr. Beattie, on the smooth dark hair of the young student, on the straw-coloured ringlets of Mrs. Outram.

Sparks of light rose from the table to the ceiling and again falling on the table struck it with audible sounds. The luminous flashing continued before the young man's eyes until the shape and size and appearance of the room were completely blotted out.

Again one of these lights condensed into the form of a hand, and this time it was small, delicate, white and rested on his sleeve; beautifully formed and dimpled, with a caressing motion it patted his cuff, then placed between his fingers a sprig that seemed to be composed of small, dark-green spiked leaves and bright star-like flowers.

James Daintry felt he was swaying and as if about to fall, but he was steadied by seeing Dr. Beattie, who from being of diminutive size had now swelled to monstrous proportions, motion him to stand up. He rose automatically, and found that he was part of a circle; they were all holding each other's hands and standing round the table at which the medium sat. The lamp was now extinguished; he could see the dead white of the opal glass of the globe in the room that was lit entirely by the balls of supernatural fire and the cascades of sparks of light that fell from them as with a rhythmic flow they pursued one another about the room.

The company stood in this circle, now quite close to the table, Dr. Beattie being so near the medium that he was almost touching her shoulder, and the young man saw the lamp vanish;

it was no longer a material object but had become a wisp of vapour that instantly had disappeared in an elongated shape rapidly across the room.

Then from the middle of the smooth and glimmering surface of the table that now had an icy appearance, as if it was extremely cold and made of rock-like substance, there rose the figure of a woman from the waist, clearly seen, of a comely shape but heavily-built, with bright hair plaited back behind her ears, a green sash under her full bosom and in her hand, small, white, and dimpled, that she stretched out towards James Daintry, a sprig of the star-like blossom.

"Harriet Bond," he said, "I expected to meet you here to-night. Will you tell me what your desire is with me?"

"Meet me," she replied, "in the usual place. You have been away too long."

The ordinary words were spoken in a dreadful tone of voice that was like the feeble shrilling of a sick child and yet had something of the harsh notes of an old woman.

The young man made a forward movement that broke the circle and stretched out his hand as if to touch the apparition; at that moment it disappeared and the whole room whirled round into circles that, spinning one round the other, made a centre-point of an exceeding brilliance that after a second absorbed the whole of the young man's vision and seemed to burst into a complete brightness that was followed by a complete dark.

* * * * *

He found himself lying on a sofa with a bottle of smelling-salts being held to his nose by Mrs. Outram; the other ladies had retired, 'in a state of great disorder,' he heard someone say.

When asked what he had seen, or what manifestation had

appeared to trouble him so, he replied: "Nothing." He confessed, however, to a violent headache and a sensation of nausea.

"No wonder," said Dr. Beattie. "You fell forward insensible and struck your forehead against the edge of the table. Otherwise the meeting was without incident. The medium made some gurgling sounds from which I could gather nothing intelligible and no phenomena occurred."

The young theological student, however, who looked extremely shocked, murmured that that would not altogether be his account of the evening. He declared that he had, he thought, seen some misty shape standing behind the medium's chair.

Lord Manton felt that he should be ashamed of himself for what no doubt had been a foolish and almost hysterical display, and yet his sensations were stultified. He was conscious that a deep stupidity overwhelmed him.

Dr. Beattie gave him a prescription, telling him to get his servant to get it made up and to take it every two or three hours; while he put into Dr. Perry's hand a box containing some pills that could give the young man a good night's rest.

"I'll give you nothing now," said he, "because it may further affect your mind. I believe you are suffering from shock. Perhaps it would relieve you were you to tell me what you supposed you saw?"

"Supposed I saw!" said Lord Manton, looking sharply round. They were all gazing at him with intense but kindly curiosity. It was at once evident to him that none of them had seen anything, except possibly Coates, the young theological student, who seemed dismayed and troubled but who yet when pressed would give no exacter account of his vision than his impression of a misty substance standing behind the medium. That good woman had now taken her fee, tied on her bonnet strings, put on her shawl, and gone downstairs, where a manservant had called her a cab and seen her into it and given the directions to the respectable building where she lived.

"I think," remarked Dr. Perry, "that we meddle, sir, with things that are best left alone. I do not pretend, especially in the state you are in and the time and place, to ask you to give any account of what you may have undergone."

"Indeed, I doubt," said Dr. Beattie, "if either of us could do."

And the lawyer agreed.

"We are on the edge of the abyss, perhaps," he remarked. "We are on the edge of something that is dark, intricate, and dangerous. It would require no great subtlety either," he added, "to decide that if this gentleman has seen something, or if he imagines he has seen something, there is little difference in the effect."

He then offered to see Mrs. Outram home and the two departed together, conversing earnestly.

Lord Manton sat on the sofa that was covered with red damask and looked steadily round the room, that was now clear in the distinct subdued glow given by the lamp that stood in the centre of the table. One of the ladies must have replaced the purplish red chenille cloth, for it covered that surface that he had seen so clear and shining like ice when the figure of Harriet Bond had risen from it . . . . The room, however, appeared in every other way the same as when they had sat down to take part in the *séance*. Nothing was disordered, nothing was in the least put out of place. Again, when his senses steadied, he observed that there were no doors either of cupboards or into other rooms, no draperies, no cabinets, from which any possible tricks could have been played.

Then he smiled at himself and his pretence of being the

practical materialist. What doors or curtains or draperies could account for the lights, the figure, the hand that had pulled at his cuff?

He looked down, startled, at his wrist as this recollection came to his mind. He expected to see between his fingers the sprig of white starry flowers and green leaves. But there was nothing.

Recovering himself he took leave of his host and refusing to speak of his experiences, but trying to put all aside by saying that he had been seized with a sudden faintness, owing no doubt to a concentrated continuous gaze at the lamp . . . .

"I wonder," he added, with a sudden suspicion as another thought came into his mind, "that I did not overset it as I fell against the table with all my weight?"

"We caught you before you did more than lightly strike the edge," explained Dr. Beattie. "Besides, you'll have a slight bruise on the temple when you look at it in the morning. Nothing more, I can assure you."

* * * * *

Dr. Perry then took his young friend home. They decided that they would walk through the streets; the winter night was clear and agreeably cold after the mustiness of the shrouded parlour. The sky was filled with the radiance of the moon that was shining behind the tops of the massive, handsome houses that faced their private gardens and the high road, so that the heavens had a faint yet pure steely-blue colour.

"You believe, of course," said Dr. Perry, putting his arm through that of his friend, "that you saw the spirit of Harriet Bond? That is what you went there prepared to see. The suggestion of the place and the proceeding, which took the form of a ritual, produced the vision that you expected, perhaps desired, to behold."

Lord Manton thrust his chin into the collar of his great-coat and shuddered slightly in the bracing but chilly air.

"You suppose that I think of nothing but my fetch, as you term her!" he replied rapidly. "Well, you are mistaken. I am interested in everything that is not commonplace and mediocre. I have heard much of supernatural phenomena of one sort or another, and I always understood that at Dr. Beattie's house—maybe you yourself told me—that if I must dabble, as you called it, in this kind of experiment his was the best place to go and Miss Trent the most reliable medium. But where," he added, "is the difference?"

"Very little perhaps," agreed Dr. Perry, "but I would take your mind off these dark and tedious byways. You are a man who should be able to live a religion and not have to spend your time in these dubious experiments."

"You used the word experiments several times," cried Lord Manton. "I know what I saw. Come home with me to my rooms in Jermyn Street. Daintry House is shut up. It's a gloomy place. We're a strange family, are we not, Dr. Perry? An old man and a young man and none but distant relations who don't care for us in the least, and who never come near us."

"Well, you have your friends who will do their best for you in a social way, introduce you to what is known as the great world."

"*Great* world," replied the other, with a hunch of his shoulders. "I am investigating—I like that word, Dr. Perry, though I object to yours, experiments—something which is more interesting to me than the *great* world, and that is the *invisible* world. I am not a man of action nor a scholar nor even of much intelligence. There is no way," he added, talking and walking rapidly so that the elder man had great difficulty in keeping pace with his step and following his words, "in which I can hope to distinguish myself. I shall have, quite soon, I suppose, considering my grandfather's age, large estates, but they will be unproductive, though not, I believe, encumbered. I shall inherit a grandiose mansion that is in many parts ruinous and is not convenient or modern, a poor copy of an ancient building raised by the ostentatious taste of an ancestor known as The Folly, and a charnel-house to which is given the pretentious title of a mausoleum."

"Nevertheless, although you put your possessions in such a dreary light, there is everything before you."

"I know that. 'The world's mine oyster,' " the young man laughed again. "Such an easy thing to say to youth—'the word's before you.' Oh, yes, I know I've got advantages—an orthodox education, an old title, a seat in the House of Lords! I could enter the Services, I could have a try at a Government post—power, wealth, sensuality—the three desires, they say, of the corrupt human heart. Well, none of them satisfies me."

"Are you sure? Not the first? Is not that which you are seeking for—power, power not only over the things of this earth but over those, as you term it, of the invisible world?"

"No! No!"

They had been walking rapidly along the broad road that stretched along the iron railings of the Park and had now reached the toll-gates at Hyde Park Corner, close to St. George's Hospital. There the youth hailed a hackney-cab that had just set down a fare, and with a sudden access of strength and energy hustled his companion into it.

In the frowsy, evil-smelling, dirty interior of the public vehicle he continued to talk in a loud, strange voice.

"Why should I not be interested in the history of Harriet Bond? You know that I have an eccentric reputation. One of my ancestors was hanged for murder. I know a good deal more about that story than when I saw you last."

"I am sorry to hear it. Why dwell so consistently on an old and, after all, commonplace crime, and one that perhaps was not committed? It might be that your ancestor, who was most unpopular because of—his debauchery and extravagance and political opinions—was unjustly condemned.

"Peers were often unjustly acquitted," replied the young man, whose excitement was mounting and seemed to resemble that of someone who has been drugged, for he was talking with great fluency and moving restlessly about on his seat, "but none, I think, have been unjustly hanged. Hanged, my dear sir!"

In a few minutes the lumbering vehicle had brought them to the door of his apartments in Jermyn Street; James Daintry paid the driver, took out his key, and went ahead of his visitor to show the way.

Hackett was waiting up for him in the expensively furnished room, but telling him to set out whatever refreshments Dr. Perry might desire and then to go to bed, the youth lit the lamp. The room was already cheerfully illuminated with the glow from the fire that the servant had kept well-gathered together; the apartment was well-appointed and everything in it rich and of good taste; Lord Manton had brought back several curiosities from abroad, but had not made the vulgar error of exhibiting them in his chambers. Nor did he indulge in any modish whims of the moment, therefore the apartment was agreeable even to the fastidious taste of Dr. Lucas Perry.

The two gentlemen sat down either side of the fire, the elder having declined and the younger having no mind for the wine that the servant offered.

"You have the sleeping-draught that Dr. Beattie gave you, take that. You are in a state of excitement after your unusual experience. If you go to bed now you may suffer from further hallucinations."

"Who told you that I had any hallucinations? Thank you, Dr. Perry, for your box of pills. I should not fail to follow the directions of our good friend, but first let me show you this."

He turned to a walnut desk handsomely mounted in brass, unlocked it and drew out of it a yellow pamphlet on which once broad black letters were faded to a sepia tone.

"This I found with great difficulty. My ancestor did his best to buy them all up. It is an account . . . . "

"And I daresay a false one, I daresay nothing but some infamous broadsheet," put in Dr. Perry.

"It is an account of the murder of Harriet Bond," replied James Daintry, sinking down on the leather chair, the other side of the fire. "That is to say of the woman I was to-night. But that is not what interests me so much as this letter that was sent to my grandfather in his youth and by him most unaccountably not destroyed but slipped in the leaves of a book he was reading at the time—Bishop Glanville's *On Witchcraft*."

"And why were you reading that?" asked Dr. Perry, holding out his hand, chilled by the walk through the winter night, to the steady glow of the fire.

"I was in the library at Charters and chanced to take it down. A book full of absurdities, but interesting, too. And this letter fell out. One can see how it happened, it is simple enough. My grandfather was reading the book, I suppose, there is his name on the fly-leaf written hastily with the date beneath. No bookplate, just his name. It seems to have followed an interview which he had with the writer, who signed himself 'Arthur Haywood.' "

"Sir," said Dr. Perry, "I think that the hour is late and you are in an excited state and I, to tell the truth, am too indifferent to the matter, for us to go into this old, sad, and wearisome subject now."

"You must listen," said the other, detaining him. "I swear I shall not sleep until you have. And then I will not speak of the subject again. Do you think I can be calm after what happened to me to-night? Certainly it seems already a long time ago, perhaps a century has passed since I stood in that room looking——" he checked himself and turning to the letter began to read:

" 'Sir, having understood from our conversation to-day your lordship's desire that I should put into writing what I knew concerning a person who was acquainted with a spirit, to his own destruction, I have made bold to give you the trouble of this letter, hoping my design, to gratify your lordship in every particular may be an apology for the length thereof.

" 'When I was curate to Doctor Falconer, a post that I have lately relinquished, as your lordship knows, when he was Rector of St. Jude's, Mullenbridge, I began to be acquainted with one Thomas Gifford, about twenty years of age, by trade a gunsmith, who lived with his father, with whom I contracted an intimate acquaintance, he being not only a good-tempered man but extremely well skilled in the mathematical studies, which was his constant delight—arithmetic, geometry, gauging, surveying, astronomy, and algebra. He gave himself up to astronomy so far that he could not only calculate the motions of the planets but of an eclipse also, and demonstrated also every problem in symmetrical trigonometry, from mathematical principles which he could discover by a clear force of reason.

" 'Your lordship, I dare say, as I suggested to you, has heard something of the fame of this young man. I advised him to go to London, where a friend of mine, a Mr. Bailey, had set up a mathematical academy.

" 'There he went and I heard from his master that he had found in this Gifford greater proficiency in those studies than he had suspected or could imagine. After this he applied himself to astrology and would sometimes calculate horoscopes and resolve nativities, and sometimes they were only too true. But he was not satisfied with it, because there was nothing in it that extended to mathematical demonstrations.' "

"And so far, sir," interrupted Dr. Lucas Perry, "we must confess there is nothing in this letter to hold our attention, and the hour being late and I asking your hospitality for a bed——"

But the young man put him aside and continued reading rapidly:

" '—when, by the providence of God, I was settled in Mullenbridge parish and not having seen Gifford for some time, he returned home to his father and waited on me. And we being in private, he asked me my opinion very seriously concerning the lawfulness of conversing with spirits.

" 'After I had given my reply in the negative, and confirmed it with the best reasons I could, he told me he considered all those arguments and believed they only related to conjuration, but that there was an innocent society with them which a man might use if he made no contact with them, did no harm by their means and was not curious in prying into hidden things. And that he himself had discoursed with them and heard them sing, to his great satisfaction.' What is the difference," demanded Lord Manton, breaking off in his reading, "between singing of spirits and the rappings by them on tables? But to continue this letter——"

"Which is tedious," protested Dr. Perry, but he could not,

even by this brusque remark, check the young man, who continued to read.

" 'This fellow, and I am repeating what I told your lordship in the interview, gave an offer to me at one time, to his master at another, to go with him to a piece of ground at the back of your lordship's estate in which the new building known as the Folly had later been completed, and there we should hear the spirits and see them talking and singing, converse with them whenever we had a mind to and return very safe. But neither of us had the courage to venture. I told him it was the subtlety of the Devil to deceive mankind and transform himself into an Angel of Light.

" 'But he could not believe it was the Devil.

" 'I proposed to try him at questions in astronomy relating to the projection of the spheres, which he resolved, and afterwards did so demonstrate from the mathematics as to show that his brain was free from the least tincture of madness or distraction. I asked several particulars of the methods he used for the discourse with the spirits, and he told me that he had a book where were the directions he followed——' "

"A *grimoire*," interrupted Dr. Perry, with a sigh. "This is all commonplace enough."

James Daintry continued reading:

" 'Accordingly, in the dead time of the night he went into a causeway with a candle and lanthorn to concentrate on the purpose of incantations, and that causeway was near the building known as the Folly. He had also compounded chalk, consisting of several mixtures with which he used to make a circle within which no spirit had power to enter.

" 'After he had invoked the spirit by several forms of words, some of which were taken from Holy Writ, those he called appeared to him in the shape of little girls about a foot and a half high and played about the circles. At first he was affrighted, but after some small acquaintance this antipathy in nature wore off and he became pleased with their company. He told me they all spake with a shrill voice like an ancient woman.

" 'He asked them some ordinary questions about the existence of God, Heaven and Hell, all of which they replied to in the affirmative, saying about Hell that it was a dreadful subject to relate, "that Devils believe and tremble."

" 'They also gave him a description of the order they had amongst themselves, as to their chief and his residence in the air, who had about him several counsellors who were placed by him in the form of a globe. Another order was employed in going to and fro from Heaven to the earth carrying intelligence to those lower spirits, and a third order was on earth, acting according to the directions they received from the air . . . .

" 'This made me conclude, my lord, that they were devils, but I could not convince Gifford thereon, yet the account was contrary to that we have in Scripture of the hierarchy of the Blessed Angels.

" 'The young man then told me that he desired these spirits to sing and they disappeared behind some bushes from whence he heard a perfect concert of such music the like he had never heard, and in the upper part he could hear something very harsh and shrill, like a reed, but as it was managed it came with particular grace.

" 'About three months after he came to me again and said he wished he had taken my advice, for he thought he had done that which would cost him his life but which he could hardly repent of. He appeared to me as if he was in great trouble and seemed much altered.

" 'I asked him what he had done, and he told me that being bewitched to his ruin he was for ever going further in the black arts and wished to have a familiar spirit to follow him as might be according to the directions in the book. He followed these directions and went as usual to the path, which is beyond the Folly, called up a spirit to be his familiar and attend on him always. He gave me a particular account of all the incantations used, with which I shall not trouble your lordship now, having given you some hint of them during our interview.

" 'The spirits appeared, according to his account, faster than he wished and he was in a most dreadful state, very much affrighted, the more so as he found it was not in his power to lay them, he expected every moment to be torn to pieces. It was in December, about midnight, when he came to me in a great sweat with this tale. He had the fortitude, however, to continue the incantations and to repeat the charm which he had written upon a piece of virgin parchment.

" 'One familiar then appeared, larger than all the other shapes, and attached itself to him, while the others gradually vanished into a snowstorm that at that time began to cloud over the landscape.

" 'This spirit was that of a woman. She said her name was Harriet Bond, and that she had been betrayed and murdered by one who had promised to love her, and her body buried near by, and that she would be this man's servant as he who was her master had desired her and as she was bound to be through the power of his incantation.

" 'Now this fellow had never thought of having a spirit of the dead for his attendant, but rather some fiend or goblin. He had heard something of the tale of Harriet Bond and knew that it was forbidden even to mention her name, so he endeavoured to lay her, or the devil that took her shape.

" 'But she would not be put off and continued to follow him, repeating her story, wringing her hands, her hair hanging down over her white dress that was tied with a green sash under the bosom, her hair thick with snow and white itself. And so she came through the door that he bolted in her face and stood by his bedside and even lay down beside him so that he felt her cold despite the blankets that he huddled about him.

" 'And in the morning he came to me and was a sick man. And I took him to the apothecary in Broad Street concerning a cure, but I could not tell the apothecary the cause of this disease.

" 'Gifford owned the whole matter to me, said he had now heartily repented but that he felt he could never shake himself free of this familiar who haunted him. He had believed at first that what he did was lawful and now he was convinced to the contrary. He told me he had made no contact with these spirits, never did harm to others by their means and never pried into the future fortunes of himself or others. But he felt that this meddling was likely to cost him his life.

" 'I reasoned with him and prayed for him and used exorcism to rid him of the spirit who, he said, was closely attached to him and standing behind him even while he spoke to me.

" 'I was unable to see it for myself, but I saw the man, though in the depth of winter, in a great sweat as in a great fever and looking constantly and uneasily over his shoulder. "I thought," he muttered, "to have had a fiend for a servant, and might have commanded it. But I cannot endure a Fetch." This was the old word, my lord, he used; it means one who is brought back. And I suppose that the poor man's mind was confused with his abstract studies and was teased by the memory of this story.

" 'As your lordship's family is so intimately concerned with it, I thought that it was only dutiful for me to wait on you and tell you the matter, so that this poor man might be treated with every tenderness in the hospital to which he is now removed, and some money be spent on his comfort so that he has a separate apartment and does not talk or rave to the other inhabitants of this sad place. And that his delusion may not be the least prejudice to his relations who have the deserved character of sober, honest people. I am, with due respect, your lordship's servant.' "

"If you read that letter before you went to Dr. Beattie's house, it is no wonder that you also thought that you saw the apparition of Harriet Bond," remarked Dr. Perry.

James Daintry did not appear to hear him. He folded up the letter and returned it to the walnut-and-brass desk, having first placed it inside the pamphlet. He locked both away, returned to the fire, and resting his folded arms on the edge of the table sank suddenly into profound sleep.

Dr. Perry went quietly to the door, called Hackett, who was not yet in bed, he had not liked his master's looks and was waiting lest some assistance might be required, and between them they carried the young man to his chamber, took off his boots, collar and coat and laid him, still insensible, as if he had taken the drug that Dr. Beattie had given him, on the narrow bed.

* * * * *

"It was a fine ceremony," said Mrs. Fenton. And then she added doubtfully, as if not sure if these words conveyed a compliment or the contrary: "And old-fashioned, too, with all the shields hung up and the black draperies on the gates, they were quite in the old style. And outside the Mausoleum, too."

"Mausoleum's an outlandish word," remarked Caroline, sucking a long, vivid-coloured pear-drop. "What's it mean, Mother?"

"I don't know. You ought to, you've been to boarding-school. Ask Adelaide. She's had more education."

"It means a place where they bury people," replied the elder girl, indifferently. "What's it matter?"

"Oh, it does matter," said Mrs. Fenton. She spoke flatly but with a flash of excitement in her cheeks. She moved heavily about the rooms, putting the white-and-gold tea-set on the table, polishing cups and saucers with a clean cloth as she did so. "There was a number of people," she added. "Fashionables, from London. All the relatives, I suppose."

"Yes, and friends, too," smiled Adelaide. "And acquaintances, all the great ones——"

"But they all went away again at once," remarked Mrs. Fenton, pausing by the round table with her air of half-baffled suspicion. "They didn't stay, not any of them. He's only got those two men with him. Dr. Perry and the Reverend Timothy Chalmers."

"Oh, and one or two other old friends," said Adelaide. "He'll be going abroad again soon, and when he comes back and is out of mourning I dare say we shall be married."

She made this statement in a careless tone. Caroline smiled slyly.

"I wonder if you believe her now, Mother? You saw how he looked at her to-day, didn't you? He even came as far as the gate with her, a few days ago, and his grandfather not yet buried."

"Yes, I saw him myself," said Mrs. Fenton, and her dull yet intent look turned on her elder daughter.

"And I've shown you his letters. You could read them all if you had the patience."

"Yes, miss, and you've shown me the bills, too. Fifty pounds' worth of stuff to be paid for——"

"Oh, that's only because he's careless. He orders the things and don't trouble about the accounts."

"Well, why aren't they sent in, then, to him?" demanded Mrs. Fenton.

"Well, that would give the secret away to his grandfather, wouldn't it?" replied the girl quickly. "They don't know who he is at the shops. I call him Basil, and he calls me Cara."

"Yes, I remember all that nonsense. I thought your aunt would have taken it out of you."

"Well, she didn't," and Adelaide smiled in a satisfied way. "Aunt Martha was very interested in the whole story. She saw me post the letters, send off the handkerchiefs, and she saw the letters I received in return."

"But did she see the postman deliver them?"

"Oh, you are suspicious!" answered Adelaide, in a complacent tone. "I used to go to the town to get them at the post office, of course."

"Well, my girl, you've certainly managed to make a tangle of it, one way or the other. I thought it would be all over when you and he went away, but now you're back again and it seems——"

"More certain than ever," put in Caroline, licking what remained of her pear-drop and looking with her clear, round eyes steadily at her mother. "Don't forget, Mother, you *did* see him twice."

"I saw him many times," put in the woman sharply; "what are you talking about, I *did* see him?"

"Well, I meant you saw him ogling Adelaide to-day."

"I wouldn't call it ogling; it was his grandfather's funeral, wasn't it? He looked at her very steady when she sat in church. I should say it was more a kind of affrighted glance."

"He was dazzled with her charms, isn't that the expression, Adelaide?" sneered Carrie. "It's out of one of your novels—'dazzled with her charms,' like somebody who tries to look at the sun and is nearly blinded."

"Both you girls talk rubbish," said Mrs. Fenton stolidly. "Yet I suppose there must be something in it. Eccentric, that's what they are, the Daintrys. What's he going to do now—shut himself up here?"

"Oh, he's going away again, a little, for a change of air, to Wales, I suppose," simpered Adelaide.

"Why to Wales?" asked Mrs. Fenton suspiciously.

"Oh, to take the waters at some Wells there; I mustn't tell you the name now. But we're to go up and see him, meet him there presently. He has some of his lady friends with him—those two ladies whom you saw to-day, the one in the taffeta, Caroline."

"They were all in black, in heavy mourning, I couldn't see which was taffeta and which wasn't," said Mrs. Fenton, sullenly.

"Well, will you come with me to Wales?"

"If I get an invitation and feel that I'm not going to be made a fool."

"That is too business-like," said Caroline, pertly. "You can't expect to use it in a fantastic love affair like this, Mother."

"Father's pleased," smirked Adelaide.

Mrs. Fenton turned with the large china tea-pot in her hand.

"You've told your father?"

"Yes, and he said he was quite willing, it was a good match, that you ought to be proud of me. I showed him Basil's letters, and read him those I was writing."

"You didn't tell your father about the bills, I suppose?"

"Yes, I did," said Adelaide, "when I showed him Basil's letters."

She opened her reticule, took out a small packet as she spoke and set it on the table. Her mother looked at this keenly, greedily; Caroline, indifferent, continued to suck her sweet and stare from the window where the rain was falling in a heavy drip of grey. All the women, in respect to the lord of the manor, were in mourning, heavy, shining bombazine with a few jet ornaments, that smelt of camphor balls with which they had been packed away for a long time—since the death of their own grandmother.

Adelaide held out a letter which was headed in a rude handwriting 'Charters,' and which read:

'Please calm all apprehension as to bills. These I will attend to when the funeral ceremonies are over. This I say for fear you should be vexing your dear self unnecessarily.'

"This is for Father: 'Sir, it is my will and wish to instantly pay for all given to Adelaide as soon as may be. This much I say and I feel very grieved that any indiscretion of mine should cause vexation to Adelaide. Allow me to remain, truly yours, Seagrove.' "

"You said there was another letter, properly asking for your hand from your father—where's that? Not that I believe in them," added Mrs. Fenton quickly, in self-defence.

"Then why are you bothering to read them, Mother?" asked Caroline. "And who do you think could have written them if it wasn't Basil?"

Mrs. Fenton laboriously placed her spectacles on her nose and read slowly the letter that was written in a most irregular script:

'My dear sir,

This note ought to have been with you long ago—better late than never is the old adage. It may apply in my case.

Without entering into particulars, I am aware you know that in secret I have long sought your eldest daughter, and now openly I ask her of you for my wife. I hope you will not refuse me her. Ere this, I should have come personally to have made the request to you had not unforeseen circumstances prevented.

I hope shortly to see you. Then, if convenient, we can arrange about her settlement, etc. I have mentioned the August month to her. I hope when we meet everything, all things, will meet with your approbation and that you will give me your consent.

Allow me to sign this note,

Very faithfully yours,

James Seagrove.'

"There is proof here of a constant attachment," cried Adelaide. "It is natural that it should have been kept secret seeing the differences in our rank in life."

"Don't talk so much like a book, miss," put in Mrs. Fenton. "I'll go up to Charters myself."

"You can if you like, Mother," returned Adelaide, still with a casual air, "but you'll spoil it if you do."

"Mother, I think it would," agreed Caroline slyly.

"Did you tell your father this—" she hesitated over pronouncing the august name, then added sombrely: "this *gentleman* came here?"

"Yes. Father said he'd never seen him, but I said that didn't matter. Caroline had, and you did the other day, didn't you, Mother?"

"He only came as far as the gate, and then he turned back—why didn't he come in then and see me and your father?"

"Well, his grandfather wasn't buried, was he?"

"Well, he might have come in and settled about the bills, anyhow." Mrs. Fenton moved about the room heavily. "Well, what did your father say?"

"I told you what he said. He was pleased. I let him see a great number of the letters I had had, ten at least. He was in one of his good fits and read them quite well. He replied to that letter, accepting. I wrote it down at his dictation, sealed it for him, and slipped it in the post."

"Did he keep a draft?" asked Mrs. Fenton.

"I don't know. What's it matter? You do make a fuss over these silly business details, as if anything can concern any of us except that I'm going to marry in August. I showed Father some verses and presents that Basil sent me."

"There's fifty pounds to pay for them," complained Mrs. Fenton. "I don't know who I'll get it from—your aunt, perhaps."

"Haven't *we* got as much as fifty pounds?" asked Caroline shrewdly. "To save us from—well, the disgrace of unpaid bills?"

"Never you mind what we've got and what we haven't got, miss," retorted Mrs. Fenton. "I shouldn't have spoken so plainly in front of you. Well, I sent you away, as I was warned to do. And he was sent away, as I suppose he was warned. And you've both come back and begun the affair again. You've shown me the letters and he's written to your father proposing for your hand. And I've seen you seal up and take letters to the post with handkerchiefs in them. It all seems fair and square."

She looked at her daughter with a sly intent glance that affected nothing but candour.

"Well, I suppose the banns can be put up now," she added.

"How insistent you are, Mother! I tell you we're going to be married in August, but it must be quiet for a while. Basil has to visit an aunt of his who lives in Brighton. She's sick and he has to stay with her for a while. See, this is the letter in which he says: 'If wishes could transport me to you there would be no need for this writing, but as I am anxious, most anxious to hear of your well-being and also to tell you that business relating to my grandfather's will may detain me from you longer than I thought, I send this. I have seen chairs I think will do for one of our rooms at Charters. Won't all be bright and happy when its future mistress takes possession of it? Pray take care of yourself, dearest, forget not you are the only hope of one to whom a palace would be but a desert and England no home without you, far dearer to me than each earthly blessing. Adelaide, who are all in all to me, take care of yourself and mind when you return from walking to change your shoes. You may laugh at me, but you know how particular I am in this respect, and you may catch cold. It has often struck me there is something untold to me, some secret affair I know not of, that troubles you. Why not, dear girl, tell me if it is so, for I have often seen you look sad and unhappy.

" 'I hope even this will cease in August when you may be my bride, my wife, then all that is mystery now will be cleared.' "

"It doesn't mean anything to me," said Mrs. Fenton. "I think I ought to see an attorney, Mr. Bisset."

"Lawyers!" exclaimed Adelaide sharply. "What's the good of that, Mother? You don't think these legal men have got anything to do with love and romance, do you?"

"They have something to do with promise of marriage and breaches of it. Many people have seen you about now, and I *did* see him look at you to-day. Well—I can't tell you any more about it at the moment, but be careful."

"You don't need to tell her that," said Caroline, yawning lazily. "It don't matter what you tell her."

"A number of people," continued Mrs. Fenton, thoughtfully, "must have seen you posting letters to him by now. I've seen you take them out to the post myself, all sealed up with that little cornelian you have with the roses and cupids cut on it."

"Yes, it's a pretty little thing," agreed Adelaide complacently. "Well, I shall be glad when the will is read and all the ceremonies are over. How dreary it was, everybody in black and those sombre silver shields hanging up and the horses' trappings down to the ground! Romantic, too, don't you think? Something grand and stately about it."

"It was old-fashioned." Mrs. Fenton repeated her charge stubbornly. "Things haven't moved here as they ought to during that old man's life-time. When he was a lively youth he was away, and when he came back here he was too old to do anything but sit in his room and nurse the gout. I wonder if the estate is rich. I wonder if the young man's got a fortune or nothing but those broken-down mansion houses?"

"Oh, indeed, Basil has a great fortune," said Adelaide. "He has large sums of money invested abroad, too. It is true that he is a gambler and often loses piles of gold in a single night, but I am going to reform him. For my sake, too, he has promised not to drink too much wine."

"He didn't look like a young man who either drinks or plays cards," observed Mrs. Fenton. "I always heard he lives a very quiet life."

"Well, since he has met me he has been more temperate in his ways, but at one time he was extremely wild, a roving gallant. He entertained the dancers at the Opera to supper in his own mansion. On one occasion he gave to each of these ladies a bracelet of real pearls."

"Who told you that?" asked Mrs. Fenton sharply.

"He did himself. He wanted to show me what a changed man he was."

"You shouldn't meet him so often Adelaide. If he wants to

speak to you he must come here and sit in your father's parlour, be presented to your mother."

"And so he will, so he will," sighed the girl with her first impatience; hitherto she had relished her mother's conversation, even though much of it was peremptory and suspicious; it had been sufficient for her to talk about her romance, even if the listener was not wholly sympathetic; now she was fretted. "Basil came over to see me when I was staying at my Aunt Martha's," she added.

"Your aunt said nothing about it." Mrs. Fenton's suspicion deepened.

"Oh, no! She was too kind and agreeable. She likes him. I made her promise not to say anything; I wanted to reveal all these things myself." Then, with a sudden change of tone, Adelaide remarked: "He knew much about the story of Harriet Bond——"

"What a name to mention! Here and now, and like that!" exclaimed Mrs. Fenton, openly shocked.

"Is it? I was always interested. Why shouldn't I be? We've met by her tomb, you know. He passed up there just now. I suppose having buried his grandfather he was thinking of graves. He keeps it very neatly with his own hands. Sometimes I put a wreath of flowers on it, and that pleases him."

"That's a tale," muttered Mrs. Fenton, with much uneasiness, "not supposed to be talked of here, and don't you mention it before your young sister . . . . "

"You can't frighten me with it." Caroline looked up and smiled. "Such horrors don't concern me at all. There's all manner of stuff about ghosts and spirits and murdered brides and people coming back from beyond in those books that Adelaide gets from the library. I don't take any notice of them."

"But *this* is true," put in Adelaide with relish, "*this* really happened. I overheard someone say to-day that it was strange they haven't moved the Folly, and the Mausoleum, too, if that's the name of the place where you bury people."

"That's where she was buried before she was moved, wasn't it?" asked Mrs. Fenton with increasing uneasiness and indignation, "and put into sacred ground—not that she deserved to be—— She was a hussy and a slut if there ever was one. I shouldn't have thought your aunt would have repeated that story. Anyhow, I expect what she tells you was all lies."

"No, it wasn't. She had a copy of the *Gentleman's Magazine* for the year that Harriet Bond was——" Adelaide paused tactfully. "When Harriet Bond met her tragic end——" she continued.

"Murdered, that's the word you're trying to say, isn't it?" demanded Mrs. Fenton. "Now, don't let's talk of that nasty stuff; it won't be a relish for your tea."

"I read all about it," persisted Adelaide. "Imagine that *he* was Basil's ancestor! Quite distant, you know, something like a great-great-uncle as far as I can make out. But *they* have always been eccentric. There was a picture of him, an engraving, in the magazine. He's quite fine-looking, rather like Basil, and of her, too, rather plump. It said she was wearing a white dress with a green sash when she was found. That sounds ordinary, doesn't it? I heard it before—at the Fiskes'——"

Mrs. Fenton poured out the tea and the girls began to eat and drink lustily. Adelaide, who was not able to talk on any subject but herself, ran on: "Don't you think I was generous to give so many of Basil's presents to Caroline? She's already got aunt's paste necklet and then I've given her the bag with the white beads on, and a set of the *Waverly Novels*——"

"Which you keep reading," put in Caroline, "and that you know I don't care for at all. What difference does it make whose name is on the first page?"

Adelaide ignored this and continued: "I've given her a pair of the white slippers and a coral comb."

"I wonder you didn't keep them yourself," sneered Caroline. "You seem to prize them too highly, always remembering them and talking about them. You can have them all back if you want to," she added, with sudden viciousness. "And you know what will happen if you do."

"That's not a kind, sisterly way to talk," protested Mrs. Fenton indifferently. "I thought you girls were so fond of one another, and now you always seem to me to be bickering. Well, I must go upstairs to your father."

In a heavy, inconclusive, puzzled manner she glanced from one of her daughters to the other, then slowly made her way out of the room, leaving her cup half-empty and her bread-and-butter broken on her plate.

"She went away very suddenly," remarked Caroline. "You *are* tedious, you know, Adelaide. Can't you talk of anything else? There's quite a number of interesting things in the world, but it's always you and your love affairs, as if one believes in any of it! I can't understand what you're up to."

"You talk very vulgarly," rebuked Adelaide. "You have no imagination, you haven't a romantic disposition—but you can be," she added, in a suddenly practical tone, "a pretty good liar if you want to."

"When I'm well paid," retorted Caroline steadily. "But don't keep making references to those trifles that you gave me. There wasn't so much *gift* about them, was there? You know that I told you I'd have to have them if I was to say what you wanted me to say."

"Poor Basil," sighed Adelaide, ignoring this speech and putting her rounded elbows on the white rough cloth. "A pity there's this aunt whom he's going to visit at the seaside—that keeps him away; when he returns he's going to purchase a conservatory for a thousand pounds, and he's promised me that he will gamble no more. He lost five thousand gold pieces the last time he sat down at the tables. That is a warning to him. He says I am not to laugh at the odd bits of paper on which he sends his letters; he has a fondness for writing on little pieces. He gives me news of his friends. They are all titled, live in high style with carriages, horses, rich clothes."

The girls continued to eat the dark plum cake and slices of new bread loaded with butter that their mother had placed before them, and to drink the strong Ceylon tea thickened with milk and lusciously sweetened with knobs of loaf sugar.

"Mother wants to send me away to school again," remarked Caroline. "You're to tell her I'm not to go."

"Oh, Carrie, I don't want you to go! You're such a sweet companion, such a charming *confidante*."

"I suppose I'm useful to you," replied the other girl, flatly. There was something of her mother's solid look about her, but her shrewdness, even at this age, was more acute than worldly wise and was not baffled and clogged by ignorance like Mrs. Fenton's. "Mother," she added with a mocking air, "wants to make an accomplished young lady of me, like you are, Adelaide."

"Oh, you're quite accomplished already, Carrie. You can have lessons at the pianoforte and harp in Mullenbridge. And I dare say French, too, then you could help Mother about the house.

There's always such a great deal to do for Father, with reading to him and sitting with him."

"Ah, yes, I can see you want me to stay, darling Adelaide," cried Carrie, bursting into a sudden loud laugh. "Well, persuade Mother that I'm not to go. I'd rather stay here; I don't like taking orders from school-mistresses, being teased by the other girls because I'm cleverer than they are but not so well-born."

"You're a queer creature," declared Adelaide, as if she suddenly realized the personality of the younger girl, and was, for a moment at least, diverted from her own entrancing and engrossing interests. "What do you want to do? What do you hope to be?"

"I might write books."

"A lady authoress!" exclaimed Adelaide, in sharp astonishment. "But you never look at novels, you never read romances. I thought you despised it."

"They don't interest me, those fairy stories. I'd like to write about what I see round me: you, for instance, Mother, Father, and Susan, oh, all kinds of people. Perhaps I shall—one day."

Adelaide considered her for a moment or two, then lost interest because this was something that did not immediately concern her; with a high laugh she said: "You have a wonderful romance to write if you ever try and write about me, Caroline! Will it be *Memoirs* or something of that kind? I can think out the title for you, and the fancies, and the turns of phrase. You are very stolid and downright and even clumsy in your diction. I wonder if we can take off this mourning? It's very unbecoming," she added with a restless air, "and very hot. Mine does not fit me at all. I like to have gowns that are made especially for me. I wonder how often this mourning has been worn before? It's such an old-fashioned cut and the material so heavy."

"We need only wear it to-day, I suppose," said Caroline. Having drunk all her tea she went to the chimneypiece and took down a china pot that was half-full of lollipops.

"Oh, do stop!" cried Adelaide, pettishly. "You've been sucking those pear-drops the whole afternoon. I noticed you in church during the funeral ceremony, that was so beautiful, so magnificent. You had your cheek all swelled out with sweets."

"I had to do something. The seat was hard and I found it all very tiresome. Mr. Chalmers sounded very stupid, don't you think? None of those people from London really cared anything about any of it. I saw the ladies yawning behind their handkerchiefs, and you could see that a great many of the gentlemen had already had too much to drink."

"Caroline, how vulgarly you talk! And what a ridiculous statement you make. It was nothing of the kind. The old Earl was greatly respected."

"I heard he had a monkey when he was a young man and loved it very much and when it died he gave it a proper funeral. It is supposed to be buried near the Mausoleum. They had a little procession with banners and drums beating——"

Adelaide shuddered, and broke out: "Don't talk like that, pray! It's horrible on the day when there's a real funeral, too!"

"Well, that was a real funeral and they are an eccentric family, aren't they?" said Caroline. "One of them was hanged for murder, you know, you must never forget that. I suppose you don't want to as you looked up the account of it in the *Gentleman's Magazine*. What was she like, this Harriet Bond? Did you see a picture of her, did you say? Those engravings, they all look the same, they might be anybody. There was a picture of her down at the 'Seagrove Arms,' I heard, but Mr. Fiske sold it, or gave it away, I don't know which. The new heir is interested in Harriet, too, isn't he? Standing by her grave, and keeping it tidy. Do you know what I heard, Adelaide—when he goes to London he goes to one of these queer meetings, whatever they call it, where they raise spirits. They're little better than witches or wizards, aren't they, these people? And they call themselves Christians! Has Basil told you anything about that?"

"Where did you hear such nonsense?" cried Adelaide, hotly.

"Oh, I meet people about Mullenbridge, and these stories get around. Mr. Chalmers is not very discreet, you know, and everybody knows Dr. Perry's reputation. *You* ought to if you're going to marry the young Earl. He must have his time occupied, mustn't he, Adelaide, between gambling and the opera dancers, visits to his sick relatives, getting out plans for a new conservatory for you, the white horse, and raising spirits?"

Adelaide took no notice of this, but whispered reflectively: "Oh, I suppose that's what he would do, to try to think it out——"

"Think what out?" asked Carrie, cunningly.

"Do be quiet for a time! I've got a sick headache now. I must go upstairs and lock my letters away and then take a little walk in the woods."

"You won't meet him to-night; he's still got so many people to entertain."

"Of course I don't wish to. I shall leave him to his sorrow. Do you think I have no delicacy of feeling?"

Adelaide went upstairs, and quickly into the little bedroom that she shared with Caroline, took off her mourning and put on her plain white gown. It was of dimity and printed with lilac sprays; this design was so small that a little distance away it could be observed only as a faint blur in the fabric.

She drew quickly out of her drawer, from carefully folded tissue paper, a length of dark-green ribbon which she had bought when staying with her aunt, and passed this under her full bosom.

Peering out of the window she perceived the daylight still held; as Caroline had remarked *he* would certainly be engaged with what company had remained of those who had come to attend his grandfather's funeral——Adelaide was impatient, restless and could no longer endure the mean little house, which seemed to clip her desires and confine her dreams in humdrum routine.

* * * * *

The day's ceremony was by far the most magnificent that she had ever beheld and it shifted her mental vision like some phantasmagoria produced by fever, rising and falling in lines of distorted perspective an unnatural shapes. The funeral procession itself, the hearse, boldly carved black and silver with clusters of plumes at the corners, the six horses with black feathers bound on their foreheads and their fringed trappings trailing on the ground, and the funeral carriages one after another, black after black, the ladies in their full skirts and their shawls, all black again, some with white faces, pale with fatigue and the melancholy of the occasion, others flushed and rosy and dabbing lips and cheeks with thin cambric handkerchiefs that gave out the odours of orange-flower water and lavender. The gentlemen all in mourning also with their shining top hats and their surah silk cravats and their clear white linen, the nearest relatives with stiff sable weepers tied round their hats, the church that seemed dim as a hollow cavern under the sea to the girl's excited imagination, the windows filled with thick green and coloured glass through which the light filtered with difficulty and fell in smeared lurid patches, red, yellow and blue on the faces of the worshippers as they knelt in their tall pews or on their rush-bottomed seats, the coffin with the embroidered pall and with the arms of the Daintrys standing on trestles in front of the altar, and the Rector uneasy and overborne by the formal tediousness of the ceremonies.[18] The Reverend Timothy Chalmers had delivered a sermon that was quite incomprehensible to Adelaide Fenton and appeared, she thought, much older than she had ever seen him, his face sagging in weary lines, his eyes bloodshot, his speech rambling every now and then . . . . He had been a friend as well as a dependant of the dead man's. He glanced sideways now and then at the coffin with a glance that had more sincerity than anything he declaimed . . . .

The air had become heavy and Adelaide Fenton, proud as she was of her place before that of the tenantry and before that of the respectable shopkeepers, almost near the genteel families who might claim a slight acquaintance with the dead nobleman, could almost have sunk in her seat with a feverish fatigue . . . .

Now she reflected on the scene and saw it all touched with phantasy, as if fever was still stirring a slight delirium in her mind. She was glad that the air cooled as she walked through Mullenbridge . . . . How long since she had seen him? Some months——

Many gossips lolling at their doors or leaning from their windows looked at her curiously, some with a very friendly and respectful glance, she thought; her story was beginning to get blown abroad, there must be a good many who were talking about her; she smiled to herself and passed through the town, the last straggle of cottages; she had to walk the entire length of the High Street

---

[18] Surah is a type of soft, twilled silk fabric. A weeper is a scarf-like length of black crêpe that is tied around a top hat with the excess trailing down at the back.

to reach her objective, the great gates that led into Charters Park and directly to the pavilion known as the Folly that had been built a couple of generations ago and never used, though from economy the late Earl's stewards had always kept it in good repair. It was, to Adelaide's untrained eye, a clumsy building, and to anyone of taste it would have been incongruous in the English landscape, for it was a copy of an Italian villa, as the Mausoleum was imitated from the Temple of the Four Winds at Athens.

Although the late Earl had been 'laid to rest,' as Timothy Chalmers had phrased it (and Adelaide always remembered conventional terms like that; they pleased her ear), only a few hours before, she had no supernatural terrors about visiting this spot, which was in the vulgar estimation haunted by the ghost of Harriet Bond, though this story had been with much success repressed and was hardly ever whispered aloud. Indeed, Adelaide had only come to a clear knowledge of it lately through the article in the *Gentleman's Magazine* which she had read when she resided with her Aunt Martha.

She knew now clearly, what before she had only imagined and put together, the entire story. It had not been at all to her liking, it was too coarse and crude, and in a way her mind had refused to absorb it, dwelling only upon the more fantastic details and transfusing it at once into the kind of unreality to which she was used. It had already become to her the story of the handsome young noble and the beautiful village maid who had engaged in a secret love affair. The jealousy of some powerful relatives of the young man had been aroused and through some machinations that Adelaide Fenton's untidy mind did not trouble to unravel the girl had been slain and the blame of it put upon the youth.

Here she stopped—she would not face the sordid end—the

trial, the hanging. She was quite able to throw out of her fancy anything she did not care to keep there; the story that, in its downright details had been rather shocking she thought, she had been able now to transmute into something pale, faded, and romantical.

Her aunt had given her some further fables that she had eagerly absorbed, of the fetch, a version of the very ancient tale of the mysterious bride, the ghost of the wronged and murdered woman who returns from the grave to claim as a lover a descendant of her murderer. This pleased Adelaide Fenton keenly and in a vague and uncomprehending way she pictured herself as the reincarnation of Harriet Bond and so had bought herself the green sash . . . .

'I believe,' she mused now, as she passed under the elms already in bright leaf and approached the Folly, 'that Mrs. Fiske said in that picture they used to keep at the "Seagrove Arms" she wore a white dress with a green sash.'

The path to the Mausoleum was trampled by the horses that had drawn the hearse and the mourning carriages and by the feet of the mourners when they had descended for the final ceremony.

Adelaide moved daintily on the bruised soiled grass; she glanced down to see if she had strained her fine and expensive shoes, glanced up again and saw to her great delight the man of whom she was continually thinking until he had become her obsession, standing not far away and staring at her with intense surprise. The black pelisse was thrown open—she had put it on more to conceal her green sash from the gapers in the town than because she needed it for warmth, and he could see the white gown and the dark ribbon twisted under her bosom; but his expression startled her; she felt like somebody caught playing a game, foolishly, who is taken seriously—by whom?

But her lightness soon returned; she looked at him, her lips parted, her eyes staring as he came towards her, raising his hat, and asking her, puzzled, who she was and if he had seen her before.

"I am Adelaide Fenton, sir. You have seen me a great number of times. You came across the churchyard with me and stood at my gate a few days ago."

"Ah, yes, indeed I did. I saw you—in the churchyard——You must forgive me. You must have considered me most uncivil. I have been a little confused of late. I had an attack of sickness in London; I'm afraid my mind is sometimes not very clear."

He was gazing at her most earnestly and her blood warmed with delight.

"Why do you come up here often, as I think, do you not? But this is the first time that you have worn that gown."

"Oh, you notice my gown, sir, do you?" she laughed, prettily.

"Yes, I have occasion to remember a white gown with a green sash. Forgive me, Miss Fenton. But this is a curious place for you to choose to promenade. Have you any *reason*?"

"None whatever," she murmured, faintly. "What *reason* should I have? I seem drawn to the spot, that is all."

"Do you like it? This gloomy, rather ugly building, this dark grove of trees, these ugly unpleasant associations . . . . "

He had used the word 'ugly' twice and she winced.

"I don't know anything about that, I never listen to old stories." She spoke meekly in her natural tone, turning her head aside.

"You wonder, perhaps, why I am here on the day of my grandfather's funeral? I observed you in church; I hope you didn't think that I was impertinent to stare at you?"

"I was only too flattered, sir, that you should notice me among so many."

She did not know how to complete her sentence, she felt herself becoming foolish, formal. She faltered and turned aside again. She need not have concerned herself, for he was not thinking in the least of what she was saying; he was as deep in his obsession as she was in her obsession; each stood in a separate magic circle.

"I must return to the house," he muttered quickly, as if endeavouring to gain some control over himself. "I have had but half an hour to spare from my guests—I felt I desired some air."

He made the conventional excuse in a distracted manner and then added: "I do not know why I came here. I must give up the habit of so melancholy a walk."

"It is beautiful, is it not, sir?" asked Adelaide Fenton, anxious only to detain him in conversation of some kind or other, hoping that someone, anyone, might pass and see them together. She came nearer to him and observed that he was gazing at her with an intense, almost horrified earnestness.

"It's sacred, where the dead, your dead, are buried," she whispered.

"Where one is buried who should not have been," he replied, lifting his lower lip.

She affected not to understand; indeed, she was quite indifferent now to the old tale.

"Love," she simpered with a stare of rapture, "can triumph over death—it can continue from one generation to another. It may seem to be destroyed, but it will return."

"Why do you talk like that?" he asked sharply. "It might be nonsense, it might have a great deal of meaning——"

"Surely, sir, it's the plain, Christian truth—the abiding power of love."

"If they come back," he muttered, "we cannot tell in what

shape it might be; there would be some kind of a likeness and some kind of a disguise."

"Were you thinking of spectres?" she asked, sidling nearer still, encountering steadfastly his troubled and searching gaze. "Do you believe, sir, that they do walk again?"

"Come back! Come back! *Revenants*, the French tongue has it. That is a fearful thing, is it not, Miss Fenton, that one should pass away and seem to be at peace, and *return*?"

"I've never thought of it, or been afraid of it; I've had my mind too full of other matters, what I'm here for and what I have to do."

"You don't speak like an ordinary young lady. I must not detain you. Pray, do not come here again. It is a spot that has evil memories, that might in time produce in you a certain sickness of spirit. You have been away, I think, Miss Fenton, staying with relatives?"

"Yes, my mother thought I should have a change of air."

"I, too, have been abroad, and must go again. Charters is too large for me—yet I might use it to make experiments."

"Of what kind?" she asked eagerly.

"I should not tell you, but what I do will be quite lawful. Indeed, I must seem to wander, to gossip and talk frivolously. I pray you, excuse me. I ask you," he added with a certain sternness, "not to come here again. The grounds are my private property. For your own good, I might forbid you the use of them."

"If I don't come to the Mausoleum, might I go to the Folly?"

"That is worse, worse! The grove between the Mausoleum and the Folly . . . . "

"That is haunted?" asked Adelaide Fenton, with a childish curiosity.

"I don't know. Pray don't concern yourself with local gossip. I bid you good evening, Miss Fenton."

He turned with a matter-of-fact manner, abruptly away. Adelaide, sauntering homeward, was thrilled with pleasure to observe the maltster passing along the road beyond the Park wall with his horse and cart—he had paused to stare at the two of them . . . . he must have seen them deep in talk; a lovers' tryst it must have seemed . . . . So Adelaide Fenton moved complacently in the large formless plot that was of an intricacy not in the least clear to herself, and about which she did not concern herself at all.

* * * * *

"The Swedenborgian will distract your wits," said Mr. Chalmers brusquely. "I am glad that you have dismissed him. You must, James, to use a phrase that I dare say sounds to you contemptuous but that I declare to be well applied in your case, consider appearances."

"Sir, you are bound to read me a lecture and preach me a sermon, I suppose," sighed the young man, with a look of affection at his former tutor; his tone, however, was not altogether unmingled with reproach.

The Reverend Timothy Chalmers, sprawling in the worn leather chair by the empty hearth, where highly polished steel andirons gleamed on the marble, was no very respectable figure. He had lost, and with a sudden stroke, what remained of his florid comeliness; he appeared an old, a dissipated and soured man in his dishevelled attire—the hanger-on of a great house whose master was dead. He knew that the young man whom he had bear-led round Europe and whom he had treated with a great deal of indulgence and whom he had advised with a very vague and amiable philosophy, would give him a pension and a home. But the death of the old master of Charters had broken his own one link with all that was desirable in life. Now it was almost automatically that he mouthed over what he considered his good worldly advice.

"You should shut up this place or pull down half and rebuild the other portion. It is old-fashioned, gloomy, rat-ridden, and dilapidated. It is natural that your grandfather, being so old and solitary a man, should refuse to have anything modernized except the few apartments in which he lived, but you—you must either give up the Charters or have it altered."

His former pupil did not answer and the Reverend Timothy sighed and continued his discourse, in his deep rumbling voice.

"You must turn me off, of course. Your grandfather left me enough to live on and I daresay you'd add a pension to it if I wanted it. It won't make much difference to me what money I have in the future. I suppose I shall spend the time reading, a few companions. I might got to Oxford. But we must think of you, not what I'm going to do. As I say, I'm glad that Swedenborgian's gone. I wish your relatives and friends had stayed a little longer. Only a week after the funeral and the house is like a vault itself, and as melancholy."

"It doesn't appear so. Indeed, most places are the same to me."

"When one has been bemused by mystical speculation," interrupted the Reverend Timothy sarcastically, "or rather in a melancholy of idleness, it would be so. This is your Swedenborgian's Heaven and Hell about you! No doubt, James, you encounter angels on your path—I would rather be a plain, practising Christian."

"You do Dr. Perry an injustice," smiled the young man. "He is practical himself, I believe he has taken some trouble over my affairs. His ideas and concerns are not what you think them to be. Nor have I dismissed him. He left Charters because he considers that while I am in my present mood he cannot do much good by remaining here; and he has other interests—his medicine for one. I do not miss him as much as I thought I should——"

"You wouldn't miss *me* at all, James." Timothy Chalmers sighed. "Charters is sombre and dreary, now, yet it used to be merry at one time, the company your grandfather entertained here, and the young gentlefolk there were about in your father's and your uncle's lifetime."

"Do you want to remind me that all came to what is known as violent deaths? Yet that is an absurd saying, as if death was not always *violent*——"

The Earl rose and walked up and down the long room.

"Yes, I know this is an unnatural life I am leading, that I should be wise to pull down, as you so often suggest, the Folly and show it to be nothing but lath and plaster and stone indifferently cut. The Mausoleum is hideous too. The entire grove should be cleared, ploughed up, perhaps—sown with salt——"

"You should certainly try to forget," said the clergyman with a heavy sigh, "the old scandal on which you have so set your fancy. That is a perversion, my dear James, a case of misapplied ingenuity, a disease, I am afraid, of sheer idleness."

"We have been over too often that question of my idleness. I shall have enough to engage my time on in looking after the estates. I know that Marks is an excellent steward, but my uncle used to do much of the management himself."

"Yes, he did. He was a shrewd man of business and an active controller of his affairs. You will find that Marks will turn to you for a great deal."

"Well, I have learned something. I haven't been altogether unoccupied when I've been here. I do at least understand my own affairs, but I realize that you consider my life extremely, shall we say, empty."

"Indeed, my dear James, I do not desire to pass any such reflection upon you. I only would like to point out to you that by avoiding all the usual pursuits and occupations common to your age and rank you leave a very dangerous gap in your existence. By what do you intend to fill it? By what we used to term the practices of black magic, and now I believe is named occultism."

The young man's answer surprised the clergyman.

"No, sir, I intend to give up that study. I find it difficult, dangerous, and absorbing. Since that illness I had after the visit to Dr. Beattie's house in Bayswater I have not been able to get the matters, either of this world or, much as I regret to admit it, the spirits of the next, in very clear perspective."

He put his hands over his eyes as he spoke and stood straight and rigid as if endeavouring to force some vague and trembling thoughts into words.

"Everything," he said, "is out of focus, as if seen through a distorting lens. Yet the colours are vivid, the outlines definite. No, you may be assured that I shall make no more experiments. I intend, too, to shut up Charters. I shall have an architect to oversee it. Sir Henry would come, I think. The cost of renovating it would, of course, be enormous. Verities is a more reasonable mansion. Shall this be demolished?"

"You should marry. You know that several good matches were designed for you."

"Yes, and I know that I have several amiable relatives willing to match me with any amiable girl that I should choose. But I should not be a good husband for any lady, I can assure you, sir. I am still young, leave me a year or two in which to——"

"You talk like a man stuck with a fit of stupor——" The clergyman rose, took the youth by the shoulders and half-led, half-pushed him into a chair. "Sit down, you are overwrought. Your grandfather's death was very sudden. Often the decease of the old will surprise and shock us as much as that of the young. These old people seem to be permanently here—I know what you must feel. There's responsibility too; the title's ancient."

"I don't think of that."

"No, you will still brood on what I beg you to forget, eh? What you must, if you wish to help your body and soul to health, forget."

"Dr. Perry, whom you so dislike a distrust, told me the same thing. What do those lessons mean? There must be a deep thrill," he added, as if abstracted, "in seeing a disembodied spirit, or seeing a spirit reincarnated in another's body."

"You're talking very wildly and a great deal of rubbish, sir. But I might point out to you that you have been seen now several times with that Miss Adelaide Fenton, who lives beyond St. Jude's the other side of Mullenbridge. You were staring at her the day of your grandfather's funeral, you have been seen with her walking by the Folly, you stayed your horse the other day when you met her in the lane. Oh, you're observed, believe me."

"I can believe as much," replied the young man, indifferently, "what does it matter? It gives me no concern at all."

"It soon may do."

"Of course, I have had enquiries made about the Fentons. Dr. Perry told me he went to see the mother a year ago. He thought that the girl might have some matrimonial design on me. It is nonsensical. She is completely without any worldly experience or knowledge, a very simple-minded creature. Adelaide Fenton, you call her? I could give her another name. Are you sure," he added rapidly, "that it was Adelaide Fenton you saw walking with me?"

He threw out this question with such a force and emphasis that Mr. Chalmers was slightly taken aback.

"Why, of course, sir—I've not had you watched or followed, or anything of that kind, it's only the local rumours and my anxiety for your safety and Dr. Perry mentioning this——"

"My safety! What do you mean?"

"Oh, we're getting into a confusion."

"It is true," admitted the young man, moodily, "that I have seen the girl once or twice. She wears a white dress, green sash, and a black pelisse.[19] She speaks in the most curious and outlandish fashion. I'm not sure who or what she is. I've seen her in the churchyard by a certain grave that I sometimes visit, and I've seen her in another place——"

"In another place that you should not visit," said Mr. Chalmers abruptly. "You've never written to her, I suppose?"

"Written to whom?"

"Why to this girl Fenton."

"I hardly know her name. I suppose Adelaide Fenton is the woman you mean. Once I was puzzled, I followed her to the gate of a mean house—her own dwelling, I suppose. Then I turned back. I have spoken to this girl, yes, on the various occasions you mention I suppose we were observed and I suppose it was Adelaide Fenton. But write to her? Why should I write to her?"

"I don't know. Mrs. Fenton's been visiting her attorney

---

19 Publisher error. In the UK edition, the following text is missing: ' "It is true," admitted the young man, moodily, "that I have seen'. The paragraph therefore begins with the words: 'the girl once or twice'. The US edition does not contain this error and has been consulted to check and correct it.

lately and talking wildly in the town, in the milliner's shop and the haberdasher's——It was my duty to keep a note of this."

"What does it matter what people say, anywhere? And I think you are mingling the true and the false, and the creature——"

"Did you not receive some foolish anonymous letters a little while ago?"

"I believe so. Why, several, of course. Anyone who is at least conspicuous, who is supposed to have any kind of position or money, receives dozens of such communications."

"But there were several, in particular—the love letters of some ignorant and stupid schoolgirl, as they seemed to me. I remarked on them at the time. They were written in the language of the circulating library, trash many of them, copied from popular romances."

"They were all torn up immediately," said the young man, impatient at this diversion from his obsession. "Why should you remember them now? I daresay there have been others. You know that I have asked Hackett to deal with all my letters. He only brings me those from friends or likely to be important."

"Perhaps it is a pity that all those scrawls have been destroyed. At the same time they may be no matter at all. As you say, such things are common enough, even I have received amorous missives from unknown females written to relieve the boredom of mean lives; they try to cure their silly idleness by imagining themselves the heroines of romances."

"What has this to do with what we were talking about? You were trying to give me some direction as to the future. I think I shall go to Verities. Yet I like Charters too. But my grandfather dying so suddenly has rather upset my schemes——"

"Yet you were always wanting freedom, James, freedom from

him, from me, even from your own servants, from your friends, everybody. And now you've got it, I suppose, as much as any man has—your title, it's old I say."

"Not respected," sneered the Earl. "*I* say."

"It's old," repeated Mr. Chalmers stubbornly, "the estates bring you in a good income, you have a respectable town house—well, everything that everyone in this state of the world's history and in this part of the world could wish for——"

"No one can be free who has an unsettled mind and a perturbed spirit. I have read much lately, and conversed with many people learned in occult science, and, believe me, there is something there not easily to be understood nor lightly to be mocked at. *They do* return—that's a hideous expression, is it not? *They do* walk again—that's a lamentable statement to have to make!—Well, then, why should not I have been chosen to be the victim of her eternal malice?"

"You scarcely know what you're saying, James, you ought not to know what you're saying. You have your wits, if you've got any, troubled. I've got to talk to you as if you were at college again and I were your tutor. You mustn't get so much nonsense into your head. This Swedenborgian——"

"You mistake him. He disbelieves in this family as you do—as I do—I do not know what I'm talking about——Can't a man express himself on some fantastic theory that he is engaged on in amusement without being taken so seriously?"

The young man paced the room again, his manner was much calmer, he laughed.

" I daresay I shall be cool and practical enough in my time, these are the steams and heats of youth, are they not, sir? You must expect them in one form or another."

"Yes, if they're not worked off in honest debauchery or honest toil. It's this solitude that's so dangerous for you. What can you expect? You keep away from everyone of your own age. Why don't you court some young lady of your acquaintance—honestly or dishonestly, what does it matter? A little feminine company——"

"I've too much feminine company," replied the other with a sudden return of violence. "Why must you keep on that theme?—it's one I wish to have disregarded."

"What theme? Truly, James, you alarm me. Is this some melodrama that you're playing, some sort of romantic trick? Do you intend to philander with that town girl and let people suppose that you're conversing with a spirit? Fie, James, that's not worthy of your intelligence."

The youth gave a flashing glare, but quickly controlled himself and moved aside.

"I'm going down to the Folly to-morrow. It has not been opened for years—save to be cleaned. I shall certainly have it demolished, but I should like to see first quite what it is like inside—my idle curiosity no doubt."

"Well, if it's not been opened for years, as you say, I should think it's falling to pieces, damp, full of vermin."

"Oh, I spoke generally—I believe the servants go in now and then, open the windows, give it an airing, sweep it out, pull own the cobwebs, and all that kind of thing. I mean that none of the Daintrys had ever gone in there, curious, isn't it? Built for pleasant, frivolous amusement, and never anything but a tomb—because *she* must have been buried—well, she was, was she not, buried in the foundations? Some wanted to cease building," he continued, "as an act of defiance——"

"Who knows what is the truth of that? So old, so garbled a tale."

"Well, *he* was hanged. That was true—you cannot escape that. But by error, by mistake, who can tell? Some other may have strangled her for all we know, played a trick . . . . "

"Do not let us dwell on vulgar details, it is ugly and sordid, James. And you know, as a Christian, that the dead do not rise till the Resurrection Day and that all these fables of ghosts—are, why, ancient folk-lore, superstitions of the peasantry, the effects of powerful crimes on weak minds."

"I daresay it is so," returned the young man, with careless indifference. "I'll take your advice. I'll ask Sir Henry to look over Charters and the Folly also, I believe that there are some antique pieces inside that might be worth preserving—a statue or a vase or so brought from Naples and Pompeii."

"I'll come with you, and we should take Hackett."

"Why?" the question was suspicious. "Don't you trust me to go alone? Do you think I've got a tryst with a spectre? Not only you, but Hackett is to watch on me!"

Mr. Chalmers affected to yawn.

"Well, I daresay it would be very interesting if you had, James, but nothing so romantical is likely to occur. And you'll meet there in that miserable place where there are rats, spiders, mice, pockets of dirt, damp and fungus, I daresay, too. A pity your forebears did not have more sense than to fling their money away in useless extravagance."

"Oh, Follies were the fashion at the time," the young man spoke with weariness as if his burden, that of some oppressive secret, prevented him from being interested in what was said. "Everyone had to have his Folly, did he not?—a custom taken from the French, the Italians? Half of them went out of the fashion before they were used—like this did. I wish my grandfather had had it demolished."

Then he was quiet for a while, and the older man studied him with a sad, concealed apprehension. His aquiline face was pale, his eyes, that usually had a clear falcon glance, were downcast, a muscle near his lips twitched.

'He don't look well,' the clergyman thought, 'in mind or body. I wonder if it is true that there is a taint in the family' (in his mind he avoided the word 'insanity'). 'Eccentric' was how the dubious characteristics of the Daintrys were described.—'Well, I'm too old and tired. Nobody's interested, I suppose, at my time of life to take in hand a youth wilful, obsessed. And his opportunities! What would I not have given at his age for a title, a fortune and estate and good looks, instead of being as I was the younger son of a younger son and having to drudge for a living! Well, I was lucky in meeting Seagrove, he was a generous friend—I suppose it was my fault I didn't make more of his gifts.'

The Rev. Timothy roused himself to carry on the conversation, to press home or to enlarge on the lesson that he had thought it his duty to administer . . . . Well, he had scored one point in getting the headstrong youth's consent to having the musty old building with the ill-repute, built in defiance on the grave of a murdered woman, demolished. Yes, the grove ought to come down too, the timber must be valuable . . . . No doubt it would make a stir in the neighbourhood, bring up the old tale, people would begin to talk and remember and ask each other why this was being done?—so late. But all that gossip would pass away . . . they could not plough the land so near the house, it would have been as well if they could—ploughed it up and sown good grain there . . . . Well, they would have grassland, or perhaps other trees, or might they have a formal garden . . . Sir Henry could suggest something, no doubt.

The old man's thoughts lumbered lazily on as he took his candle from the stand in the hall and went upstairs to the large, comfortable bedchamber in the modernized wing of Charters he had occupied for the great part of his life—it had been his abiding place when he had been in England; he had always used it when he had been tutor to James.

He looked round now at the lavish furnishings and the many luxuries not only with regret but with remorse. 'He was thinking of me, not of James, when he gave me the post of looking after the boy. I wonder if he'd have done better with another kind of man? I haven't got much influence over him, in fact none at all, I daresay. I found him rather tiresome, melancholy, austere. I let that Swedenborgian become too intimate with him. The man's honest, too, I suppose. Well, I daresay it's all a passing whim, a manner of youth, "the steams and heats of the imaginations" as he said himself, occultism and spiritualism, practised now in London drawing-rooms! What is it but sorcery and witchcraft?'

* * * * *

Mrs. Fenton showed Mr. Bisset, the attorney snug in his bleak back office—he was a small man in a small way—the packet of letters written on odd scraps of paper that her daughter had given her to read.

Alfred Bisset rubbed his chin . . . he had promised secrecy before this matter was broached to him, now that it was revealed he was puzzled, doubtful, wished he had taken it more seriously. Was it a hoax, a trick, had he got his dirty finger on a great prize—at last?

"There's his letter asking her father to allow them to become engaged to be married," stated Mrs. Fenton, slowly and flatly, pointing out a three-cornered piece of paper.

"It's an odd business," said Mr. Bisset, not committing himself. "I know they have been talked about lately. The young man is peculiar. So is his tutor, the Reverend Timothy. And that New Jerusalem man, whatever he calls himself, who was with him so often, and the old Earl lived too long, Mrs. Fenton, he was senile and allowed his heir to become intimate with some strange people."

"That don'e affect what I've come to you about."

"No, of course not. But you'll admit that it is all very extraordinary."

"I'm not so sure," countered Mrs. Fenton, with a touch of defiance. "Adelaide is very pretty and genteel, she has been to a good boarding-school, they're both much of an age, they've met in the woods and lanes."

"She's a *good* girl, I suppose, ma'am?"

"You see the promise of marriage," answered the mother stoutly, a slow dull red mounting to her face. "You see how he writes to her in tones of the greatest respect."

"Too much respect, it seems unnatural. The hand is like that of a charity schoolboy, too."

"Well, he never had much education, taken away from Eton early, sent about with that old parson——"

"Maybe, maybe! I can find out something. It'll be a question of identifying the handwriting. Have you seen him with your daughter?" he asked suddenly, looking up, his small eyes keen either side his pointed nose.

"Yes, indeed." Mrs. Fenton was slow but triumphant, she fingered the broad brown ribbons of her bonnet. "I saw him come as far as the gate and then turn back, not liking to intrude on us, I suppose. Caroline, that's my second daughter, you remember her, she's seen him often. She's looked through the window and seen him sitting there with Adelaide. She's gone into the parlour, the drawing-room, when he's been there and they've told her to run away. He's given Adelaide a number of presents. You see, he speaks about them."

"Yes, and there's a letter here about not paying for them. What's that?"

"Well, the bills came in."

"You paid them yourself? How large was the sum?"

"Fifty pounds."

"Fifty pounds!" Mr. Bisset pursed his lips.

"Well, that's not a great deal, I suppose." Mrs. Fenton was half-uneasy, half-defiant, "for a man who's a lord."

"No, certainly not for the lady of his choice—I don't understand the matter at all, but something might be made out of it. She's pretty, as you say, I've noticed her. A fine, fresh-looking girl. Very simple and innocent, just a country maiden, I suppose, Mrs. Fenton."

"Yes," replied the mother, looking aside. "Adelaide's very simple and innocent, I don't suppose she's ever had a mischievous thought in her life. Why should she? Carrie's a good little girl, too. They're like angels, I can assure you. They say their prayers every night; it makes your heart ache to see them kneeling by their bed in their white nightgowns with their hands pressed together, looking upwards."

The attorney again carefully and gingerly turned over the pieces of paper, some of which were so frail that too rough a touch might have damaged them. Many of them were written in pencil, some in what seemed to be a cheap ink. The address at the top of many of them was 'Champits Hotel, London,' that of others 'Charters,' of others again 'Verities.'

"You see he tells her all about his family, the cousin who's sick at Brighton and all the relatives and the great people whom he knows."

"Yes, I suppose all those details could be verified. Why are you bringing them to me, Mrs. Fenton?"

"For advice—I told you that—for advice. It can't go on like this, can it?"

"What does your husband say? I know he's a permanent invalid, but I suppose he has some good moments."

"Yes, he does. Adelaide has spoken to him. I don't know that—myself I shouldn't have disturbed him——When the girl got this letter written to my husband she took it up and he answered it. He can't use a seal himself, but Carrie did that for him, sealed the letter and we took it and put it in the post."

"But Lord Seagrove has not presented himself at your house, has not been formally received as your daughter's suitor by either your husband or yourself?"

"There might be good reasons for that, mightn't there? While his grandfather was alive?"

"Yes, there might even be good reasons now. It would hardly be a match that would please his friends. He has many and powerful relatives, a circle of influential acquaintances. One could suppose that he might wish to keep—this—secret. One might suppose, too, Mrs. Fenton, that it's merely a quizzical play on his part and that he never intended to marry your daughter at all. Young men will have their romances, you know."

"Yes, I know," scowled Mrs. Fenton, "and they have to pay for them. Adelaide is quite in earnest. If he is playing—she *is* deceived."

"Oh, she would be, of course. As you say, a simple, innocent girl. How does she spend her time, Mrs. Fenton?"

"She reads a little to her father, the Bible and the *Pilgrim's Progress*. Sometimes she gets an improving book out of the library, one of those brought out by the Society for Promoting Christian Knowledge, she's a taste for botany, too, and pressing flowers and ferns in a book, and does embroidery. She's quite clever with her needle. She helps Carrie with her studies, a little French—I hope to get them a pianoforte by the turn of the year. They play on a harp, as it is."

She spoke rapidly, as if she was throwing up defences against the man's silence. When she paused and he still did not speak she challenged that silence by demanding: "Both my girls have very good characters, you know that. Nobody in Mullenbridge speaks ill of them. They've never done anything foolish or indiscreet."

"I know, indeed, Mrs. Fenton, that's perfectly true. But there seems some indication of a slight indiscretion or foolishness here. It would be a most unlikely thing for Lord Seagrove to marry your daughter, you realize that, of course?"

"I suppose I do." A dark flush of humiliation came over the women's flat face. "I was ambitious myself once, when I married Mr. Fenton. I tried to think things out ever since, but never got them clear."

"Well, there are many stories—the prince and the beggar maid and all that kind of fable. These two are both the same age, she is pretty and he is young, and moody and solitary. Well, I suppose it might be. But I don't believe it's serious, Mrs. Fenton, I'm afraid."

"It's got to be serious. That's what I've come to you about. It can't go on like this. He'll have to present himself to me and to her father. If he's playing about with her he'll have to pay for it. There's such a thing as breach of promise, isn't there?"

"There is indeed, Mrs. Fenton, and if these letters could be proved authentic——"

"Well what should they be but—You mean that they might be——"

"Well, someone might have forged them, I suppose. We'll have to prove his lordship's hand, get witnesses—those who've seen them together."

"There's plenty of them," said Mrs. Fenton with a swift eagerness. "They've been seen walking up by the Folly."

"An ominous place for a lover's tryst. It has a bad name still, you know, Mrs. Fenton, though the story's not supposed to be talked about. She's never been received by any of his lady relatives or brought up to Charters to see the old Earl?"

"How do I know?" parried Mrs. Fenton sullenly. "She won't tell me everything. Carrie's the one she confides in."

"Yes, your daughter Caroline. She seems a sweet child. Well, leave the letters with me, Mrs. Fenton, and rest assured that I shall be extremely prudent and not mention the matter to anyone. Impress on your daughter to behave with the utmost circumspection. Remember that the Daintrys have not altogether a—well, they have a slight reputation for eccentricity."

"What we used to call when I was a girl, bad blood in the family. But there's nothing against the young man. I think he'd make a good husband, be kind to her, I suppose? Apart from the title and the honour and the riches?"

"Oh, yes, Lord Seagrove has an excellent character. I've never heard anything about him except that he's, as I say, moody, solitary, and shuns all the usual pursuits and companions of his age. He has come into the title unexpectedly; though the late Earl was of a great age, he was very healthy and expected to last much longer.

I daresay for the moment the young man is a little confused as to his prospects."

"He couldn't be about his heart," said Mrs. Fenton, rising, "not about the sentiments of his heart. I'll take those letters back, you can't keep them."

"Oh, but I should like—Mrs. Fenton, I should like to study them——"

"No. Adelaide don't know I've come here. She'd be shocked if she knew of it, bringing a lawyer into her love affair. But I thought I had to have advice." She stretched out her large hand. "Give them to me. I promised to return them. I'm only supposed to look at them and take them back again."

"Very well," the attorney put the letters between two clean sheets of foolscap. "Be careful how you handle them. The paper's so poor and thin and the pencilling so faint that they'll soon have disappeared altogether. Strange that his lordship should use such odd scraps of paper."

"You see that he mentions it in one of the letters—that's a way of his. He wouldn't take any risks with crests, or whatever they put on them, or gilt-edges, would he, if he was writing secretly?"

"No, I suppose not, but a careless young man like that might do something reckless. Well, it's a queer case, and I'll keep my eyes open, Mrs. Fenton, and let you know what I can find out. If you have any influence on your daughter impress on her, even at the risk of offending her girlish simplicity, that she must bring the young man forward to meet you and her father. He must, by word of mouth as well as by letter, offer himself as her future husband."

"I've told her that before, but she won't listen to me. Her head's in the air with all that novel-reading."

"Ah! Novel-reading, Mrs. Fenton? I thought you said that she only got improving books from the library?"

"So she does." Mrs. Fenton turned a baffled stare on the sharp features of the lawyer. "Improving books, stories about the rewards that come to virtue, and to those who wait. I say it puts her head up in the air a bit, she's always thinking of noble deeds and how to sacrifice herself. She's planned all she's going to do when she's—when she's up in Charters." The woman stumbled over giving her daughter the magnificent title of Lady Seagrove, and the lawyer noticed that halt in her clumsy boasting.

He tapped his pencil on the desk and looked down at the floor cautiously and shrewdly. This was an uncommonly strange story, and unless he was greatly mistaken, something uncommonly good could be made out of it . . . for himself.

"You know," he said, rising to open the door for Mrs. Fenton, but standing in front of it to prevent her leaving, "that Lord Seagrove studies occultism, as they call it now, and is, so the gossip goes, extremely interested in raising a certain spectre."

"I heard something about it, some talk in the town, I don't see what it's got to do with what we've been talking about."

"No, but it's a strange subject for so young a man in such a position to take up. It might have the effect of rather unsettling his wits, of making him—well, perhaps that expression's a little too strong—not out of his mind, but of making him do something he doesn't quite realize the importance of——"

"Well, he knows my girl's not a ghost."

"I suppose so," conceded the subtle lawyer with a wise smile. "Miss Fenton is very much charming flesh and blood, a well-developed girl for her age. Does she know that unhappy story connected with the Folly?"

"No, she never heard it. She doesn't think of concerning herself with anything so horrid." Mrs. Fenton Lied smoothly. "I was in this place for years myself before I heard anything about it."

"Yes, it was kept very quiet," agreed the attorney. "The late Earl had it hushed up and all the papers and books and everything bought up and destroyed years ago now——That reminds me, Mrs. Fenton, what brought *you* to Mullenbridge?"

"My husband came into a little property of his uncle, just a house and a garden and an acre or two at the back that we let out to a farmer."

"It's your own place, you're not a tenant of the Earl's?"

"No, it's our own place." Mrs. Fenton was impatient at this diversion. "My girl goes up to the Folly—she never knew, she never knew——" she stumbled, "what . . . what happened there."

"Well, there need be no mystery between us, Mrs. Fenton. An unfortunate rustic by the name of Harriet Bond was murdered and buried in the ground that had been turned over for the foundations of the Folly, then partly built. She had been, by the common report, seduced by the fifth Earl, who was a wild and reckless rake of the type common enough at the period—she was of superior bearing, and being beautiful it was believed that she had a promise of marriage from him. And he was supposed to be quite infatuated with her——"

"Well, there now, you see it can happen," interrupted Mrs. Fenton violently, "that's what I thought. There's the old story to prove, that's what made me feel there might be something in it."

"Might be! But you must be sure there is when you've looked at these letters——"

"Of course I'm sure," panted Mrs. Fenton, cunningly, "now that I have *seen* the letters. When Adelaide first gave me the hint, well, it seemed astounding and I remembered this old story that I had heard, as I say, after I had been here ten years. A pity they hanged him for it, isn't it?"

"Why? He had powerful enemies. Besides, he was guilty."

"Her fetch is supposed to come back," said Mrs. Fenton, complacently. "I've heard that story, but I've never been up to the Folly myself, I'm a woman who stays in her home and just goes up and down the high street—I've seen the Folly in the distance when, of course, walking down the road, but who takes the trouble to go down that avenue of trees across that field to see an old, ugly, disused building?"

"Not many, I assure you, especially after dusk, Mrs. Fenton. The phantom of Harriet Bond is reputed to walk there! Ha! Ha! Local superstition! In the late Earl's youth a man who took to sciences with which a peasant's brain could not cope declared that he had raised this spirit as his familiar and attached it to him. He confessed this to a clergyman who went to the Earl—the tale got about—how soon these stories do get about, a servant at the keyhole, I suppose! And then all was hushed up again and the man was removed to an asylum."

"Well, it don't concern us," said Mrs. Fenton, obstinately.

She took the letters, rolled them carefully between the two sheets of foolscap and put them into her reticule.

"She ought to have an engagement ring," leered Mr. Bisset. "Ask her to press him to give her an engagement ring. I see that one of the letters fixed their marriage for August—well, that's not so very well ahead. You'll have to watch and wait, Mrs. Fenton, and be very careful. And be sure you let me know—I understand that in your husband's poor health it makes him incapable of protecting you and your girls. Be sure and let me know every move."

Behind the commonplace flow of conventional words was an emphatic meaning. Man and woman looked at one another cunningly. Mrs. Fenton gathered up her heavy skirts of brown merino and with a sigh went slowly down the stairs, while the lawyer, holding the door open, looked after her, for his articled clerk had sprung from the neighbouring closet and was conducting the lady to the door. 'Too good to be true,' he sighed, 'and yet—when dealing with a fool——'

* * * * *

Lord Seagrove decided that he did not wish to see the Folly in company with his ancient tutor, the steward, or any of the servants, it was an experience that he dreaded and yet looked forward to with horrid relish, and he resolved to undergo it entirely by himself.

He chose a morning forty-eight hours after his interview with Mr. Chalmers to make this experiment—for such in his mind he considered it. The clergyman was confined to his bed with a more violent than usual attack of the gout and seemed to have forgotten the project of visiting the Folly, for when the young man visited him he made no reference to this suggestion.

Two friends had ridden over to condole with him on the death of his grandfather, and he had had to entertain them to luncheon. He endured their company, pleasant as they were, with some impatience, and was glad when he saw their horses disappearing down the avenue of trim chestnut trees. 'Once,' he thought to himself, 'one gets on the borderland of such realms as these, anything in the ordinary world seems utterly tedious."

The day was of pure sunshine and a high wind that had blown all vapours from the sky. The young man walked rapidly over his own parkland, leaving the sward by the avenue and reaching the fields where a heavy yellowish-white cluster of meadowsweet showed in the hedgerows and cowslips grew in yellow and golden patches on the short grass, and passed the Mausoleum without any concern. The funeral escutcheons were still hanging on the grille, their long crêpe draperies tossed by the strong breeze. He had no concern with the old man who was recently dead, nor with those other members of his race who lay in their handsome coffins within the pretentious building that vanity and ostentation had raised in imitation of classic splendour in that English park.

He wondered why he had not desired to enter the Folly before. Such a wish had never indeed crossed his mind, save once when he had suggested it idly and his grandfather had forbidden him, giving no excuse but merely a flat refusal to allow him the key. Then, though this seemed strange now in the recollection, the wish had vanished and the Folly had begun to seem to him like the Mausoleum, like the grove of elms and ash that stretched between the two buildings as part of the landscape, something to be taken for granted and never investigated. Now, however, his desire to enter and examine the building was keen, it had revived suddenly, a few days ago when he had met the girl whom he supposed was Adelaide Fenton.

Was it a few days or a few weeks ago when he had seen that figure in the white dress, the green sash, and the black pelisse standing there almost exactly where another girl must have stood a century or so ago?

*   *   *   *   *

The key turned in the well-oiled wards, the interior of the pavilion, built for idle pleasure, the scene of a murder and never used, was neat and decent. The old Earl always kept capable stewards who saw that those whom they employed worked well.

The westward window was unshuttered and the long chamber held a subdued light, dim, like thin wine in a thick glass.

"Often have I passed this door and never thought to enter here before; well, the place is ordinary enough, and shall be demolished, as Dr. Perry advised. It was a foolish bravado that allowed it to be completed—to stand so long."

The young man was not interested in his surroundings, but in a small volume that he drew quickly, furtively from his pocket; this contained a few pages that he had eagerly read and re-read and that he was determined to read again, in this place.

A large chair of wood, painted yellow and blue, with wreaths of convolvulus in natural colours, now much rubbed, stood by the tall window; the youth seated himself there and once more read the precise and dryly written account of the trial and death of his ancestor, one not so far removed from him in time, but related to him distantly, through involved relationships. How many lies they had all told him—foolish lies, but successful, too, in casting round this vulgar crime so many mists of confusion that it had become a fable. Had not that been a mistake, to give this incident the horrid air of a ghastly legend?

Was it not a mistake to try to destroy all accounts of this affair, to hush up all remembrance of it, to let sullen silence grow over it, as the fat weeds had grown over her grave?

It had taken him some time to find the hidden portrait, longer to find the hidden report, but here it was at last . . . at last.

'I am not yet twenty-one years of age.' It had not, after all, been a very long business, this satisfying of his curiosity. That talk of a trial and a judge . . . that now, did they not realize that he would know better, or had they, in the eagerness of their desire to deceive him, forgotten, or never known?

A man is tried by his peers . . . .

This was the date, the day, all details in the sepia-tinted print . . . February the 13th, the year 1750 . . . .

'The neighbours, some of them being armed, came up to Charters, the servants giving them way, they came into the garden and saw his lordship with a young boy, who was faithful to him, going towards the stable door that is under the clock tower, and one of them stepped forward as if to take him, the others being close behind, but he gave them a high look, so that none durst touch him, clapt his hand to his sword and went into the house, the boy with him. Some constables now came up and there was a great press in the garden, none venturing on forcing an entrance into Charters, for the constables were themselves the Earl's tenants, and the gentry for whose orders these waited kept away. So for two hours there was a murmuring and a waiting, then my lord appeared at a garret window (a place where they little looked to see him) and asked what they wanted. Then one of the constables was bold enough to say that a murder had been discovered, and his lordship's friend had up for it and his confession brought in his lordship.

'The Earl said: "That is a lie. I command you to disperse, but first, as the day is cold, come into the kitchens for victuals and drink."

'One said: "There is none to serve them, but all have forsaken your lordship, and we are here to apprehend you."

'Then he swore that none should take him and went from the window, and the boy came down and spoke to the people, asking for a surgeon, for he thought that his master was likely to do himself some mischief.

'A farmer went to find Mr. Ryder from Mullenbridge, and

still none had any clear idea of what to do, but they searched about the grounds, and two of the yeomen found my lord walking on the bowling green, wearing his travelling coat and carrying a blunderbuss; he was much disordered in his attire, and asked them of what he was accused, and they replied that a barbarous murder was laid to his charge and he must come with them. By then he was surrounded and taken to the Seagrove Arms. An inquest was held on the body of Harriet Bond, and a verdict of wilful murder brought in by the coroner's jury against the prisoner, and he was committed to Winchester gaol.

'On his appeal to be tried by his peers he was taken to London, in his own landau with six horses, with a strong guard, and carried before the House of Lords; there, being put into the custody of the Black Rod, he was ordered to the Tower, where he had apartments in the Round Tower, near the draw-bridge.[20]

'Several of his friends waited on him, among them the distant cousin, then an ensign in His Majesty's Guards, to whom his estates would go, and the ablest of legal gentlemen offered for his assistance. He would, however, have none, nor disclose himself to any, but appeared, indifferently, to admit that what his false favourite had disclosed was true enough, and that he had instigated this fellow to put away Harriet Bond, yet, when the moment had come, had taken a hand in the crime himself—"to silence," as he said, "her importunities, yet I know now that they will never cease."

'This wild talk so alarmed his friends and in particular some ministers who came to wait on him; they tried to reason him out

20 Landau: a heavy, four-wheeled, horse-drawn carriage. It was a luxury vehicle with two folding hoods that could be drawn up to form a box-like enclosure.

of it by declaring that the crime was so mean and pitiful there could be no excuse for it; the prisoner declared that there might be an attachment to a noble gentlewoman that was a sure way to be returned, but likely to be blasted by the jealousy of this cunning creature who had what she believed was a promise of marriage. This talk (that came near a confession) was so distracted, there was no knowledge even among his lordship's intimates as to who this pious lady could be, for he had always put aside all talk of a marriage, that his friends induced him to put in a plea of insanity, to which he readily agreed, yet with a disdain, as if merely to please them whom he had so much offended.

'After having been in the Tower two months and two days, the Earl was brought to trial before the House of lords, the Keeper of the Great Seal being Lord High Steward.

'During his journey to London and his confinement, the Earl had behaved with great propriety and moderation in his diet. It was noted by the curious that he had a mere basin of tea with a spoonful of brandy and a muffin for breakfast, and that with his dinner and supper he had no more than a pint of wine.

'Witnesses were called and examined at great length, the trial taking three days; his lordship took up his own defence with an elegance and clarity of understanding that disproved his own plea, that of insanity, a plea that he declared he was much averse from, that he did not think would avail him, and that he made to gratify his friends only. This plea spared him, however, any analysis of his supposed crime, that he passed over in silence save for a sarcastic comment about the fuller's dream—"for," said he, "if this be admitted to evidence, who is safe?"

'He was found "guilty" by his peers and sentenced to be hanged and anatomized, being given, in consideration of his rank, ten days' grace.[21] In this interval he behaved decently but refused all spiritual aid, even making a mock of some zealous friends who tried to induce him to repent his sins—for said he, "the time allowed him was not long enough for that."

James Daintry read no more; he had, rolled in his memory like a parchment in a case, the account of the hanging, the drive to the gallows in a phaeton with six hoses, the press of people so great that from the Tower to Tyburn the sweating beasts took many hours, the cool gentleman conversing elegantly with the Sheriff, wearing a coat of copper-coloured satin with intermingled braids of gold an silver, 'that I designed,' he remarked, 'for my wedding.'[22]

But none had heard of any marriage proposed for him unless he referred to his promise to Harriet Bond.

As he reached the black-hung platform the chaplain who accompanied him warmly and earnestly begged him to make a confession, but the condemned man merely replied: "That lately he had had so much to distract him that he had hardly been in his right wits," but agreed to repeat the Lord's Prayer, that had always, he said, seemed to him what any man might subscribe to. Then he declared that he saw a lady in a coach near the edge of the crowd, where a company of foot kept the mob from the toll gates, and that he must speak to her, but no such lady could be seen, wither by the sheriff or the chaplain, and both begged my lord not to make a delay in searching for this person, the press and the commotion being so great. So the condemned man died

---

21 During the 18th century, the bodies of murderers hanged under the Bloody Code underwent post-mortem anatomisation and dissection as part of their punishment.

22 Phaeton: a light, open carriage.

with much firmness, and though his family could not prevent his powerful enemies from bringing him to this horrid end, yet, they had enough influence to have the account of the case suppressed, it was not reported in the news-sheets, related in broadsheets, nor indeed anywhere printed, while all the details of his career were expunged from the family records.

Newsmongers made their secret copies, however, and a relation of the strange affair appeared in *The Gentleman's Magazine* some twenty years afterwards, owing to a Daintry having offended the owner of this publication. Yet the Seagroves had this issue suppressed, and most copies destroyed . . . only here and there in an old cupboard . . . There were rather too many old cupboards, dark receptacles, not only in ancient houses but in people's minds where secrets were stored. Anyone who really wanted to discover something, especially something that had the flavour of being forbidden fruit, sooner or later seemed bound to do so.

The young man looked round the Pavilion. It had been decorated with some skill in monotone, after the manner of the Pompeian frescoes. False windows were painted on the panels in shaded tones of grey. The imitation lights were crossed by trellis, now faded to the hue of umber, and beyond were colourless and unreal scenes of lake and mountain in what had been once named the Italian style.

He looked from one to another of these landscapes meant as trivial and fashionable decorations, the lightest of amusements, but to him now full of at least a sombre, if not sinister, meaning. The fact that these scenes were all without colour—perhaps the artist had been meaning to add brilliant southern hues to his light and shade and had cheapened the work at the last—seemed to make them part of a dream, for in themselves the views were commonplace enough, the stock-in-trade of the journeyman decorator. No one more important surely had been employed for the Folly when it had been finished in a spirit of bravado without any intention of ever being used. Most of the panels had fine cobwebs at the top. These spread over the latticed shutters, also in the *persiani* manner.

He had only unlatched two of them. Now he rose and opened the others so that as much light as was possible came into the Pavilion, and the landscapes between the windows were cast into a further blight of shade which had the effect, to his perturbed imagination, of making the small figures of peasants to move, the streams and cascades to stir, the trees to bend in some invisible wind.

The furniture of the room was old-fashioned but had been kept in good condition. It was uncomfortable, stiff and painted Italian chestnut, carved, with gold inside the little flowers of Florence, and hard cushions of purple and green velvet with long tarnished tassels.

He gazed down at the floor with a dark glance that seemed to gaze through the plain drugget and the boards beneath.[23] He had no idea where the spot was for which he was searching. It might be that the chair he had taken, half-way down the room, was over that empty grave. It might be in that far corner where a mirror from which most of the tinfoil had worn off, and that seemed to reflect nothing but greenish depths of water, was hanging in front of a tapestry, which time had changed to hues of indigo and mignonette.

The monochrome paintings took his mind to Italy and to the day when, as he had told the Fiskes, he had first heard of Harriet

[23] Drugget: a flat-woven wool rug.

Bond in Rome. He recalled Rome, all his tour, now . . . . The sharp colours of the South overlaid the monochromes, the austere blurred shades, the dull half hues of the Pavilion that had never been used, and it came into his mind that he had not lately been to see Mr. Abraham Steel, the botanist employed by his grandfather, who lived in the modern brick house by the great conservatory and who, with his two gardeners, was totally absorbed in horticulture.

The young man had made botany his obsession before he had come to be concerned with Harriet Bond. It had been the one subject on which his grandfather and he had agreed. Many thousands of pounds had been spent on the greenhouses, which were supposed to rival some of the smaller glass-houses at Kew, but Abraham Steel and his exotics had not been part of Lord Seagrove's life for some years. He wondered now, if the man would continue in his place, he, too, must be set, as in a magic circle, in his obsession. The hot glass rooms with the water-pipes going round them, the steam on the thick green dome, the unnatural, luscious flowers, the silent gardeners with their cans disappearing, and then the *herbarium*, the collection of priceless books on botany, the presses in which were the dried specimens. It was a curious, unreal life, yet at one time he, James Daintry, had liked it, had gone down there to learn botany and to paint and draw the flowers and fruits that Mr. Steel cultivated with such silent and austere care.

This almost forgotten pleasure had partly been brought into his mind because that morning, without a word or a note, a canister had been sent to him that he had opened in some surprise. A cascade of strange flowers had fallen over his breakfast table, succulent, fresh, most of them to him nameless. Pearl and lilac and sea-green colours, bearded and fringed with long stamens and curling petals, all sharply fragrant. Some of the stems were loose and broken, some of the leaves dark, glossy, and strong, some pale and fragile. He had understood that this had been Mr. Steel's reminder to him, the new master of Charters, of what had once been his pastime.

'I must go and see him,' he thought drowsily. He had had the flowers placed in a large dish, but some of them had sunk half under the water and appeared like sea-shells or even small marine animals.

He remembered now between these flowers and the half-eclipsed Italian landscapes, the Southern journey with Mr. Chalmers and the brightness of everything, that clear perspective that made even the most distant castles stand out in every detail. 'The farthest hills had a sharp violet edge, so that it seemed as if they were made of cardboard and you could put your hand behind them. There was never any blur, or mist, or twilight; the dark came down suddenly, like a mantle over your eyes.'

He remembered the journey to Naples, the visit to the volcano and the pause that he, Hackett, and Mr. Chalmers had made in a wayside habitation that they learned from an Italian priest who joined the party, was the dwelling of a recluse. A flask of wine, and bread and apples had been put on the table before them by a quiet man who was presumably the hermit. There had been many flowers there, the solid scarlet bells of the pomegranate and pepper trees, the oleanders and camellias that had a thick substance as if cut out of mother-of-pearl. He and the Reverend Timothy had collected specimens for their cases . . . he had been full of enthusiasm then for the endeavour to grow them in 'the great stove-house' as he called it, using his grandfather's out-of-date term, at Charters.

They had passed through these brilliant valleys towards the crater where the ashes lay sprinkled, feathery, on the hardened lava, dull colours of dark blue and putty from which the cameos, so displeasing in texture and colour, were cut that were sold with the coral and amber at Portici. It was quite senseless for him to think of that now . . . Portici—there had been nothing there! He had turned back with his party as soon as the mules began to get restless because of the hot cinders. He had taken, he was sure, no notice of the Reverend Timothy's orthodox comments and commonplace, if learned comparisons, between the crater of Vesuvius and Hell's gates.

He had never been to Sicily, nor had any wish to see that larger monstrosity Etna, where the plumes of smoke shot by flame spread out continuously like a canopy over the haunted island.

His mind came back to Rome. One of the painted scenes in the Pavilion resembled Lake Nemmi. He had gone there on horseback with his tutor, Hackett, and the courier, a man with swarthy Roman features and the pure Roman accent, who had acted in the same capacity to his father. James had been impressed, as all must be, by the sombre lake that light never seemed to touch, the trees sloping down to the very edge either side so that the waters seemed to lie as if at the bottom of an almost empty black cup. The saplings were marked with chalk to guide those at the top down to the waters. There was a small track round part of the shore and at one place a barge that seemed as dark and gloomy as that of Charon was moored.[24]

It had been spring, and the white violets and the cyclamen in their three colours of vivid pink, pearl pink, and pure white, like butterflies with nipped-back wings, were thick among last

---

[24] In Greek mythology, Charon is the ferryman of the underworld who ferries the souls of the dead over the Rivers Styx and Acheron.

year's mosses. They gave, however, no air of light or gaiety to the scene as did the primroses, violets, speedwells, and cowslips of an English April.

When the tourists reached the shore of the lake, and there was but room for them to walk in single file between the water and the sudden up-rise of the wooded slopes, the courier told them the usual legends, against which Mr. Chalmers had already warned his pupil. They had, of course, scholarly works at the hotel which would give him the true story of Lake Nemmi. But the courier told them of the barge of Tiberius that was sunk beneath those smooth black waters, and how it had gone down by a devilish device invented by the tyrant when it had been loaded with singing girls, young musicians and the youth of Roman nobility; while they were at their music, their wine, wreathed with flowers and redolent of perfume, the emperor's stratagem had taken effect—a plank had shot from the bottom of the barge and it had sunk through the lake, which was supposed to be fathomless.

"I don't think," Mr. Chalmers had said serenely, "that there is any water that is fathomless. It merely means that man has not been able to fathom it."

The courier had smiled. "Well, signor, it is a good many miles down that the bones, if there are still bones, of the youths and maidens are lying. Whatever men can fathom, he has never so far fathomed Lake Nemmi."

"For that reason," the tutor had said in conventional tones, "it was chosen by the ancients as a sacred grove. Priests, disguised to alarm and intimidate the ignorant, set up their temples here and affected to answer oracles. They hung their shields emblazened with mystic signs upon the trees. From those pagan days many fables have come down which no doubt even in our enlightened times would at the proper moment cause a shudder to the superstitious or the sensitive."

Lord Manton had replied quickly that they caused *him* no uneasiness, but in truth he was oppressed by walking so near the water that had a dull gleam on it like the surface of lead; and so close to the steep groves, once sacred to pagan divinities and since Christian times supposed to be accursed.

"I suppose I should tell you," Mr. Chalmers had said, "that this is a spot that to you should be very painful, while at the same time one that you should regard with reverence. I don't know," he added with some hesitancy, "if I should have told you in our pleasant *salon* or here, but I think . . . " he nodded towards the guide, "Pietro should be the one to tell you in his own language. He was present at the accident."

The Italian, who spoke a moderately good English, replied like one taking up his cue: "Yes, sir, this is where your father met his death through his own headstrong obstinacy."

"My father?" the young man had repeated. "Yes, I remember hearing he had died by an accident abroad, it was here, was it?"

"Your mother, my poor boy, had died of cholera in Rome. She caught a chill, sketching in the churches like so many foreigners do, you know, when the sudden cold comes down."

"Yes, I knew my mother had died of cholera in Rome," the boy repeated, "but my father—was he drowned here?"

"Yes, he and his manservant. They were warned that it was dangerous to ride a horse round the lake, but they would go and I——" the Italian shrugged, "well, I went with them. We had sure-footed beasts and it *might* have been perfectly safe. We had had a long drought and though the lake never shrinks, there was no slippery mud but a dry foothold. It must be admitted that the gentleman was in much distress of mind, not only through the unexpected death of his wife, but because six months before only his younger brother had been shot by a French journalist in Paris over a foolish *punctilio*.[25] There had been much attachment between the brothers, and your father, sir, had come to Rome with his wife to ease the sharpness of his bereavement. He had me with him very often. Some nights, when he was much agitated, he would sleep, fully clothed with his pistols beside him, on a table, and I would sit holding his hand all night. He had, as people will in such a condition of their intellect, many whims. He had gone to a vast expense and a tedious trouble to have his wife's body sent back to Charters, and he had gone also to Carrara to order her monument from the marble quarries. Though she was to have been buried with his other kin in a Mausoleum at Charters, which he told me was the copy of an Italian temple, yet he intended to set up a magnificent show-piece for her in the church of St. Jude's. He employed the best artists and gave himself much concern about the design. All was completed to his satisfaction and the monument packed in seventeen cases and sent by ship from Leghorn to an English port."

"Yes, I have seen it," Lord Manton had said. "I think it is stiff and ugly, but I have such a mission too. Mr. Chalmers and I have also to go to Carrara or Massa to select a monument for the man of whom you are speaking. There is nothing but a small tablet in Charters. Tell me how this happened."

The Italian looked at Mr. Chalmers and the boy felt his flesh prickle.

"There seemed no reason at all—something startled the horse.

---

25 *Punctilio*: a fine or petty point or detail of conduct or procedure.

We called out to my lord to be careful. He was a fine horseman, of course. The servant tried to overtake him and help him by seizing the bridle, but he was thrown out of the saddle. The horse scrambled up and got a foothold somehow on the bank, but the servant, whose name I recall was Prickett, seemed to take a plunge forward after his master, calling out to me that there was a woman with a green bonnet who *would* come between him and the sun. Then he, too, lost his footing and horse and man were in the lake. I could do nothing," added the Italian with grim placidity, "the young Englishman was sucked under almost at once. The horse struggled for a little and swam ashore; I managed to get him landed, but the servant had gone, too. It was not until three months later that your father's body was cast ashore, though the peasants, after this horrid event, came down frequently in their goat skins and their black hats with ribbons, as you may have observed them, sir, to stare at the lake, and they saw your father's hat, which, I remember, was made by Scott's of Bond Street, floating on the still water."

The young man remembered now this touch of absurdity which had yet been a touch of horror . . . . The modish hat had floated on the lake that lay above the remains of the festival yacht of Tiberius.

"Well, I suppose it was an ordinary accident," he had admitted half sullenly.

"I suppose so, sir," smiled the Italian. "Your father had told me that his house had a ghost, or fetch, as he said his wife termed it. It is possible in the state of mine he was in that he believed he saw this woman before him."

Then, in these austere and sombre surroundings, James Daintry had heard the story of Harriet Bond, but it had been a very different version from those afterwards either recited to him or discovered by him.

As the Italian took his little party up the chalk-marked trees to the flat ground above the lake, he had told how, with a few suave and energetic comments put in here and there by the florid, panting clergyman, that Harriet Bond was an imbecile of great beauty of person who worked as a servant at the 'Seagrove Arms.' Her origin was unknown, and the Italian, who was a Roman Catholic, was quite ready to give it some supernatural or evil turn, but Mr. Chalmers had said briskly: "It is nothing. The girl was half an idiot." She had fastened her attentions on the fifth Earl, who went, when he was at Charters, freely about his estates. He was a man who insisted very little on the dignities, in those days thought so much of, of his rank. He had spoken to her once or twice, impressed by her strange beauty and her heavy manner, and she had taken to following him, to waiting in the park at twilight, to creeping along the hedges while he rode the highway to meet him in by-lanes; to leaning out of the window of the 'Seagrove Arms' when he passed until he had felt her spying to be a persecution, the more so as he was engaged, having already tired of the debaucheries of his age, in chemical and metaphysical experiments. He had always had the reputation of being eccentric, and a great deal of his large fortune had been spent on what were then known as 'follies,' but what afterwards were considered to have had some value.

The Italian was not sure, but he had had some hints from his employer that the fifth Earl, who was a bachelor, was much attached to a lady of a most pious complexion who had, if not actually refused his advances, at least kept them at a distance, and that he began to feel that the persecution of Harriet Bond, which covered him half with scandal and half with ridicule, and that had become the matter of sarcastic jests among his companions, was debarring him from any progress in the affections of this other woman. But Mr. Chalmers had put in emphatically that they were not sure of that, and that it was an old story, anyhow, and now, once it was told, it must be forgotten.

"Well," continued the Italian as they suddenly came on flat land, as if they had crawled over the edge of the cup within which the lake lay, and stood in the sunshine, "he was supposed at some time when he was half demented between his experiments and his heavy drinking to offer a considerable bribe to anyone who would rid him of Harriet Bond and to enter into a good deal of talk with one of his hangers-on for the disposal of the girl. The details of the crime that followed we need not go into. The girl was certainly murdered with a collier's pick which was being used to make the foundations of the little Folly my lord was having built at Charters. There was a man, a fuller, supposed to be unsettled in his wits, who pretended that he had seen visions of the girl after she had been for some weeks missing, and who lodged an information with the magistrate. It was commonly believed that he had seen something of the crime when crossing the park after dusk and that he used this story of a ghost as a means of disclosing what he knew without offending great personages. Since the disappearance of Harriet Bond the fifth Earl had lived much retired at Verities and had had in his service and confidence several foreign doctors, of what sciences or universities I know not, who were regarded by the neighbours as little better than necromancers, alchemists, or wizards. After the discovery of the body of the girl, the man whom the fuller accused, and who certainly had gone to the 'Seagrove Arms' to take the girl away, was arrested at the

Newmarket races, made a full confession exonerating himself save to the point that he had been an accomplice or accessory after the fact, and accusing the Earl, who was arrested, taken to London, behaved in a strange yet decorous manner, and, having made many enemies at court, mainly among the Prince of Wales's party, for he had a sarcastic turn, was tried before his peers and finally hanged."

* * * * *

This was the episode that the young man recalled as he sat in the little Pavilion, that had seemed so far away, so insignificant when mentioned by the Italian on the narrow borders of Lake Nemmi. It had been two years after that that small-pox had killed his elder uncle and a sudden squall on a Scottish lake had taken his aunt and his cousins. Some others had 'died in infancy,' as the trite saying went. . . . He had often read, and they had no meaning for him, their names on the marble tablets in the old church. So he alone had been left with the full burden of it!

If it was true, was she not at last satisfied, and he demanded aloud, rising to his feet: "Who was Harriet Bond?"

His fancy overlaid the monochrome pictures, the neutral, correct tones of the decorations of this room built for pleasure but never used, with those vivid and brilliant colours of the flowers that Abraham Steel grew in the steaming glass-houses, with the flowers and plants, some of them so hard in colour and looking so hard and stiff in texture as to appear metallic, that he had seen in Italy . . . the orange before it ripened, the colour of dark jade, the citron, long-shaped and greenish-yellow, the golden polenta spread out before the small Tuscan farmhouses to dry, the maize growing in the fields with the hues of precious metals—silver tassel, golden seed. That canister of flowers this morning—the dark purple, the violet that seemed to gleam, the crimson that had passed into white like a spreading stain, the textures of velvet, of satin, a sheen like hard pearl, a yielding softness like feathers. He seemed to see the prism as if each colour had divided into its component parts . . . it was like seeing a pack of cards jumbled on the table, a broken puzzle that he must put together, yet always as intangible as it was fruitless.

There was really nothing for him to know, nothing for him to understand. How often Lucas Perry had tried to help him from his stumbles in this benighted world of fog and shadow into a clear spirituality where he might see angels, but not fiends straying about his path; but he did not know if the Swedenborgian had really affected him favourably. The man was odd, too, and the founder of his doctrines little short of a madman. Strange that a great brain should slide late in life from the precision of mathematics to the whirligig of hallucinations, and that another man of mean extraction and capacity should put all this rainbow shifting fancy into the rigid rules of a dogma! Yet he would have been glad of the company now of Lucas Perry. He remembered his gracious old house at Camberwell, where he kept a well-equipped dispensary; though he held a high degree for medicine he seldom practised, save when some case of bitter distress was brought before him. But his workshop, as he called it, was an agreeable place with large jars of Delft of a dull blue, with a dark blue design, or Majolica with the shifting, iridescent glaze like some seashells have, and the dry herbs—cumin, saffron, hellebore, and other drugs, ointments and unguents of which the youth had long since forgotten the names; yes, it had been a pleasant place, with its air of serenity, of peace, of healing. Outside the window had been a large tree, a flowering lime that bore flowers the hue of amber, the boughs pressed close to the long windows, and in summer were filled from dawn to dusk with the incessant murmuring of bees, themselves the hue of the long dry blossoms that presently loosened and lay on the ground like a faded carpet.

The odd man had told him many curious things all intended to soothe and distract him from his own foolishness.

Heartening tales of voyages and difficulties that he had overcome; or of some rare flower, hardly discovered, from which excellent properties of healing and cure had been obtained; of long travels over distant mountains where there was nothing but slides of snow and lakes of salt until suddenly a crevice would be passed and the traveller, bewildered by cold and lack of colour, would see beneath him valleys full—yes, full in the sense in which the canister had been full that morning—of the most superb blooms, unknown in this western island, tall as a man, and they were of strong colours of yellow, blue, and violet that had been growing and fading and seeding and growing again as long as the world had existed, without the eye of man looking upon them. Now perhaps all that remained of these trophies gained at such exertion and peril would be with some dried seeds at the bottom of a small alabaster box, or a description in ink already beginning to fade, in an old notebook; one such he remembered in particular, bound in unshaven goat's skin; or a pressed plant, a ghost of itself in a book with wooden covers. But Lucas Perry had told him that these mean-looking prizes yet bore in them the germs of relief of suffering to mind and body, or perhaps future and most important discoveries.

"But here," said the young man, rising, "is nothing—a bare room that has never been used. I think my wits are not settled, I cannot divide this moment either from the journey out of Naples—or was it Portici?—the visit to the recluse? I remember how the apple shone in his hand and how, after a little while, he took our plates away and put another repast on the table as if bidding us to depart, for other travellers wanted refreshment. No, I cannot understand why I have this all confused, or why like a palimpsest with the canister of flowers that was spilled over my breakfast table and the copy of *The Times* this morning, and the letters I never read but Hackett took up, and the visit to Lake Nemmi and what Mr. Chalmers and that Italian told me . . . . We saw the peasants on their way home—high-crowned black velvet hats with the ribbons and the fur leggings, some of them were ferocious and threw stones at strangers, but Mr. Chalmers gave them small coins and then they ran away. The *campagna* is barren now, but it once used to be orchards or corn . . . . This brings me to my native landscape, where among the corn will grow pleasanter blooms than anything I saw in Italy. The blue speedwell and the azure corncockle and the poppy that seems nothing but a stain in your hands when plucked but means what we all need—sleep and oblivion. I like, above all, to see those flowers in the ripening wheat, and now this room that has nothing but the sunlight, that my material eye tells me is very pale, falling in shafts through the windows, and those old poor paintings in monochrome, is all blurred and blotched with those ancient colours.

It is *in my eye* like the rainbow, or the mirage that one sees in the desert; or in the highlands when troops of phantom soldiers rush down the glen and disappear along a path too narrow for even one mortal to conceal himself in—where in the early dawn the shepherd going to his flock sees a mocking giant bowing at him through the mist. Aye, optical illusion, we know that and how it can be produced; but does that get us much further as to why it is there and why it torments us? I should brush all this aside and face this bare room and the pallid English sunlight and my own fortunes. Not so easy, but to be done."

He closed all the *persiane* save one.[26] The light from that was sufficient to illuminate the room clearly, and he tried to look at it now with critical judgment. It was an imitation of a well-known pavilion of a villa on the Brenta. It had no especial merit of any kind and he was quite sure that Sir Henry, apart from any superstitious fancy, would advise its demolition. It was, above everything, out of date; as out of date as hermits or ghosts or mausoleums built in copies of ancient temples. It was, as Dr. Perry had not hesitated to tell him, in exceedingly bad taste, nothing but lath and plaster and canvas and a few boards. In a day or so half a dozen men could have removed all trace of it, and for ever.

* * * * *

A light scratch on the door, it seemed to him as if he had been expecting it, he said firmly: "Enter whoever is there." The handle was turned and the girl whom he knew vaguely as Adelaide Fenton stepped with a mincing air, not quite suited to her graceful but heavy limbs, into the Pavilion. Her rather full eyes were sparkling with pleasure and excitement. She wore the green sash, the white gown, and her ordinary dark coat.

"Oh, it is a shame for me to disturb you," she said in a prim voice, keenly glancing round, "but the Pavilion is a curiosity, you know, to Mullenbridge, and I saw you go in as I happened to be passing. I was plucking cowslips." She showed a handkerchief that she held at the four corners. "We think to make some cowslip wine, but here is not nearly sufficient flowers."

She continued talking rapidly as she came into the centre

[26] *Persiane*: shutters.

of the Pavilion and, as it seemed to him, into the centre of his dreams, as if their two circles had now closed into one. Her words were absolutely commonplace as was his demeanour.

"You don't mind me coming up here, do you?" she said, as if with the air of a pretty girl sure of her ground with an amiable young man. "You see I'm interested in all these old things. I read something about this in a book I found in a cupboard at my Aunt Martha's."

The young man did not wish to hear anything about books found in cupboards; the patterns were fitting together too quickly in a manner that was not agreeable to him. He looked at her with a very keen scrutiny. Flesh and blood—an ordinary miss, surely, surely . . . and yet who knew what disguises these creatures took? He had read a great deal too much of in what forms they returned. He wondered how the fuller had seen the spectre that called on him for revenge, and in *what* manner the poor fellow who ended his days in a lunatic asylum had seen the shape that he had conjured up from the causeway near by where the little girl fairies sang behind the bushes in the harsh voices of ancient women.

Adelaide was triumphant because of her good fortune. If the young man did not seem very desirous of her company, at least he did not rebuke her . . . it was just a case of keeping one's wits . . . .

She knotted the four corners of the handkerchief together. The pale green and the thick yellow of the flowers showed between the folds of fine linen.

"You received my little present?" she asked rapidly. "I ventured to mark them with my own hair. You got my letters, of course? I am not impatient at waiting, you know, but if you could come down to the——" Something in his look made her pause, and he filled in the word.

"To the grove? You want me at the grove or in the churchyard of St. Jude's?"

She giggled foolishly. "Well . . . we have met there, you know—but it is rather a sad tryst, don't you think? Why can't we go about more openly. You know I'd like to come to Charters."

"I swear to God you've been there," he said solemnly. "That you know every hole and corner of it, every place from which you can leap out on a man who is not suspecting."

"Oh, la!" cried Miss Adelaide. "That's an odd way of talking! Why, you know perfectly well I've never been up to Charters, nor Verities either, and there's a number of things I want to see. Now this Pavilion, what was it for, why was it built? It's not a tomb like the Mausoleum, is it? A cenotaph, I suppose?"

He agreed solemnly. The light seemed to him to be failing suddenly, like it did in Italy, not with the long melancholy of an English evening. It was because he had shut all the windows but one, of course . . . .

She smoothed out her pelisse and took, uninvited, the grey-painted chair. Out of the bundle of cowslips she slipped small pieces of paper.

"Mother's getting worried about these. It don't look well to ask her to keep on paying. You know there's a lot of presents I'd like to have. Won't you just sign your name to an order? It's no more than fifty pounds, and that's not much for a man to pay for a girl he's fond of."

"Fifty pounds? Why should I pay you fifty pounds? I didn't think it was money she came demanding."

"Of course it's not. It's love and romance and affection—but you know how careless you are, dear—and the money's needed, I need the things. You see there's always so many bribes to be given to Caroline, and the little wretch watches—well, I declare, I might as well have a constable behind me; and you know that your people have set their spies on me too."

"Are they trying to lay you, the wise men and the priests? Who are you—just a village girl."

"Well, they call Mullenbridge a town, don't they?" countered Adelaide.

She looked at him with greedy eyes, a likely youth but not altogether to her taste. He was not dressed in such a showy way as she really would have approved.

"Well, I don't like all this kind of half-light talk," she sighed. "If I were married I should like to go . . . "

" 'In blue and green,' " he quoted, " 'which is only to be seen, on the back of an Irish queen,' and in a chariot which would take us at a speed of sixty miles an hour to Ireland."

"Oh, la, no, I don't want any nonsense like that, I read in one of the ladies' papers that Mother takes in, of a fashionable wedding where the bride wore a dress worth £7,000 and the carriage was painted yellow and the servants were all in liveries of yellow and blue and all the maids had bouquets of sapphires on golden wires. That's the sort of show that I should care for. I should make a good display, I assure you."

"I don't know what you are talking of," he replied, walking up and down. "You begin to distract and oppress me, you certainly do, like *he* and those that followed *him* (and my father too) were distracted and oppressed."

"Well now," protested Adelaide stolidly, "you mustn't go thinking of those silly old stories. I was a bit interested myself, and there was a book in the cupboard . . . "

"I don't wish," he interrupted, "to hear of the book in the

cupboard, of anything hidden in the cupboard, of anything hidden away." He glanced again through the doors of the Pavilion. "Tell me what you want of me and leave me at least for a while. It may be that you have got me in your power."

She had her pencil ready and thrust the ragged piece of paper in front of him. "Why don't you sign that? That's all I want. Aunt Martha will be asked for fifty pounds and there will be a scandal and talk and you will be embroiled. And I think you like me," she breathed with amateur coquetry.

"Do I like you? I don't know. I've got to see those marbles set up in the church to my father's memory. They are still there in the packing cases after four years. My grandfather didn't care about seeing the work done after all, but I must. One of them is broken."

"Can't you get your mind of that sort of horror?" asked Adelaide. "Churches and ghosts and people coming back from the dead and fairy tales? Oh, sir, I am sorely in want of this money and you do owe it to me, you know, with all the letters you wrote."

"Did I write you letters?"

"Why of course you did. I've got quite a packet of them. You see, although Father's paralysed he's got to know something, and he put his seal to his consent."

"Tell me where I should sign and go," demanded the young man. "What are you talking about—fifty pounds?" He pulled out his pocket-book. "I haven't as much."

"What you have got will do, and that ring—I'm sure it's nothing you value much."

"It's my gold signet, I couldn't give you that. I don't know why one keeps these trifles; habit, I suppose."

He counted some sovereigns out of a long knitted purse. "Ten pounds, nothing like enough. She said she wants fifty pounds. I'll send it down to you to-morrow. Where does your shape in which you dwell reside? Close to the church and the grove, of course, I've often met you there."

"Send it Miss Adelaide Fenton—the house has got no name, it's just one of the houses by St. Jude's in the lane."

Adelaide's hands, though firm and usually well under control, were fluttering on the handkerchief full of cowslips and the scraps of ragged paper. In a corner of the cambric she tied up the ten sovereigns. With a movement that was suddenly warm, human, and caressing, she moved towards him and he felt as if a glow of heat, agreeable and enervating, had enveloped him.

"There now," she coaxed, with her soft full lips close to his ear. "Don't worry and trouble yourself over all these silly tales. They've let you lead an unnatural kind of life. I used to think so when I was a chit myself, seeing you walking about with that old man and the steward or the stove-house fellow, and never or seldom companions of your own age; and you don't like those stiff formal young ladies they bring down, do you? I can make you happy, dear. I'd get you far away from this, but not in any of your fairy coaches going at sixty miles an hour, but in a well-built barouche with four good horses."[27]

"He had six to take him to the Tower and to Tyburn," interrupted the young man.

"That's what you're not to think of," said Adelaide, firmly. She took his cold hand between hers. "They'll drive you crazy between all of them. Wouldn't you trust me?"

She pushed back her white bonnet and he gave her an anxious,

---

[27] Barouche: a large, luxurious, four-wheeled carriage with a collapsible hood.

searching look, as one who is half awake from evil and terrifying dreams may gaze into the countenance of him who awakens him in order to discover if he be a friend or an enemy.

"Yes, I think I can trust you," he said. "You're quite beautiful too."

"More beautiful than those ghosts and phantoms, I suppose," replied Adelaide with a laugh that showed her fine teeth. "Don't you bother with them, you leave everything to me. Now I must be going home, or there'll be the wrong sort of talk. You see it's Carrie that's so difficult."

"Who is Carrie?"

"Caroline, my little sister. She's a minx that ought to be at school; lazy and greedy too. Pretty in a way—one could get rid of her. We've never had a chance. You've got to do something to keep her quiet, and my mother's going to Mr. Bisset."

"What for?" muttered the young man with an air of disinterest.

"Oh, I don't know, some nonsense, I suppose; but if you'd come and see her, if you'd give me something, if you'd write letters . . . . "

"I have told you I will send the money down to-morrow. Is it to keep the grave clean?"

"Well," answered Adelaide casually, wondering what use she might make of this further delusion. "I suppose you *might* call it that. Well, I'm not going to leave you till I see you out of this place."

With quick movements of her strong arms she closed the last shutters. The young man had risen and was staring at the handkerchief with the cowslips, the heavy coins knotted in one corner, and the scraps of paper he had signed, two of them, with the pencil she had pushed into his hand . . . .

She took his arm and led him through the open door. A slight gale was blowing through the groves of lime and oak.

"We will walk down to the park gates together," suggested Adelaide. "You look sick to me, as if you ought to have a little brandy. Do you carry it with you?"

"No. As far as the park gates, is that your limit?"

"Why no, of course not, but I don't want to be seen with you on the high road." She thought to herself: 'I hope there's a number as *will* see us.'

She was really rather concerned about his appearance. He was as chalk white, she thought, as his cravat, but the air and the kind of rosy warmth from the declining sun seemed to revive him. The blank look left his eyes to a certain extent. 'He is good-looking,' she thought critically, 'but not what you call very manly. I wonder if his head is really turned, or his *mind*? I wonder what he imagines, and I wonder how far I can trust my own common sense? Sometimes it all seems quite unsubstantial, then again a practical affair that would make one's fortune.'

She stood looking at him, having loosened her hand from his arm, and he paused a few steps away from her as if hesitant as to whether to leave her or not. She had a solid and monumental beauty with her bold contours, her fresh colouring, her upright carriage, her full limbs. She seemed to promise support and consolation, a rounding-off of all his mental wondering. Her glance was certainly steadfast. He did not remember to have seen that look in any human eyes before, not even in those of his old grandfather, or Lucas Perry, or Mr. Chalmers.

"I'll send down to you to-morrow," he said. "I understand, of course, that you are Miss Adelaide Fenton, that you live near her grave. I understand all the implications. You must allow me to think it over."

As he was hatless, he made a conventional bow, a half-salutation with a raised hand. She watched him go across the field where the cowslips were so thick, and then she tuned and briskly went through the park. It would have been well if he could have accompanied her a little farther, but she had not done so badly, native shrewdness had triumphed over native vanity.

When she came into the lane she carefully put the money and the pieces of paper in a second handkerchief that she pulled from her bosom and laid them at the bottom of the other handkerchief that held the cowslips, so arranging them that there was no sag in the cambric. When she had completed this little bit of trickery she glanced up and saw, with a horrid sense of apprehension, Carrie sauntering in the lane, sucking a large pear-drop.

PART FOUR
CHERRY PIE

'The dead do sometimes break through the boundaries that hem in the ethereal crowds; and if so, as if by trespass, may in single instances infringe upon the ground of common corporeal life.'

ISAAC TAYLOR.[28]

THE sight of the solid gold sovereigns seemed to Mrs. Fenton to have a touch of reality that everything she had ever seen before lacked. Adelaide had shown them to her on the palm of a steady hand, and shortly afterwards a manservant (well known in Mullenbridge as coming from the great house), having a disagreeable and precise air, had delivered a package at the door of the cottage. It was unsealed and had no sentimental trappings of ribbons or tresses of hair, but the flame of triumph was clear in Adelaide's round face as she pulled the covering apart. It contained a brief note that she hastily thrust into her bosom and Bank of England notes to the value of fifty pounds.

These she placed on her mother's worktable beside the spools of thread that seemed to the girls to have some magic quality, for their mother had been using them since they could remember, since as children they had watched the kitten play with them, and they never were empty, only soiled.

"Ten sovereigns and fifty pounds," whispered Mrs. Fenton.

---

[28] From *Physical Theory of Another Life* by Issac Taylor, published by Bell and Dalby in 1858.

"Well, it looks like business."

"It is supposed," interrupted Carrie tartly, "to look like love."

"I don't think," said the mother, labouring with her own heaviness, "it much matters what it looks like or what it is, so much as it is money."

"Well there's your money, Mother," sneered Adelaide with an air of contempt. "I told you he'd pay up. I saw him yesterday up in the Folly, the Pavilion. Poor boy, they'll drive him crazy with their tricks unless I can get him away soon. Now you needn't go to Aunt Martha, you can pay everybody."

"Yes, I suppose I can." Mrs. Fenton's suspicious mind had fallen on a dark aspect of the case that had at first not been apparent to her. "But who is to know where the money comes from? It might be your Aunt Martha's or even mine. People won't believe——He should have paid himself."

"Here is his name," countered Adelaide, opening her reticule, still with firm fingers. "A proposal asking for my hand. He'll come up to see Father and you whenever you wish."

Mrs. Fenton clutched the ragged piece of paper. "Always the same," she muttered, "more like a charity school boy than a great gentleman."

"Well," said Adelaide, "you know his whims and my explanation."

"And you know," put in Carrie, coolly, "that if he wasn't queer in his head he wouldn't be marrying Adelaide, so why don't you make the best of your good fortune, Mother?"

"Good fortune . . . I don't know. It seemed to me good fortune when I ran away with your father, and look what it ended in. If the man is likely to get into a lunatic asylum, it don't seem to matter how much money he has got."

"That's a silly thing to say. Even if he were put away I should have a handsome allowance, shouldn't I, and everything I wanted?"

"What *do* you want?" demanded Mrs. Fenton. "What have we got for those fifty pounds we've got to pay away? I mean to keep the gold to put in a mesh purse and look at it."

"He's got a mesh purse made of silk, sewn with tiny rings," sighed Adelaide.

"Money on trumpery," Mrs. Fenton continued to grumble. "What's it meant—a pink bonnet, a string of coral, cheap it looked to me; some pots of stuff for your face, and you don't need it yet at your age, and that jet bracelet far too old for you and a lot of other nonsense that you and Carrie count out at night like a couple of magpies."

"Oh, Mother, you're so difficult," protested Adelaide, and tears of genuine rage and disappointment were smarting in her clear eyes. "Don't you see *what I've got*—his signature and the money and ten pounds in gold that you can, as you say, put in a net and look at. Why, it would be very pretty up there by the statue of John Wesley."[29]

"That old bit of Staffordshire pottery!" said Mrs. Fenton dubiously.

"Yes," urged Adelaide, "you could hang it there because the firelight would catch it."

"And what would people say coming in—they'd think we'd gone crazy too. No, I shall put it away."

"That's what people always do with gold," remarked Carrie calmly. "Hoard it, bury it. It's a pretty thing, it should be made into

---

[29] John Wesley (1703-1791) was an Anglican clergyman and founder, with his brother Charles, of the Methodist movement in the Church of England.

a necklace or a bracelet or a clasp for a bell. What's the use of it shut away in cupboards?"

Adelaide moved quickly at the last word. "We don't want any craziness," she declared firmly. "There's been too much talk of things being shut away—that old Pavilion, and the burial place too, is coming down."

"I've heard talk of a great architect from London coming to Mullenbridge," remarked Mrs. Fenton, still with an air of suspicion.

"Oh, yes, Basil and I were discussing it. Charters will be pulled down and so will the Pavilion and the Mausoleum. Sir Harry is most up to date, he will have it all rebuilt in the ornate Gothic style. It will look sweet. There might be a little drawbridge and some ivy growing over it, and I think I might set the rage for a kind of Tudor costume—you know, Mary Queen of Scots or Anne Boleyn."

"For a silly fool of a girl that you are," complained her mother, exasperated, "it is a wonder you do what you do, it seems to me as if the half-witted have their own luck."

"I quite agree," sneered Carrie, "and their own patron saint. Well, Mother, aren't you pleased after all, and aren't you going upstairs to dangle the sovereigns in front of Father? I've no doubt that however ill he is he will recognize them, though I daresay it's a long time since he had one between his finger and thumb."

"You always talk so coarsely, Carrie," protested Mrs. Fenton with dull resentment. "I don't know what to do with you, you ought to go back to school."

"No, she's not to go back to school," Adelaide said firmly, "she's to stay here and to help you, and to be my bridesmaid and to have a really smart costume from Paris—anything she chooses—and a necklace of real stones."

"I don't know." Mrs. Fenton spoke as if she was battling against some tangible object, "how to get away from all this nonsense. I've been to Mr. Bisset, you know," she added sharply.

"Well, I don't care if you have," Adelaide was at once pert. "Of course, he won't be the man that Basil or I shall employ, he's just a village attorney, not used to managing these splendid affairs; but you can take him the letters if you like, and say how often I have received them, and how often I've sent them, and tell him about the handkerchiefs, too, that I embroidered with my hair, and the sweet notes that I found in the old beech tree, the one with the hole in the trunk in the grove."

"He don't take any kind of nonsense like that," said Mrs. Fenton, "but the written words and the circumstances—and now this money. He did say it was a family gone to bits and people might believe of it what they wouldn't of any other gentry. That queer man Dr. Perry, as he calls himself, coming round here so quiet and sly, and the Reverend Timothy—what sort of reputation has he got? What is he?—still hanging on at Charters?"

"I don't know," Adelaide was still flippant. "Of course, he will leave when I am married, ugly, bloated old wretch. I'll be bound he's got too large a pension anyway. Oh, it is all going to be changed, Mother, and those ugly, dark recesses and cobwebby places, that I swear do not get properly cleaned out, for everyone knows the housekeeper and her servants are careless—everything will be pulled down and we shall have the most charming little castle, of which I shall be *chatelaine*."

"With a white horse," put in Carrie firmly, "don't forget the white horse, Zimro, who can go, I suppose, like the fairy chariot at sixty miles an hour."

"There will be a white horse, of course," maintained Adelaide with a slight flare of her nostrils. "Don't you try to poke fun at everything I say and do."

"I'll take this up to your father just to show him." Mrs. Fenton spoke with the air of a person of slow wits who has at last come to a definite decision.

"Mind you bring them back," said the girls at once.

"Oh, I'll bring them back alright, your father won't be left to spill them in the bed or crumble them up in his shaky fingers." Then, as if recollecting her orthodoxy, she added smoothly: "It will soon be time for one of you to go up and read him his chapter. He wants a bit from one of the last chapters of *Pilgrim's Progress*, where the children are urged to eat the green plums and have pains afterwards."

"That isn't the *Pilgrim's Progress*," said Carrie, "but in the other story that is bound with it. I think it is rather stupid, as if you needed the devil to tempt you to eat fruit hanging over a wall."

"Well maybe it is the devil," argued Mrs. Fenton uneasily, "that does make you eat the fruit, especially if it's stolen and makes you bad and need medicine."

"Of course, its not the evil," said Carrie. "It's human nature. I don't like reading that chapter to Father, what does he care about green plums, or plums of any kind?"

Mrs. Fenton did not pause to retort. She left the room, closing the door heavily behind her, and allowed the girls to hear her firm footsteps up the stairs, as a kind of signal that she did not intend to spy on them."

"You're a pretty good liar, Adelaide," continued Carrie, digging her fingers into her pretty ringlets and then yawning. "I cannot quite make out what you are up to. I thought you were nothing but a sheer fool, but you seem to me to be doing some pretty clever things."

"Never you mind what I'm doing," retorted Adelaide.

"Remember it's your part to believe in them—and I *was* up in the Pavilion."

"I know you were. I followed you, then walked up and down the lane. I saw you go in. Did you feel frightened?"

"Frightened, why?"

"Well, there's the story it's haunted, you know. That story that interests you and me so much. I saw him after he left you, I was standing by the five-barred gate where the blackthorn's fading . . . . I noticed that as I stood there so long—the little flowers are turning brown and falling off. I thought he had an odd walk, a queer hunch of the shoulders. I wonder if he is going crazy, Adelaide. Of course, I agree with you it would be worth while even if he were. I don't think he's so good-looking, not what you would call a hero of romance—and living in that peculiar way also. Why, he what you call throws away all his advantages. There don't seem no money spent on the place."

"How vulgarly you talk," Adelaide interrupted with a burst of irritation. "What was the good of you going to that school at Clapham! It's the people you mix with in Mullenbridge, you gossip with everybody!"

"Everybody gossips with me," said Carrie coolly, "there's a difference you know."

"You ought to go back to school for your own good." Adelaide knew she was fighting a hopeless battle, but made some efforts at self-defence. "I daresay," she continued hurriedly, "I could have you sent to Paris or Brussels."

"I don't wish," said Carrie, "to go to Paris or Brussels—the best chance I am ever likely to get is here."

"Best chance of what? What do you want?" demanded the other sister.

"Well, something more than I have already. After all, what's it been, as Mother said, but trumpery and finery and I have had some hard work to do. What's the use to me of a set of books I don't read?"

"You have no hard work to do," protested Adelaide hotly.

"Oh, yes, I have, following you and him and his servants, and putting two and two together and finding out what this person thinks and what the other person says. It's hard enough work, I can assure you."

"Well, you can leave it for the minx you are, and go and stay with Aunt Martha. I think you're hard and disagreeable, Carrie."

"It doesn't much matter what you think, does it?" the younger girl spoke in a voice that was touched with brusqueness. "I want to get away from this place, I want to get away from all of it; from Father lying upstairs with the curtains with that embroidery of foxes and acorns, and Susan in her lindsey wolsey . . . ."[30]

"Don't bother about lindsey wolsey," put in Adelaide, "you shall have *poult de soie*, the most beautiful material. I saw a sample the other day . . . ."[31]

"Maybe I'd like that, maybe I'd not," said Carrie, stretching in the chair. "I want a little money, that's all. You seem to be able to get it."

"I'm sorry I showed you that to-day. I had to impress Mother," regretted Adelaide, "and in front of you. Of course I can get money and everything I want, but I do not desire to have you spying about," she added viciously.

---

30 Lindsey wolsey: linsey woolsey, a coarse sturdy fabric usually woven with a linen warp and a wool weft.

31 *Poult de soie*: ribbed silk taffeta.

"I shouldn't wish to stay," added Carrie with a flash, "you forget I'm more than eighteen now. I think that all this stuff you're playing about with is dangerous. I think he's half mad—and *you* don't know truth from reality. But I also think I might get the two of you to do something for me."

"It's unnatural," cried Adelaide, the tears again springing to her eyes. "You have always been tormenting me and holding something over me, ever since the days when you got Aunt Martha's red paste brooch for pretending you'd seen me up with him in the Folly."

"Ah, there's the word," cried Carrie, "*pretending.* I've been your false witness for a long time, haven't I? I suppose if Mr. Bisset thought it worth while trying to hook this fish, I might be your false witness again in a court of law."

"I hadn't thought of a court of law," replied the elder girl with a rather desperate look, "it's all been romantical."

"Maybe, but romances sometimes end in courts of law—breaches of promise—the village maiden and the Earl's heir, now the Earl himself! It would fit in quite well, Adelaide. There would be a number of people who would say they had seen you together and he's such a fool I don't know how he'd defend himself. And then they'd have the letters of course, no one would think an innocent girl like you could have written them yourself. Why that would horrify everyone, wouldn't it? And Father could be got to sign a deposition that he had seen the young man who had asked for your hand. Do you know that the rector is beginning to get uneasy that *he* is coming so often to her grave? He's had peculiar pains taken with it by the sexton so that there may be no excuse for my lord to come down, and with his own hands adorn and clean it."

"He doesn't go there now," said Adelaide hurriedly. "I told

him about that myself. I never go there either. What is that odd gloomy part of the churchyard, Carrie, where the sun never seems to fall?"

"It is gloomy, but it is not cold," replied the other girl. "It is dark because of the yew tree. They used to grow yew trees for the archers to use for their bows. And then there's the fir from a cone one of the Daintrys is said to have brought back, and you know, those strange plums that no one will ever eat," smiled Carrie with zest.

"Yes, I know," said Adelaide with disgust, "and I don't want to hear the story over again."

"Well, they are quite unknown over here in England. They grow from the grave of a foreign sailor who died here without giving his name. He was found exhausted on the road and he only said a few words in a strange language—out of his grave a little tree grew. Of course he'd been eating plums just before he died, quite natural, isn't it? Those plums come from Normandy."

"I think you're a horrible creature, Carrie."

"That's quite enough to make that part of the churchyard gloomy, as you say. It's a sort of potter's field," said Carrie with a sneer. "There's a Jew there and a carpenter who they think, but they are not quite sure, hanged himself. Perhaps he was a Judas to someone; and there was a blackamoor who ran away from his master, and they tried to saw the collar off his neck, but he died before they could, and they buried him there. All their graves are unmarked, the place is lush and dark and very suited to your tricks."

"Well, there's a stone over Harriet Bond's grave," said Adelaide with a sigh. "It's quite neat and proper, don't you think?"

"Well, it states, matter-of-fact, quite clearly: 'Harriet Bond, aged eighteen,' " recited Carrie, " 'late of this parish, barbarously murdered and done to death by one beguiled by the devil—a warning to all young maidens to be circumspect in their ways.' and underneath the date's scratched out. You can see that—the trouble it's been hacking it out! Then: 'A broken and a contrite heart, oh, Lord, Thou wilt not despise.' "

"I don't know how you can sneer about those things, you might have a broken and a contrite heart yourself one day."

"I don't know," Carrie yawned again. "I've got a good digestion, I sleep well, people amuse me. I've an idea I can get what I want, but don't you go on fooling too long, Adelaide. You bring things to a climax and you can do something worth having for me. I have a plan to go to London."

"*You* to go to London!" cried Adelaide, for once startled out of her intense absorption in her complicated and confused affairs.

"Yes, I can stay at the school in Clapham for a bit and look round. I've got some ideas—but you hurry up, Adelaide, with the cash."

The girl left the room and Adelaide took the rocking chair that belonged to her mother, it had, hung to the back by worn tape strings, a bolster composed of bright crochet-work in coarse wool. The girl was, at the moment of her triumph, rather more disturbed than she had supposed it possible she should be. She also confessed in her innermost heart to a most poignant disappointment in the person and bearing of the young man from whom she had obtained so easily the money and the signature yesterday. Never would she admit that she did not really 'care' for him. She had formed from what she knew of him, from what she had seen of him walking with his tutors or friends, an image that satisfied her as being that of the perfect lover; but now she had spoken to him face to face. He looked ill, his cheeks were unnaturally hollow, his complexion unnaturally sallow for one of his age. His dress was extraordinarily plain, even a little rubbed round the cuffs. She feared he stooped in his walk, that he had almost a shambling step, and what he had said to her seemed, as far as she could recollect it, almost crazy.

All that was normal and healthy in the girl shrank back. Perhaps after all she had better leave this odd affair, that had so exclusively occupied her for the last three years, alone. And yet everything had seemed so easy; that was it, too easy. He seemed to have no spirit, no will of his own, and then his talk—at cross-purposes with hers surely? And yet she did not know. She sighed. Was she one to distinguish truth from reality? What did they all mean? What did this girl, dead so long ago, matter? What was this talk of experiments up at Charters? Well, if she once got up there she would know what to do. There would be no experiments of any kind; there would be solid facts like a French maid and a staff of liveried servants, and the gardens set out in a modish style like those at Chatsworth, with fountains set playing and perhaps one of those metal trees that played an amusing trick on visitors and sprayed them with jets of water when they came too near . . . .

How stupid of people to be meddling with all this moonshine when there was everything that was fine and lusty and jolly just to one's hand. Did she know enough, and had she the strength to battle with these half-comprehended dangers? A vicious look came into her fine features. The falsehoods which she had persuaded herself were the truth fastened on to her unstable, excited mind. Impatiently she rose from the rocking chair and went out into the garden. After Charters you couldn't call it a garden—just a strip of ground divided by a clipped lilac hedge from these peering, leering neighbours—vegetables and a few flowers, primulas and violets. Nothing better than you could get in the hedgerows. The wallflowers were miserable too; they looked in their right place growing on the ruined wall near Charters with tufts of brittle weed and last year's brown mosses; and pale Venus's slippers, rising frail beside them—but here put out in rows it was as if someone made a display of weeds. And the damson tree that was always diseased and the pear tree next door which never bore fine fruit, but always had leaves pierced by caterpillars, and the view beyond of the sloping churchyard, and the church of St. Jude. Norman, of course—Gothic, but not of the modern, elegant kind. Adelaide despised it, the wooden steeple seemed to her foolish. She disliked hearing the rustics practise their bell ringing—and then that dank and dismal spot behind, with the one visible grave and the three trees that had no kindly history . . . .

Adelaide turned away to the house the other side. One of the old women had died since Adelaide had been to visit her Aunt Martha, and the other was continually, as it seemed to the girl's irritated fancy, in the garden, peering under the bushes, grubbing up the weeds, rearranging dozens of pebbles round the borders and, without raising her back, looking upwards, spying.

Adelaide challenged her now and went to the hedge of clipped lilac that separated the two gardens.

"You seem to be always working in the ground now," she said flippantly. "Don't you find anything to do in the house since your sister died?"

"Well, to tell the truth," replied the old woman nervously, "I don't much like to be in the house now I'm alone. It's strange how much more cheerful one feels in the open air, handling bulbs and roots and seeing the birds hop about."

"Well, it's an ugly little cottage, there's not likely to be ghosts in it," smiled Adelaide contemptuously. "There's only one ghost, you know, in Mullenbridge, and that's up by the Folly."

"Oh, I don't like to think about that," replied the other hurriedly. "I don't often get as far as the Folly. I'm really crippled by rheumatism."

"You will have your back locked bending over the beds as you do," replied Adelaide, losing as she often did, when she forgot her geniality, the pretty varnish that the Clapham boarding school had given her. "Do you know," she added, "it makes me quite uneasy to see you always there whenever I come in and out."

"Oh, does it," sighed the other woman in a nervous flutter. "Well, I should never have thought of looking if you or—your young man——" she stammered, "or anything of that kind . . . ."

"Oh, you've seen my young man, have you?" Adelaide was gratified. "But it is a secret and you are not to say a word."

"Oh, I am sure I would not say anything, but it gives one something to think of, doesn't it? Do you know I came over all queer when I first went up and found that poor wretch's grave had been looked after like that—clean white stones put on it and little plants set . . . ."

"Well, the sexton does it now, everyone seems to bother about such foolish things."

"I wonder," the other woman chatted on, standing as apart as she could and looking at her shaking fingers that were covered with damp mould, "who put that text on her stone? After all, who knows she had a 'broken and a contrite heart'? All we do know was she was killed by a collier's pick at a place where she oughtn't to have been. I should call her no good and as near a hussy as could be. I expect if she hadn't been murdered she'd have come to the ducking-stool. They knew how to deal with them in those days."

"Have you ever heard anything about her?"

"No, why should I? It is an old story, I've not always lived here and for my part there's never a spot of England that I've stayed in that hasn't got its tale of something of what oughtn't to have been done. It is always the ghost in the nut walk or the ghost by the pond," she began to laugh. "Who cares for 'em, they don't do no harm. You know that by saying the psalms right off six times without taking breath you can exorcise them and make them plead for mercy. But you mustn't give them their terms," she added hurriedly. "They always ask to be fastened up in a bridge and that means they'll kill every man, woman and child that passes over it. No, you must keep on like the good clergymen used to, even when they were on their faces with fatigue, and go on saying the psalms till the spirit gives in. And then perhaps if you've no more strength at all, you can make an agreement with them to stay in the local pond, and then your only trouble is that you mustn't let the cattle drink there or the ducks swim in it; but if you're really clever you can send them to the Red Sea, you know that's where they all go. There was a place I was in when I was a girl where they had a very clever person, a truly holy man he was, and there was a roaring ranting spirit there of a farmer what had murdered two wives and used to disturb all godly folk so that no one went out much after dark. Well, they got him proper into a bottle, and the bottle was there when I left the church. A nasty reddish colour it was and the parson wouldn't let you have a look at it, but a young woman what had seen it said she saw something black hopping about inside."

Adelaide looked doubtful. She had no answer to such a story. She was incapable of being much interested by anything that did not greatly concern herself, and had neither education nor imagination sufficient to deal with anything like this.

The old woman added with a touch of malice: "Aren't you afraid of the ghost, going up, as they say you do, so often to the Folly and at twilight, too? You know there was the fuller who saw her and that's what got my lord hanged, and there was that man Gifford who was studying astronomy—he saw the fairies and heard 'em too. He went off his wits, they put him in a Bedlam."

"Oh, I daresay if one talks too much of such things," agreed Adelaide, "one might get in a Bedlam. Why don't you get somebody to live with you? You've got us next door and other folks beyond, and there's a cottage or two down the lane. You ought to read your Bible more, I have to to Father. That and the *Pilgrim's Progress*, which I suppose is as good."

"No, it bean't as good," denied the old woman with precision. "It's nothing but a story book. I don't believe the half of it. I'd read my Bible more, but it's such a fine one, it was given me when I left service and it's red leather, all stamped, with markers and a box to put it in, and gilded edges and big letters in red, and my name inside writ all proper; and I don't mean to thumbmark it, taking it out to get consolation from it, and I say if the Lord be what He claim, He can keep the evil spirits off without you opening a Bible. It ought to be good enough for Him who sees through everything, to have His book by your bed. That's what I and my sister did to protect ourselves without spoiling the handsome book."

"Our Bible's ready to drop to pieces," said Adelaide, "and who cares? How long the days seem," she added with a sigh. "Spring does always appear to me melancholy."

"Why don't you go down to Mullenbridge and enjoy yourself with the shops?" asked the old woman, taking her trowel and making some aimless jabs at the loose stones at the edge of her path.

"There's nothing in Mullenbridge," complained Adelaide discontented, "everything's old-fashioned and out of date. It is all right for Carrie, who only wants lollypops and cakes, but for anything modish . . . "

"There's Miss Herle's," grinned the old woman spitefully, "I did hear as you got bonnets from her."

"Well, even if there was, where have I got to wear them?"

"I suppose you'll be going to the Assembly Rooms dance this year, on the right side of the rope, too."

"Well, of course I shall," replied Adelaide, who had not before given the problem any consideration. "I shall wear a single white rose and a gown of heavy corded silk in a peach colour, and perhaps I shall have a fan . . . I don't know."

"Well, as you said yourself, you won't get all that finery in Mullenbridge."

"You won't speak so harshly to me when you know who I am and what my destiny is," replied Adelaide.

She sighed and turned away to the gate and looked up the verdant lane that was so seldom trodden that the soft grasses and mosses were worn away only in the centre; either side they grew lusciously into the hedges where the coral horns and pearl-coloured trumpets of the honeysuckle were beginning to entwine among the delicate tendrils. The sky was fading to a saffron colour against which the trees, not yet fully clothed with leaves, had a dark clear outline. Flights of small birds in arrow formation were flying homeward and their chatter filled the air with a noise not only incessant but that seemed perpetual like the whispering of the poplar leaves on a day of high breeze, or the running of the water by the old mill wheel.

The Assembly Ball . . . . Adelaide, with her wits absorbed in other concerns, had not given this a thought. Of course she would have to go to it, even if it was only, as she termed it, *incognita.* She might even wear a mask, would not that heighten the romantical effect? Her mother must go with her as a matter of business, and Carrie, she supposed, as a matter of blackmail. She had got the word out of one of the novels she had read. The subject had been very discreetly treated. Some great lady was being blackmailed for some slightly imprudent letters she had written before her marriage, by an entirely disreputable mad, and as Adelaide had read the story—first soaked in its sensuous charms, the description of the satin-lined boudoir, the lady's amorous adventures—she had at last grasped on the fact that Carrie was blackmailing her, and that Carrie was not easily to be silenced or shaken off.

This was not at all an agreeable thought. She had always detested her younger sister, and she was angry with herself that during these years of her day-dreams, plots and schemes she had allowed Carrie to so get the upper hand from the moment when she had by threats obtained from her the red paste brooch. Carrie was no longer a child, she seemed indeed older than did Adelaide herself. She was beautiful in her massive way and formidable with her cool talk, her audacity, her perfect command of herself.

Adelaide's triumph seemed tarnished by her close view of Basil and the ill-effect on her of his incoherent talk was further disfigured by the thought of the implacable Carrie.

* * * * *

Mr. Bisset received an unexpected visitor when the same Carrie, looking tall and womanly in her neat summer attire, walked into his office with an air of curiosity that seemed, however, to be soon and rather contemptuously satisfied. She noted the deed boxes with no very important names painted on them, the genealogical trees of no very distinguished families hanging up on their glazed cards, the lawyer's desk with its bundles of documents tied up with pink tapes.

"Well, I'm surprised to see you, Miss Fenton, I must say," Mr. Bisset tapped his teeth with his quill, a little dubious, a little excited as he had been from the first by the Fenton 'affair,' as he termed it.

He knew it to be, from his point of view, a very delicate business and he had been shrewd enough to keep his head and not to utter a word of it to anyone, though he longed to have the advice of some London lawyer on what he could not help thinking was his 'but of luck.'

"Mother's been coming to see you," said Carrie, "and everything Mother does she makes a muddle of and this . . . well, romance . . . " the word did not sound prettily on her smooth young lips, "has been going on for a good while now. You see, Mr. Bisset, we are in a rather foolish position. My father is paralysed and doesn't know about anything, there is a very stupid old servant in the house and my mother is ambitious and intriguing, but didn't have any education and hasn't made much of her own life, has she? While Adelaide has got so confused with her day-dreaming and her seeing herself as a heroine of a novelette that she too hardly knows real from false."

"Well, young lady," remarked Mr. Bisset dryly, "that is a very sensible speech, though not a very dutiful one. How old are you?" he added inquisitively.

"I'm rather more than eighteen," said Carrie coolly, "and so far I have not done so well for myself. Life in Mullenbridge don't offer anything for me. I'm not going as a chambermaid or a lady's servant or behind a haberdasher's counter, and I know well enough that no likely young man will look at me. That's where Mother is so stupid, she just don't understand. Can *you* understand, Mr. Bisset, what out house is like, with a sick man upstairs wrapped in a grey shawl and four women living on themselves in a house near a churchyard away from the town? We've no relatives here and few friends. Mother is always uppish and yet don't know how to play the lady."

"I should think that a cool-headed young woman like you could get some sort of position in London," said Mr. Bisset, still guarding his defences.

"I daresay, but I want a start, don't I? I learned a bit of gentility, that I can put off and on like a bonnet, at that school at Clapham, but that won't carry me far. I've got a bit of . . . well, I suppose you'd call it comonsense. I seem to know why people do things, I can see through them——I suppose you're like that yourself or you wouldn't be a lawyer, even," she added coolly, "in a small way."

"We are all in a small way in Mullenbridge," said Mr. Bisset, drawing his quill pen up and down the paper in front of him, "but my way's not so small as I can waste time endlessly on you nor on your mother either. She hasn't paid any fee, I can tell you, and the stuff she has brought me seems like a farago of nonsense—the proof of that is I haven't dared touch it, I haven't ventured to go forward with it and you may be quite sure that if I had seen the least chance of being able to do so . . . well, it would have meant a fortune for me, wouldn't it?"

"You think it's all nonsense?" asked Carrie eagerly. "That is why I wanted to see you. Mother lies, of course, and foolishly. I tell you there's something in it. He—we won't mention names—

has been to our house, I've seen him. I've seen him walking with Adelaide by the grave of . . . well, Harriet Bond . . . . "

"That was a stupid bit of scandal," frowned Mr. Bisset. "Made half the country-side think he is loose in his wits like his ancestors have been."

"Is he?" asked Carrie, and her firm bosom rose. "That is what I want to know. I can't do much spying, I'm too conspicuous and people won't tell me the truth, but it seems to me an unnatural life he is leading."

"The family history is not good," remarked Mr. Bisset, "there's no disloyalty in saying as much. They had a series of tragedies which left this young man the sole heir. The old Earl—well, I don't know that he was more than eccentric—but it was the present Earl's mother who was Irish and began to get the fetch talked about. Well, there was a series of accidents and they all died unfortunately, and of course they have got all the friends they want in London. It don't seem as natural for a young man to live up there in Charters with that small staff and that half-drunken parson, as it did for his grandfather. It is a queer establishment, I'll admit. Thousands must go on that conservatory. I envy that man Steel his job—he has got his own libraries, and they say he can spend what money he likes; and what is the sense of it all, what is the good of it?—flowers and herbs and tropical trees! The old lord was very keen until a year ago, and they say this one's taken little notice. Then the old man Chalmers—well, I suppose you've heard something about him, you seem a shrewd young lady. He's of a good family, he belongs to the past, he's got low principles. He wasn't the right kind of person to take a young boy about. He should have been sent to school and college."

Caroline listened patiently, she felt that all this dull stuff must have something to do with the affair that lay so near to her heart.

"Then," said Mr. Bisset with his slow cautious air, "there is the Swedenborgian who visits them. Up to no good I should say—wants a slice of the money."

"They have got a good deal?" asked Caroline. "It looks to me as if the whole place was falling to pieces. I suppose they have a fortune in consols and town property."

Mr. Bisset laughed loud and coarsely. "My dear young lady, do you suppose I know anything about that, or that I could tell you if I did? They have their own attorneys and their own affairs. I should say there is a good deal of money and there are a great many treasures, I have been told, at Charters, brought back from Italy and France and Greece, that haven't been as much as dusted for many years. What are you trying to make out and what are you trying to tell me?"

Caroline, looking with her clear sparkling eyes at the ashy, ruined face of the attorney, said: "He sent fifty pounds in paper and ten pounds in gold to pay for Adelaide's finery. He put his name to a letter she'd written asking her hand in marriage; my father's seen him standing at the door of his room, no further because the old man was sick, you understand. I've seen him often enough walking up and down by the Folly. Adelaide sent him some handkerchiefs worked with her hair and she has a pile of letters from him—here are some of them," and she placed a box on the lawyer's table.

He fingered them greedily. "This is the same sort of stuff your mother brought me. I don't know what to make of it. Maybe he has been so ill-educated and got his head so in the air that he would write like this, and then we might come in for heavy damages. Why not—the young lord and the village maiden and their attachment to one another as they wandered freely in the woods; and then the alarm of both families and the youth sent abroad and the maiden to one of her relatives—and then their return and the renewal of affection and the exchange of a pledge. It might be quite a good case even for a London lawyer. We should have to prove his hand, of course, and get together as many witnesses as possible who have seen them talking or walking."

"Two days ago they were in the Pavilion and Adelaide came home with his signature to the paper and ten pieces of gold, and the next day Hackett, that is his body servant, came up with a letter in which was the fifty pound notes."

"Ah, the servant," said Mr. Bisset quickly. "Now what did he say?"

"Nothing. He looked disgusted, he went away menacingly—but that wouldn't matter, would it?"

"I don't know. It would be very useful if we could——" the lawyer hesitated on the word suborn, "if we could get hold of somebody in Charters who sees the young man receive the letters and perhaps could witness to him sending them off . . . but it's a long affair."

"It can't be such a long affair," said Carrie with a touch of impatience. "Suppose he is half-witted and goes off his head and is taken away to a lunatic asylum before we've got anything out of it. Don't you see, that is why *I* am here. Mother is so silly and clumsy and don't know her way about. It is not my place to go up to Charters and face him with this, and it isn't Adelaide's, I suppose, and Mother would only make a failure of it if she tried. Wouldn't you or somebody else just face him with it? I suppose," she shrugged, "he'd pay quite a good deal to have the whole thing hushed up."

"Well, my dear young lady, you seem quite willing to make a

trade of your sister's affections."

"Oh, Adelaide's affections!" said Carrie. "She would soon get over it if she had some money for clothes. She'd like to get away from Mullenbridge, the same as I should, but I see things as they are and she don't, and she keeps reading those stories which put queer ideas into her head—like white horses called Zimro, and wedding dresses that cost seven thousand pounds."

"Everybody I've got to deal with seems to be a liar," said Mr. Bisset. "I daresay the young man would lie too. What's one to expect when he's half under the influence of a crazy Swedenborgian and half under that of a drunken parson, don't enjoy any natural pleasures and spends all his time going to spiritualistic meetings, whatever they call them. Those who had the looking after him ought to have seen to it that he didn't ever hear of that story of Harriet Bond. God knows there was trouble enough to hush it up and influence enough and money enough to, but it comes out."

"In cupboards," simpered Caroline, "people will keep these things—odd copies of magazines and daubs that ought to have been signposts. What do you think of it all, Mr. Bisset—did that man who was hanged at Tyburn murder Harriet Bond or not?"

"I should doubt it—not a man of his breeding with a collier's pick. I think it is quite true from what I've been told here, that she was half-witted and persecuted him; of course he might have paid the other to do it and have been there himself. There is a room in one of the towers in Charters, you know, that is still fitted up for his experiments. Those were great days, the 'sons of fire,' or alchemists they call them, and there was hardly any man of wit and money who was not tired of cheap pleasures who didn't experiment in his laboratory. Well, it comes back to them both being half-crazy. If she persecuted him, you might understand that he, in the state of mind he was in then, might have had her done away with. The peers might have well accepted his plea of insanity, but he'd outraged the ruling party. I don't know . . . it's old stuff. It seems to hang about Mullenbridge and Charters. I hear the young lord is going to have the place pulled down and done up again in the new gothic style."

Caroline pursed her lips and clasped her hands. The lawyer looked at her; she was too tall, too heavy, but might be a great success as a fine bouncing beauty. It was certainly easier dealing with her than with the sly, stupid, ignorant mother.

"Those few years you had at Clapham were a great deal of use to you after all," he said ingratiatingly. "Well, keep your letters, I've seen them, I have known they are there and I will do what I can. I tell you I should be kicked out if I went up to Charters. I might get hold of someone in London who would take it up. Of course, we couldn't hope for a marriage, you know."

"We only hope for money," declared Carrie coolly, "that is all Mother hopes for, that is all I hope for."

"What have you got to do with it?" asked Mr. Bisset. "It is all you hope for! You were a child when this started."

"It gave me an interest in life. It is the only means I have of getting money of any kind."

"So you are doing a little blackmail, are you?" said Mr. Bisset. "What have you had so far?"

The girl put back a tress of bright hair that had fallen in between her bonnet and her cheek. "Nothing," she said, "but a little trumpery—two years ago, a paste buckle or a set of books I don't care to read, or one or two little things like that might have meant something to me; they don't now. It is pretty dull and dreary watching Adelaide and telling lies for her . . . ."

"Ah, telling lies for her—you must be careful there. It wouldn't do to go into the witness box and make an admission like that, would it?"

"I shouldn't make an admission like that. What I have told you is true."

"I daresay," replied the lawyer, "it might be accepted as true."

"Now," said Carrie, "there's this question of the Assembly Ball."

"Well, that's nearly two months off," said Mr. Bisset.

"He has asked her to be there and she's made up her mind that she is going. Some of the money isn't to pay the debts, but to buy her a white dress and a new green sash and a white rose for her hair. How is she to get the ticket or an invitation, Mr. Bisset?"

He reflected a moment, his brows drawn together.

"I should think you'd better ask the young man. Why don't you get hold of him, Miss Carrie? You might, he wanders about without his tutor now. He don't have many people staying with him—Sir Henry Dering, I believe, is coming down about the reconstruction of Charters, and there may be a few friends, but, clever as you are, you ought to be able to get hold of him. Try to sharpen your wits on him like you have on me to-day. Perhaps you'd get more out of him than you have out of me. I daresay at least," added the lawyer cunningly, "you'd be able to discover if he was in his right mind or not."

Caroline rose and smoothed down her pelisse. "I got a good story for coming to see you, and also for covering up Mother's visits here. I have told everyone—that is the few people whom I know—that it is about the bit of property we have in Mullenbridge."

"That'll do, my beauty," laughed the lawyer, "I shan't give you away. I don't know whether you are wasting my time or if I am on a good thing . . . . "

"There can't be much more waste of time," said Carrie, "His relatives will get hold of him whatever his state of mind. He's supposed to be going to Wales. They'll marry him off to some woman who won't care about his fancies as long as she is a countess and got a fortune."

"I think you're right," argued Mr. Bisset. "But maybe we could get a little picking first."

*   *   *   *   *

Lord Seagrove had visited Abraham Steel in his neat and cheerful house attached to the large conservatory which was built on the model of Sir Joseph Paxton's glass and iron pavilion that had been used for the Great Exhibition of 1850 and afterwards copied in the Duke of Devonshire's place at Chatsworth. His ancient interest in horticulture had certainly revived, but he was not so free of his obsession that he could not link the two together.

He found Abraham Steel, who had been so in the background of his life for the last three or four years that he had never even mentioned his name, to be a dry person given to no freaks of the imagination, neither ignorant nor superstitious, but apart from ordinary work with plants much interested in out-of-the-way experiments.

He had a small but well-fitted laboratory in his house, and when he had shown his employer the wonders of the conservatory where the flowers seemed to flame and sway, to quiver and droop like imprisoned birds, among the monstrous leaves and the steaming heat, he explained to him, quite dryly, what he was doing.

It was an experiment on a subject that the young man had never heard of before, though it had first been put forward in a book published in 1650. It was known by the name of Palinganesia and Mr. Steel believed that it had been practised, though rarely, by the more intelligent of the alchemists of the middle ages.

At first the youth was not particularly interested, but suddenly one remark by Abraham Steel drew all his attention; the botanist was careful to preface his comments with many cautionary this and that, but he declared that it had been mooted by many that the forms of plants, though invisible, might still be retained in their ashes.

"You may, sir," he observed, "think this very strange if you have never attended to the subject, but there are some of the best French chemists, and a certain Polish physician, who are supposed, on good authority, to have possessed vases which contained ashes which when subjected to a gentle flame showed the forms of various plants. A small obscure cloud was first observed which then took on a faint form and showed a rose, or whatever plant or flower the ashes consisted of . . . . I had one successful experiment," remarked Mr. Steel, with satisfaction, "but was never able to repeat it until recently. Last winter I succeeded, as I believe, by chance. I had for another purpose extracted the salts from some burned nettles and left the lye outside to cool. In the morning, the frost having been severe, I found my salts frozen and the shape of the nettles exactly represented on the ice so that the living plant could not be more perfect. I had staying with me at the time several botanists and herbalists who were able to notice this curiosity and all were agreed, sir, that when a body dies its form or figure still resides in its ashes. I then went deeper into the subject and found that many of my predecessors, including the famous Sir Kenelm Digby, had practised this art of bringing back the forms of plants from their ashes, and he had said that we may suppose that the earthly husk remains in a retort while the volatile essence ascends like a spirit, perfect in form, but void of substance."

Lord Seagrove was now intensely interested; Mr. Steel remarked his pallor and offered him a chair and suggested that the heat of the stove-houses had overcome him?

"No, it is what you are telling me, pray proceed."

"I don't know there is so much in this, men have fallen on stranger discoveries unawares. One day we may get further with this. I have heard of a Swiss chemist who laid a large bunch of palm under the tiles which were yet warm, where it dried, but the frosts soon came and contracted the leaves without expelling the volatile salts. They lay there till summer when the chemist chopped up the palm, put it into a clean retort, poured running water upon it and placed the receiver above, he afterwards heated it; thereupon there appeared on the water a patch of yellow oil about the thickness of a knife-blade, and this oil shaped itself into the forms of innumerable palm leaves which did not run into one another, but remained perfectly distinct. He says he kept the fluid some time and showed it to a number of people. At length, wishing to throw it away, he shook it and the leaves ran into one another with the disturbance of the oil, but resumed their distinct shape again as soon as it was at rest, the fluid form returning to the perfect signature."

"The perfect signature, that might be so with *human* bodies."

"Why, sir, that is the interest in our labours. This is supposed to have a great deal to do with what is known as wraiths or apparitions. I do not know how far such experiments are really practical, but I must say that I have had some success . . . . "

"If you can burn a rose or reduce it by some means to ashes, and then by some other means restore its form, pallid perhaps and faint—well, it makes one wonder . . . . Might that not be a solution?"

"The line of thought is confused and uncertain," sighed Mr. Steel. "We make *experiments*. You know that when gas was first discovered it was supposed to be a ghost. There is a great deal that lies beyond our comprehension."

"You are engaged with flowers and plants. I, too, am interested, in another direction. I should like to take part in your work. There is a laboratory at Charters that has been much disused. Now if you were to take some heliotrope . . . cherry pie . . . . "

"Oh, cherry pie!" interrupted Mr. Steel. "A modest little flower; you know we call it from the Greek name . . . . It turns to the sun—like the sunflower or giant artichoke, but cherry pie the villagers call it from the perfume.[32] I take it to be a resolute plant and one of a peculiar shape and I will, if you wish, continue my experiments at consuming this plant and bringing it back again in the phial as its own ghost."

"You know," said the young man hurriedly, "that we have a ghost at Charters, one that is supposed to walk by the grave near the Folly."

"Why, I have heard so, my lord, but—well . . . where can you find a place in England that has not some such tale?"

"It's called the fetch, that might apply to your flowers also. It returns."

"Here again," remarked Mr. Steel, "we must use a little reason. I think it was your own mother, sir, who first applied this term fetch, which I take to be but the Irish for the Scotch word wraith—

---

32 Publisher error: in the UK edition, the first two lines of this paragraph have been swapped around, so the text reads, 'you know we call it from the Greek name . . . . It turns to the sun—"Oh, cherry pie!" interrupted Mr. Steel. "A modest little flower;'. This error does not appear in the US edition, which has been consulted to check and correct it.

and in this case it was not correctly applied, for a fetch is the apparition of someone who still lives; but the word was taken up here and applied to the spectre who was supposed to haunt the place where she was buried."

"I thought," said the Earl, with an effort, looking away, "that I saw her at a séance I went to in Bayswater."

"That might be a freak of the imagination, for who knows that the dead do return?"

Mr. Steel looked curiously at the young man whom he had not seen for so long, but about whom he had heard so many peculiar tales. To have an eccentric master who paid him well and left him alone suited him perfectly. He was a man of science who had lived a solitary and, in a way, a selfish life. He never left the brick house and the conservatory at Charters and had long seen the last of any relations, nor had he many friends. He was quite ready in a cool way to undertake any curious project on his own lines, and had already made some few discoveries and created some strange flowers, all of which, however, he usually kept secretly and to himself.

The problem of the ghost that haunted the grove did not greatly concern him, though he had heard, on the rare occasions when the late Earl or Mr. Chalmers had visited him, that the heir, now the master, had been unhealthily concerned by these legends.

"Now," urged he, " you must again get the matter straight, sir. My experiments with flowers, the ghosts that I obtain of roses—suppose I obtain this ghost of heliotrope . . . it will not be the same as an apparition of a woman who is already dead and whose body has not been consumed save by decay."

"I suppose not," said Lord Seagrove, "but it might conclude the matter, it might settle all uncertainties once and for all. Supposing we tried the human body or what is left of a human body . . . supposing we took some corpse from the churchyard . . . . ?

"Well, really, sir, I could not play the part of a resurrection man—well, there's something unholy and unpleasant about it——"

"There is? That's what I should like to decide. I say, supposing we obtained what was left of a corpse, perhaps only a few frail bones, and you reduced them to ashes and then treated them as you will treat the heliotrope, we might see *her* as she really was. That might decide whether the apparition of Bayswater and this woman who so often crosses my path really is Harriet Bond."

"It is a fantasy beyond discussion," protested the botanist. "I should not let your mind, sir, dwell on such things. It would be unlawful if you are thinking of disturbing the grave of Harriet Bond—remember that it lies in sacred ground—the talk and the scandal would undo you and the result, I am convinced, would be null. Rather come with me again into the conservatory and mark the beauty of my tropic plants, the orchids growing out of these brown damp feathered trunks, the waxen lilies," and he took the young man's arms, gently removing him from the library and closing the door behind him, "that float on those still waters—the lotus of the Egyptians, the most exquisite of pink and white petals . . . . "

"I prefer our flat English water lilies. I suppose there were water lilies on the pond . . . " He broke off. "But it wasn't a pond, it was merely a pit of water where they had been digging for the foundation of the Folly. You know I'm going to have it destroyed."

"Yes, sir, I heard that Sir Henry Dering was coming down and that you were reconstructing Charters. It seems a pity in a way. It is a fine building, surely it needs only a little reconstruction here and there."

"It's too large, there are too many presses and cupboards with things hidden away."

"Well, when you marry, sir, I daresay your good lady will find a use for all the rooms and all the presses and cupboards too—your establishment is very small, if I may say so."

"It's all I need," said the young man slowly. "I think I'll go to Verities. If you were in my place, would you have that ugly copy of the Temple of the Winds taken away and the coffins put in the family vault in the churchyard?"

"Yes, I certainly should, the building is shoddily made and looks incongruous in an English landscape; besides the design was too common. There were so many great families who came back from the grand tour with sketches of these ancient temples. The Folly is the copy of a pavilion of a villa on the Brenta . . . well, it was the mode of the moment. I should certainly have it removed now . . . . But cannot I beg your attention to my stove-plants?"

"Your men work here all day stripped to the waist?" remarked the other idly.

"Yes, in a sweat. These plants could not survive in anything less than this tropic heat. I fear we cost you a great deal for tons of coke."

"Yes, they are very beautiful and strange and seem worth being kept alive in this unnatural manner. The canister of flowers that you sent me the other day had a peculiar effect on me."

"I often send you specimens, sir. I don't know if Mr. Chalmers or Hackett allow you to have them."

"These fell all over the copy of *The Times* and my breakfast service. Yes, you may be certain," he said in hurried tones, "that whatever I cut down here, I shall not cut down any expense on your horticulture . . . and I wish we could make that experiment with a human being."

"But, sir, consider that even if anything so fantastical was possible, and the wraith did appear, what use would it be? No more than your Bayswater spectre. It wouldn't speak or explain itself. The recalled rose has no colour, no light, no radiance—it is at first but a dim cloud and afterwards but a vague shape."

"It has risen again from its ashes. That would be all I should want."

* * * * *

Adelaide wrote boldly to Charters . . . one of her usual letters, signed with her name of Cara, addressed at the top to 'Basil,' but inscribed on the outside to 'The Earl of Seagrove.' In this she demanded a ticket for the Assembly Ball and begged him to take this opportunity of acknowledging her before everyone as, in her own words, 'his destined bride.'

Carrie was not told of this piece of imprudence. Adelaide posted the letter herself at the small village post office; she told Carrie as little as she could. She began to feel increasingly from day to day the weight of the espionage, the blackmail. She turned to her mother for a little support, but that woman was confused and heavy and kept sullenly and obstinately to what she called 'facts' . . . what Mr. Bisset would advise, what they might get before the young fool went out of his wits, so she was not the proper confidant for Adelaide's softer emotions.

There was a drag in time, as it seemed, to all three women, for Lord Seagrove went to Verities and stagnation fell upon the place. The Spring passed without any of them noticing it; the seasons meant nothing, not even to Adelaide, as a romantic background. All her thoughts and wishes were artificial and fanciful. She fretted to go to London to spend some of the money she had obtained from the young Earl. She eagerly read again and again the ladies' magazines that were sent for her from London; dwelling on cosmetics, bonnets, modes of wearing the hair in ringlets, what was the fashion at the court, what was worn in the *haute monde* as these elegant annuals termed high society. What was the use of the money in Mullenbridge? Miss Herle, who was the best *modeste* there, asked too many questions and looked at her too keenly.

Adelaide brooded, became dissatisfied with her destiny to an even more acute degree, and finally developed megrims and retired sullen and sulky to her sole privacy, the bed in the room she shared with Carrie.[33]

There she brooded over the Assembly Ball, the fact that he had not answered her letter, and what she had heard of his visit to Wales and how she could combine all her schemes. At times she felt a little light-headed and scarcely knew what had happened or what was likely to happen, and moaned in a half-delirium for her lost lover.

Mrs. Fenton, also waiting for the report from Mr. Bisset, outwardly concerned herself with the cherries that grew on a small wall at the back of the house—an espalier of morello cherries that had been there when she had taken over the house, nailed by strips of cloth to the bricks, themselves of a rosy colour, the smooth branches spread the length of this low wall over which Adelaide had to step every time she went into the sloping churchyard. The crop this year was abundant and Mrs. Fenton remarked on the bitter-sweet smell which exactly resembled that of the few plants of heliotrope that she had planted next the cottage wall. It was not heliotrope to her but 'cherry pie,' and the two, fruit and flower, became associated in her mind. Cherries . . . as they, small, even

33 Megrims: migraines.

coloured, and almost translucent, ripened, she decided to make them into brandy. She was skilful at these small household arts and both she and Susan took a considerable interest in neat labours.

She set Carrie to pluck the cherries one summer morning when the clouds were curdled overhead like slightly souring cream touched by an idle hand, and in between were vistas of sky the colour of a bluebell. Carrie gathered the cherries skilfully, breaking them off with the stem. She knew if you left the stem on the tree the fruit would rot before it could be put down with the brandy and the bay rum in the earthenware crocks to wait the long transformation into brandy. She did not dislike her work as a means of passing time. It pleased her to see her smooth, well-kept white hand against the rough pink brick, the clusters of pointed leaves and the small shining fruit. She filled her baskets, took them into the kitchen to Susan and Mrs. Fenton and then went out again to see if by any chance she had overlooked some of the cherries; but the tree was stripped of all save the fine yellowing leaves. So while Adelaide was sick and Mrs. Fenton was absorbed in making cherry brandy and waiting for what Mr. Bisset would say, Caroline thought she would go up to the town to see if she could find out anything . . . .

She vaulted the wall and took the well-kept path than ran up between the graves on the slope. These were all of the native stone and had weathered into the colour of the landscape. They were covered with small mosses, cups of gold and silver, that had pitted them like a disease. On many of them grew stout tendrils of ivy that clung to the stone with hairy suckers; the work of long dead stonemasons still showed faintly—here a cherub's head, there a text hardly to be deciphered, there again perhaps some crude ornamentation.

Carrie reached the church, and peered in. Well, nobody troubled about the new marble tomb to the young man who had been drowned in Rome. It was there in its strong wooden packing cases taking up a great part of the church. Where were they going to set it up? There did not seem, to her, any space. She peered curiously between the straw, admiring the beautiful texture of the stone, trying to make out something of the design, but this was impossible.

She passed out again into what had been called 'the potter's field' where lay the Jew, the blackamoor, the escaped slave with the collar of steel on his neck, and the French sailor from whose grave grew the plums of pale amber hue that no one would eat—and the neat tomb of Harriet Bond. "A broken and contrite heart," sneered Carrie. Her keen glance, and it was very keen lately, observed that the tomb had lately been cleaned. 'I wonder if he is mad enough to send people down from Charters to do that,' she thought, 'or does he come himself?'

She passed out of the lych gate into the road and the first straggle of houses that comprised the beginning of the town of Mullenbridge. The sun was clear on the bow-fronted shops, with their green glass and their poor display of goods . . . on the gossips, some old-fashioned enough to still have spinning wheels, others knitting or merely drowsing in the sun. In the town square she saw Mr. Bisset's boy leaning against the old weigh-house with a straw in his mouth and talking to a lad of his own age who came from the haberdasher's shop.

Caroline put her fingers ostentatiously into her reticule. Mr. Bisset's lad saw her and sauntered away from his companion.

"Do you know anything? Have you found out anything?" asked Carrie.

"My master doesn't tell me anything," muttered the boy sullenly, keeping his eyes on the sunny cobbles, "and I don't think there's any chance to look at his papers—he is cunning-like and locks everything up. But the Earl's back; he came to Charters this morning."

"That's worth a shilling," said Carrie. Coolly, she took this coin from her bag and pressed it in the youth's hand. "I hope next time I see you, you will bring me something that's worth more."

She sauntered on along the High Street. They were taking the harvest in and the day was closing. The wains passed by piled with stooks of corn, labourers in their smocks were outside the 'Seagrove Arms' drinking their ale. Carrie nodded pleasantly to all of them.

She was soon free of the town and out into the lane where the briony and the bramble trails had replaced the blackthorn, the honeysuckle and the wild rose.

"He will go straight there, of course," she said, "and I shall have a chance of talking to him."

She passed into the park and through the grove, looking at it with a cold incurious eye. Those two buildings meant no more to her than if they had been of cardboard and she could have pushed them over with her fist or foot, nor did the still trailing draperies and shields set up for the late Earl affect her at all.

She went to the Pavilion, noticed two of the windows were unshuttered and scratched on the door. As she expected, his voice bade her enter. She did so at once and with an air of confidence. He was seated where he had been seated when Adelaide had found him, with a pile of books before him. He frowned and looked at her with distaste and suspicion.

"I didn't know," he remarked, "that anyone was aware that I

had returned to-day—and who are you? Does she take another form that I must talk to in the language of this world?"

"It would be to your advantage to listen," said Carrie. "I have some likeness to my sister I know, but I am not Adelaide any more than Adelaide is Harriet Bond."

She looked at him with a more observant and a kindlier eye than had Adelaide; having never made out of him a fantastic, romantic figure she judged him more favourably. She thought he was comely and she was sorry for him; yes, compassionate, for this young woman, who was so hard and worldly, and so despised and used her own relatives, was capable of pity and compassion. She had on occasion saved flies from spider's nets and drowning birds from streams or from the coarse netting that Mrs. Fenton put over the currant bushes. She noticed, too, that the young man had a thick greenish glass beside him, in which was a small spray of a common plant—cherry pie; the perfume was just perceptible in the damp stale air of the Pavilion.

"I'm not more to you than, I suppose, a servant girl," added Carrie, "but I'd like you to think of me as another human being. Our stories are both, I dare say, a little odd."

"I don't want to hear yours, nor to brood on mine now. I'm always intruded on—these grounds are private; I have told everyone this. I will not have trespassing."

"It would be well for you to listen to me," insisted Caroline firmly. "If you don't, I shall take everything I have to say to those old men—the parson, or the Swedenborgian. I rather respect Dr. Perry; as I told you, we used to have talks when he and I were in the lanes together. Now, sir, will you listen to me? My sister and my mother are trying to involve you in some sort of a scandal and a confusion that you will find very difficult to cut your way out of; my mother is ignorant and clumsy, but she has a sharp, vulgar attorney as her accomplice, and my sister, whom I regard as almost unsettled in her wits, is capable of the strangest actions in the furtherance of her plans. Now you've played into their hands . . . . I suppose you've been warned . . . " continued Carrie, looking round, "that you've played into their hands?"

"What are you looking for—the place where she was buried?" asked the Earl. "I think it is over there, but of course they dug the foundations over. If one wanted what was left of her—a handful of bones or ashes—one would have to go to St. Jude's."

"That is not the way to talk. It is over and done with, there are no spectres but in your mind. The girl was done to death by a common brute as I suppose, who had both her and the young man in his clutches . . . half-witted, there you have it; but if you are in a big enough position, people don't use those words. Well, I'm the key point of this conspiracy."

"Conspiracy?" repeated the other. He gazed at the spray of heliotrope; the word did not startle him for long. "Do you believe that *that* could be reduced to ashes and then brought to its own form again?"

"No, of course not," smiled Carrie. "It's a bit of cherry pie, ordinary enough. I was picking morello cherries this morning; maybe we'll have a pie or two before Mother uses them all for brandy. They are put in a crock and pickled and change——"

"Well, there you are again," he broke in, "everything is changed—the flower, the spirit . . . changed, you know, not a shadow left."

"Not even a shadow left," agreed Carrie. "There is not even a shadow of Harriet Bond; my sister is rather like her, or thinks she is. She got a white dress and green sash after she had seen that picture. She found the whole story at my Aunt Martha's in an old *Gentleman's Magazine*, in a cupboard."

"Too much in cupboards, too much hidden away."

"Well, sir, I know you are a great gentleman, but I don't somehow feel afraid of you. I'm sorry for you. You see, I want to get away from here—this place is only a stepping-stone for me. I am past eighteen and I have got other ideas in my head. You sent money down to Adelaide to pay her bills—of course, nobody, not even a sharp lawyer, would be able to prove what you sent it for—but it will look a bit queer, won't it?—and then you sent a letter. And what about the Assembly Ball, are you going to send her a ticket? She's made herself ill worrying about that. She don't know you are back from Verities. I thought it was time this stopped . . . ."

"I don't understand," said the young man, rising in great agitation. "Indeed, I don't understand—maybe . . . I feel that my mind is a little cloudy . . . I think I should have advice before I listen to you."

"And I," said Caroline firmly, "feel that you should understand before you take advice. You may find yourself paying for a breach of promise case—and a number of letters and presents will be put in, and a number of people will be brought forward saying that they have seen you and my sister together, and this old story of a ghost will just be left out. They know you are a rich man and they'll make you pay. I must say my sole concern is money, too, and I think I'd rather have it from you than from them."

She took off her bonnet, which was of grey merino, and swung it by the coarse ribbon strings. "Don't you see that I'm not afraid of you, or the ghosts, or this place, or Mother, or Mullenbridge—I think I was born fearless. When I wasn't so long from school, I was satisfied to lie for the bit of trumpery that Adelaide used to give me. I knew what she was doing even then; but now what she can give me isn't worth while. I don't think they'd get that case, and there would be nothing for any of us, and we should be shamed and disgraced and have to leave Mullenbridge under a cloud, with Father in the state he is—and Adelaide, I suppose, would fair go off her head and have to be clapped up, so I thought I'd come to you. Have you understood what I have said?"

"In a way," said the young man nervously, "in a way, but I still believe what I believed before you came."

"Well, keep the two things separate in your head if you like, *I* don't know what you *do* believe. I don't know how far it has gone with you; but I'd like to make you an offer. You see, I'm their principal witness."

She paused, hoping these words would have some effect. The youth only nervously tapped the table with his fingers and stared at the little spray of heliotrope.

"Don't you understand I've got it all in the palm of my hand? They rely on me, the innocent schoolgirl, who wouldn't be able to make up a falsehood, who saw you visit us, who took you up to Father's bedside, who heard you promise Adelaide a pianoforte, who saw her receive your letters. Well, I can go back on all that for a price, and the whole thing would fall through, wouldn't it?"

"I suppose so," he said sternly. "What difference would it make to me? I don't think that I have quite understood."

"There isn't much time," said Carrie. "I wish I could have found you before, but of course it is difficult, we being of such different stations in life; but if you could get away from here your wits would settle, and if I was to go to Mr. Bisset or to your lawyer and say that I'd been lying, the whole thing would fit together like a puzzle; and *nobody has seen Harriet Bond.* It's an old wives' tale—and nobody will see her."

The haunted man looked with great attention at the bold, handsome creature who made him this proposition that he could not, indeed, completely grasp but yet seemed to him kindly and to hold something of comfort.

"Money is nothing for me to give," he said. "You could have what you wanted as far as that went." Then he added in great trepidation: "But she insists on being present at the Assembly Ball—is there one? I didn't get her letter, though."

"No, I expect your letters are intercepted. I don't know whether they keep them or burn them, I don't know what good advice you've got—the old parson's drinking more every day, everyone can see that, and Dr. Perry hasn't been here for some time and he's got half his head in the clouds. You ought to rely on me. Pay me. I hate them anyway—I hate my mother, and hate my sister . . . I don't love my father . . . who could? I'd give Susan a pension and with the rest I'd get away, and you should get away, too, then there'd be an end of it. If you don't do it, mischief's going to happen."

"Mischief's happened already," he said gloomily.

"Yes, but you could get out of it, like the fly gets out of the spider's web. It's not closed you in yet. Look at you now—sitting here in this place! What is it? Nothing. What is that old burial place? Nothing, either. Be done with all these bones and ashes."

"Bones and ashes? Queer you should say that. Mr. Steel's making an experiment . . . . "

"Don't have anything to do with it," said Carrie contemptuously. "We're flesh and blood and got to deal with matters of flesh and blood. If you'll give me a thousand pounds in Bank of England notes, I'll save you from all of it. You can get away from Adelaide and the ghost and the gossip and the things they are saying about you—and this silly old story and everything, for a thousand pounds. I'll go with you to the parson or your lawyer or anyone you like and tell the truth."

"But nobody knows the truth."

"*I* do," she insisted. "I know a certain aspect of the truth that would set you free. Don't you see, they're only trying to bleed you? Soon they'll be faking spectres. It's done, you know . . . lights in the churchyard—I know; somebody in a white sheet . . . . I tell you, I'm sorry for you, for all you've got and don't know how to use. A thousand pounds is not much to you, I'll be bound. I expect I'm asking too little."

"No, it's not much," the young man admitted simply. "I have not gone into my fortunes yet, having had little interest, but I know it's not much for me. I'm going to have Charters pulled down—no hiding places, you understand, no cupboards and presses where things can be found. *This* is going, too, and the Mausoleum. Sir Henry Dering is coming to-morrow."

"Well, then, why do you hesitate? Give me the money and set yourself free. Do me a good turn at the same time, and those other fools, too, because they won't know how to manage the thing and they may find themselves in prison . . . . "

"But how," he said sternly, "can I respect anyone who comes asking me for money—a young girl, too?"

"Money is the one solid thing in this case. Without it—well, I'll keep to my lies and let you go on struggling in the snare, and take my chances with them; and I don't say they won't be ruined—but there's a fair chance you will be, too."

"I'll think it over," he said hurriedly, "I'll think it over."

"Don't be a fool," said Carrie with some violence. "There's no time to think anything over. I know what you're brooding over,

I know what she's brooding over—tossing about on her bed and making herself ill—the Assembly Dance and the white rose in her hair! It's all—well, evil, I think. I don't believe I'm doing a wicked thing in asking you for a thousand pounds. It will be put to a good purpose, I can assure you."

The young man was glancing uneasily at the sprig of heliotrope. "There are a few experiments I want to make," he muttered. "Of course you shall have your money."

"But not like that—you've got to understand what you're paying it for; you will have to get a lawyer, or at least Mr. Chalmers, if you can get him sober now, or Dr. Perry, or somebody. Well, you've got friends in the great world, haven't you?"

"I suppose so—too many friends, but my mind has been set in one direction only for a long, long time."

"Yes, so has Adelaide's, and I don't know which is the bigger fool! What are these ugly pictures that you've got here?"

She looked at the monochrome landscapes between the windows and touched with a firm white finger the scene of the lake that was for ever connected in Lord Seagrove's mind with Lake Nemmi. "They mean something to you, they make you shudder," she added. "Well, you should have them all burnt." She took her bonnet from the chair, where she had left it hanging when she rose, and swung it on her arm and said earnestly, and still with that note of strong compassion: "You should give me the money, you should make haste or it will be too late . . . . and it always seemed to me, even when I was a child, that those were *awful* words—too late!"

*　*　*　*　*

Sir Henry Dering, who brought with him a company of friends and fellow artists, decorators and sculptors, men of the first rank as he pleasantly termed them, arrived at Charters with an air both of complacence and pomp. He was a fashionable architect who had already remodelled in the Gothic style many Tudor and Jacobean buildings. The owner of Charters disliked him immediately and was inclined to fly to the company of the Reverend Timothy, who, however, refused to support him in his half-defiance, half-rebellion.

"Exactly what you want, James," said the cleric, who had got a flavour of his lost days of pleasure and power from the intrusion of these strangers into Charters. "The place seems more normal now, more human, with people measuring up the cupboards . . . ."

"Why do you talk of cupboards?" exclaimed the young Earl. "Isn't there anything more important in the place than cupboards?"

"Well, you know what I mean," smiled the Reverend Timothy. "Presses and closets—and it's a medley, anyhow; the house, a wing built on here and a wing built on there, and that curious screen inside the door with the busts of the Cæsars. They think that was put there in the reign of James the First but it will have to go anyhow."

"I suppose it will cost a good deal of money."

"Oh, Sir Henry will let you down lightly; it will add to his reputation to make the place what he calls 'civilized.' "

"I shall never live in it!" declared the young man moodily.

"Oh, perhaps you will," nodded the Reverend Timothy. "One never knows, at your age one's moods change, and often quickly. Why, I've known Charters all my life; I've had my pleasant times here. Well, I'm not sorry to see it change. There come times, you know, when the oldest things have to be rebuilt."

Sir Henry expressed himself in many elaborate terms on the task before him. He considered Charters and the ruined keep an ugly medley of various styles—inconvenient, in a way ostentatious, and by no means worth preserving; and although that was not altogether his province, he advised that some of the timber should be cut down. "It is encroaching too near to the house, it casts a shadow into all the windows. It must be worth a good deal of money—those walnuts and elms in particular I should get a contract for."

The young lord agreed without much enthusiasm one way or another. He honestly endeavoured to let these numerous strangers have their way with him; he tried to join in their conversation, which was of topical events of society, gossip from London or of international affairs. They were all worldly men, cool and competent. They brought their servants with them and there was an increase in the staff at Charters. The place became better kept, better lit and in every way more comfortable.

Sir Henry, who was a connoisseur and held a fine collection of pictures in his house in Portland Place, discovered many treasures that had been ignored by the old Earl and were not known of by the young Earl. There was a picture that had been hanging in a bedroom that had not been slept in for a century or so. Sir Henry, delicately flicking the canvas with an elegant thumb, declared it might be a Titian. There was an exquisite cabinet of inlaid tortoiseshell, ebony and ivory that had small painted panels that might perhaps be worthy of a famous name being attached to them. There certainly were some splendid tapestries long since rolled away in the wardrobe room, but kept carefully from moth and mice by diligent servants.

"I cannot imagine," complained the young master wryly, "what the place is going to look like. I cannot see it as Charters."

"Well, you'll soon get used to it," said Sir Henry. "You know if we didn't move a bit with the times we should all be living in the wattle huts of the Saxons," and he laughed foolishly at his own joke.

There was the question of the Pavilion and the Mausoleum, the heart of the whole problem really. The architect was at once for their instant demolition. About the Mausoleum there might be some difficulty; the ground was consecrated and the bishop would have to be consulted. It would mean the removal of a good many bodies to the vault in the church of St. Jude, which perhaps was not large enough. But it was, the architect declared emphatically, an ugly, shoddy piece of work and looked ridiculous in the English fields and as a copy of the Temple of Winds it was absurd. He showed by a rapid sketch and by reference to notebooks that it was out of proportion and only bore a remote likeness to the beautiful original. Still, the question of its demolition had to be put aside for the moment. That of the Pavilion offered no difficulties; all the gentlemen agreed that it should come down at once. Set like that in the grove of elm and lime inside the great gates and too near the Mausoleum, it was positively hideous.

"I do not wish to cast any reflections, sir, upon your ancestor's taste, but it must be confessed that it looks like a schoolboy's effort, something run up by the local mason and daubed by the local painter from a student's design."

"I never considered the taste of it much," said Lord Seagrove harshly; "it has other connections in my mind than those of architectural fitness. I suppose you know the story of it?" he added defiantly—but in all honesty they did not know the story. The local traditions of this out-of-the-way place had never come their way.

Mr. Chalmers, smooth and benign, told them with a yawn that the Pavilion was supposed to house the local ghost. Sir Henry smiled.

"There is hardly anywhere I've been that there is not a local ghost or apparition or wraith," he said. "I am afraid we cannot in our profession pay much attention to the supernatural. You will soon find that people will stop talking of the ghost when the Pavilion's gone."

"It was a Folly," muttered the young man, "such as they used to have in the eighteenth century. You know, sometimes a hermit cell set with skulls, sometimes a tower with a lantern on the top to guide the travellers at night, sometimes a bagatelle, a gaily coloured summer house like this is supposed to be . . . but this was never used, the man who built it died before it was finished and his successor completed it out of bravado."

Sir Henry was polite enough to inquire into these family legends, but received little satisfaction either from the clergyman or the young man. Hackett, however, took an opportunity to enlighten him as to the immense importance of the Pavilion and the way the Mausoleum played in his young master's state of mind.

"I have been with him, sir, since he was a boy . . . I mean, a little fellow, before he went to Italy with Mr. Chalmers. The family had what you might call a run of bad luck; one after another had a violent death when young, leaving just my old lord to reign until he was very old indeed and had forgotten almost everything, and that gives young people a nasty sort of shock. They grew up feeling as if death had mowed a wide space round them."

Sir Henry glanced covertly at the servant. "That is a picturesque expression," he said. "Is there anything really of moment that you have to tell me? I thought I had merely been asked down here by a young man who wished his home reconstructed in modern style."

"It is a bit more than that, sir," urged Hackett. "He is suffering in his mind; he goes to those strange meetings in London. I was in his rooms in St. Jermyn Street when he came back once from one at Bayswater. There was a nasty piece of work around that Pavilion—a girl who was half-witted, as I take it, was murdered—and there was a lot of talk of ghosts and wraiths, and then my lord's ancestor . . . oh! he is of the cadet line, it is not a direct descent, but it is the name and the blood . . . was hanged for it."[34]

"I remember that," said Sir Henry, "yet, moving about as one does and meeting so many people, I had not associated it with Charters. Hm, the Earl of Seagrove who was hanged at Tyburn—an odd tale, but they were odd days; but the best way in which I can help your master, and I thought he seemed rather listless and disinterested, is to at once demolish the Pavilion. It will only be a matter of three or four days if I can get the workmen in from Winchester."

* * * * *

Sir Henry owed a great deal of his success to his business-like temperament. He was, therefore, as good as his word and the frail walls of the Pavilion—wood, stucco, painted canvas—were soon levelled with the fresh summer grass lying in Seagrove Park, rather like a child's monstrous toy destroyed in a fit of temper. A considerable amount of dust, stale and stifling, rose up among the groves of elms and limes, as if some evil creature was offering oblation to some evil deity. It was old-style plaster, the workmen said, bound together with human hair, and had a filthy smell; cheap work, too, and the painter who had accompanied Sir Henry simpered at the poor daubs in monochrome between the latticed windows. He supposed they had been done by some journeyman painter, such as in those days used to go from one village to another,

34 A cadet line is that descended from a younger son.

re-painting the boards outside the inns and, if they were lucky, portraits of the notables of the rural districts at so much a head.

The foundations were, however, solid. The Folly, for some crazy reason, had been built upon a rocky piece of ground. When all the clutter that had formed the long room had been carted away, there remained a considerable scar on the parkland. Sir Henry asked the young owner of Charters what he wished done with it. It would be a long time before grass grew on it, he remarked, "they seem to have been making foundations of a much larger and more important building, and then to have satisfied themselves with this trumpery affair."

"That is exactly how it would have been," replied Lord Seagrove sullenly. "Don't you understand that my ancestor intended to have an expensive and extravagant building here? and that when he was——" he checked himself and looked aside, "when he was taken away . . . " he went on forcing himself to use words that were distasteful to him, "his successor was advised to let the Folly go, but by no means would do so, but put up this shoddy affair—just as a token."

"The workmen must dig out the foundations," Sir Henry decided, "and try to level the ground, and perhaps a small grove of trees might be planted, when we have filled it in with earth. That is where Mr. Steel would come in; he is an extraordinarily able man as regards botany and horticulture." Sir Henry, as one at the top of his profession, knew that he could always afford to pay a compliment to those equally eminent in other professions, and never failed, with mechanical benevolence, to do so.

"Mr. Steel," said the young man, "is entirely for the conservatory, for the exotics, the tropical plants . . . . "

"Yes, yes, I know, but he would be able to advise what you

might plant here. You don't want to see an ugly scar—unless my men chip it away and you have a sort of rugged precipice. There is no water near by that could be brought to rush down in a cascade?"

"No water that would wash it away," replied the young man solemnly.

He stood with Sir Henry on the broken ground where the Pavilion had been. It was most peculiar to him to see empty space with his outer eye and with his inner eye the Pavilion. He would never lose that, he knew; even if he lived to extreme old age it would never vanish—always when he chose, and sometimes, he feared, when he did not choose, it would be before him . . . with its latticed windows, its pictures in monochrome, one of which would always remind him of Lake Nemmi, with the chairs of Italian chestnut painted grey, and the hard cushions, with those figures of women crossing up and down, there seemed to be three of them now—Harriet Bond, who had once been buried there, the girl who had come to him with her handkerchief full of cowslips and had asked for money, and the other girl who had so much of her likeness who had demanded of him a thousand pounds. He meant, when the time was favourable, to think that proposition over, to endeavour to get it clear in his mind. Perhaps he would ask Mr. Chalmers' advice about it, or travel to London and search out Lucas Perry, but when by himself he endeavoured to get the matter clear he found that his brain jolted all the circumstances into a broken pattern; the steep banks of Lake Nemmi with the cyclamen and the trees marked with chalk that showed the way from the water to the campagna, his father's hat floating on the black waters and the faces of the horses as they struggled towards the shore; Harriet Bond, in the form of a fairy, a child with an ugly old woman's voice on the causeway meeting the crazy young man who had ended in a lunatic asylum . . . and the girl who had met him by the grave in St. Jude's so often, who had stared at him across the pews, across the faces and decorous black draperies of all his relatives at his grandfather's funeral . . . the girl who had come with a handkerchief tied full of cowslips; and the other girl who had spoken to him in such different tones and asked for a thousand pounds and said something about the Assembly and a ticket. Were they the same? If one believed in evil spirits, if one believed that *they* came back, one must believe that they could take very different forms.

These three fused and shifted before his eyes as had the balls of fire in the fusty back drawing-room at the Bayswater house . . . always the white dress and the green sash . . . so she had appeared from the table that assumed an icy surface. Who had taken from it the pearl-coloured globe lamp and the chenille cloth? He had not noticed any of the women doing that.

He tried to put these matters out of his mind. He must have advice, good advice. For three days or so he had not seen any version of the spectre. He admitted that the house was more cheerful with these companionable worldlings about it, with more servants, with newspapers here and there and discussions of what was happening abroad; he admitted that he seemed in a great way rested.

He supposed he was glad that the Pavilion had gone. He wondered if there would be any talk about it in Mullenbridge. He watched the bonfire they made of the wood and canvas. There was so much clay and rubble and plaster that for a while it burned, as it were, reluctantly, but the dry wood soon caught and the pictures in monochrome and the slats and the *persiane* shutters and the table, by which he had sat when the two girls had come to him, and the floor boards and all that outlandish furniture that was, Sir Henry declared, worm-eaten, took on beautiful colours of violet, gold and crimson. Something that had been decaying so slowly, with such noisome odours and over hideous tarnishings, was now transmuted suddenly into a brilliant splendour.

"It's the best way to get rid of it," said Sir Henry. "There's nothing cleanses like fire. You may suppose," he added with a smile, looking rather askance at the pale young man, "that your ghost is going up in those flames. Let's say that's an end of her."

But it was not this aspect of the case that Lord Seagrove thought of, the word *transmutation* had taken his fancy. That seemed to be behind everything . . . the flowers were transmuted into ashes, then into their own ghostly likeness; the human soul, when the body was decayed, was transmuted into a fetch or wraith.

He left his companions much to themselves, with their blue-prints and their discussions and their plans and schemes that, after all, did not concern him very much. Sir Henry was quite interested in his work and had been promised a handsome fee; he was an enthusiast in the mode of the moment, nineteenth-century Gothic . . . . He believe that he could turn Charters into a very pretty building, and that if he pleased this moody and rather careless young man, who seemed to have more time and money than was good for him, well, then, he might get the commission for altering Verities, that he had not yet seen, in the same style. So, with the laboratory at his disposal, and his assistants coming and going, his friends the painters and sculptors advising this and that in the way of paintings and statues, he was a busy man and scarcely noticed that Lord Seagrove withdrew more and more from his company.

It was to Mr. Abraham Steel, at the small brick house and neat precise laboratory, that the young man went whenever he could with decency neglect his guests. Mr. Steel wished to discontinue his experiment with the heliotrope. It was difficult, it was whimsical, it was slow . . . it meant the reading of a great many books in Greek, Latin and German. His employer was not sufficiently accomplished to be a useful assistant, and Mr. Steel became rather agitated in trying to explain to the eager youth what was to himself incomprehensible; but Lord Seagrove insisted that they should continue to see if they could produce, from the salts of the heliotrope, the cloudy ghost of the flower.

On arriving at the laboratory one day when the scene was veiled by a continuous cloud that seemed to overspread sky and earth with an equal density, dimming both light and colour, he found to his deep vexation that Mr. Steel was absent and had, without asking permission, gone to London. This left Lord Seagrove with blank hours heavy as weights in his hands. His distaste for Sir Henry Dering and his companions was growing. The day, too, lowered on his spirits, no breath seemed to stir even in the topmost branches of the highest tree. There was no air of summer, though herbage was brilliant with those flowers that began to take on the most vivid and superb hues of the end of the blossoming of the year.

He went up by-lanes to St. Jude's, and visited the church and noticed more with vexation than remorse the cases of marble brought from Massa, still unpacked. He was faintly aware that this negligence was entirely his fault, the rector had written to him several times about it, Mr. Chalmers had spoken to him and he had done nothing. He knew he had no interest in this; his mind was lulled, lazy, turned in another direction. He had not even unrolled the design given him by the Italian artist.

He looked languidly at the walls of the church on which were the cenotaphs of those buried in the Mausoleum.

'All,' he thought contemptuously, 'ostentatious and useless people with their bragging motto and their coat of arms meaning now so little.'

High up in the gloom of the church, heavy with dust and cobwebs, was an ancient tilting helm, worn by one of the Daintrys at some battle of which no one now troubled to remember the date; and in a much mutilated chantry lay another Daintry and his wife, precise in the defaced alabaster, with their rigid features, she with her tight bodice and pleated skirt, every fold hard in the stone, her pointed shoes on a favourite peevish-looking collared hound; he with his feet set against the back of a lion, their hands folded in eternal prayer. Round the bottom of the altar tomb walked the weepers, small figures in monkish attire with long draperies about their heads and cloths to their eyes, much as all those relatives and friends had looked in their weepers and cloths when they had filled this church on the day of his grandfather's funeral.

The place was filled every Sunday and kept cleaned—it had a musty, charnel-house air, and there seemed to him something sinister even about the stiff table on which was written in large letters the Ten Commandments. He had a curious desire to mount the few steps to the pulpit. What must it feel like to stand there with the great Book under one's hand, preaching words of doom and judgment? But he turned aside and by the other door came out into the churchyard. Passing, and without temptation to pause, the spot that he had long haunted, where the French sailor, the blackamoor, the murdered girl and the Jew lay, he came down the slope to the small wall that divided the churchyard from the cottage of the Fentons.

There was a curious smell in the air, different from the smell of must in the church, or the smell of the ancient plaster of the Pavilion. Cherry pie, that was it, someone was making cherry pie. It was like the perfume of the heliotrope . . . one of those vulgar names that were very fitting.

He lingered by the wall; there was no one to be seen. Where was the girl, or the girls? Would it be as well to pay her a thousand pounds? Would she really save him from some tangible annoyance or danger? . . . and which was the girl who had asked him for this large fee, and which was the one who had demanded the ten golden sovereigns and the notes for fifty pounds?

He looked over the wall and saw the stripped cherry tree, with the dark red ringed branches, the small serrated leaves, bare now, not one single fruit. A cherry pie . . . one could smell it . . . the fruit cooking. Well, they would perhaps have one or two dishes of that homely fare and the rest would be laid down, as Mr. Steel was laying down the heliotrope, with spirits, with salts and transmuted into the potent liquor of brandy, he supposed; or would that come back again into the shape of sprays of cherries?

The silence was complete, a storm must be approaching. Like everyone who has lived long in the country, he knew by unconscious observation that before a tempest the birds and insects take shelter and stop their curious noises; this gives that ominous stillness that to the townsman is alarming.

The three women who were so concerned in him and his destiny lost this opportunity of speaking to him, for they were, as he had supposed, enclosed in the kitchen busy with their cooking. Mrs. Fenton was putting the cherry pies, three of them, into the brick oven, and the girls were placing the cherries, layer after layer, into the crock where they were to be salted down for brandy.

Adelaide had not forgotten her passionate need of the ticket for the Assembly Dance, nor had Carrie forgotten her interview in the Pavilion that was now demolished. She intended to wait a day or two longer and then to endeavour to see the Reverend Timothy Chalmers. She knew that her mother had visited Mr. Bisset the day before, under the excuse of carrying to his wife a cherry pie. She herself had helped fold it in the clean napkin and place it in the wattle basket. A delicacy, indeed; there were no morello cherries in Mullenbridge, at least not in any way as fine as those that grew on the wall between the cottage of the Fentons and the churchyard of St. Jude's.

Carrie had accompanied her mother. On the way both of the women had looked up at the large amber plums rotting into decay on the tree above the unknown French sailor's grave. Some of them were on the ground and the wasps were busy with them. They might sink into the lush mould and send up other plum trees, but no one would ever eat of that fruit.

Lord Seagrove turned back again and, as he reached his own ground, met Sir Henry, who approached him with the air of a man who has something important to say.

"A most extraordinary discovery, my dear sir," he exclaimed. "Perhaps you would like to come and see it for yourself. You know the trouble," he went on, in his exact, pompous way, "I have had with the foundations of your Folly . . . we have had to have picks to break the stone . . . . "

The young man said nothing, but whispered to himself: 'She appeared with five wounds in her head, made by a collier's pick.'

"Well, we discovered when we had gone some way through the rock that there was a hole or a tunnelling that had been made for some heavy supports, but never used for it, and in it there were bones, my dear sir—bones!"

"I suppose," said the young man, "there would be. Of course, they never took her to consecrated ground."

"Well, I don't quite know to what you refer . . . to this old crime, I suppose? I couldn't even be sure that they are human bones. I suppose there will have to be an inquest, but they are laid out with portions of a woman's attire . . . mere shreds, you know, that will perish when the air gets to them. There's a white gown and a bit of a green sash and some leather and buttons. Would you like to come and see them for yourself?"

"Not now. I'll go to Charters. I'd like to speak to Mr. Chalmers about this."

* * * * *

The Reverend Timothy Chalmers was much disturbed. To him, no incident could have been more unexpected or more horrible. There had never been in all that he had heard or read of this accursed affair any hint whatsoever that the body of Harriet Bond had not really been moved to consecrated ground, but he could understand that a number of people had banded together, probably pledging themselves by sacred oaths, to play this trick. The rector would not care for the body of the slut (and the foundling who was supposed to be an unlaid spirit) to rest in his churchyard, even if she were given a meagre foot or two in that part where the yew grew and the cyprus. It would have been difficult also to find anyone willing to move the body of the murdered girl.

What about the inquest, he puzzled. Perhaps they came and looked at her as she was there, or more likely she was taken in some crude casket to the 'Seagrove Arms' and then put back again at dead of night, the same way that they used to bury the suicides at the cross-roads. What a trick to play—and that simple grave there—I suppose they buried a coffin with sawdust or stones in it—and then for it to be found like this!

"I suppose, sir," he turned in deep agitation to the young man who sat quietly, too quietly, in the window place, "that you will consider this the reason why her spirit has walked . . . that she desires burial in holy ground? She might be so buried even now . . . the whole affair is so complicated. We don't even know if the coroner sat upon these bones . . . it may be impossible to identify them."

"There will be no need," sighed Lord Seagrove. "I can identify them without the least difficulty."

"Well," rapped out the parson, taking a heavy drink from the glass beside him; this, in his opinion, was not a matter to face when sober, "your fancies won't do, James! It'll have to be a matter of fact from now on. The affair was too hushed up, too many lies were told . . . Well, what does it matter? Perhaps this will lay at rest your 'fetch,' as you call it."

"I'm not thinking of that at all," replied the young man with a smile. "Oh, no, not in the least! I have given orders that the bones are not to be disturbed . . . I haven't seen them yet. In my mind's eye I can behold them very clearly . . . a few fragments of white dress . . . a few tatters of a green sash . . . nothing else. No jewel, no ornament, no reticule in which might be miraculously preserved some papers bearing on the secret . . . ."

"Nothing of that kind whatsoever," agreed Mr. Chalmers briskly. "If you'll take my advice you'll go to Verities or to London—leave this to Sir Henry, who, mind you, is not in the least concerned, who views the whole matter as a curiosity."

"They had to use a collier's pick."

"Not a collier's pick—a workman's pick."

Mr. Chalmers felt his burden was becoming too heavy for him. He must have advice; that night he would write to London—to the young man's nearest relations, to physicians, to lawyers, to any and everyone whom he could think of . . . . This had gone on long enough . . . it ought to have ended before they found the bones . . . .

The old tutor sat down conscientiously to a heavy correspondence and with his own hand wrote out the bare details of the case, and his conviction of what he considered the state of his one-time pupil's mind. The labour was hard for one of his years and habit of body; it was done as a duty, and he helped himself, as he sat in the old library, with constant drinking. There was no one now to prevent him ordering what he would from the handsomely stocked cellars. Shortly before he died the old Earl had said to him: "Drink yourself to death, Timothy—we ought to both have done that years ago."

His letters finished, he sat back with a sigh of physical weariness. Well, Charters was to be destroyed, and he probably . . . well, he hoped as much . . . would be dead before this new sham Gothic castle rose on its site. All the volumes in this library now, those tomes of theological works, those sermons and exhortations, those treatises and editions of the classics bound in the vellum and parchment that was cracking for lack of oiling over the long sepia lettering and the purple dyes . . . would there be a bonfire made of them as there had been of the Pavilion? They were only rubbish . . . so many books in the world and no need to read one of them. He had written a few himself, he remembered, in his time; he had been obliged to—a younger son thrown into the Church because there was a safe living in the family's gift. Well, he'd had his pleasant days, his gay and dangerous days, too.

Lord Seagrove had been a good friend to him. They had stood together through all those dismal tragedies . . . the young dying one by one, so close together . . . the two deaths in Rome—cholera and the horse slipping into Lake Nemmi, the *duello* in Paris over some crazy nonsense and the children as if snatched up by the angel of death one by one until there was only James left to bear it all. "And it's been too much for him, poor lad. Well, I'll get him free if I can. He'd be better in a lunatic asylum than here . . . . I wish the storm would come."

He rose, shuffling down the long room, holding in his hand the candle by the light of which he had worked. He had had to renew and snuff the candles continually during his tedious correspondence. Well, the letters were all signed and sealed. Hackett could take them to the post to-morrow. Surely somebody would come and help him—he was only a poor old man at the end of things who had done his best.

The Reverend Timothy went to the window, putting his candle apart on a table where the draught would not at once quench it, and opened the shutters, lifting the heavy bar with some difficulty. The night was dark and very still, there was not enough air to put out his light. He could hear nothing . . . not even the rustle of a tree, not even the bay of a watch-dog. He could see nothing . . . not even the dimmest sparkle of a star.

Well, those Fentons seemed to be quiet; they had given up their ignorant, crazy game, whatever it was . . . . He had not seen either of the girls creeping round the grave for some time. Sir Henry, tiresome and boisterous as he might be with his pretentious crowd of fellow artists, at least had kept off something not so wholesome as their vanity.

It was uncommon to look into such intense darkness; he

remembered when he had been in Rome with James, and they had glanced out, by chance, moving aside a curtain of cerise-coloured velvet, on to a night that was laced by glittering fireflies. One had no such pretty freaks in England . . . . There would be a spatter of rain soon and the storm would come up with vivid lightning that would seem to cut the earth and the sky in half; thunder and lightning that could now be more or less explained, yet that nevertheless made the worldly think of the last judgment and hell-fire.

He wondered what they had done with those bones . . . left them untouched, he supposed, covered by sacking. That was an odd business—that would be either quite cleared up or entirely forgotten. This leaving of things in cupboards, he thought . . . yes, old magazines with garbled stories in them . . . and crude paintings . . . things hidden away. Had not her bones been hidden away, too? The sham in the churchyard . . . sawdust or stones with the mocking cross above . . . If the rain came down heavily it might wash away that frail memorial of Harriet Bond (if it were she)—the old man, in his tired excited fancy, saw the shreds and fragments of what had once been a human body flowing, with the heavy waters of the Heaven, down the disturbed, hacked earth on to the high road, through Mullenbridge into, perhaps, at last, consecrated ground.

* * * * *

The Earl's thoughts were far different from these. He had left Charters and the company of Sir Henry Dering and his friends, who were amusing themselves in a moderate kind of way with card games and learned conversation, for the brick house of Mr. Abraham Steel. The botanist had returned by the last train from London and driven home in his little gig. He was surprised and rather uneasy at finding his employer waiting for him and was the more perturbed when he heard related in curt tones the discovery which had been made in the foundations of the Folly.

"Well, I suppose it's one of those 'finds' which are always happening." He tried to make his voice matter-of-fact. "They never take down an old house, do they, but some kind of bones or relics are found in the walls or under the laths? I shouldn't make anything of it, sir—if it is to do with what you think it has, it's an old wrong-doing and been paid for. I don't know the legal aspect of it, of course . . . coroner's jury, I suppose?" he added doubtfully.

"But there was a coroners inquest on Harriet Bond," replied the young man. "You see, they were superstitious. After the fuller's story of the ghost they did not want her in the churchyard. Who would have crossed by St. Jude's at night if she had been buried there? Everyone was agreed on that . . . so they put her where they found her. After all, they didn't know who she was. A foundling, a half-wit, a changeling perhaps . . . ."

"Well, sir, that's the language of fairy stories; we know now in this scientific age that there is no such thing as a changeling . . . ."

"You with your scientific age," replied the other sternly, "know only enough to confuse the issues. I could put to your most renowned man of science question after question that he could not answer."

"I dare say, sir, but life's scarcely worth living if one keeps puzzling about these incomprehensible mysteries."

"Life is scarcely worth living if one is surrounded by incomprehensible mysteries. Now, Steel," he put forward his thin hand and took the other by the cuff, "here is our chance . . . put, in an almost miraculous manner, in our way. You can make with those bones the experiment you intended to make, or are making with the heliotrope."

The botanist drew away.

"Why do you turn aside? Your very look seems to refuse me," urged the young man. "You're not superstitious, are you? You're not even, as I take it, an orthodox Christian? I can, without the least trouble, have those ashes of humanity brought here. They can be reduced further, to their essence as you reduce the plants to their essential salts. They can be placed in a large jar of crystal and perhaps from the obscure cloud that arises from them we shall see the likeness of Harriet Bond."

Mr. Abraham Steel had gone far in speculations of many kinds in his time. He was a man of independent thought and rather cold feeling, who lived for his profession alone, and he could not himself have explained why this suggestion filled him with horror, almost with terror. Young Seagrove appeared sane enough—there was nothing wild in his look or his demeanour; and Mr. Steel knew well enough of the experiments that were made, and had been made for many hundred years past, not only in colleges and universities, but in the laboratories of private houses where there was enough leisure, wealth and learning. Yet he was uneasy. He made the excuse of fatigue, he could not talk to-night.

"What did you go to London for?" asked the young man impatiently. "There was no need . . . I have been waiting here for hours. It's not so easy to get away from that crowd that Sir Henry's brought with him."

"Well, that is a thing I cannot understand either," said Mr. Steel, glad to divert the conversation. "You do not like Sir Henry, you do not care for his style of architecture, you do not want Charters made into a sham Gothic appearance . . . it will cost you a good many thousands—why do you put up with it?"

"Because it doesn't matter to me one way or the other. My mind's set on another path. Why won't you help me?"

"Well, I suppose, because apart from everything else it is nonsense, it is a confusion of ideas. Supposing we were successful—and I don't suppose we should be for one moment—and brought back this wraith, or fetch, or whatever you call it—what would we have but a shadow, a cloud? It wouldn't be able to speak, to tell you anything——"

"I don't know . . . . I thought when I saw her in that Bayswater drawing-room she was on the verge of speaking, and then I fell forward and hit the table—but all that is odd, Steel, there was not any bruise on my head afterwards, and it seems to me that if I'd fallen forward as they said I did, I should have upset the lamp."

"Well, you see, sir, what it comes to is, that everything to do with this business *is* a confusion—you want to go away and clear your mind. I think you should give up this experiment with the flowers; I'm not very keen on it myself. I can tell you of others equally interesting; a man who has just returned from Egypt gave me some seeds to-day that I believe will produce the most stupendous blooms. We could build a hot house for them alone . . . you used to be interested in horticulture . . . take that up again, sir, or leave Charters altogether. Turn your mind from these old tales."

"It's no good," frowned the young man, "for all of you to try to discourage me. I am, after all, the master. I can send you and Chalmers and Hackett and everybody who has been spying on me and watching me for so long, away. I can ask Sir Henry to go, then I can do exactly as I please."

"That's rather childish talk, if you will allow me, sir. As for me, you've not seen me for some years, save perhaps passing in the gardens, and there has been no more than a polite salutation between us. If you were to behave in a peculiar manner to Sir Henry, he would be offended, but forget after a time . . . Chalmers has his pension, Hackett too. The person on whom all this would rebound would be yourself. We should all know where to go and what to do, we've all got our interests and our lives. There are other conservatories in the country that would employ me. Don't you see what I'm coming to?" He looked keenly at the young man, and the earnestness of his speech held Lord Seagrove's distraught attention against his will. "We should all go our several ways in our normal occupations, and you would be left alone in Charters and probably lose your senses."

"That is very presumptuous of you to speak to me like that! I am as sane as any of you; I, perhaps, see a little further than any of you."

"Well," sighed Mr. Steel with something of a yawn, for physical fatigue was really beginning to tell on him, the train journey had been tedious and exhausting and he had transacted much business in London going here and there in a hansom cab that had shaken him over the cobbles, "it's a heavy night, with a storm coming up, I think. Will you sleep here instead of going across the park to Charters? It's very dark and you don't seem to have brought anyone with you—or shall I send my man?—I expect he's abed, but I can arouse him."

"I have got a dark lantern if I wish to return," said Lord Seagrove, "but first I wish to come to an issue with you. I think it childish and ungracious of you to refuse to help make this experiment. Why, it has been put, as it were, in our hands—how else could we have hoped to have had such a chance."

"Well, I don't know—I daresay the Royal College of Surgeons could have provided us with some specimens if we'd asked them.

Forgive me, sir, but you are not very experienced. Science has been rather more inquisitive than you suppose perhaps, and more by-ways and, shall we say, forbidden ways, tried out than perhaps you imagine."

"Oh, I know I've read very little," replied the other impatiently, "and I don't want to hear any of your diatribes. I want you to help me with what I have in my mind now . . . there is no one else," he added, with an appealing note in his voice. "only you can do it. The others would . . . well, if I don't get the bones to-night they'll be taken away. I don't suppose they'd allow me to bring them here, but you and I, with this darkness and a lantern, even without any help, could take them. There won't be a guard over them, I don't suppose, and if there were, I have the authority to remove him."

"You don't see very far ahead," remarked Mr. Steel without much interest.

"What do you mean by that? I see past this earth into, perhaps, Hell."

"And I see for you nothing at all so grandiose—merely I see the madhouse."

* * * * *

Adelaide went to Miss Herle's shop to inspect disdainfully her store of finery, at the same time that her mother went on a more serious errand connected with the same subject to Mr. Bisset. Adelaide was weary and languid. She had been moping too long and had seemed, even to her own self-absorption, to have come to the end of her powers of intrigue. It was queer that he had not answered her last letter; the money was all very well, but sent by a servant without a line?

She asked Miss Herle, who regarded her with sharp inquisitive glances, if she had any white roses.

"You know, those Parisian flowers that are so lifelike, made of velvet and silk—not the ordinary cambric ones."

"We hardly have much opportunity to sell such luxuries in Mullenbridge," replied Miss Herle briskly.

"Perhaps you could get me one," urged Adelaide. "I want it for the Assembly dance."

"Why, haven't you heard—there's not going to be an Assembly Ball this year because of the old Earl's death? My dear Miss Fenton, whatever have you been dreaming about, or wherever have you been? There won't be—any festivities held this year. That would have been anyhow . . . besides now . . . . " She pursed up her lips and narrowed her eyes with the air of importance due to someone in possession of a valuable piece of gossip.

"What about now?" said Adelaide. She was half disappointed, half relieved about the Assembly Ball; it would save her face, of course, and yet it swept away the prospect of she knew not what gorgeous triumph. She could not easily dismiss the picture of herself in the white gown and the single white rose, being received and recognized by her lover at the public gathering.

"Well, there's a good deal of fuss up at Charters, isn't there?" said Miss Herle. "It's extraordinary how many of that young man's relations have been arriving with every train. They bring their own servants and the town seems quite full. They are noticeable, of course, because they are all in mourning, even if it is only bands."

"Why should they be coming?" asked Adelaide. Her cheeks burned with a sudden pang of hope. Was he going to acknowledge her before all his relatives, friends and acquaintances?

"I don't know," said Miss Herle. "Those sort of folks keep their secrets to themselves. They say there was something . . . well—odd found when they pulled that old Pavilion down, and some people venture to hint that the young man himself—well, shall we call it, has had an attack of illness? You must always remember the history of the family."

Yet even as she spoke Miss Herle was not quite sure that she might not be making a considerable mistake and offending and perhaps losing in Adelaide Fenton the best customer who was ever like to come her way; so she brought out with her precise, businesslike air, several boxes full of silver paper and showed the girl feathers, knots of velvet scarves and other novelties that had lately arrived, so she declared, from Paris.

Adelaide was distracted, but not for long. Her visions had long since flown far beyond the contents of Miss Herle's cardboard boxes.

"It's heavy, like a thunderstorm," she sighed. "I'm sorry you haven't got the white rose."

"But if there's not going to be an Assembly Ball, it don't matter, does it?" snapped Miss Herle shrewdly.

"No, but there might be some other kind of private festivity at Charters, I suppose; when the time and date for the ball comes the old man will have been dead a long time."

"These great people keep up mourning for a long time," the milliner was prudish. "You know—black and crêpe and bombazine, and then grey and violet, and then sometimes white and pearl colour. It's a couple of years sometimes . . . . "

Adelaide came down the narrow street slowly. She hesitated as she passed the door of Mr. Bisset's neat and commonplace house in the High Street. She knew that her mother would probably be there. Mrs. Fenton had been saying for days that she meant to go to the attorney's and, more than that, the attorney's lad, who seemed on fair to good terms with Caroline, had several times come to the cottage. On the last occasion his visit had certainly been official. He had brought and voiced openly a desire for Mrs. Fenton to come to see his master as soon as she conveniently could. The appointment had been for to-day at four o'clock . . . it was, by the clock in the market place, twenty minutes past that hour now.

'I don't see,' thought Adelaide, 'why I shouldn't know what they are talking about. It's something to do with me, I suppose.'

Without ringing the bell, she went into the narrow hall, up the shiny clean stairs and knocked at the door of Mr. Bisset's office.

It was the attorney himself who opened it to her. He seemed alert, surprised and after a while, she thought, pleased at seeing her there.

"Well, I didn't ask you to come, Miss Adelaide, but perhaps it's just as well that you have done so. I've been giving your mother a warning."

Adelaide glanced round the room. Carrie wasn't there . . . well, that was to the good. She was haunted by the thought of Carrie. Mrs. Fenton looked sullen, almost at bay. She was seated in a four-square fashion, her hands upon her knees, staring down at the floor, her best bonnet tied firmly under her chin. On the lawyer's table lay all the scraps of paper that Adelaide knew so well.

"This is a queer case," pronounced Mr. Bisset, "a very queer case indeed. If things had gone a little differently I might have made something of it, but as it is I'm afraid I don't see that I can. In fact, Miss Adelaide, I've been advising your mother to leave Mullenbridge—to get out of the way before there's trouble. You see," he added sharply, "there may be some more of these letters. They may have all been pushed into the fire for what I can tell, but on the other hand they may not—and there's a great number of people being called to Charters. Well, you might say the town is black with them, as they are all in mourning."

"I don't see what that's got to do with anything," said Adelaide with an air of stupidity. "I knew Mother was up here to-day, seeing you, so I thought I'd come too. Why shouldn't I? Those are my letters, Mother needn't have interfered."

"Well, I doubt if you could have done much yourself," smiled the attorney. "Nor could I—we should have had to have a London lawyer on it. A breach of promise case against a man in his position . . . well, it isn't so easily worked, you know."

"Who is talking of breach of promise cases?" demanded Adelaide hotly. "You don't understand, either of you. You want to make my romance sordid and vulgar."

"It isn't a case of what I want to make it, it's a case of getting at the commonsense of the whole affair. I think you've been wasting my time, and I've little chance of being repaid for my trouble; but worse than that, I may have put my head into a good deal of worry. It might mean me having to leave Mullenbridge, too. Somebody," he added with a sudden coarseness, "has discovered the whole game."

"What do you mean by 'the whole game?' " demanded Mrs. Fenton defiantly, while Adelaide rose with an air of nervous indignation.

"Well, I mean that *someone*—since I've had this business in hand, I've kept an agent, such as he is, at Charters, one of the servants—and I think this *someone* was Mr. Abraham Steel, has had his suspicions caused, by what crazy act I don't know, of Lord Seagrove's and spoken to *someone* else—probably Mr. Timothy Chalmers, who is not so far gone in his cups that he cannot start the alarm round all the relatives, and they've come down, or sent representatives to deal with the matter."

"What matter?" demanded Adelaide. "Those are letters from

him to me, aren't they? And you've seen the presents he sent me from the first, that was a pink bonnet."

"All that could be faked nicely," said Mr. Bisset.

"You're not going to say that my innocent girl . . . " the indignant woman began to cry out.

"I am not going to say anything," interrupted the lawyer. "We might even yet get a few hundreds—a few thousands out of it, if we could get at the young man himself. I don't know what they know, you see—I don't know what there is at the bottom of it. Maybe he's been foolish; perhaps even he did write some of these, but I doubt it."

"Who do you think did write them?" asked Mrs. Fenton foolishly.

"Why, the fair young lady standing in the window, of course. It's been done before, girls writing love letters to themselves—yes, and giving themselves presents that were supposed to have come from lovers. But this is certainly bold and audacious, and I shouldn't have been altogether sure that I was on the right track, knowing the character of the young man and all the rest of it; but, anyhow, I think now we are up against . . . well, what is a little too much for us."

"It isn't possible to move my sick husband . . . " began Mrs. Fenton in great agitation.

"No, but I suppose it's easier to do that than to face what you might have to if some of these great folk begin to, shall we say, turn nasty?"

"I saw him myself in the Pavilion . . . " began Adelaide, "not long ago . . . . I walked with him in the grove often enough . . . can't you understand? How ridiculous just because the circumstances of our births are slightly different! How can such accidents affect the course of true love?"

"Don't use any of that novelette language to me!" said Mr. Bisset. "I wash my hands of the whole affair . . . . I am sorry I touched it. It was a temptation, I know—but here you are, here are all your letters back, and no matter what you tell anybody about my meddling with the business, I shall always say I refused to handle it."

Mother and daughter both recognized the finality of these words. Without more debate they accepted at least a temporary defeat and, not touching one another, but moving in single file, moved slowly down the worn stairs to the street.

"I'll not go away," said Adelaide. "Mr. Bisset's an ignorant man. Why should I be afraid of all these people who have come from London? they don't know what's happened between me and Basil."

"We'd best be quiet . . . we'd best go away," replied Mrs. Fenton nervously. "After all, we've been repaid for the money we've spent and I suppose I was a fool to listen to you, even for half an hour. It's all very confusing to an ignorant woman like me."

"I won't give it up," insisted Adelaide.

As they passed through the street of Mullenbridge she noticed several strangers and people of the meaner sort who must be these same strangers' servants . . . carriages passed along the cobbles in which were smart ladies wearing mourning, and there were maids and lackeys peering into the windows of the humble shops.

The two women went sullenly, each absorbed in her own uneasy defeat, back to the cottage by St. Jude's. Susan met them at the door and they noticed that the neighbours, the solitary woman who lived on one side and the decaying couple who lived the other, were in their gardens regarding them with greedy glances; but Susan had her own prudence. She kept her lips tight until she had her mistress and her daughter inside the little parlour with the shining ornaments, the horsehair sofa and the workbox of sea shells.

"The parson from the great house has been down here," she then said. "He's coming again . . . . I didn't like the look of him."

"He was half drunk as usual, I suppose," interrupted Mrs. Fenton, but she shivered and put out a hand to steady herself, gripping the varnished chimneypiece close by the Staffordshire figure of John Wesley.

"He seemed in a fair state," admitted Susan, whose own hands were fluttering. "He said you'd know what he meant by advising you to leave Mullenbridge."

"How can I?" asked Mrs. Fenton, speaking at random. "How can I move my husband?"

"I suppose it could be done," said Susan. "Better that than getting into any trouble here, wouldn't it?"

"Why should there be trouble?" cried Mrs. Fenton. "I've never told you my secrets, have I? Have you been listening at doors and spying and watching?"

Susan shook her head with a blind, weak look.

"Indeed, no, but one can't help feeling when something seems to grow up in a house and spread all over it like a fungus."

"Did he say anything," asked Adelaide, "*definite* about me, or that young man at Charters?"

"No, but I dared to ask him about some of the stories as is going about."

"No stories have been going about worth listening to," put in Mrs. Fenton angrily.

"I asked him about those stories of the bones," continued Susan. "He said it was a lot of nonsense and they was monkey's bones. Well, I've heard of an old story of how one of the lords up there did bury a monkey. I met a man whose father had seen it leaping about the trees—queer outlandish kind of pet I call it—and when it died, they gave it a funeral and dressed it up like the family ghost."

"*You're* talking a lot of nonsense," cried Adelaide angrily. "I shall have to take this matter into my own hands. Where's Carrie?"

"Carrie's upstairs with your father. She's reading him out of the *Pilgrim's Progress* the story about the sour plums. I don't like it when she does—it reminds me of the plums on that poor fellow's grave what no one ever picks or eats. But I think ma'am," she added timidly, "it could have been real bones, do you?—and that grave there, with 'a broken and contrite heart' on it . . . merely a mocking of the Lord?"

"I don't know," said Mrs. Fenton gloomily. "I suppose we meddled with what was too big for us. With all these people here I feel as if there was a darkness over the whole place . . . interfering, coming from nowhere . . . what good will they do him—unless they shut him up!" she added viciously.

Adelaide went upstairs, leaving the two women muttering together. That day there seemed no talk of tea, the shining kettle was not put on the hook, the tray of pretty bright china was not brought out. Carrie seemed to have forgotten her appetite for cake and chocolates. Where was she? Adelaide felt that in her only might some strength, some clarity be found . . . . Reading to old Mr. Fenton out of the *Pilgrim's Progress*. There she was by the invalid's bed, and the curtains that were embroidered with acorns and foxes . . . and there was he, neat and placid, with his grey shawl pinned over his withered chest. Was he really listening . . . ? Was he capable of discerning a tale that pleased him and one that did not? Adelaide gave that matter a brief and contemptuous wonder. She passed round the tester to Carrie, who did not cease reading until her sister touched her on the shoulder.

"Pull the bell and make Susan come up . . . she and Mother are only gossiping downstairs . . . I want to speak to you."

Carrie finished her paragraph, closed the book decorously and jerked the embroidered length of wool.

"You've made a mess of it, I suppose," she complained. "Got into a muddle and a confusion . . . I ought not to have had anything to do with it."

"Hush!" warned Adelaide. "Don't talk like that . . . Father might hear."

They waited impatiently until Susan, perturbed and wiping her eyes, appeared and took her accustomed post.

"Don't come up, Mother," Carrie shouted down the stairs. "I and Adelaide have got to talk together a bit."

The two girls went into the small bedroom that they had shared as long as they could remember. Beside the long straight beds were the trophies of their elaborate deceits . . . the mantua-maker's boxes, some sets of novels, the chest of drawers that held the ornaments of paste, coral and pinchbeck, the pots of cosmetics that Adelaide had ordered from Bond Street . . . .

The evening was sultry and tawny clouds had obscured the scene. Carrie set the window wide . . . the prospect looked over the wall, where the stripped morello cherry grew, towards the sloping churchyard and the dun-coloured tower of St. Jude. The smell of the brandy-making and of cherry pie still lingered about the little house.

Adelaide sat down, her look was fixed.

"I don't know what to do. It's all those people . . . how is one to outface them?"

"I don't know," answered Carrie. "They're not to be *outfaced* at all, of course. It was nothing but lies and tricks from the first . . . and you couldn't have done it if he hadn't been—well, what I should have called half-witted."

Adelaide patted her foot impatiently and protested. "But he's not—and he's fond of me . . . and those letters *were* written to me . . . and he did promise me a white horse, and a conservatory . . . and I've been deceived."

"I suppose you didn't mean Mother to take it up with Mr. Bisset?" asked Carrie in her businesslike way. "I suppose you weren't thinking of London lawyers and breaches of promise? No, I daresay you weren't," she continued thoughtfully, "you were thinking of more romantical things . . . of being a countess and married in a satin dress worth seven thousand pounds . . . . "

"I don't know what you're talking of," said Adelaide with a frightened look. "What was that Susan was saying about bones . . . ? I didn't hear anything about bones being found . . . . "

"Oh, some rubbish—when they took the Pavilion down. Who cares . . . ? It's nothing to do with us. We've had a great deal of trouble over this—at least I have—and I don't see why something shouldn't be got out of it after all. Of course, one cannot do anything with all these great folk—but I mean with the young man himself, or even with that Dr. Perry if he's up there. It wouldn't be so difficult for us to move . . . there's an empty farm, or was, close to Aunt Martha's . . . Mother and Father could go there and Aunt Martha would give her an eye. She'd be back where she started, which is all she deserves—and you could get a job as a lady's maid."

"Ah, you've set all your fortunes pretty nicely," said Adelaide. "Mother and Father back where they started, as you put it . . .

well, there was gentility on Mother's side and Father had a good position . . . but still they're old and their time's past."

"Susan could go to the Poor House," added Carrie coolly. "I daresay she's got some savings—if she hasn't, she'd have to go to the Poor House, she's too old for work elsewhere."

"And what about you, my beauty?" asked Adelaide furiously. "You've parcelled us all out—Poor House and farmhouse and a servant's place—but what about you?"

"Oh, I daresay I could do a bit better for myself. You see, I didn't have the same kind of education as you did, but I have a much better intelligence. If I had a little capital I might do well for myself in a manner of ways. I've got the addresses of several people from the Clapham days. They might help me to make a start."

"And where do you think you are going to get the capital?" demanded Adelaide.

"I've got an idea about that. It's daring, it's touch and go, but so has been everything I've done. Don't you bother about me or yourself—you keep quiet. I can guess the advice Mr. Bisset gave you. You take it."

Before Adelaide could reply, Caroline had gone downstairs and faced her mother who was sitting rocking to and fro in the chair by the small fire.

"I've been speaking straightly to Adelaide. I humoured her for a while—well, partly for fun, it's dull here—and partly for what I could get out of it; but you see, Mother, you were rather clumsy going to an attorney with all that flimsy nonsense. I dare say the young man is half out of his mind—look at his family history and the way they brought him up, the fools! Did you see who's come down here now? There must be a dozen relatives and lawyers and doctors, too. I should like to know," she added curiously, "what it was he did that brought them all on him of a sudden like that."

"What do you suggest, Carrie?" begged Mrs. Fenton in a cowed voice. "What do you suggest?"

"Well, you'll have to draw out some of your savings—you can sell this place, but it'll take time—and you and Father will have to go to Aunt Martha's. He could travel in a special kind of carriage. You can take Susan with you, if you can afford it—there's a little empty farm there, and you're still hale. You can hire a man and work it and go back to what you came from."

"I suppose I can," whispered Mrs. Fenton. "I suppose I can, there's no doubt of that. And what would Adelaide do?"

"Adelaide had better get out of Mullenbridge as soon as she can. She'd better take a train to London."

"To London?" echoed Mrs. Fenton in a tone of horror. "Where's she going to stay in London?"

"There's the Clapham people—she'll have to go there. As long as she's got a little money, they'll be civil. She could put an advertisement in one of those papers she's so fond of reading. I dare say she'd do as a lady's maid, she's not bad at the packing and the mending and the ironing. She's fond of finery—I suppose if she was always handling other people's trumpery, it would keep her from worrying about where she's going to get some for herself."

Mrs. Fenton gave a sigh that was not wholly of disillusion. This brisk and capable young woman certainly took a great many burdens off her shoulders, eased her puzzled brain of a good many intricate problems.

"*Will* Adelaide go, do you think?" she whispered.

"Oh, she'll go all right—she's scared. You won't find her up at the Mausoleum, if it's still standing, or that grove of trees, or playing at being a ghost any more. She'd only to see those great people about the streets of Mullenbridge and all her courage went."

"But of course," protested Mrs. Fenton, "he did write her those letters . . . there was a love story . . . . "

"Oh, of course," sneered Caroline. "No innocent young girl could possibly make it all up, could she?"

Another thought struck Mrs. Fenton, and darkly.

"Carrie, supposing Adelaide does it again?"

Carrie smiled. "You're shrewder than I thought, Mother, but it won't matter to us—we shan't be involved in it; she'll have to pay the penalty herself, won't she?"

"I suppose so," agreed Mrs. Fenton indifferently. "I don't like casting the girl off."

"It won't need any casting—she'll go quick enough now. I shall find her packing when I go upstairs. She only wants a few clear directions and she'll follow them."

* * * * *

Lord Seagrove was intensely irritated when he realized his house was occupied by so many of his relations and friends. He could not discover the reason of this; when he spoke to Mr. Chalmers, or to Dr. Perry, who had suddenly appeared, they put him off with what he felt to be ambiguous answers.

"Why, there are as many people here, as many as there were when my grandfather died," he demanded peevishly; "a great number of them I don't know or like, and why should I be suddenly interviewed by lawyers?"

Mr. Chalmers repeatedly told him with steady monotony that he had a big estate and much to settle, and that he could not expect to live like a recluse; Dr. Perry told him more earnestly that these people were his friends and had come to help him, and there were not after all as many as he might have supposed.

"The house seems *black* with them to me," replied the young man with indignation. "Wherever I go, there they are like shadows."

"It's because they are in mourning that they appear like shadows," replied Dr. Perry. "You've got a long way from me, James, I feel as if I couldn't reach you."

"Who was it told them to come?" insisted the young man. "Someone must have asked them—I'm sure I did not. My one desire is solitude and I was about to make a most interesting experiment with Mr. Steel."

Dr. Perry did not enlighten him to the effect that Mr. Steel and the interesting experiment had been exactly the reason why Charters was so full of his friends and relatives. Indeed, the Swedenborgian endeavoured to keep the young man away both from the laboratory attached to the conservatory and that which was fitted up in the house.

"I wish," he declared earnestly, "that I could make you see the fair and clear spirits that stand either side of you willing to help you forward, but you have turned your eyes upon a forbidden path and perhaps it is now past my power to make you look in any other direction."

Lord Seagrove sulked in his own room. He had taken an intense dislike, not only to his guests—strangers they seemed to him—but to Sir Henry Dering and his colleagues. There was no restriction put upon the youth's movements and no company seemed forced upon him, yet he felt himself watched and spied upon, confined even more than he had been when he had only his tutor, his grandfather and Hackett to fear. He was suspiciously conscious that an elaborate liberty, that was entirely false, was allowed him; that he was permitted to roam from room to room, to walk over the park, to go riding—to do anything, in fact, he wished—but that always, not far away, was someone who chanced to be passing through the same room, or riding near, or walking in the same direction—someone who would give him a casual, jovial salutation and go his way.

"But still, it is never solitude. I'm never alone—and why does Steel make so much ado of that experiment? It's simple enough. The heliotrope . . . he says he has finished with that . . . that he didn't think he had got the formula complete. Then there are the bones . . . ."

They would not speak to him much of the bones; they said they were those of some poor pet animal and that the bulk of the dress, green sash and white gown, was mere nonsense.

But he was not in his own mind satisfied. He asked to be allowed to see the excavation where it had been discovered, but Sir Henry told him smoothly that all had been levelled with the ground and that the site of the Folly would soon be on a level with that of the parkland. But the young man knew the place where that grave was; he could see as clearly as if they had allowed him to have a sight of it, the small white bones laid out . . . the bonnet . . . the sash . . . the dress. To him the affair was perfectly clear, reasonably exact—just as if he had read it in one of those articles, like that in the *Gentleman's Magazine*, where he had discovered the truth. He repeated this word to himself often, as if it were a charm . . . the truth. Then he considered that she was not human . . . an evil spirit always. "They knew she walked . . . that she would come back and haunt us all until there was no more of us to torment. I am the one destined to take that mysterious voyage over land and sea to those distant haunted hills of Ireland. I cannot escape my destiny—and do they think by putting me off from a few necessary experiments they are thwarting me, or holding me back? Spies, all of them, and even Lucas Perry not the friend I thought him. I am disappointed in Abraham Steel and the heliotrope . . . . " The youth had, in his uneasy, perturbed mind, constant, shifting pictures of sprays of heliotrope being reduced to ashes, of morello cherries being pulled from a churchyard wall, of dust . . . and then the form again . . . .

He became angry with the answers, soothing and respectful but, from his point of view, worthless, that he received from everybody whom he asked about the discovery in the foundations of the Folly. 'After all, I am master here and I shall do what I choose and I will not be put off with these excuses. I will get hold of the books that Steel has and make the experiment myself. Indeed, I rather doubt if there is any need for an experiment. Very likely once I saw them they would come together again and show me the girl as she was. Now, who were those two who came to me in the Folly before they destroyed it, when I was looking at the picture of Lake Nemmi . . . that was an absurd touch, my father's hat floating on those waters where the dark priests used to gaze when they came down from the thickets and where the barge of Tiberius sunk . . . or was it a hat? A handkerchief full of cowslips . . . a purse of gold pieces . . . and she looking at me almost as if she gave the signal for us to flee together.'

He had been down to the site of the Pavilion several times, but always with a fairly large company and the talk had been of most commonplace matters; now the attention of the great architect was turned to the demolition of the Mausoleum. The consent of the bishop for the removal of the bodies had been obtained and the shoddy copy of the Temple of the Four Winds of Athens was to be removed after all and those grandiose coffins, with their rotting palls, now to be taken to the church of St. Jude's.

"It was an ugly fashion," said Sir Henry in his authoritative way, "and one quite out of date. That gone, and the Folly demolished, we have now a clear sweep of parkland which in the new landscape style ought to look quite handsome. I should suggest some exotics that Mr. Steel ought to be able to provide, to break the homely look of the elms and limes."

The young man listened to all this ungraciously. They had rather, had they but known it, overdone their casual air; though he outwardly acquiesced, inwardly he was making his own plans. He was one against many, and knew it; but he had the cunning of the peculiar world to which he belonged, and this was sharpened by necessity. He was aware they had made plans for him to go to London, the Portland Street house that was near to that of Sir Henry's, quite soon or, if he objected too much to town life, to Verities, while the alterations were made to Charters.

"All the cupboards——" he said to Sir Henry, "you'll have them all opened, I suppose—nothing hidden away in cupboards?" and the great man had smiled suavely and said that there would be a great many dark presses, closets and cobwebs swept away with the house that had been left too long unchanged. Certainly it had been added to, but rather uncouthly, and when my lord returned he would be surprised at the transformation that he, Sir Henry Dering, had been able to work in Charters.

The young man, who was outwardly at perfect liberty, went to St. Jude's on foot, on a day that was the first of autumn to those with a keen sense of the weather, for the clouds were low, the air chilly, and the trees shedding their leaves so that trails of gold and amber and scarlet were on all the paths and roadways.

He passed quickly down the sloping graveyard, vaulted the wall where the morello cherry was now but a dry skeleton, and rapped on the back door, that of the kitchen of Mrs. Fenton's residence.

*   *   *   *   *

It was Adelaide who answered, and immediately. She showed no exultation at the sight of the man whose presence would have been so welcome to her only a few weeks ago. She had entirely lost her confidence and uttered a broken cry, putting the tea-cloth she carried to her lips.

"I thought I'd try and see you," he said. He spoke now always in a quiet tone, as if afraid of being heard. "There's so much I don't understand, and you might be able to help me."

"We're leaving," replied Adelaide quickly. "We're leaving Mullenbridge—we don't want anything to do with lawyers or your relatives. Mother's arranged it . . . ."

Low as she had kept her voice, Carrie, in the parlour, had overheard; there was always Carrie to overhear.

The younger girl now came in softly with her finger to her mouth. She was not altogether surprised at the visitor.

"You had better leave this to me, hadn't you, Adelaide?" she suggested. "And talk very quietly, please; Mother is upstairs packing with Susan. It's strange how much one gathers together, even in a small house, in twenty years or so."

"Why are you going?" asked Lord Seagrove in a confused way. "Everything seems to be disappearing . . . they are taking down the Mausoleum now, and will bring the coffins to St. Jude's . . . and this cottage will be empty then . . . ."

"We shall be able to sell it perhaps to the sexton, who has always complained that he is poorly housed. Why have you come here?" said Carrie; but Adelaide had now begun to assert herself.

Over her confused mind came some flash of hope and courage; perhaps after all the crazy dream might come true.

"We can't talk here," she said quickly, "we never could—but I'll meet you up by the grove."

He lifted his lip in a way that she had never seen him do before. She marked, with a kind of inner horror, how pale and shrunken he seemed.

"Do you suppose they leave me long enough to make any kind of tryst?" he replied. "I suppose there's somebody after me now. I cannot stay long . . . ."

"But you could get away," urged Carrie, in a matter-of-fact voice, "if you wanted to . . . if you arranged it properly. I'm afraid that you don't know, sir, how to manage your own affairs, any more than Adelaide or Mother does. The world has to be run by sensible people like me. I suppose that your relatives have discovered that a great deal of nonsense has been going on, a great deal of wicked foolishness," added the girl with a prim air. She glanced with a slight apprehension upward as she spoke, as if she feared she might be overheard. At sunset to-night *I'll* come and meet you at the grove. Do you remember what I asked you before? Well, I still want it and it is going to make a great deal of difference to your peace of mind and to how all those people pester and badger you . . . it will set you free."

"You will come . . . not the other one?" he said, still dubiously, looking from one girl to the other. "You know what they found in the Pavilion . . . you've heard about the heliotrope and the experiments Mr. Steel's been making . . . ."

Adelaide began to cry. "I want to get out of it!" She was wringing her hands.

"You *are* out of it!" said Carrie contemptuously.

She took the young man by the arm and led him out of the small house. There was no one in sight. The sunshine, that had the reddish sombre tint of autumn, was tinted over what most people would have called a peaceful scene . . . the sloping churchyard, the weathered tombstones, the path leading to the church porch.

"You must rely on me," urged Carrie with a firmness that did seem to communicate itself to Lord Seagrove. "You mustn't let them torment you so . . . why, the place is black with them like a flight of bats! It's all over . . . it's been nothing but a lot of story-book nonsense from first to last. You'll grow out of it . . . you'll look back upon it as a foolish kind of dream. Well, I think you owe me something . . . ."

"I want to make that experiment . . . " he confessed. "I want to come to the bottom of it. If it's true, why shouldn't she and I go together to Ireland . . . ? That's the place—the far-off hills of Ireland and the chariot that travels as quick as the wind. Yes, a fairy story as you say, and that's what we are all looking for—to get back into the fairy story. I've been up there trying to find out what they discovered."

"It don't matter," declared Carrie, walking slowly with him up the church path. "Don't you be seen here now . . . you get there to-night on some excuse or other before it's quite dark, for it is more difficult for me if I have to bring a lantern—*and you have the money with you*—the others are provided for. St. Jude's cottage will be empty and you'll forget about us. It was only silly play-acting. Mr. Bisset will give up everything he's got, every scrap of paper; he's scared, I know; one look from a London lawyer and he'd be on his marrow bones!"

"I don't understand what you are talking about!" protested the young man peevishly.

"No, I don't suppose you do—but *they* do, those people who have come down to look after you. Now I'm going into the church; I often do, you know—I do some sweeping and dusting there sometimes—shaking out the hassocks and putting the hymn books in order . . . . And you'll go round on the high road and back again, and to-night, just before it's dusk, you'll meet me where the Folly used to be."

"I will," he promised with sudden earnestness.

"And don't forget to bring the money," insisted Carrie calmly. She thought it better to deal with the matter in a commonplace, crude fashion.

"I will not," he replied. "And then you will help me with my experiment?"

"Certainly," said Carrie. "Why shouldn't I?"

They parted with no more than that. The girl looked up and down the road, she could see no one, but it was certain that some member of his household was not far away. They had not much time, they must be gone from Mullenbridge within another twenty-four hours.

She went into the church which often served her as a private place in which to think and plot. She was afraid that this enterprise was a desperate one, and that she had very little chance of getting that thousand pounds, but in her opinion the man was little more than half-witted and might be induced to part with the money. She had not dared to be too explicit, but surely there was at least a chance that he would come with it, in gold or in notes, that she, going instantly to London by the first train from Mullenbridge in the morning, could turn into cash before they were stopped by his bankers.

She very much prided herself on her common sense and her

level head. Her contempt of her mother and Adelaide, and even of the lesser villains of the plot—silly Miss Herle, knavish Mr. Bisset—increased considerably until there was a firm sneer marked upon her well-cut lips.

There was a great number of things that she would do when she had her money, She did not intend to continue any attempts at blackmail. She knew for one thing that it would be pretty well hopeless. Mr. Bisset, in a panic of terror, would give up all the letters. Adelaide had already crumpled, she would probably try other tricks and make failures of them; but for the moment she was frightened.

Caroline sat primly in the pew that chanced to be that of the Seagroves. She liked it because it was tall and shut her in. There was a receptacle for Bibles and Prayer Books, there were footstools of fine leather, and cushions, too—quite a comfortable place. Well, she could indulge herself in a little rest, but she must keep her eye on Adelaide, who might run blurting the whole thing out to Mrs. Fenton, or even to a neighbour.

What an utter fool Adelaide was! It had interested Caroline to watch her from the first, how she had spun her daydreams into some sort of coherent romance of which she was the heroine; how, idle and inert, she had sulked from day to day 'only half alive,' as Caroline put it. She was more to be despised that poor Mrs. Fenton, who was so ignorant and whose brains had been fuddled by ambition, and Adelaide's wild and foolish stories.

Caroline rose and with raised eyebrows remarked that the marbles that were to form the monument to the present lord's father were still unpacked.

'I suppose they'll either have to put them up or take them away,' she thought. She lifted her skirt as she passed them for fear of catching her hem, which was neatly braided, in any of the wooden packings.

It was quite pleasant in the churchyard, agreeable even in that no-man's-land, that potter's field. The forbidden fruit no longer hung on the plum trees; they fluttered a few yellow leaves on thin boughs. The blue bloom of the Lebanon cedar was accentuated with the season; the grass had not yet faded and the solitary tomb was neatly kept.

'What's this silly story,' mused Caroline, 'that they wouldn't bury her here after all because they thought she might be a changeling, or some rubbish like that? Of course she's here, and if they really found anything up at the Folly, why, it *would* have been the bones of a monkey. I've heard that story—and anything might be true of the Seagroves.'

She went across the graveyard and opened the gate, not choosing to jump the wall, for she was ladylike and precise in all her movements. Adelaide was, as her sister had expected, crying in the kitchen.

"You ought to have let me go, Carrie," she began to moan. "Maybe it's coming right after all."

"Maybe it is," agreed Carrie firmly, "but not in the way you think. You listen to me, you fool! Would you like to go up there alone, at night, in the state of mind he is? If you'd seen his eyes and heard what he spoke of you'd be afraid. You were really afraid last time when you got the money out of him, weren't you?"

"Well, I suppose I was a little," sobbed Adelaide; "everything seems so strange now and everywhere one turns there is a stranger looking at one suspiciously."

"We are marked down, we're got to go, and quickly. I'm going to see him to-night because I think I may be able to get something out of him that will make this nonsense worth while."

"It all seems very stupid and sordid," sighed Adelaide.

She seemed, her sister was glad to remark, extremely frightened, frightened of her own dreams that had gone sour in her fancy, frightened of the crude actuality that, in the form of lawyers and even constables, had suddenly sprung up across her make-believe.

"It'll be a good thing to be away from Mullenbridge." Her facile mind, already turning to new adventures, went on. "We oughtn't to have been here so long, Carrie, I always hated the place!"

"Yes, it'll be a good thing to be away," agreed Carrie.

Her sister pulled at her sleeve. "Why do you want to go up there to-night? I don't suppose he'll come. I don't suppose he'll be allowed."

"It's a chance," said Caroline. "I'm just taking a chance. What I want from him will make no difference to him, but all to me. I don't see why I shouldn't get something."

"What do you mean 'get something'?" said Adelaide, beginning to cry again. "What have I got but a broken heart?"

"Rubbish! You and your broken heart! You go upstairs and read some of your novelettes and think about some more great lords who are going to give you white chargers and hot-houses."

Adelaide said: "You're unkind! You're vulgar! I wish you wouldn't talk to me like that, Carrie—and I wish you wouldn't go up there to-night."

"Well, I'm going. There's nothing in it, is there? Everybody's got a right to stroll along towards the Folly—and don't you say a word to Mother or to Susan, and don't you disturb Father, and you keep inside the house, Adelaide. You're not to let anyone see you, even in the garden. You've got to be very careful."

"No need to warn Mother," said Adelaide, still sobbing. "She's packing, packing—we'll be gone, gone!"

*   *   *   *   *

Caroline Fenton, without the least sense of discomfiture or agitation walked along the single street of Mullenbridge, quite conscious of the curious eyes that were glancing at her, out on the high road towards where the Folly had stood. A scaffolding had been erected around the Mausoleum to allow, with due reverence and decorum, the dead Seagroves to be removed to St. Jude's.

Caroline thought, and for the first time, that the man who was supposed to have committed the crime which had caused, as the girl put it in her mind, 'so much fuss and nonsense,' was among those whose magnificent coffins would be taken in stately procession to the church.

The day was fair and the sky entirely transfused by a pale sapphire light.

'I don't see why, if I play my cards properly, I shouldn't get it out of him. Of course, it all depends whether he has brought it with him. I don't suppose I could venture on going back to the house with him for it, although I might. After all, I don't suppose any of them know the truth, and I dare say they'd be glad to get rid of me and all I might say for that sum. I wonder what's in his mind?' She dwelt on with a cool, passionless curiosity. 'I suppose he's half-mad . . . he and his spectre bride, and the two going together to the green hills of Ireland—never grown up, I suppose."

She opened the large gate that admitted to the Seagrove estate and crossed the grass that had a dry autumnal look. The last gale had loosened many leaves and the lime grove was sparsely covered; when Carrie looked up she could see the boughs interlacing against the sky that was beginning to take on a twilight pallor. There was a number of workmen's scaffoldings, planks and tools about; a small hut had been built for the men's accommodation. They had only just left off work, she could see two of them in the distance walking towards Mullenbridge.

The ground where the Folly had stood had been already skilfully smoothed down, although it was too late in the year for any turf to be put on the site, and the part that was of rock had been left a jagged hole; over a portion of it was spread some sacking.

'Queer,' thought Caroline, looking round, 'that this is where the Pavilion stood with those pictures of foreign parts. Well, here's the end of one ghost story. I'm a bit early, I don't suppose he'll venture to come out till it's darker. Perhaps it's stupid of me to wait here, I might be noticed.'

She sauntered on, now and then stooping to pick up a twig, examine it and throw it away, all the while looking furtively to right and left; but there seemed no one to spy upon her. She came to the Mausoleum with its elaborate scaffolding. The day faded quickly, as it seemed to her, and for the first time in her prosaic life she had the sense of space and distance and eternity not being entities that could be measured by any commonplace terms.

* * * * *

Lord Seagrove had not forgotten his tryst at the Pavilion. He determined, whatever opposition was put in his way, to keep it, and he made his plans very cunningly. Of the people who were about him he had taken so little notice that they were no more than dark shadows hemming him in like a flight of bats or birds. He knew the faces of Hackett, of Dr. Lucas Perry, of Mr. Chalmers, of one or two of the women . . . he knew how to keep up an ordinary conversation . . . but the rest were but so many phantoms that he might beat back by a quick blow of the palm of his hand.

After dinner, when the candles had been brought in, he went into the library. Mr. Chalmers followed him. What the man said the youth did not know, but he was aware that he replied himself quickly:

"I'm very tired to-day—I think I should like to go to bed early. We're going to London, are we not, quite soon? I shall be glad to get away from the place. I don't particularly want to see Sir Henry demolishing it."

"Well, he won't altogether demolish it," said the Reverend Chalmers suavely. "He's a very able architect, you know . . . he will only take down a wall here, a wing there." The parson spoke with the assurance of ignorance. "When you return it will look different. You will feel it will be more your home."

"No cupboards left . . . " said the young man, moistening his lips, "no places where things might be hidden . . . . "

"Are you really going to your chamber? It's quite early, you know, and there are a number of people to entertain."

"But it's understood, is it not," replied the youth petulantly, "that I'm not well? Hackett can come up and attend to me."

He lit his candle from those standing in the hall, and the parson, who was tired and who had drunk quite his share of port, thought wearily: 'Well, I suppose he's safe enough. He seems to me to have given up all this nonsense, anyhow.'

He watched the youth's bent figure go up the stairs with a halo of light from the candle around it, spacing it from the shadows.

'I, too, shall be glad when we are in London—let other people take on this damned bit of work.'

He pulled the bell and when the servant came, told him to ask Hackett to attend the Earl and stay by him until he was asleep.

"Mind you, he mustn't know that he is in any way being

watched; that would drive him frantic."

The servant nodded. Those words were always being whispered over Charters: 'He mustn't know he's being watched!'

Hackett was for once something off his guard. Indeed, he considered that far too much nonsense, as he termed it, had been made about what was, after all, nothing very important or difficult. He was quite prepared to believe that his young master was in a strange state of mind, and to accept the verdict of the doctors who had come on the summons of Mr. Chalmers to Charters; but he was not himself a fanciful man, and he did not think that the youth, to whose whims and vagaries he had been used when he was a boy, was likely to do anything dangerous or disgraceful. Yet Hackett was another who would be glad when Charters and Mullenbridge was left behind and the train had brought them into London and they would be able to start a different kind of life; he thought it a good thing that the old house should be pulled down; it would be a much finer, smarter place when Sir Henry had done with it, no doubt; of course, the old Earl had lived too long and let life, as Hackett put it, 'get rather the upper hand of him.'

He talked on these lines cheerfully enough with his master, who was not prepared to go to bed, but said he had a quantity of letters to write.

"I shall stay in the closet for a little while, Hackett, and you, if you will, can go to bed."

"Very good, my lord," said the servant, but he intended to keep his trust and to remain awake and so on the alert until the young man was asleep in the old-fashioned tester bed. He forgot what the cunning mind of Lord Seagrove remembered, that there was what is known in French as an *escalier dérobé* in the closet, a small spiral staircase leading from one floor to another and finally to a postern door that opened into the garden.[35] It was awkward and had not been required for many years; indeed, a bookcase stood in front of it. Many people had forgotten its existence, but to-night, sharply and clearly, it had come into the young man's mind.

He left the door into his bedroom, where Hackett was moving about, ajar and sat down and scribbled aimlessly for a while by the light of the handsome silver lamp. He was trying to focus his mind on to what he had to do. It was the tryst of trysts to-night, when everything would be made as clear as crystal . . . when the heliotrope . . . strange how that cottage by St. Jude's had smelt of cherry pie . . . would receive its own ghostlike form, when the bones would be consumed into ashes and arise again as the spectre of Harriet Bond . . . when that girl—whoever she was who had made the tryst with him—would explain everything. Perhaps she was the spectre and he need not go any further than that.

Money was required, he believed—for the expenses for the journey to Ireland perhaps. It might be that even fairies required their fees. He opened the secret drawer in his desk where a certain supply of money was kept, and pulled out a quantity of notes without counting them, and his order book on his bankers, and put them in his pocket. Then, very softly and quietly, he edged aside the bookcase. Hackett was still moving about. 'What does the fellow find to do, I wonder?' thought his master petulantly. 'Why doesn't he sit down? I dare say he'd like to smoke a cigar, but daren't for fear I smell it.'

He called out: "Hackett, I shan't be ready for a while yet, don't keep moving about like that, you disturb me; I have got my letters to write."

---

[35] *Escalier dérobé*: a concealed staircase.

The servant murmured some decorous acquiescence and there was no sound from the bedroom.

'I suppose,' the young man thought, annoyed with himself, 'I ought to have allowed him to go on moving, it would have covered up the sound of the bookcase,' but he contrived to lift it, without any noise, on to the rug.

There was the door . . . it might be locked and he might not have the key; but it seemed to have no lock. There was a small knob that turned easily, and below—darkness.

The young man left the lamp where it was. He knew that Hackett would be watching the light through the half-opened door—then slyly and cautiously he edged through the doorway of the secret stairway and, with the exquisite precaution of a child at a mischievous pastime, made his way step by step down the staircase from one floor to another. Sometimes he passed doors under the cracks of which he could see lights, and through the cracks of which he could hear voices—but always he went cautiously, quietly, making no sound himself; and then there came the end of the staircase and a door was in front of him. The handle was turned easily and the evening air was on his face.

He would be rather late for the tryst. The sun seemed to have set, yet there was light about, either of earth or Heaven or Hell—light enough for his purpose; it seemed to emanate from his own mind. Clearly he could behold all that he wished to see.

He made across the courtyard, still retaining enough cunning to keep close to the wall, in the shade, and then was in the park, and walking, then hastening almost to a run, to the site where the Folly had stood with its picture of Lake Nemmi. He went exactly to the spot where a piece of sacking lay across a rocky hole. That was where they had found her, of course, and where he would find her, too.

The English landscape was blurred, not by the increasing dark but by his own mind. He saw the Italian lake with the dark slope of trees to the still water on which floated his father's hat . . . where the two horses and the grooms struggled in the steel-blue water . . . where the fetch had risen to snatch at her faithless lover . . . where the chalk-marked trees rose up between the cyclamens to light and air . . . . Not a picture on canvas—the lake itself . . . .

He fumbled a little, sat down and felt the sharp stone—and there was something else there. Of course, exactly what there should have been—a collier's pick.

He heard someone speaking to him, sharply as he thought, calling him to order, beckoning him. He peered. There she was, exactly as he might have expected she would be—a white gown, something dark round her waist.

"Have you brought the money?" demanded Caroline Fenton.

He did not hear what she said. He raised the pick and struck her. She fell down and then rose. He struck again—three times. And then, Caroline Fenton, slipping into the long empty grave where once the body of Harriet Bond had lain, did not rise again.

THE END

'The Ambiguities of Miss Smith', is taken from *The Fatal Countess: And Other Studies* by William Roughead, published by W. Green & Son, Limited, in 1924. The endnotes that accompany this essay were written by William Roughead and appeared as footnotes within the *The Fatal Countess;* the placement of endnote reference numbers follows that used for the original footnotes.

The Ambiguities of Miss Smith: A Romantic Tale

"This action, Sam," said Mr. Pickwick, "is expected to come on, on the fourteenth of next month."

"Remarkable coincidence that 'ere, Sir," replied Sam.

"Why remarkable, Sam?" inquired Mr. Pickwick.

"Walentine's day, Sir," responded Sam; "reg'lar good day for a breach o' promise trial."

—*The Pickwick Papers.*

MR. Weller's "wision," as we know upon the best authority, was limited. Had he enjoyed those ocular powers the possession of which he expressly deprecated, he might have descried in the not distant future a "coincidence" equally remarkable. His intelligent gaze, thus projected, would behold certain proceedings, instituted before Mr. Justice Wightman and a special jury in the Court of Queen's Bench, Westminster Hall, on 14th February 1846, for a breach of promise of marriage, in which the damages were laid at £20,000.[1]

Even *Bardell* v. *Pickwick*, that memorable trial, must yield the palm to this amazing lawsuit, whether we regard the situation of the parties, the nature of the documentary evidence, or the amount of the damages claimed. Mrs. Bardell was a widow of years and experience; Mr. Pickwick, despite his boy's heart, an elderly gentleman in tights and gaiters. Miss Smith was a damsel of nineteen; Lord Ferrers had but just attained majority and an earldom. The famous correspondence read to the jury by Mr. Serjeant Buzfuz pales into insignificance when set beside the series of letters produced in this case; what are chops and tomato sauce, or even warming-pans, compared with the wealth of corroborative detail in which these effusions abound? The £1500 at which Messrs. Dodson and Fogg rated the blighted affections of their client is a mere bagatelle in comparison with the sum required to compensate the sufferings of Miss Smith. Finally, one day sufficed for the disposal of poor Mr. Pickwick, whereas the settlement of this young lady's claims occupied four.

I confess to a certain sympathy with Mrs. Bardell. The behaviour of Mr. Pickwick was ambiguous and calculated to mislead a confiding and susceptible female, who had conceived for him a passion which few will be disposed to blame. And if we thus pity a mature landlady denied the privilege of becoming the consort of her stout, bespectacled lodger, how must we condole the disappointment of a maiden who loses the coronet almost within her grasp, to the gracing of which she felt herself so admirably fitted? The wicked nobleman, too, that stock figure of Victorian romance, all whiskers and no heart; how shall we sufficiently reprobate the baseness of *his* conduct in frustrating these amiable and tender hopes? But this, as Major Bagstock would say, is weakness, and nothing shall induce us to submit to it. Let us therefore approach the facts in the calm and dispassionate spirit proper to a narrator of history.

It was a brilliant bar. The Solicitor-General, Sir Fitzroy Kelly, led for the fair plaintiff, his jurors being Mr. Chambers, Q.C., Mr. Robinson, and Mr. Symons. The noble defendant was represented by the Attorney-General, Sir Frederick Thesiger, assisted by Mr. Crowder, Q.C., Mr. Humfrey, Q.C., and Mr. Barstow. Mr. Symons having opened the pleadings, the Solicitor-General[2] proceeded to state his client's case to the jury. The defendant, he said, was a nobleman of very ancient family and vast landed possessions in the counties of Leicester and Stafford. He came of age in 1843, and had succeeded to the title and estates on the death of his grandfather, the eighth Earl Ferrers, on 2nd October 1842. As Viscount Tamworth he received his education from a private tutor, Mr. Echalaz, at the village of Austrey in Warwickshire, until 1840, when he went abroad. The plaintiff also lived in Austrey with her father, a gentleman of moderate means but high character. Her mother was extremely well connected, being descended from the Curzons, the family of Lord Scarsdale.[3] As early as 1839 Miss Smith attracted the notice of Lord Tamworth; occasional meetings led to conversations and correspondence, and before going abroad his lordship made to her the most passionate declarations of love, of unalterable, enduring attachment. These feelings were reciprocated, the parties became engaged to be married, and it was agreed that the ceremony should take place so soon as he reached majority. The attentions of the young Viscount came to the ears of her parents; in view of the disparity in rank they regarded the matter with some apprehension, and for the protection of their child sent her to school in London and afterwards to France, where she might complete her studies remote from the dangerous fascinations of the peerage. Two years passed, and when Lord Tamworth returned from his travels Miss Smith was fortunate to find him still faithful to his plighted troth. He sought every opportunity to continue the intimacy and saw her as often as possible, riding over from Chartley Castle or Staunton Harold, his country seats, respectively situated thirty and fifteen miles from Austrey. The intervals between their meetings were bridged by a voluminous correspondence. When on the death of his grandfather he succeeded to the title, and in the following year came of age, it was agreed that the union should take place in May 1844, the date being afterwards at his request postponed to August. Every preparation was made, the trousseau and the cake were ordered, the bridesmaids chosen, when in July, within sight of the ceremony, this unhappy lady read in the newspaper the announcement of his marriage to another.[4]

With regard to the correspondence counsel said that Lord Ferrers' letters, some of which he would produce, were in the earlier stages written upon scraps of paper, in a hand scarcely legible, and many of them had been lost. By the beginning of 1844, however, they increased not only in fervency of affection but in legibility and volume. It was remarkable that in writing to this young lady his lordship should constantly allude to things and persons having no existence save in his own imagination. Some explanation of that would no doubt be given later; meanwhile the habit appeared unintelligible, and on the part of an educated gentleman, inconceivable.

Deeming her not finely enough dressed to suit his aristocratic taste, Lord Ferrers desired his betrothed to purchase, as presents from himself, certain articles of apparel, for which he was in due course to furnish her with money. Carried away by this singular act of generosity she blushingly incurred liabilities to the tune of £200; the tradespeople pressed for payment, and though in delicate and reserved terms she hinted to her noble lover that it would be well to settle these accounts, no remittance came to enable her to do so. Tenderness for Lord Ferrers' reputation led her to withhold from her parents the fact that she had been obliged to buy his presents herself. "Please calm all apprehensions as to bills, etc.," airily wrote his lordship, "these I will attend to when I come down; this I add for fear you should be vexing your dear self unnecessarily." "Gentlemen," continued the learned counsel with true Buzfuzian emphasis, "he did *not* come down, and she *did* vex herself, not unnecessarily." The importunity of the creditors at length compelled her to tell the truth to her parents, who were much perturbed by the absence of business habits thus manifested by their future son-in-law. Mr. Smith wrote to Lord Ferrers on the subject, and in due course received the following reply: "SIR,—It is my will and wish to instantly pay for all at Tamworth as soon as may be. This much I say, and I feel very grieved that any such indiscretion of mine should have caused vexation to Mary. Allow me to remain, truly yours, FERRERS." As the wish remained father to the thought and the Earl sent no cheque, Mr. Smith had to borrow the money to pay the bills himself, the lender being the lady's maternal grandfather. But, owing to her distress of mind, Miss Smith concealed from her parents a debt of 30s. due to one Miss Wyman in respect of a certain pink silk bonnet, and even went to the length of denying to that lady's face that she had ever ordered it. This, counsel admitted, savoured of dissimulation, but was a trifle when compared with the perfidy of Lord Ferrers.

The Solicitor-General then quoted extracts from the correspondence between January and July 1844, which will come in more conveniently later, when the letters were read in full to the Court. The postponement of the marriage further alarmed the parents, but all doubts were set at rest on receipt by Mr. Smith of the following letter:—

> MY DEAR SIR,—This note ought to have been with you long ago, but "better late than never" is the old adage. May it apply in my case. Without entering into particulars, I am aware you know that in secret I have long sought your eldest daughter; now, openly, I ask her of you for

> my wife; I hope you will not refuse me her. Ere this I should have come personally to have made this request to you, had not untoward circumstances prevented. I hope shortly to see you; then, if convenient, we can arrange about her settlement, etc. I have mentioned August as the month to her. I hope when we meet everything, all things, will meet with your approbation and that of Mrs. Smith. Allow me to sign myself, very faithfully yours,
>
> W. FERRERS.
>
> Chartley, June 24th.[5]

In view of the intimate and affectionate character of the correspondence, proving meetings, unchangeable attachment and abundant evidence of the promise of marriage, the jury would participate in counsel's astonishment when they learned the nature of the defence: that Lord Ferrers never spoke to this young lady in the whole course of his life, that he did not know her, and that all these letters were from beginning to end one tissue of fabrications and forgeries! That the girl of nineteen should conceive and execute the atrocious design of entering into such a conspiracy, making her parents and others parties to that conspiracy, and carrying it out by means which would defy the skill of the most experienced experts, was impossible to believe. It was madness to suppose that a girl could sit down and forge the writing of this nobleman in the long series of letters which would be laid before them; the task was beyond the ability of a professional imitator of hands or an inspector of franks. Instead of contenting herself with a few words importing a promise of marriage, that she should expose herself to attack in every one of the ten thousand lines throughout these letters was incredible.

The parties were fighting with unequal weapons. The defendant's cousin, Mr. Evelyn Shirley, so continually mentioned in the correspondence, had refused to give any information. Adkins, his lordship's confidential man, through whose hands the letters passed, took up the same position. As he—counsel—did not know what these persons might say he could not call them, but he would produce the Rev. Mr. Arden, Lord Ferrers' domestic chaplain, and other gentlemen familiar with his writing, who would establish beyond dispute the genuineness of the letters. He would also call witnesses as to meetings, people who had seen the parties together at sundry times and in divers places, he would prove the gift of an engagement ring, and he would put the lady's parents in the box.[6] Both Lord Ferrers' father[7] and grandfather[8] had married women of low degree, and his education, as shown by the style of his letters, was below that of a charity schoolboy. The plaintiff was a highly educated and accomplished lady, and would never be guilty of the faults of grammar and spelling exhibited in these letters. The terrible wrong, the dreadful agony of mind inflicted on her, the destruction of her whole prospects, and the attempt to stigmatize her as a criminal, the jury would bear in mind, along with the great wealth and station of the defendant, in appreciating the amount of damage she had sustained at his hands.

One can conceive the sympathetic murmur—what the reporters of the State Trials would term "a great Hum"—amid which the learned counsel resumed his seat. An admission having been put in that the defendant was born on 3rd January 1822, and was married at St. George's, Hanover Square, on 23rd July 1844, the Rev. Edward Francis Arden, Clerk in Holy Orders, was called. He had been chaplain both to the late and to the present Earl, and had known the latter intimately as Lord Tamworth. When his lordship returned from abroad until 1844 witness was his constant companion. Lord Ferrers' education had been imperfect. Witness was well acquainted with his handwriting. Shown ten letters to Miss Smith and two to her father, he said he believed them to be Lord Ferrers'. He recollected an accident happening at Staunton Harold when, fencing with swords, he cut the Earl's finger. Lord Ferrers used to disguise himself, "after the fashion of the toll-gate breakers," by putting on a nightshirt and blackening his face and whiskers. Witness had seen him wearing a ring similar to that produced.

Cross-examined by the Attorney-General, he had officiated at Stowe, at Staunton, and at Chartley. He had seen Lord Ferrers in disguise there. Witness also disguised himself by putting on his shirt outside his clothes, etc., and the Earl painted on his face "moustachios," which as a clergyman of the Church of England he was not in use to wear. They went about together so disguised several times—"just a mere bit of a schoolboys' lark." He acknowledged, under pressure, that his age was about thirty-seven. Asked whether on these occasions he was sober, the reverend gentleman replied, "I am sure I do not know; that is of no importance." He denied that complaints were made of his being often drunk: "it was merely the chat of the country that he was a little careless," but whether of drink, of his clerical duties, or of his reputation he was unable to say. "People will talk; if you had been there they would have talked about you the same," added the witness. "I should probably, Sir, have been more secure from the observations," retorted the Attorney-General. Witness swore that on no occasion between 1842 and 1844 was he ever the worse of liquor. In June 1844 he left Staunton of his own accord; he was not dismissed. He then stayed with Mr. Ingram, a surgeon at Chartley. It was untrue that he and his host's daughter were turned out of the house for misbehaviour. He and Mr. Ingram afterwards quarrelled, not on account of his improper conduct with the daughter, but because her father was a fool and a blackguard. Witness was searchingly questioned as to his relations with this lady. He denied that they had lived together or that he had driven her about the country, but admitted that occasionally he had been with her by rail to Birmingham. When after leaving Chartley he went to Stowe he put up at the Cock, a public-house, where he was accustomed to meet his parishioners. He was not frequently intoxicated there, though he was in the habit of drinking with the landlord. He had received half-a-dozen notes from Lord Ferrers: the letters produced he believed to be in his handwriting. Accompanied by Miss Ingram he had called upon Mr. Collis, a jeweller, with reference to a ring which had been mended for the Earl, and asked whether Collis knew his lordship's writing. He told Collis that Lord Ferrers had refused to receive him and had cut him in public; but this was not in reply to Collis's question why he was helping Miss Smith to get up her case. He had been shown by Mr. Hamel, attorney for the plaintiff, letters, other than those now produced, purporting to be the defendant's, which were not in his handwriting. He admitted saying to Mr. Eld, the lordship's steward, that there was only one letter which he thought genuine, and *that* he could not swear to. A long re-examination failed to rehabilitate the reverend rogue, whose reluctant and evasive answers led to some sharp passages with judge and counsel. He now said that the two letters signed "Devereux Shirley"—the defendant's brother—were the other letters to which he referred. He had no knowledge of or acquaintance with Miss Smith or her family before the trial. The impression left upon the jury by this deleterious divine can hardly have been favourable.

Major Majendie, who had served with Lord Ferrers in the Staffordshire Yeomanry, was next called. He had seen his lordship's signature to pay lists and had some slight correspondence with him. He thought the letters produced very like his writing. Cross-examined, he had received at the outside four notes from Lord Ferrers, inviting hm to shoot, etc., and never saw his signature to any pay lists but two. Willian Perkins, paymaster of the Staffordshire Yeomanry, gave similar evidence. Cross-examined, he had never seen any of the defendant's writing except his signature. He had been shown three letters signed "Devereux Shirley," one of which he thought more like Lord Ferrers' hand than the rest. Timothy Colborne, footman to Lord Ferrers at Chartley from February to August 1843, said that his lordship often went with his own horses to Rugely and would take post-horses there. Rugely was on the way to Austrey. He had seen the Earl write and knew his hand; the letters produced were certainly his. Lord Ferrers was in the habit of writing on scraps of paper; witness had dried his letters for him at the fire, and had seen him sign "Washington Ferrers." Cross-examined, he had seen at least fifty letters so signed, and over a hundred signed "Ferrers." The former were addressed to members of the family: his lordship's brother, sister, and cousin. Prudence Cotton, daughter of the Chartley postmaster, said she knew Lord Ferrers' writing and identified as his the letters produced. On cross-examination it appeared that she was not employed in the post-office.

Such being the evidence for the plaintiff on the question of handwriting, let us now hear that adduced as to actual meetings between the parties. William Stanton, butcher in Appleby, knew them both by sight. He saw them together upon two occasions: near Austrey brickfield in the summer of 1840 or 1841, and walking on the road between Austrey and Appleby in the summer of 1843. Cross-examined, they passed his garden while he was digging potatoes; he did not stop to watch them, but "kept working like a rum 'un." The plaintiff was "hanging on Lord Tamworth's [Ferrers'] arm." He did not remember telling one Saddington that he had never seen them together. Thomas Trennadine, maltster in Appleby, knew the parties by sight. Several times in the autumn of 1839 he saw Lord Tamworth come out of the Smiths' garden-gate between 9 and 10 p.m. Cross-examined, he had been absent from the district for five years before 1839; he did not go away to avoid a prosecution regarding some malt. The evidence of the next witness, though rather irrelevant, is too amusing for abridgement and must be given in full:

> *William Taylor, sworn, examined by Solicitor-General.*
> Do you live at Austrey?—Not when I am in London.
> Did you live there?—Yes.
> Do you live there when you are at home?—Yes.
> Do you remember Lord Tamworth, who is now Lord Ferrers, being at Austrey?—Yes, I do.
> Now did you at any time see him and Miss Smith together?—I passed them both at one certain time, and a horse as well.
> How long ago was this?—I think it was about 1814.[9]
> *Mr. Justice Wightman.* This man seems exceedingly tipsy.
> *The witness.* No, I am not.
> *The Solicitor-General.* I will not ask this witness any more questions.[10]

William Tell, Austrey, saw three years before Lord Ferrers talking to Miss Smith on the Appleby Road. Cross-examined, it was in November, about four o'clock, but he would not swear to a quarter of an hour "no way." "There might be two yards between them" at the time. Emma Base, the Smiths' servant, said that she used to walk out with plaintiff and the children. They met Lord Ferrers many times; he was on horseback and would dismount when he saw them. On these occasions by Miss Smith's order she walked on with the children and plaintiff afterwards rejoined her. Cross-examined, she never saw them in conversation. Elizabeth Bircher, Austrey, once met them walking arm-in-arm when Lord Tamworth was with Mr. Echalaz. Three times she saw him ride past the Smiths' house and turn to look at it. Cross-examined, he was fully two minutes riding past, with his head on his shoulder. "It must be a good long house," commented the Attorney-General. John Page, bailiff's follower, at 2 p.m. in July or August 1841, 1842, or 1843, saw the parties walking side by side three yards apart, in the Butts field behind the Smiths' house. Cross-examined, he was then going to buy a sickle, and 1843 was the last year in which he reaped.

This, with the notable exception now to be mentioned, is the whole evidence of Lord Ferrers ever having been in Miss Smith's company. Ann Smith, aged thirteen, sister of the plaintiff, said that she had often seen Lord Tamworth at Austrey. One day in the spring of 1843 she looked in at the drawing-room window at her father's house and saw his lordship standing at the chimneypiece; her sister entered the room, and she left the window. On 9th December 1843, the day of Austrey Wake—the local fair—on going into the drawing-room to tell her sister that the Wake-cake woman had come, she found Lord Tamworth playing the piano. Her sister was with him. He rose up, and the witness went out so soon as she saw "who it was." Her sister took cakes and wine into the room for the noble visitor's refreshment. She was told she would be whipped if she went in while his lordship was there.

Cross-examined, she used to see Lord Tamworth at church. The first time she saw him in the drawing-room was after breakfast, about Easter. Her mother had told her not to go into the room and she guessed Lord Tamworth was expected. The second time was at midday. She was sure of the date because of the cakes. Her mother was in the sitting-room when the Wake-cake woman called; the servants were in the kitchen. The piano could be heard all over the house. Re-examined, Lord Tamworth could get into the garden by the fields without being noticed. He used to gaze at her sister in church.[11]

Thomas Nicklin Smith, father of the plaintiff, said he was an invalid, much confined to bed. He first heard of Lord Tamworth's attentions in December 1839, and sent his daughter away to school until his lordship had left Austrey. After Lord Ferrers' return from abroad in 1843 witness understood that he came to the house, but never saw him there. In 1844 his daughter showed him from time to time letters which she had received from the Earl. He identified the ten letters produced. In June 1844 she handed him a letter,[12] proposing for her hand; he replied, accepting; read his answer to a friend, Mr. Holgate; and gave it to Mrs. Smith to seal and post. He had destroyed the draft. His daughter afterwards showed him an acknowledgement from Lord Ferrers, which was not among the letters now in Court. In February or March last he was shown by Mrs. Smith and John Lees two handkerchiefs, enclosed in letters from his daughter to the Earl, addressed to his lordship at Chartley Castle. The preparations for the wedding and the shock of the newspaper announcement of Lord Ferrers' marriage concluded the examination-in-chief. Cross-examined, Mr. Smith said that his daughter was fifteen and Lord Tamworth seventeen when the latter was with Mr. Echalaz. He made no communication to that gentleman regarding his pupil's behaviour, not being on friendly terms with him. He knew his lordship by sight but never spoke to him. In 1843 he saw dresses, books, etc., which he was told were presents from the Earl. His daughter had no allowance of her own. He was unable to seal his letters himself. He had seen letters, others than those produced, and some pieces of poetry, received from Lord Tamworth. Shown certain documents which he was not allowed to read, he believed them to be in his daughter's handwriting.[13]

Mrs. Mary Anne Smith, the plaintiff's mother, was in her own way as unsatisfactory a witness as the Rev. Mr. Arden. She described herself more than once as a truthful woman, anxious to tell the truth; but perhaps she was if anything too full of that virtue, which was so compressed within her bosom that it was hard to come by. She said she learned from her daughter of Lord Tamworth's attentions while he was with Mr. Echalaz. When he returned from his travels her daughter said she had met him again, and showed her from time to time letters receive from him. The handkerchiefs were sent at different times; she saw her daughter write the letters, fold them up, and put in the handkerchiefs. Both were posted by John Lees. In April 1844 she accompanied her daughter to Stafford where they were to meet Lord Ferrers, who had invited them to Wales; he failed to come as arranged, so they returned home. From Syerscote Manor, her father's house, her daughter wrote to the Earl a letter, posted at Tamworth. She wrote again, the letter being posted at Lichfield by Mrs. Perry, a sister of witness. Lord Ferrers replied, proposing to Mr. Smith for his daughter's hand; Mr. Smith's answer, accepting, was read to her and to Mr. Holgate; she sealed it, put it in a drawer overnight, and posted it next day at Ashby in presence of Mr. and Mrs. Holgate. When everything was ready for the wedding she learned of Lord Ferrers' marriage.

To the cross-examination of this lady by the Attorney-General no summary can do justice. Anything but obtuse, she was swift to mark the bearing of his questions, saw his points almost before he made them, and indeed was so wary and acute a witness that she proved at times more than a match for her learned adversary. She "hedged" with a persistence which made it well nigh impossible to pin her to any definite statement. For instance, the judge would observe: "We are not sure what her answer is"; "I find great difficulty in taking down an answer that is immediately retracted"; "that is exactly contrary to what she said before"; "she states first she believes it is paid, and then says she does not know," and so forth. Mrs. Smith said that everything was prepared for the wedding; linen, dresses, etc., were ordered, four bridescakes bespoke, two bridesmaids engaged. Yet she had never spoken to Lord Ferrers in her life. He "signified" that he would come to see the parents of his fiancée, but never appeared. The preparations were all made by his desire. After the Earl's return from abroad she and her daughter attended a ball at Tamworth. *Her daughter, who was tall and dark, wore a single white rose in her hair.*[14] Lord Ferrers, though expected by them, was not present. Her daughter afterwards received from him many gifts of dresses, jewellery, and books: silks, cashmeres, muslins; rings and brooches; the Abbotsford edition of the Waverley Novels, etc. Two or three months later bills came in; witness paid them; they amounted to £200. She saw only the totals, the detailed accounts were sent to the Earl. *Her daughter sometimes used the name "Marie."* Witness never actually saw her receive a letter from Lord Ferrers. A pink silk bonnet was delivered on 29th June 1844. The box contained a note from Mr. Devereux Shirley. An account for it was rendered at Christmas which she showed to her daughter, who said there must be some mistake. On 6th January 1845 she and her daughter, accompanied by their solicitor Mr. Hamel, went to Ashby and saw Miss Wyman, the milliner. Miss Smith did not then repeatedly deny that she had ordered the bonnet, nor did Miss Wyman remark "she wondered she (plaintiff) wasn't struck dead." Witness did not say that if her daughter would confess she would forgive her. The latter told her that Devereux Shirley personally at Ashby handed her the note, which was to be put in the box to deceive her papa and mama. Hamel paid the bill. She saw Miss Wyman again after the present action was raised, and asked her not to mention the bonnet episode till the case was decided. Shown certain documents which she was not permitted to read, Mrs. Smith said that they were in her daughter's writing.[15] She identified the two handkerchiefs produced as those sent by Miss Smith to Lord Ferrers. She had no recollection of a conversation with Miss Neville, when that lady pointed out the resemblance between the handwriting of the Earl's letters and that of her daughter; she might have said that the likeness had been remarked in the family; she did not say that Miss Smith had got some of his lordship's writing and used to imitate it. She was much upset at the time, because the defendant's agent had said "they [the Smith family] would all be put in Warwick Gaol as forgers." "I am a truthful woman," exclaimed the witness; "I am glad to find one," cynically retorted the Attorney-General. Her daughter never wrote to her lover before his return from abroad. She was not a great reader of novels.

Application was here made that the defendant's witnesses might have an opportunity to inspect the letters; this was opposed, but the Court allowed it, on condition that only those to be called should do so.

John Lees and Mr. and Mrs. Holgate, friends of the Smiths,

Mrs. Perry, aunt of the plaintiff, and Susan Hopely, one of their servants, severally swore to the posting of letters, addressed by Miss Smith to Lord Ferrers, at Atherstone, Tamworth, Derby, Ashby, Leamington, and Lichfield respectively; and an official of the Dead Letter Office proved that no letter to Lord Ferrers had been returned to his department.

The famous correspondence of which we have heard so much was then read by the Associate. In view of its extent, the great variety of topics touched on, and the spaciousness with which these are treated, it is impossible to give the reader more than a mere taste of the writer's epistolary gifts. The first, dated "Mivart's, February 11th," was addressed to "Dearest Mary":—

> If wishes could transport me to you there would be no need of this writing; but as I am anxious, most anxious to hear of your well being, and also to tell you that business relating to my grandfather's will may detain me longer than I thought from you, I send this . . . . I have seen chairs I think will do for one of our rooms at Chartley. Won't the old Hall be bright and happy when its future mistress takes possession of it! Pray take care of yourself, dearest; forget not you are the only hope of one to whom a palace would be but a desert and England no home without you; far dearer to me than each earthly blessing. Mary, you who are all in all to me, take care of yourself, and mind when you return from walking you change your shoes. You may laugh at me, but you are not particular, I know, in this respect and you may take cold . . . . It has often struck me that there is something untold to me, some secret care I know not of that troubles

> you. Why not, dear girl, tell me if it is so, for I have often seen you look sad and unhappy . . . . I hope even this will cease in May, that you may be my bride, my wife; then all that is mystery now will be cleared, and your father will not have to look for the marks of horse's shoes in that hovel of his, but that "Zimro" may be found in his stable.[16]

He tells her of visiting his sister who is ill at Brighton, of a dinner party he has given at Mivart's, of his intention to purchase for £1000 the conservatory at Staunton, and of his regret for "the loss of that foolish £5000," which will be a warning to him: his father and grandfather lost much money in that way, and he is not minded to become "a second Lord Huntingtower." He draws a pathetic picture of the married state of his cousin, Evelyn Shirley's daughter, "who wedded Walker," a gentleman, as appears, of a proud, cold-hearted character, a man unloved, married for wealth or station, and his lady "more like a corpse than anything else." He concludes as follows:—

> 'Do not laugh at the various pieces of paper I send; you know my fondness for writing on little pieces. Adieu; every earthly blessing be yours, is the sincere wish of your much attached till death, WASHINGTON FERRERS. *P.S.* This Atkins [*sic*] brings. Write and say how you are; he will post it. Let no one see this, 'tis so bad a specimen.[17]

In his next letter, also dated "Mivart's," his lordship acknowledged receipt of a handkerchief marked with her hair, the gift of his betrothed, which he will prize beyond all mortal mouchoirs. He hears from Devereux, who has seen her, that she has been ill, and reproaches her for not communicating the fact direct. He had much interesting gossip to give her concerning his friends Sir Robert Peel, Lord Clive, Lord Claude Hamilton, and other high company. "Mrs. Walker no better; I hate her husband." The claims of fashion are not neglected by this observant nobleman: "Bonnets are not very pretty, plumes are universally worn." His hand is paining him—"that foil and Harding [*sic*]." While he was buying a beautiful casket for her boudoir at Chartley, his cousin Evelyn came into the shop, asked what a bachelor wanted with such an article, and "supposed the next thing would be a wife."

> Send the other handkerchief with a note when finished.... Lord Brougham dined with me yesterday. I like him well, he comes here to-morrow . . . . My promised wife will be all on earth to me. I am reading much now, as I really find myself wanting here amongst all these great men. I was surprised to find what a good Italian scholar Evelyn is, he knows it well, the language. Adieu now, dearest, ever think of me as your only truly attached, WASHINGTON FERRERS, Remember me to your sister Ann.[18]

The next letter thanks her for the other handkerchief. He has been staying with the Shirleys at Eatington, the house-party including one Sir Terence Volney of Berkshire, "a strange person, very pleasant, quite an enthusiast as regards religion, rich, and not over young." The family name of this amiable baronet ought, by the way, to have been Harris, for no human eye but his creator's ever beheld him in the flesh. After these practical details the writer thus waxes lyrical:—

> Lady of my heart and earliest love, what fond remembrances enfold themselves round thy image! All my hopes and fears, boyish and manly, are with thee; with thee my happiness began, with thee will end the rose of my existence. Pure white rose thou may'st be compared to, for thy thoughts are pure as drifted snow, and as such I prize thee, my own love, for thou wilt make my life blissful and happy. Only take care of yourself, and remember—[not this time, to change her shoes]—you are mine.[19]

He must see Jessop, his confidential attorney, one of the tribe whom Evelyn calls bloodsuckers; "I cannot do without Mr. Jessop." Devereux has joined his regiment, Evelyn has lost some thousands in a speculation with Mr. Wilberforce, and there is further mention of the unhappy wife of "that brute Walker," who seems to have been his King Charles's head. This is all the family news. The next letter, written from 26 Park Lane, after certain pertinent reflections upon mutual trust and confidence as the true foundations of happiness in married life, proceeds:—

> I shall certainly come the day before our wedding and stay with you at your home, judging it cannot be objectionable to your parents. Perhaps before that time I may introduce myself in due form, but this we will talk of when I come. 'Tis, as you say, strange for Papa and Mama not to know the intended husband of their child till so shortly before the ceremony which unites the two; but I hope the hereafter will make up for the now in these things.[20]

He has been at Brighton again on a visit to his ailing sister, who despite her broken health keeps much company.

> I saw some right queer young ladies there, Scotch women, Miss MacTrevors; very rich, very ordinary, bold—in short anything but nice. And these are called fashionable women—Heaven keep me from such! Oh, in the evening they exposed to view such shoulders! 'twas more than kind. I quite longed for Devereux to see and quiz them, and sketch them, which he would have done to perfection! . . . Adieu, dearest and best, take care of yourself, and let each thing you want be in a state of preparation.[21]

The next, dated "Deanery, Bangor, April 30th," deals with his disappointment at the miscarriage of the Cambrian excursion: "It seems we were not to meet together in romantic Wales, that land of mountain and heath blossoms." He is sorry to hear about the bills for his presents, but looks forward to "the pleasure of reimbursing your grandfather"—the pleasure would doubtless have been mutual. Let their marriage take place in June; when he returns home he will instruct Jessop to prepare the settlements. The next, without date, is from Chartley. Holding her as he does "the choicest gift of God," he conjures her to disregard anything she may see in the newspapers respecting his impending union with a Welsh lady: "what lie will not the papers tell?" He is sensible that people must think him a rogue or a fool, but he finds comfort in the knowledge that she will never forsake him. The next, from Chartley, undated, further postpones the ceremony till August. He is full of troubles; Eld, his steward, talks of leaving him, and he is like to lose the ghostly counsel and support of Rev. Mr. Arden. He hopes her parents will not object to "this putting off our bridal," though he has heard that Mr. Smith is stern and unbending. "The bridecake will keep," he prudently reflects, "and be the better." Devereux is to get leave to attend the wedding. The next has reference to her engaging a waiting-woman for the first week of August. Then on 24th June he writes from Chartley Castle, enclosing the formal proposal addressed to Mr. Smith already mentioned.[22] The last of the series is dated "Shirley Wich, July 13th"—ten days before his marriage to Miss Chichester. He has been laid up with fainting fits, but so soon as he is allowed to travel he will be with her.

> Do not be surprised if I come quite *incog.* and stay with you at the Swan. Remember you the quantity of wigs and the potent stain of the walnuts? Look out for me on Tuesday . . . . Tell Mama to look well if she will not recognize me in the pale and sallow young man she may meet at the Swan. Till then adieu, my own, my promised bride. Ever yours till death, FERRERS.[23]

The series concludes with certain letters of Devereux Shirley, written from the sickroom, giving a harrowing account of the sufferings of the noble invalid.

The case on the part of the plaintiff being closed, the Attorney-General[24] addressed the jury for the defendant. Much must have seemed to them, he said, unintelligible, many questions put by him have appeared pointless, but all would presently be made plain. The alternative before them was a painful one: if they decided against the plaintiff they dismissed her from Court with ignominy and disgrace; if in her favour, they must find that a young nobleman, having engaged the affections of a girl, had afterwards denied his attachment, and used the very tokens of his affection as a means to fasten upon her the odious crimes of forgery and fraud. His learned friend, adverting to the nature of the defence, had dwelt on the improbability of a young girl, even were she bold and wicked enough to contrive such a scheme, being able to carry it out. But to that argument the cases of Elizabeth Canning and of Maria Glen afforded a sufficient answer.[25] The case could be conveniently divided into two periods: (1) from February 1839 to June 1840, during which, as Lord Tamworth, defendant was with his tutor at Austrey; and (2) from January 1843, when as Lord Ferrers he came of age, to July 1844, when he married his present wife. The notes and poetry alleged to have passed between this boy and girl were said to have been destroyed by her. It was remarkable that a village maiden should not have preserved such flattering proofs of her patrician conquest.

Counsel then reviewed the evidence of meetings during the first period, remarking that it seemed rather a weak foundation for so imposing a superstructure. It was to him wholly immaterial whether these two young people met at that time, occasionally walked together, or exchanged a word of two. No one had come forward to say that they ever *conversed*. If it were true that his lordship frequented the house, why were his visits not proved by the family and servants? After his return from abroad, coming of age, and succession to the title, the defendant alleged, and the jury would probably believe him, that no communication of any kind took place between him and the plaintiff.

With regard to the letters produced, while the plaintiff was enabled to select her witnesses to handwriting, the defendant first got a sight of them in the course of these proceedings. His advisors expected that the postmarks would form an infallible test for detecting the fraud, but they found that there were none, that all the letters were said to have been delivered by the Earl's servants! He might tell the jury at once that this was an entire fabrication and falsehood; that neither Adkins nor James ever received from their master for, or delivered to Miss Smith one single letter. The letters were admittedly full of fictions, which the Solicitor-General sought ingeniously to account for by saying that Lord Ferrers was constitutionally incapable of telling the truth. But what conceivable motive could he have in making these false statements? They would, however, under Providence, be the means of exposing and defeating this shameful fraud.

Passing to the second period, they heard of meetings even under her father's roof, of letters breathing ardent affection, of the naming of the very day, continuing to the eve of his marriage to someone else. Now Lord Ferrers was his own master; family circumstances would make him less scrupulous than usual about marrying beneath him; there was absolutely no reason for his not approaching the parents. Why remain concealed and correspond through agents? Why, engaged to another lady since May, write to Mr. Smith in July, proposing for his daughter's hand? There were two witnesses only to alleged meetings at this time: Page, the bailiff's follower, who couldn't say whether it was in '41, '42, or '43—the sort of evidence it was impossible to meet—and Ann Smith, the plaintiff's little sister, whose evidence was, to him, the most distressing incident in that painful case—a child brought forward to tell a story utterly false. From the mother's evidence it appeared that Lord Ferrers had never been beneath her roof, and this new statement took the defence completely by surprise. She said that she twice saw the Earl with her sister in the drawing-room, the first time "about Easter"; that her mother warned her not to go in, and that she knew perfectly well that he was expected. So the visit was notorious in the family; yet neither the parents nor the servants said a word about it. As to the second occasion, fortunately for Lord Ferrers, they had a definite date: 9th December 1843, the day of Austrey Wake: which enabled him to meet *that* falsehood. It would be proved that on that day he posted with his sister after breakfast from Chartley to Welshpool, where they lunched, and thence to that lady's house in Wales. Even "Zimro," the swift horse, could not have enabled him to cover the fifty-eight miles to Austrey and back, to play the piano there at midday, and to lunch at noon at Welshpool. His sister's oath, his steward's accounts, the bills for the posthorses and for the meal, would establish the fact beyond dispute.

As to Lord Ferrers' education, so far from being like that of a charity boy, he had been at two private schools and for two years at Eton, before he went to Austrey. Five persons had sworn that these letters were in his handwriting. Of these the Rev. Mr. Arden and the footman might be dismissed as unworthy of credit. The disgraceful exhibition made by that "respectable clergyman" was fresh in their memory; Colborne, the six-months' servant, dried 150 of his master's letters at the fire between June and August! He said that 50, signed "Washington," were addressed to Mrs. Hanbury Tracy, to Mr. Devereux, and to Mr. Evelyn Shirley, who would swear they never in their lives received from their relative a letter so signed. The two military experts founded their belief on having seen his lordship's signature to two pay lists; the postmaster's daughter did not assist at the post-office. That was the evidence as to handwriting.

The falsehood of these letters was established by internal evidence. Some were dated "Mivart's," where Lord Ferrers had never been in his life; one in 1844 from the Deanery, Bangor, where he had not been since 1840. He bought the conservatory at Staunton in 1842 for £400, and is made to say in 1844 that he is thinking of purchasing it for £1000. He took his seat in the House of Lords on 11th August 1843, and on 11th February 1844 writes that his "good cousin Evelyn" advises him not to take it yet. His sister, Mrs. Hanbury Tracy, whom he is represented as often visiting at Brighton during her illness, had never been there and was in perfect health. His brother Devereux, who is said to have been interviewing Miss Smith in 1844, joined his regiment in Scotland in March 1843 and was not absent a day from that country till March 1845. As to the £5000 gambling debt, Lord Ferrers never touched a card in his life. Evelyn Shirley's daughter, the victim of the villain "Walker," was an infant six months old! The finger cut by the Rev. Mr. Arden in 1842 is still unhealed in 1844. That Lord Ferrers knew Lord Brougham, that his steward talked of leaving him, that Jessop was his lawyer, that he had a horse called "Zimro," that Evelyn knew Italian or had speculated with Mr. Wilberforce, were all statements equally and wilfully false.

After vainly searching the evidence of Mrs. Smith in quest of truth, so lamentably lacking in the letters, of which that matron boasted herself the depositary, the Attorney-General asked how, in view of his contention that the whole story was untrue, could the fact be accounted for that letters addressed to Lord Ferrers by the plaintiff were proved by divers respectable persons to have been posted by them at various times and places?The very handkerchiefs therein enclosed are produced by the defendant himself: is he then mad enough to maintain that there was *no* correspondence? "Now let us begin to unravel the mystery; we are coming to the third volume." No sooner had Lord Ferrers succeeded to the title than there began to arrive a succession of *anonymous* letters, plainly the production of a lady enamoured. Neither knowing nor caring who his fair correspondent might be his lordship threw most of them in the fire; but fortunately for him four had survived. *These, put to the parents in the witness-box, were identified by them as written by their daughter.* The first letter, dated 19th December 1842, was posted at Derby:—

> MY LORD,—Strange it may seem to you, no doubt, to receive a note from a stranger, and a lady too; but it signifies little to me, as I know well you will never know the writer of this letter, never see her. Now for what I have to tell you it is this: there is a public ball at Tamworth every Christmas, generally about the 6th or 8th January; go, I advise you, go; there will to my knowledge be a young lady at the ball who I wish you to see and dance with. She is very beautiful, has dark hair and eyes, in short she is haughty and graceful as a Spaniard, tall and majestic as a Circassian, beautiful as an Italian. I can say no more; you have only to see her to love her, that you must do; she is fit for the bride of a prince. Go, look well round the room, you will find her by this description: *she may wear one white rose in her dark hair.* If you see her not there you will never see her, as she is like a violet hid midst many leaves, only to be found when sought for . . . . Keep your own counsel, my Lord, and deem yourself happy in the idea of knowing one so talented, beautiful, and young. Ask her to dance and fear not. And now I have fulfilled my mission and shall rest in peace, more peaceful, though, did I know that you would meet this bright young girl. If you, like other men, love beauty

> you will love her. Adieu, burn this letter, and remember she is my legacy to you. You have hurt your hand, I hear; I am sorry. Farewell for ever. ISABEL.[26]

"Do you understand the case now?" asked the Attorney-General. "Have I kept faith with you? Have I redeemed the pledge I gave that however dark and mysterious it might appear I would disperse all the shadows and present it clearly and distinctly to your view?" Here was the very letter proved by the mother to be in her daughter's handwriting, put into the very post-office described; and when other anonymous communications, even containing handkerchiefs, were received by Lord Ferrers, could they doubt that this artful girl, deceiving some, assisted, it was to be feared, by others, had been contriving a scheme of the most arrant falsehood and of the grossest and most scandalous iniquity; that but for various providential circumstances Lord Ferrers would have fallen a prey to the snares with which he was encompassed, his honour blasted, his reputation gone, and his wealth invaded by this infamous engagement. Another letter, dated 5th June 1843, contained the following gems:—

> Washington, beloved one, when shall I see you, when behold the form of one dear to me, how dear! . . . You are young, and have no father or mother to guide your steps. The world, I am told, is deceitful and wicked; you have no one to advise you, to whisper words of affection and of love, to watch over and be with you. You have some wealth and rank; if these could constitute happiness then you might be happy; but your household hearth is not warmed by affection. Do you never sigh for one to

> love you, one whom you could put faith and trust in? . . . Alas, in secret I write to you, in secret love; would we could meet. Do you never visit Staunton? Beloved one, adieu, adieu, ever your friend, MARIE.[27]

In a third letter of March 1844 "Dearest Washington" is informed that despite his persistent silence she cannot banish his image from her heart.

> It is, I am aware, unmaidenly thus to write, but you know not the writer . . . . Oh, that we might meet, and that you could love me even as I love you! But we dwell far apart—[what about "Zimro"?]—and thus music and flowers and birds must still be loved by me . . . . Perhaps these notes may never even reach you. If you are at home, write and say if you have received a packet of anonymous letters directed to you at Chartley. An envelope with "yes" or "no" written in it will be sufficient. Direct to Miss A. B., post office, Leicester . . . Washington, you are mine, and you are very dear to me. Let me still think of you, and if you write then I shall have something to look at as yours.[28]

"I think," commented the Attorney-General, "the lady will indeed be *very dear* to Lord Ferrers, for these proceedings will not be conducted without considerable expense to him." This last is dated 1st May 1844 and bears the Tamworth postmark.

> MY DEAREST WASHINGTON,—Days even weeks pass on yet hear I nothing from you . . . . How I long to see

> your face; shall I ever again do so; to hear your voice and see you smile, but perhaps I may never behold you more.

"This is very odd," was counsel's comment, "because May was fixed for the wedding and all arrangements had been made."

> Something whispers to me we shall once more meet, be it in lighted hall or church, or under the shade of the hawthorn tree; we shall meet, though you may not dream you are there holding converse with your anonymous correspondent. But time hastens, and as our carriage passes through the borough from which your second and prettiest name [Viscount Tamworth] is derived, while our horses are baited at the Castle Inn, so shall I post this to you. Dearest Washington, with best wishes for your happiness and future welfare, allow the lady who thus writes to subscribe herself, most devotedly, MARIE.[29]

These letters were written by the plaintiff. Could the jury doubt, apart even from proof of handwriting, that artful and ingenious as she had shown herself to be, she also wrote those attributed to Lord Ferrers? Could anyone after that exposure stand up in a court of justice and in the face of the public maintain such a case? If fatal consequences to the plaintiff followed she had brought them on herself; the stern demands of justice imperatively required their interference for the protection of the defendant.

The evidence for the defence, so far as led, need not detain us. Mr. Evelyn Shirley, Mr. and the Hon. Rosamond Hanbury Tracy, and the Hon. Devereux Shirley, amply confirmed the statements of the Attorney-General, and the indispensable Mr. Jessop said that he had never acted for Lord Ferrers. All five emphatically denied that the letters were in his handwriting. A clerk from Mivart's proved that Lord Ferrers had never stayed at that hotel. At this stage the Solicitor-General, who had been absent from Court for the last two days, intervened. He said he had only that morning seen the four anonymous letters, which took him entirely by surprise. In these circumstances, being unable to account for or explain them, he felt it his duty in the interests of truth and justice to withdraw from the case; the plaintiff would elect to be nonsuited. Mr. Justice Wightman approved; it was quite impossible, he said, to believe that the letters purporting to be written by the defendant could be his. His lordship ordered all the documents to be impounded in court. The plaintiff was nonsuited accordingly, and the case was at an end.

If the Fair Circassian of the letters were again to invite the attention of the law, one would naturally have expected her to grace the dock as the subject of a criminal prosecution. Instead of this, however, on 4th December 1847, before Mr. Justice Cresswell and a special jury in the Court of Common Pleas, Westminster, she resumes her civil rôle of plaintiff, in an action for damages for libel against the *Britannia* newspaper. Mr. Serjeant Talfourd, the friend of Dickens to whom he dedicated *Pickwick*, and Mr. Symons, who must have been strong in the article of faith, appeared for the injured lady; Mr. Cockburn, Q.C., and Mr. Barstow, for the proprietor of the offending journal. The plaintiff explained the learned Serjeant, had lately published a pamphlet, denying the charges brought against her in a recent trial, which was severely commented on in the *Britannia* of 7th November 1846 in a review, headed "Miss Smith and Earl Ferrers," extending to several columns. The libel complained of was contained in the following passages:—

> We will not follow Miss Smith further. Her pamphlet is a curiosity. It may take its place among the monstrosities of literature. It is not equal either in romance or talent to the revelations of Marie Cappelle,[30] but it belongs to the same class, and shows the same kind of perverted ingenuity. But it is for its singularity that we notice it. This girl, though young, is old in the art of deceit, and it is necessary that she should not be deceived as to the opinion that must be formed of her infamous conspiracy, and of the recklessness she displays in coming forth with a string of wretched falsehoods—some avowed, some still concealed—to defend it.
>
> * * * * * * * * *
>
> She is to be pitied; but as she is dangerous, those who have the charge of her should be careful to keep her under some kind of restraint and prevent her from exercising her mischievous propensities. It is fortunate for her that the nature of her plot did not require more fatal instruments than those she has employed.

It was admitted by the defendant that the libel in question had been published in the *Britannia*, of which he was the proprietor and publisher. Serjeant Talfourd explained that as the defendant had not pleaded justification for the statements that the plaintiff was a foul conspirator and all but a murderess, he was unable to call Lord Ferrers to give evidence of the true facts. He could only prove the circumstances in which the libel was written and ask the jury to give his client reasonable redress for the injury that had been inflicted upon her. Mr. Thomas Nicklin Smith, father of the plaintiff, was then called. Having admitted paternity, he said that

Miss Smith had brought an action against Lord Ferrers for breach of promise, and that she had published a pamphlet dealing with the case, which had been reviewed in the *Britannia.* He had read the article; it related to his daughter. Cross-examined, the pamphlet was published in September 1846. It was entirely her own composition; he merely corrected the manuscript. Mr. Cockburn then addressed the jury for the defendant. The plaintiff, he said, had also been plaintiff in another action: "the most remarkable case ever tried in Westminster Hall since the erection of that venerable edifice, which would be handed down to posterity as one of the *causes célèbres* of Europe."[31] After giving a brief account of those proceedings, counsel dealt with the history of the pamphlet. It was sent to a public journal for review, and the reviewer, satisfied that there had been a gross outrage of public decency and morals: that an action had been brought upon letters proved to be wicked forgeries: had commented on the facts in appropriate terms. As to justification, was the defendant to be put to the expense of getting up evidence to afford this lady a chance of vindicating her character? Had justification been pleaded, this action would never have been proceeded with at all. Even should the jury think that the defendant had exceeded the strict limit of his public duty, the plaintiff would be entitled only to nominal damages. Mr. Justice Cresswell having summed up the case, the jury immediately returned a verdict for the plaintiff, damages one farthing. The judge refused to certify the libel as wilful and malicious, thereby depriving the plaintiff of costs.[32]

I have but scant space left for this new "Mystery of Isabel." The pamphlet[33] follows the familiar advice for such as have no case. In her preface, dated from Syerscote Manor, she explains that it is written as the only means of defending herself and a beloved parent from the wanton attack of the Attorney-General. It appears that this innocent and guileless girl was the victim of a vast conspiracy, supported by shameful perjury on the part of all concerned. Only her mother, "than whom a more unsuspecting and artless creature never lived"; Sister Ann, "untainted by the serpent's venom of falsehood and corruption, stamped by the child-like attributes of truth"; and the Rev. Mr. Arden, "the spiritual adviser and bosom friend of two generations of the House of Ferrers"; only these survive, like the righteous men in the Wicked Cities, as saving examples of purity and truth. Scanning her vituperative and mendacious pages to find how a writer so resourceful will encounter the damning fact of the anonymous letters, we see the Haughty Spaniard taking the bull by the horns with appropriate pluck.

> I do not hesitate to say that I wrote the four anonymous letters; circumstances compel me to acknowledge that they were the productions of my pen. The first was written with the hope of inducing Lord Ferrers to come to the Tamworth ball, as he promised when at Austrey he would meet me at the first ball I went to there, and thus be introduced to my parents. I had only seen him twice since his return, and I could not summon courage to ask him myself to meet me; I therefore wrote anonymously, thinking that the exaggerated statements I made in that letter would be sufficient inducement to bring him.[34]

The others were written to test the fidelity of her noble wooer. As he afterwards told her he had lit his pipe with them, she did not scruple to deny their existence to Mr. Hamel, "thus casting a stain upon my name which I fear no after event will ever efface:

what was meant as a mere girlish frolic has proved a misfortune of the deadliest kind."

As to the Earl's letters, Hamel had conjured her to tell the truth, saying that if afterwards he found anything wrong he would throw the case, "and leave her without hope to the mercy of the world." Nay, more; on the eve of the trial the Solicitor-General himself solemnly warned her in the strongest terms that if there were any sort of deception or reservation practised by her, nothing could prevent its detection and the immediate loss of the case. But his client, "secure in her own innocence and the perfect truthfulness of her cause," stuck to her guns: the letters were written by Lord Ferrers. From which two things are plain: that her advisers had their own doubts on the subject, and that the plaintiff had the courage of her opinions.

To account for the otherwise unaccountable behaviour of her late fiancé she does not hesitate to pronounce him mad, and in support of her allegation she gives the following instances of his insanity: (1) "the erection of a gibbet in Chartley Wood for the purpose of hanging in effigy Lawrence, the Earl's great-great uncle";[35] (2) "the interring of a pet monkey after the fashion of a peer"—the deceased, having lain all night in state, surrounded with waxen tapers, in the great hall of Chartley Castle, "my lord followed his monkey friend to the grave, and beat one of the mourners to make him weep"; (3) "he had a mock riot too, which the county police were called in to quell"; and (4) his practice of riddling cinders on a Sunday, "as well as the like amusements proved in evidence at the late trial." Whether these fresh "facts" are the creations of the authoress's fertile fancy, and how far they support her thesis, is for the reader to judge.

Touching the future fortunes of the Beautiful Italian history is silent. Such social memoirs, autobiographies and diaries of the period, etc., as I have been able to consult make no mention of her or her achievement. One would have expected that the gifted damsel, who at nineteen was capable of concocting a romance so strikingly original, would afterwards have made a name for herself in the field of fiction. But if she did develop her remarkable talents in that direction she must have done so anonymously, for I have failed to trace her later works. Unlike the violet of her graceful smile, "hid midst many leaves, only to be found when sought for," she has contrived to baffle my discreet pursuit. I am persuaded, however, that she had a hand in *The Importance of Being Earnest.* You recall how Cecily, worn out by Algernon's entire ignorance of her existence, accepted him on 14th February, bought herself in his name a ring and a bangle, and kept his "dear letters" in a box.

> ALGERNON. My letters! But, my own sweet Cecily, I have never written you any letters.
> CECILY. You need hardly remind me of that, Ernest. I remember only too well that I was forced to write your letters for you. I wrote always three times a week, and sometimes oftener.

The words are the words Oscar, but the voice is the voice of "Marie."

William Roughead's Notes

1 *Proceedings upon the Trial of the Action brought by Mary Elizabeth Smith against the Right Hon. Washington Sewallis Shirley, Earl Ferrers.* London: William Pickering. 1846.

2 Sir Fitzroy Kelly (1796-1880); Lincoln's Inn, 1824; K.C., 1834; defended Tawell the murderer, 1845; Solicitor-General, 1845-6, 1852; Attorney-General, 1858-9; Lord Chief Baron, 1866-80.

3 Robert Sewallis Shirley styled Viscount Tamworth (1778-1824), only son of Robert, VII. Earl Ferrers, by his 1st wife (Jane Prentice), married 5 August 1800 Sophia Caroline, 1st dau[r] of Nathaniel Curzon, 2 Baron Scarsdale. She d. 1849.

4 The Hon. Augusta Annabella Chichester, daughter of Lord Edward Chichester, afterwards second Marquess of Donegal.

5 *Proceedings*, p. 25.

6 By a beneficent and wise provision of the law, as it then stood, the plaintiff and defendant, being the only persons acquainted with the facts, were not available as witnesses.

7 Rt. Wm. Shirley, Visc. Tamworth, b. 1783, d.v.p. 2 Feb. 1830, aged 46; m. 12 Dec. 1821 at Brailesford, co. Derby, Anne, d[r] of Richard Weston. She d. 7 Oct. 1839.

8 Washington Shirley, E. Ferrers, m. 1st. 1781, Frances, d[r] of Rev. Wm. Ward; 2. 28 Sep. 1829, Sarah, d[r] of Wm. Davy. He d. 2 Oct. 1842.

9 As Lord Ferrers was not born till 1822 and Miss Smith till 1825, the proleptic character of this testimony is apparent.

10 Proceedings, p. 125.

11 It is unfortunate that this interesting child did not tell her story *before* her mother was in the box. As it was sprung upon the defence later, they had no opportunity of questioning Mrs. Smith in regard to its many remarkable features.

12 See p. 315, *supra*.

13 The significance of this admission will presently appear.

14 The reader is requested to note this seemingly irrelevant fact.

15 The importance of this will be appreciated later.

16 *Proceedings*, pp. 279-280.

17 Ibid., pp. 281-282.

18 Ibid., pp. 284-285.

19 Ibid., p. 286.

20 Ibid., p. 289.

21 Ibid., pp. 289-290.

22 See p. 315, *supra.*

23 *Proceedings*, p. 296.

24 Sir Frederick Thesiger (1794-1878); Gray's Inn, 1818; K.C., 1834; Solicitor-General, 1844; Attorney-General, 1845-6; Lord Chancellor, 1858-9, 1866-8.

25 Counsel might also have cited the more relevant case of Marie de Morell and Lieutenant La Roncière in 1835, of which an account is given by H. B. Irving in his *Last Studies in Criminology*, pp. 89-178, London, 1921.

26 *Proceedings*, pp. 350-351. One would fain believe that Miss Smith borrowed this pseudonym from the heroine of Herman Melville's *Pierre*; but, alas, that other ambiguous damsel was not then begotten.

27 Ibid, pp. 352-353.

28 Ibid, pp. 354-356.

29 Ibid, pp. 356-358.

30 See *Memoirs of Madame Lafarge; written by herself.* 2 vols. London: Henry Colburn, 1841. The energies of this lady had been directed not to the entrapping, but to the interment of a husband. Her vindication, if equally unconvincing, is less brazenly mendacious than that of Miss Smith.

31 It was later to be eclipsed by the Tichborne case in magnitude of roguery.

32 *Times* Report.

33 *A Statement of Facts respecting the cause of Smith v. The Earl Ferrers . . . with an Examination of the Speech for the Defendant of the late Attorney-General, Sir Frederick Thesiger.* By Mary Elizabeth Smith, the Plaintiff. London:

John Ollivier, 59 Pall Mall. 1846.

34 *Statement of Facts*, p. 21.

35 For an account of the trial and execution of Lawrence Shirley, fourth Earl Ferrers, for the murder of his steward at Staunton in 1760, see Burke's *Celebrated Trials connected with the Aristocracy in the relations of Private Life*, pp. 193-227, London, 1849; and, for good reading, see the book *passim*. Burke's narrative if the present case (pp. 485-505) is confined to extracts from the speeches of counsel, "this most extraordinary case being of such recent date that any comment upon it would be premature and injudicious."

Whatever Became of Miss Smith?
A Final Note
by Gina R. Collia

William Roughead commented, at the end of his essay 'The Ambiguities of Miss Smith', that he would have expected Mary Elizabeth Smith to make a name for herself in the field of fiction, given her ability to concoct such a strikingly original romance. He made searches to discover what had become of her, but she 'contrived to baffle' his 'discreet pursuit', and he could find nothing written by her following the publication of her *Statement of Facts* in 1846. Having decided to pick up where Mr Roughead left off, what follows is the result of my own 'discreet pursuit'.

Mary Elizabeth Smith did indeed pursue a literary career, for a short time at least, and the response she received was moderately favourable. *Moscha Lamberti: Or, A Deed Done Has an End*, a poem of 207 stanzas (with eight pages of explanatory notes), was published by Arthur Hall & Co. in 1849. As Mary explains in her preface, its subject—clearly chosen with the purpose of drawing attention to her own situation—is founded upon a note taken from Fielding's *Select Proverbs*:

> 'The two families of the Amadei, and the Uberti, from a dread of the consequences, long suspended the revenge they meditated on the young Buondelmonte, for the affront he had put upon them in breaking off his match with a young lady of their family; and marrying another.
>
> At length Moscha Lamberti suddenly rising exclaimed in two proverbs, that "Those who considered everything would never conclude on anything." Closing with the

> proverbial saying—"*Cosa fatto Capo ha*! A deed done has an end!" '

And from Machiavelli's *History Of Florence And Of The Affairs Of Italy* she quotes:

> 'As soon as the fact became known, the Amadei and Uberti, whose families were allied, were filled with rage; and having assembled with many others, connections of the parties, they concluded that the injury could not be tolerated without disgrace; and that the only revenge, proportionate to the enormity of the offence, would be to put Buondelmonte to death.'

The preface to *Moscha Lamberti* is dated 'Syerscote Manor, Tamworth, Christmas, 1848', and the book is dedicated to the author's mother, Ann.[1] The dedication begins:

> Being revered! to whom I owe my birth—
> My own dear mother! this book, to thee
> I dedicate; thou'rt all to me on earth;
> Naught else have I to love; accept from me
> An off'ring trac'd in deep adversity.
> Thou wilt not spurn this effort of my muse?
> The boon thy daughter seeks, thou'lt not refuse?
> Though slander's emissaries, her fair fame accuse.'

Later, it goes on:

> 'And though thy daughter's name be vilely slurr'd,
> And the stern world, with falsehood brand her word.'

Clearly, three years after the abrupt close of her action for breach of promise, Mary was still pleading her case. Had she truly believed her own romantic fantasy, we may well be inclined to feel sympathy for her. However, the anonymous letters written by her to Earl Ferrers that were produced during her court case—four of a number received by him over the course of several years—proved that Mary was, and had acknowledged herself to be, a stranger to the earl when she wrote to him.[2] She was not self-deceived; she knew that the story of her engagement was entirely fabricated when she commenced an action with damages laid at £20,000. And yet she continued to paint herself as the injured party, and her obsession—for it must be called that considering her actions—with this 'romance' continued long after she had been proved a fraud in court.

Her dedication was considered 'earnest and eloquent'.[3] The narrative of the poem was described by one reviewer as 'by no means carelessly constructed, and the denouement, when arrived at, is signalled by an occurrence of thrilling interest.'[4] Another reviewer had 'perused this beautiful romantic poem with unmixed feelings of gratification'; in his opinion, the 'much injured lady', for which there was 'a feeling of deep and general sympathy', possessed 'intellectual qualities and poetical talents of a very high order' which would 'shed on her humble name a lustre which a coronet cannot confer.'[5] But her poem was not to everyone's taste; *The Critic* found it 'wanting the *spirit* of poetry', with no novel thoughts or original ideas, and declined to reproduce any of its verses out of 'kindness to the writer'.[6]

I have found no other published work by Mary Elizabeth Smith. And, while it is possible that she used a pseudonym—she was, after all, quite happy to write letters under an assumed name—it seems doubtful, given her purpose in writing, that she would have been content to publish books under any name but her own. Given Mary's determination, her talent for creating fiction, her unwillingness to accept defeat, and her father's willingness to fund the publication of her writing, if she had wanted to publish more books she no doubt would have found a way to do so. So, it seems likely that she gave up her writing career almost as soon as it had begun.

Perhaps Mary finally accepted that the 'romance' was over. Or, more likely, she was disappointed with the outcome of her written endeavours. When she pursued an action for damages for libel against the *Britannia* newspaper in 1847, she doubtless did so in the hope that the proprietor of that journal would plead justification, thereby allowing Serjeant Talfourd, who represented her, to call Earl Ferrers to give evidence in court. As the proprietor chose not to do so, Earl Ferrers did not appear, and Mary was denied the opportunity of having the evidence of her failed court case raked over again (with the aim of clearing her name at the *Britannia*'s expense!). As those who reviewed *Moscha Lamberti* chose to focus on her writing rather than her imagined romantic entanglements and the besmirchment of her good name, they too denied her the opportunity to vindicate her character.

What was the point, she no doubt cried in frustration, in winning a libel case if she ended up where she began and gained only one farthing in damages? And what was the point in going to the trouble of writing a book if she received in return nothing but a handful of appreciative reviews and came no closer to restoring her reputation? Whatever its literary merits, in writing *Moscha Lamberti* Mary's goal was undoubtedly to force her failed court case back into the public eye—to enable her to *clear* her name rather than to *make* one as a writer—and in that respect she most likely viewed the book as a complete failure.

In 1853, Mary's father died, and this may have had some

bearing on her decision to stop writing too, at least in the short term. During the libel case against the *Britannia* newspaper, Thomas Smith confirmed that he had assisted in the preparation of his daughter's *Statement of Facts* in 1846 and had sent it to London for publication.[7] Perhaps, without the help, encouragement, and finance he provided, Mary found writing and publishing her work more difficult after her father's death. That said, if she had found it worth her while she would no doubt have gone on with her work eventually.

On 3 November 1857, four years after Thomas Smith's death, Mary married Kosciusko Kent Newbolt, only son of Dr. William Kent Nowbolt and grandson of Sir John Newbolt, late Chief Justice of the Supreme Court at Madras.[8] Presumably, her marriage put an end to the possibility of Mary ever bringing her court case to the public's attention again. She had four children: three daughters and one son. Her husband died in 1883 at the age of fifty-nine.[9] Her son, George Palmerston Newbolt C.B.E (1863-1924), was a well-known Liverpool surgeon. Her daughters never married; Marion died in 1885 at the age of twenty-four, Annie died in 1902 at the age of forty-three, and Rosa remained living with her mother until the latter's death.[10] Mary spent the final years of her life in Liverpool; she died on 17 March 1909 at the age of eighty-three.[11]

Notes

1 Syerscote Manor Farmhouse, near Tamworth in Staffordshire, was the home of Mary's maternal grandparents, Joseph and Mary Erpe. Though Mary's mother gave her name as Mary Anne Smith when giving evidence during her daughter's court case, her actual name was simply Anne Smith (née Erpe).

2 If you remember, Mary denied the existence of these letters prior to the court case because she believed they had been destroyed. After they were produced in court, and her parents confirmed that they were written by her, she was forced to give some explanation. Within her *Statement of Facts* she claimed that she had written anonymously in the guise of a stranger to Earl Ferrers because she lacked the courage to write in her own name or that the letters were written to test his fidelity.

3 *Morning Advertiser*, 7 April 1849, p. 4.

4 *Nottingham and Newark Mercury*, 23 March 1849, p. 6.

5 *Arbroath Guide*, 10 February 1849, p. 6.

6 *The Critic*, 1 April 1849, p. 158.

7 *Northampton Mercury*, 11 December 1847, p. 4.

8 *Staffordshire Advertiser*, 14 November 1857, p. 5

9 *England & Wales, National Probate Calendar (Index of Wills and Administrations), 1858-1995.*

10 *Dorset, England, Church of England Deaths and Burials, 1813-2010*, *1901 England Census*, and *1921 England Census.*

11 *England & Wales, National Probate Calendar (Index of Wills and Administrations), 1858-1995.*

www.ingramcontent.com/pod-product-compliance
Lightning Source LLC
Chambersburg PA
CBHW020932310726
48980CB00007B/738/J

* 9 7 8 1 9 1 7 1 1 3 1 3 7 *